Volcano Street

David Rain

Atlantic Books
London

First published in Great Britain in 2014 by Atlantic Books,
an imprint of Atlantic Books Ltd.

10 9 8 7 6 5 4 3 2 1

A CIP catalogue record for this book is available from the British Library.

Trade Paperback ISBN: 978 0 85789 207 2
E-book ISBN: 978 1 78239 406 8

Printed in Great Britain by CPI Group (UK) Ltd, Croydon, CR0 4YY

Atlantic Books
An Imprint of Atlantic Books Ltd
Ormond House
26–27 Boswell Street
London
WC1N 3JZ

www.atlantic-books.co.uk

For those who stayed in the Happy Valley

When real things are so wonderful,
what is the point of pretending?
E. M. FORSTER

The fiction of one's life is the truth.
VINCENT PRICE

# Chapter One

My fault. All my fault.

The judgement sounded in Skip's head. All the way from Adelaide she had heard it, in the rattling windows, in the snores from other seats, in the tyres as they juddered over the country highway. She told herself it wasn't true, but still it came in the swish of passing vehicles: that station wagon, chalky with dust, with surfboards lashed to the roof; that farmer's truck, tight-packed with sheep, that thundered by and wafted back its sharp, shitty stench, filling the Greyhound for desperate minutes.

Marlo, with her book, had moved across the aisle. How placid she looked, how self-contained: hairband like a halo, neat across her crown; elbow crooked against the chrome window frame, propping up the hand that shaded her eyes.

Skip picked up her comic. Lex Luthor held Metropolis to ransom, threatening to destroy it with a death ray aimed from space. Never mind, Superman would sort it out. She wished she were Superman. Not Supergirl, in that dinky little skirt. Skip didn't just want to be super, she wanted to be a man. If she were a man, she would be blamed for nothing.

She rested her head against the window. September: the beginning of spring. The afternoon sun was pale and lemony. Monterey pines in neat plantations had replaced the flat paddocks, barbed-wire fences and scattered grey gum trees that had reeled by for hours. Abundant moist undergrowth seethed between the trees, testament to the cool green winter just gone.

Skip loped across the aisle, dropped her head into her sister's lap, and looked up, wide-eyed. *'Cattus cattus?'* Their old joke (If a rat's *rattus rattus*, is a cat *cattus cattus*?) had become a greeting. Usually Marlo laughed; today she sighed impatiently and shifted her book.

'I'm starving!' Skip sprang up. 'How much longer?'

'You've had lunch.'

'Soggy sandwiches from a BP roadhouse!'

'Wolfed them down, didn't you?'

'I'm a growing boy.'

The Wells sisters – half-sisters, really – might not have been related at all. Skip, small for her age, was a freckled tomboy with a head of coarse bright straw, cropped as if with pinking shears; Marlo, almost a woman and womanly with it, was porcelain pale, with hair that crested her shoulders in rich dark waves. Today Skip wore a nautical sweater, once white, over a plaid shirt, faded jeans with threadbare knees, and sneakers that were falling apart. Marlo's white blouse, blue blazer, grey skirt and shiny black lace-ups could have been her uniform from Adelaide Ladies' College, minus cap, tie and tie pin.

'Marlo ...' Do you blame me? Skip almost said, but gestured instead to the book in Marlo's lap and asked what Germaine was on about now.

'Cunt hatred.' Marlo did not drop her voice.

On the open pages Skip picked out a few words: sex, prostitute, sex, cunt, fuck, cunt. She liked Germaine. Germaine was radical: she pissed people off.

2

Sunlight flickered greenly through the pines. Sometimes it was dull to have a serious sister. Skip supposed she should shut up, but instead dug Marlo in the ribs and made a joke about the pig-faced lady who had left the coach at the last stop. Was she hurrying home on her trotters? Was she oinking?

'In a pig's ear,' said Marlo, and Skip, delighted, twisted around, hitched her chin over the seat's high vinyl back, and surveyed the other passengers. They were few: a fat man with a short back and sides who read the *Sunday Mail* with an affronted air; a thin lady in a chamberpot hat; two carrot-headed little boys who had torn up and down the aisle until the driver roared at them to bloody well cut it out. A soldier in a slouch hat, young and spotty, gazed out the window. Just back from Nam? Fascist. Skip pictured him, in grainy black and white, sloshing through a swamp. Cradled in his arms was a machine gun, and his eyes darted suspiciously through steamy haze. Skip knew all about fascists. When they got to San Fran, Karen Jane said, they'd march against the war. Everyone in San Fran was radical and marched against the war.

The chamberpot lady looked at Skip and frowned. Skip ducked beneath the seatback. 'That lady looks snoogish.'

'*You* look snoogish,' Marlo said.

'What's her name? I'll bet it's Miss Sweetapple.'

'What Sweetapple?'

'Rhonda. Can you do better?'

Marlo turned a page. 'Read your comic.'

Loneliness expanded in Skip's chest like a black balloon pressing behind her ribs, growing bigger with each breath she took. Her comic lay on the seat across the aisle. Caper, long ago, had given her a Superman comic from America. It was better than Australian ones: colour all through, not just on the cover, and the paper had an exciting foreign smell. Superman, Batman, Justice League: in the local reprints the heroes were the same, but Skip thought of them as the Australian versions, and not so good by half.

'What about school?' she said to Marlo.

'What about it?'

'It's Sunday. We'll be starting tomorrow, won't we? I suppose you can't mix with first years. You'll ignore me.' This, Skip knew, was dangerous ground. For Marlo, the worst aspect of their exile was giving up her scholarship to Adelaide Ladies' College. 'But you'll look my way, won't you, when no one else can see? Exchange glances. Roll your eyes.'

Wearily, Marlo shut *The Female Eunuch*. 'You realise I've exams in a couple of months? My whole future depends on this.' She had said so before, and Skip wondered: Whole future? What was a whole future? She could imagine next week. She could imagine next month. But a whole future?

'You'll be all right, Marlo. What do you need with that snoogish college? You'll sail through those exams. You'll be the smartest girl in Crater Lakes High.'

Marlo's laugh was bitter. 'Crater Lakes High!'

The approach to Crater Lakes discloses nothing remarkable. The highway neither curves around the several collapsed calderas, brimming with water, which give the town its name, nor affords much view of the remaining dead volcano that rises above them to no notable height. No dramatic ascent, no twisting and turning, signals that the town is near; the road sweeps on, flat and straight, as if impatient to cross the border into Victoria, leaving dull South Australia behind.

The town comes like this: abruptly, regimented grids of trees, awaiting chainsaws row by row, give way to green flatlands; paddocks with sheep; paddocks with horses; a long, rusted galvanised-iron shed; a homestead, set well back from the road; signs announcing the speed limit; signs touting business (LAKES MOTEL – YOUR HOME

FROM HOME); a sign welcoming the visitor to the City of Crater Lakes, South Australia, twinned with Gopher Prairie, Minnesota, and declaring the population (16,025 in the year this story happened); then service station, warehouse, car yard, supermarket, as the Princess Margaret Rose Highway turns for a mile or so into Volcano Street, the town's main drag.

The time had just gone five. The girls stood on the pavement. Ranged around them was all they owned: two smallish suitcases, one tartan, one leather-look; a Qantas bag; Marlo's Olivetti Lettera 22 in its zippered case; a wicker shopping basket that had been Karen Jane's before she decided it was too bourgeois.

Anxiously, Marlo turned this way and that. The fat man with the short back and sides had waddled away around a corner, *Sunday Mail* tucked beneath one arm; Rhonda Sweetapple had climbed into a Ford Falcon next to a grey, defeated-looking husband. A bustling group, all freckled, all carrot-topped, surrounded the little boys. A smaller group had turned out for the soldier: a father guffawed, a mother sobbed, and a grinning brother cuffed the slouch hat from the young man's head.

From an alley beside a newsagent's emerged an Aboriginal man dressed in dungarees. Silently, he began unloading freight from compartments under the coach – tea chests, cardboard boxes, parcels wrapped in string – while the driver stood by. Once he barked at the Aborigine; more than once he glanced at Marlo. Catching her eye, he winked at her, tongue making a castanet click. 'Got someone meeting yous, have yous?'

'Our Auntie Noreen,' said Skip. 'And Uncle Doug.'

'Doug and Noreen Puce? Kazza's kiddies! Should have known. Forgot yous was coming.' The driver was a big man with shaggy grey hair and a seamed brown face, like a surfer grown old. His rolled-back sleeves exposed hairy forearms, burned almost black, and his belly ballooned over a chunky belt. A badge above his breast pocket declared his name: SANDY CAMPBELL. 'Yous'll be living with Doug and Noreen, then?'

Marlo's reply was reluctant. 'Sort of. For a while.'

Across the street, the carrot-tops had dispersed to a battered truck; large numbers of them, piled in the flatbed, caterwauled 'You Are My Sunshine' as the vehicle shuddered away with many a wheeze, clatter and bang.

Skip scuffed the pavement with her sneaker. At several stops on their journey, Sandy Campbell had tried to talk to Marlo; Skip had headed him off each time. That was what Skip did. Boys, men, creeps of all kinds tried to crack on to Marlo, and Skip made sure they didn't. That, at least, was the idea: Marlo needed protecting and Skip protected her. But she hadn't done her job properly. If she had, they wouldn't be in Crater Lakes now.

Marlo murmured, 'Shall we ask how far it is?'

'Auntie Noreen's place?' Skip approached the driver. Smoke curled from a roll-up in his lips. She, or her question, seemed to amuse him, and he bent down to her height. Behind them, the Aborigine struggled with a tea chest, pushing it along the alley with much grunting and gasping.

The roll-up waggled. 'That Kazza was a wild one.'

'Karen Jane?' said Skip. 'Still is.'

'All the blokes round these parts reckoned so. Missed her when she went up to the smoke, we did.' The grey head jerked towards Marlo. 'Like mother, like daughter, eh?' Grinning, Sandy Campbell chucked Skip under the chin and straightened to full height. 'Don't worry, love, I'll run yous out when we've finished here – I'll take yous,' he added, raising his voice for Marlo's benefit.

Skip, outraged by the man's familiar manner, was about to tell him where he could stick his ride when an open-topped Land Rover tore down the street and drew up with a screech behind the coach. A young man jumped down from the driver's seat and gasped out, as if he had been running, 'Yous the Wells sisters? I'm late. Old Ma Puce is gunna be real pissed off.'

The new arrival was a gangly fellow, more boy than man, with a darkish complexion and prominent teeth: almost horsy, but not unhandsome. His brown eyes were limpid, his brow tall, and his bronze hair bubbled over the top like a potion from a test tube. A grey apron covered his T-shirt and jeans, with pencils poking out of a narrow, high pocket.

'So Noreen's sent the slave.' Sandy Campbell seemed a little put out. 'Girls, meet Pav – Crater Lakes' most eligible bachelor. He's a wog, but not the worst kind.'

'Pavel Novak.' The young man, still puffing, extended his hand to Marlo. 'I would have been on time but the shop floor was a mess. Stocktaking,' he explained.

Sandy Campbell dropped his cigarette butt; it lay on the concrete, smoke upcurling. 'Pav here's one of your uncle's employees,' he told the girls. 'Or should I say your aunt's? Who would you say was your boss, Pav – Noreen or Doug?'

Pavel, not answering, sprang to help the Aborigine, who, after a break, had resumed work on the tea chest. 'Lift it from the bottom. Bend the knees,' Pavel said kindly, while Sandy Campbell, watching the two of them struggle down the alley, called, 'He's paid to do that! Leave the abo retard alone.'

The Aborigine, who perhaps indeed was retarded, dropped his side of the chest, almost crushing his fingers. He was little and bent, with a broad flattened face like an ebony carving, and oil-dark curly hair, thick and long.

Uncertainly, Skip and Marlo loaded their suitcases, the Qantas bag and the wicker shopping basket into the back of the Land Rover. With particular care, Skip passed her sister the Lettera 22. 'You'd better hold Olly.'

'So it's goodbye for now, eh? Careful with the wog boy,' said Sandy

Campbell. 'Volcano Street ain't been safe since that bugger got his licence. Used to be my Land Rover, this one' – he pronounced it 'Lan Drover' – 'before I flogged it to young Pav.' He patted the vehicle's green flank. 'Wrecked it, he has. Buggered the suspension. Buggered the transmission. Spit and chewing gum, that's all that keeps this crate on the road.'

Pavel returned, sweating. He stripped off his apron and tossed it in the back. Resuming his place at the wheel, he gestured for Marlo to sit beside him in the front. Skip climbed in next to the luggage, then thought better of it, scrambled over the long front seat and thudded down between them.

'You don't mind, Pav?' She punched his arm.

'Skip, don't be rude,' said Marlo.

The Land Rover moved off down Volcano Street, and Pavel apologised again for being late. He drove carefully, even too carefully, as if in deference to the girls. Skip was disappointed: she had expected a reckless ride.

The Aborigine watched them go, his eyes deep and dark.

'Yous here for long, are yous?' The wog boy spoke in a broad Australian accent.

'I shouldn't think so.' It was Marlo who answered. She had assumed her queenly manner: straight-backed, eyes forward, hands folded neatly over Olly Olivetti. Skip understood: Marlo, bold only with books, could read about prostitutes and cunts and still be prim.

'Picked a nice day for it,' Pavel attempted next.

'I heard it rains all the time,' said Skip. 'In the Lakes, I mean.'

'Rains a bit,' said Pavel. 'Even when it's warm.'

'So what's there to do here?' Skip asked.

'Aw, the Lakes is really going forward.' Pavel (was he always so cheerful?) might have been repeating something he had heard a hundred times. 'There's Chickenland – you'll see the big chicken on the roof, can't miss it – and Coles New World. Yous must have seen that on the way in.'

Marlo laughed, and Skip, not sure if they should make fun of this boy – he might, she supposed, be a bit simple – said quickly, 'Pavel – what kind of name is that?'

'Czech, isn't it?' said Marlo. 'Czech for Paul.'

'Why don't you call yourself Paul, then?' Skip asked, but Pavel only smiled. Something in that smile, in those abundant chunky teeth, disturbed her in its guilelessness, a dreamy wonderment that made her feel older, wiser.

Shops spooled by, all shut for Sunday: pie shop, pharmacy, Tom the Cheap. A gaggle of children slouched across the road and Pavel cheerily beeped the horn. At the main corner, three two-storey sandstone buildings stood in a row. Waiting at the lights, he named them: King Edward VII Theatre; Crater Lakes Institute; and Crater Lakes Town Hall (his father worked there), with its clock tower, a little Big Ben, and gardens beside it banded by a low stone wall. Iron lace lavishly decorated an ancient pub opposite.

They were turning left off Volcano Street when a sign above a whitewashed, garage-like building, crouched back from the pavement behind a parking lot, declaimed: PUCE HARDWARE. Lawnmowers, chained in place, stretched along a fence at the side, and a placard with an arrow exhorted customers not to miss a yard at the back (NOREEN'S GREEN FINGERS) filled with plants in terracotta pots and secured today by a chain-link gate.

Skip asked Pavel if he had worked there long. He said he had been there since he left the high.

Marlo perked up. 'Where's the high?'

He jerked a thumb. 'Bit of a way from yous.'

They passed down a street of houses, white limestone bungalows with galvanised-iron roofs of red, green or blue. Each house had a concrete driveway and a carport or garage; few front yards had fences, and lawns ran to the kerb.

Skip said to Pavel, 'You must know our aunt and uncle well.'

Pavel said he supposed so. Skip feared to ask the inevitable next question: what are they like? She had been barely more than a baby when Auntie Noreen last visited Adelaide, but Marlo remembered their aunt as a big booming woman in a paisley frock who had given them gifts they didn't want and argued bitterly with Karen Jane. 'Me own sister! I'm ashamed of you,' she had finally sobbed, before leaving, vowing never to return. What Karen Jane had to say about Noreen didn't bode well.

Guilt rose in Skip again. She hated herself.

Pavel turned off the neat street and followed several shabbier roads. Tarmacadam gave way to dirt, and trees overhung the road. They passed a paddock with a pony in it, a half-built house, and vacant lots heaped with bricks, timber, and metal sheeting. The grass was richly green.

On a corner stood a service station, startlingly ruined. Twin Golden Fleece pumps rose like robot sentries before a building that looked as though it had been shaken by an earthquake. A wall had collapsed, the roof had caved in, and weeds now pushed through cracks in the forecourt. Beside the ruin, an abandoned refrigerator, several stoves, and an engine or two, brown and brittle, listed on the edge of a deep depression in the earth of the sort known as a blowhole: blasted out by explosives, it was a place to deposit junk.

'They call this Puce's Bend,' said Pavel. 'Your uncle started up that servo after the war. Went bust.'

'We're a long way out, aren't we?' said Marlo.

'Not that far.' Just down from the blowhole and on the other side of the road, Pavel drew up beside an unruly hedge. Beyond it was a sprawling single-storey house with high gables, twin triangles of radiating sunburst beams above a veranda propped up by stuccoed pillars.

'Is there a school bus?' Marlo asked doubtfully.

'Next corner.' Pavel pointed. Opposite an empty paddock, a steep, overgrown verge cushioned the crook of a ninety-degree turn; there was no visible bus stop, no shelter. Beyond the corner could be seen another house, located on higher ground: a flash of white through billows of leaves.

Pavel leaped down to the road, gallantly grabbed all the luggage, and led the girls down a gravelled driveway, indicating with a tilt of his head that they should follow him around the back. The side of the house was blank but for a chimneystack halfway along, tapering like a Saturn V rocket made of bricks, and a single high sash window. Paint, dark green, flaked from the frame; shadows shifted behind the lace curtains. Between the house and a shed at the end of the drive stood a tall wooden fence with a gate in the middle. Pavel drew back a bolt and ushered the girls inside.

At the rear of the house lay a patio cluttered with buckets, rakes, brooms, flowerpots, pine planks and garden furniture, like a distant unruly satellite of Puce Hardware; a wooden extension – an incongruous chalet – stretched from the opposite side of the house. Filling the air was a noxious tang: the damp, earthy sourness of an open sewer.

Skip laughed. Marlo reached for a handkerchief.

The sun was sinking, sending bright arrows flashing down the yard. With the glare in their eyes they had not at first made out the fellow who stood beyond the rotary washing line. Pavel thudded down the luggage and raised a hand; the fellow echoed the gesture. He was thin, dressed in grey overalls, and leaned on the handle of a shovel as they approached. Beside him was a hill of dirt; he stood, like a gravedigger, above a deep pit.

'New septic. Bloody thing backed up last night,' he said and wiped

11

his forehead with a leathery hand. 'Last thing you want to be doing on a Sunday arvo, eh?'

'Yair.' Pavel nodded sagely.

Marlo hung back, handkerchief in place. Skip peered into the pit. Five feet down was a wooden platform, squelchy like a rotted floor; several boards, pulled free, exposed a ceramic pipe, scaly, as if crusted with barnacles, in a reeking dark pool. Lengths of pipe and fresh timber lay on the grass above; the fellow's task, evidently, was to extend the pipe into another pit that would then, with new planks in place, be covered up again.

'Yous on the mains, ain't yous?' the man said to Pavel. 'Bloody wish we was. Don't know how many shit pits I've dug. Stand where you like in this yard, you're standing on shit.' He cackled mirthlessly and prodded Pavel's chest. 'Wouldn't like a go with the shovel? Yair, suppose you better get going. I says to Queen Noreen, Time we got on the mains. Didn't have mains when I was a girl, she says. Didn't have the goggle box neither, I says, and that don't stop you gawping at it all day. Wait till I'm gone, I says. Your old Doug won't last for ever, not the way you work him.'

Pavel nodded. 'Yair,' he said again, then, 'Yair,' this time with conviction, and only then did Doug Puce, ponderous as an ocean liner, turn to face the girls.

'Good trip?' he asked Marlo, and she nodded behind the handkerchief. 'Don't worry, love, this lot'll soon be fixed. Worse last night when the bloody thing backed up – all through the house you'd have smelled it then!' He held out a long hand, thought better of it, and wiped it on his overalls.

Uncle Doug was thin in every respect: thin hair, in Brylcreemed grooves, topping a head like an Australian Rules football gone flat; thin face with narrow eyes, nose, lips; neck spindly as the forearms protruding from his rolled-up sleeves. His face and arms were teak brown and his ears stuck out sharply, as if stiffened with wires.

The call rose like a kookaburra's: 'Is that me girls?'

A screen door banged, and flitting eagerly over the yard came an enormous woman in a billowing muu-muu patterned in zigzags of bright pink, lime and orange. Her smile buried her eyes in fatty cushions, and blue-dyed hair sprang electrically from her head. The bare arms she held up were swollen as if with dropsy, the hands small as a doll's at the ends of swaying, puckered swags of flesh. A startled Marlo was enfolded in doughy depths.

'Mar-*leen*! How long is it since I seen me little Mar-*leen*? I swear, you're pretty as Kazza, back in the day ... And Baby Helen!' Little eyes glinted at Skip. 'Come on, don't be shy – a big hug for your Auntie Noreen!'

Skip complied, but quickly squirmed free.

'Bugger, what yous doing in the yard? Tea's ready. Pav, love, bring the bags, there's a good boy.' Auntie Noreen pirouetted back to the house and beckoned the girls to follow. She appeared not to notice the stench in the yard.

Inside, they passed down a dim passage into the living room: floral carpeting, floral lounge suite, tasselled ornate lampshades, floral curtains tied back with braided cords. Arrayed on a low table was a massive spread. Skip's eyes brightened at the sight of cream horns, scones with jam and cream, chocolate cake, chocolate éclairs, vanilla slices, and biscuits on dainty plates. Maybe there was something to be said for Auntie Noreen. On the television, a housewife exclaimed over a box of Lemon Fab.

The girls perched on twin armchairs; their aunt assumed her throne in the centre of the sofa. Flanking her were a knitting bag with protruding needles, a Patons pattern book, and a crumpled copy of *TV Week*. Skip looked around the room as their aunt ('Let *me* play mother') poured the tea. On the mantelpiece was a clock cased in lacquered wood, and several framed photographs. One showed a boy in soldier's uniform; this, Skip supposed, was Uncle Doug in youth. The ears were unmistakable.

'I'll be off then, Mrs P.' Pavel, in the doorway, looked forlornly at the spread.

'Right you are, love. Stocktaking up to date? Now make sure you're at the shop in the morning, all bright-eyed and bushy-tailed. Old Noreen knows. Never forget, Noreen knows.'

'I won't, Mrs P.' Pavel nodded goodbye to the girls.

'This *is* nice, isn't it?' The sofa creaked beneath Auntie Noreen as if the frame might snap. 'How long's it been since I seen yous kiddies? Make up for it now, won't we? I says to Kazza when I wrote – and I *did*, whether the cow wrote back or not – it's wrong, hiding them kiddies from kith and kin. Well, now she's got no choice. Aw, this is lovely, this one.'

The last remark referred to the television, where Gordon MacRae, firm-jawed with gleaming dark hair, sang to Doris Day in a rowboat on a lake. For a few bars Auntie Noreen sang along, quite tunefully, then said that in younger years she had fancied she looked a little like Doris. 'Baby Helen does too, I reckon. Blonde, girl-next-door type. But Marlene's the beauty.'

'It's Marlo,' Skip said coldly. 'And I'm Skip.'

'Marlo? Don't like that. Marlene, that's a lovely name, like Marlene Dietrich.'

*Mar*-leen *Deet*-rich. Rhymes with bitch.

'They reckon she's had so many facelifts she can't smile. Woman to woman, lovies: never go down that route. Me, I make do with Mother Nature's gifts. The blokes always reckoned I had a shapely foot,' Auntie Noreen added – and indeed the foot, in open-toed sandals, that she raised for their inspection was admirable in its contours. If it resembled Karen Jane's, this was unsurprising; Noreen would have looked a lot like her sister, had her sister been blown up with a bicycle pump to the point just before she was about to burst.

14

'Eat up, Marlene. Eat up, Helen,' she urged. 'Can't let it go to waste, can we? There's many a little blackie in Biafra would be glad of an Arnott's Custard Cream.'

Marlo applied jam to a scone with scholarly deliberation; shyly, then with increasing boldness, Skip moved in on the spread. She would have to be quick; their aunt, on her own, did enough to eat vicariously for the children of Biafra. Reaching across the tea table, plucking here a cream horn, there a vanilla slice, levering up a generous wedge of chocolate cake, Noreen Puce moved dexterously for a woman so huge. How high she heaped her plate! When there was no room for more, she sipped from her teacup, crooking a little finger, and took up her cake fork with a ladylike air.

'So you work at the shop too, Aunt?' Marlo asked.

Their hostess seemed affronted at the idea, but explained, not impatiently, 'I'm more in what you'd call a supervisory capacity, love. The day-to-day stuff, Dougie looks after that, but of course I has to keep an eye on him. I says to him, Don't think you can pull any fast ones on old Noreen. I says, Your old man may have started that shop, but who did he leave it to? Old Noreen! Who kept that shop going through the war years when you was lazing round in Bongo-Bongo Land, eating mangoes? Old Noreen! Who's understood its history? Old Noreen! Who's cherished its legacy? Old Noreen! Stupid bugger, starting a servo in the back of beyond. Independence, he says! Be his own man! Old Noreen knew which side our bread was buttered. Established 1922: W. H. Puce (that's Dougie's dad, Willard Hartley Puce), for all your hardware needs.'

Proudly, Old Noreen lifted her jowls, like a toad bobbing its head above the surface of a pond. 'He was a visionary, Willard Hartley Puce. Before Willard Hartley Puce, where would you go in Crater Lakes for your hammer and nails, your fire tongs, your showerhead, your drill bit, your hardwood skirting board? One miserable general store, that's where, with everything higgledy-piggledy like a mad woman's undies: bolts of dirty fabric, sacks of chickenfeed, jars of pickled monkeys' balls, old copies of *The Bulletin* and nothing you wanted ever in stock! Blokes laughed at Willard Hartley Puce. Said he was a dreamer. How could a one-horse town like Crater Lakes support a hardware emporium good as any on Collins Street, Melbourne? Pall Mall, London? Chomps-a-bloody-Lee-saze? But Willard Hartley Puce didn't just see Crater Lakes as it was. He saw what it would become.'

Tears filled Auntie Noreen's eyes. Skip and Marlo struggled not to laugh, but their aunt was oblivious, assuaging her passion in fervent application to her plate. The finesse with which she wielded her fork was extraordinary; so too was the hummingbird speed with which each mouthful vanished.

She was refilling her plate when she admonished Skip, 'Eat up now, Helen love – try some of the cake.'

'I'm Skip.' There was an edge in Skip's voice.

'Skip! No sort of name for a girl.'

'It's my sort of name.' Skip recalled bright afternoons on Caper's boat, with Glenelg Beach far off, sunlight flashing on the water like scattered coins, fish thudding to the sloshing deck, and Caper, wanting her to see the latest, calling her in his Yank voice, 'Skipper … Skip!' That had been his name for her, and she had loved him for it; he had given her a captain's cap and let her reel in lines. She gave him orders. 'Make these lubbers walk the plank!' she cried, jabbing a finger at seasick Marlo, at blissful stoned Karen Jane, and Caper saluted: 'Aye, aye, Skip.'

In the road, a large vehicle heaved to a halt. Through the scrim, Skip saw to her alarm a chassis with ridged silver lines below a sea-blue stripe. Painted above the stripe was a leaping greyhound.

Auntie Noreen was saying, 'I'm sure yous girls are going to love it here. Fresh country air, that's what yous need.' She inhaled theatrically, her ample chest swelling; Skip, who was breathing shallowly due to the occasional waft from the shit pit, studied her in wonder. 'Look at yous,' their aunt went on cheerily. 'One of you's pale as a ghost and the other a little starved sparrow …' She arched towards the window. 'Eh, what's that bastard doing poking round here again?'

The screen door banged. There was a commotion in the hall, masculine laughter and the tramp of heavy boots. 'Good to see you, mate!' and 'Yair, couple of cold ones' were two of the phrases the girls heard before Auntie Noreen rolled back her head and cawed, 'Bugger, there goes me shit pit!'

A grey shaggy head appeared around the door.

'You, you old bludger!' Auntie Noreen cried. 'Didn't I tell you never to darken me doors again?'

The joke was met with a flash of yellow dentures and a wink for Marlo. 'See yous settling in all right, love. Said yous would, eh?' The grin alighted on Auntie Noreen, whose mountainous body wobbled with pleasure. 'Saw that one casting spells on young Pav back at me coach stop, I did. He'll be looking forward to seeing her in the shop tomorrow.' He addressed Marlo again. 'Be gentle with him, love. He's a country boy, not used to your big-city ways!'

Guffawing, Sandy Campbell vanished towards the kitchen. 'Dougie, you bastard,' he yelled, 'where's me beer?'

'He's a friend of yours – the coach driver?' Skip said to her aunt.

'Friend! Me old cobber Raelene, God rest her soul, was married to that bugger twenty-odd years. Things she told me, you wouldn't believe! Stops out all hours, rolls home drunk, slaps her round the chops, then expects her to take it up the …' But Auntie Noreen realised, perhaps, that she had gone too far. 'Oh, it's dreadful, the things we women endure! He's a charmer, but any girlie who trusts him has only herself to blame. Don't think he hasn't come sniffing round *me* in his time,' she added, with an air of horror. 'I'm a married woman, I tells him. Dougie's your best mate. You reckon that one cares?'

There was nothing to be said to this, though Marlo, in a perfect world, might have quoted *The Female Eunuch*. From the kitchen came bellowings (Sandy Campbell's), murmurs (Doug's), clatterings, clumpings, and the clink-clink of bottles. Auntie Noreen, drawing up her huge round-shouldered form a little, smiled as if captured by a pleasant memory.

'Aunt, what did he mean about tomorrow?' Marlo ventured. 'The shop – why should I be in the shop?'

But Auntie Noreen had applied herself to the tea table again, hovering between the remaining cream horn and the remaining vanilla slice in an agony that was no agony at all, since, with the swiftness of a buzzard alighting on a carcass, she transferred both to her plate. For so prodigal a mouth, Auntie Noreen's was surprisingly small, a puckering purplish circle that sooner or later made most people think of an anal sphincter. 'Thought I'd put you in the spare room, Marlene,' the sphincter was saying. 'You're oldest, after all. Helen can go in the sleepout at the back.'

'We've always had the same room.' Skip thought sadly of the old house in Glenelg and their room above the garage. Caper's flat, too small for them all, was far away down concrete steps and along a weedy path. She and Marlo had lived in a world of their own, one she never wanted to leave. On the walls Marlo hung foxed engravings, found in a junk shop on Jetty Road, of famous women writers: Jane Austen, Elizabeth Barrett Browning, George Eliot. Skip loved lying in bed at night with Marlo close by. Beside the garage, a Norfolk pine creaked in the wind; from further off came the gentle hiss and splash of the sea.

'Your sister needs her privacy,' Auntie Noreen was saying. 'She's growing up. I'll bet she thinks about nothing but boys and make-up, eh, Helen? I suppose she's got crushes on all the hit-parade stars. Does she drive you mad, mooning over them all day? Who's her favourite – Johnny Farnham?'

'We *hate* Johnny Farnham,' Skip snapped.

'Don't reckon your sister does,' leered Auntie Noreen, and took an oozing bite of cream horn. 'Yairs, I know yous girls are going to love it here,' she carried on. 'After all, it's your home now.'

'Only for a few weeks,' said Skip.

'Weeks? I shouldn't think so. I admit it's a stretch for me, taking on yous girls. Not as young as I used to be. And it's not as if I don't have enough to worry about with me poor boy away, doing his bit for Queen and Country.' Auntie Noreen gazed fondly at the mantelpiece, from where the young soldier stared back at her with a dutiful air.

'Your son?' said Skip. 'You've a son?'

'What, your mother never even told you that? That's your cousin Barry – Barry Puce!'

'He's in Vietnam?' said Marlo.

'Aren't you angry they sent him away?' Skip asked.

'Why should I be angry?'

'They sent him to die in an unjust war.'

Auntie Noreen blinked at her niece. Colour rose in her bloated face. 'Now listen here, missy, I'm not having commie talk in my house. My Dougie did his bit in the last show – five years slogging through the jungle, gooks to the right of him, gooks to the left – and now it's Baz's turn. Make a man of him, it will.'

Warningly, Marlo placed a hand on Skip's arm, but Skip could not restrain herself. 'If he were a man, he'd refuse to fight. He'd resist imperialist aggression. The Vietnamese are entitled to self-determination. They're fighting for their freedom.' She knew all the phrases: hadn't she heard them enough from Caper, from Karen Jane? She'd heard them from Marlo too, and was disappointed that her sister sat there shaking her head as if to say: Stop.

Auntie Noreen's toad-neck swelled. 'Vietnamese? Why the Yanks don't just drop a big one on all those slitty-eyed Wongs and be done with it, I don't know. I see one young lady's got a lot to learn,' she said, revealing the inner steel with which she ran a hardware emporium comparable to any in Collins Street, Pall Mall or the Chomps-a-bloody-Lee-saze. 'If there's one thing makes me blood run cold, it's to hear a kiddie parroting propaganda.'

Skip's face burned; she might have replied, but her sister's grip remained tight and she sank back into her chair.

Auntie Noreen polished off the last vanilla slice, dusted her little hands together, and levered herself to her feet. Her severity was gone at once. 'Yous girls have had a long day. I reckon it's time I showed yous your rooms. Dinner in an hour.' She added, with a laugh, 'If I can shift that bugger Campbell from me kitchen.'

'School day tomorrow, isn't it?' said Marlo.

'That's right, love.' Auntie Noreen draped an arm around Skip. 'This one can get the school bus. Get to know the other kiddies, eh? Your sister can ride with Doug.'

'I'll take the bus too,' said Marlo.

'Eh?' said Auntie Noreen. 'Nah, can't do that.'

'But why should Uncle Doug take only me to school?'

'School! Love, didn't they tell you? I know these social workers are slack, but I reckoned they'd have told you. Did you think I could have two useless girls on me hands? Said I'd take yous on one condition, didn't I? Helen goes to the high – has to, she's a kiddie. But the big one? She's past leaving age, and we need a new girl in the office at Puce Hardware.' The little mouth twisted into a smile. 'Marlene, you'll be marvellous.'

'You can't mean this.' Gasping, Marlo blundered from the room. A voice – Sandy Campbell's? – cackled as she ran past, and then from deeper in the house a door slammed, loud enough to shake plaster from the walls.

Wide-eyed, Skip stared at Auntie Noreen, who smiled calmly back as if unaware that she was destroying Marlo's whole future.

# Chapter Two

'Cattus cattus?'

Skip's voice was low. Carefully she made her way across the floor. The room was dark, but in the light from the passage she saw that Marlo still lay, fully clothed, on the bed. The leather-look suitcase, the shopping basket, and Olly Olivetti in his zippered case hunkered undisturbed beside the musty wardrobe.

Twice before Skip had scudded this way: once at Auntie Noreen's insistence, when dinner was on the table; and once in defiance of her aunt, who said that if Miss High-and-Mighty (just like her mother!) wanted to be silly, she could stew in her own juices. Both times Marlo had stared at the ceiling and demanded to be left alone. Now Skip had been told to go to bed, but she couldn't, not like this.

In the kitchen, the grown-ups still sat at the table. Sandy Campbell's voice boomed, anecdote after anecdote, joke after joke, punctuated by Auntie Noreen's delighted cackles.

'Dinner was nice,' Skip tried. 'Apple pie and ice cream for dessert.'

'I suppose Auntie Noreen ate mine.' Marlo drew herself up. She wrapped her arms around her knees and turned towards her sister. In the slant of light her face gleamed blankly, bright against the dark-papered wall. Her eyes were clear: she hadn't been crying. No, Skip thought proudly, Marlo wouldn't cry.

'She can't mean it, can she? You've got to go to school.'

'She means it. Damn this place!'

'Good old Marlo! This is more like it.' Excitedly Skip paced the floor, remembering plans and schemes they used to make, long ago, as they lay in bed in their room above the garage. 'They can't keep us prisoners, can they? We'll escape. We'll run away.'

'How? We've no money.'

'Hitch. Ride in trucks, up front with the driver. I'll play the mouth organ. I'll tie up my hair in a dirty red bandanna. Oh, Marlo, it'll be the adventure of a lifetime. We'll end up in Sydney – Kings Cross.'

Caper had told them about Kings Cross, where he lived when he first arrived in Sydney, a drifter up to no good. Skip imagined a shabby flat on the top floor of a white, peeling house, high above the harbour. This would be their castle and Marlo would be its queen, with Skip the loyal page boy. From a balcony frosted with iron lace they would gaze down, dazzled, at deep blue waters, while the chug of boats, the honk, the knock, the slosh, the jingle of chains from the tethering docks made merry music. In the evenings they would dine in dark, smoky cafés, hidden in basements or down snaking alleys, where poets with beards and berets argued at surrounding tables, fights broke out over the favours of waitresses, and girls who looked like Joan Baez strummed guitars and sang. Skip, who had never been to Sydney, could see it so clearly. Striding back and forth, gesturing vigorously, she did her best to convey all this to Marlo. She didn't succeed.

'You're twelve. I'm sixteen. The police would be on our trail in days.'

'We'd wear disguises. Glasses. False beards.'

'And money? What would we live on?'

'Your stories, Marlo. You're going to be a writer.' Reverently, Skip picked up Olly Olivetti, peeled back the zippered case, jammed the

typewriter into her sister's lap, and propelled her hands to the keys.
'You're already a writer.'

'Silly stories! I ripped them all up.'

'Not "Moon Escape"? Not "The Slaughterhouse Murders"? That's
the greatest story ever.'

'It's kids' stuff. I wrote it when I was your age.'

'You'd never destroy them. You couldn't.' Skip dived for her sister's
luggage. Wrenching the suitcase across the floor, she tugged at the
straps that stopped it flying open.

Marlo leaped towards her. 'Go away!'

They struggled for the suitcase and Marlo grabbed it. Skip kept up
her pleading. 'You're frightened. Don't be. We could run off tonight.
You and me and Olly Olivetti, on our way round the world.'

'You're a child. You don't understand.'

'What's to understand?'

'I don't want to hitch to Sydney. Or write silly stories. I want to
go to school.'

'What would Germaine do?' This, Skip knew, was a desperate
ploy, but she had to try it. 'That's the key, isn't it? In any situation,
ask yourself: What would Germaine do?'

'How do you think Germaine got where she is? She passed
exams. She went to university. Keep dreaming if you want to – keep
dreaming until you end up thirty-three years old, living in a squalid
little flat with a layabout criminal boyfriend and a couple of bastards
you can't afford.'

'How can you talk about Karen Jane like that?'

'She dreamed all her life, and that's what dreams got her.'

'And you've stopped dreaming, and what have you got? Puce
Hardware at nine in the morning.' As soon as she'd said them, Skip
wished she could call back the words.

'Don't preach to me,' Marlo said in a pained voice. 'You made our
mother go mad.' Gently but decisively, she hustled Skip to the door.

Skip slid to her knees in the passage as the door slammed behind her. Her breath came in gasps. Yes, she had made their mother go mad. Karen Jane was in the funny farm because Helen 'Skip' Wells was a stupid girl. From the kitchen still came the bellowing, the laughter. She leaned against Marlo's door. There was no lock: if she tried, she could burst in again. But she held back. So much had happened: too much. And some things, Skip was beginning to see, could never be undone. She tapped faintly on the door and whispered, 'Marlo? I'm sorry.' There was nothing else to say.

Only silence came from behind the door.

How late was it now?

Skip squatted on the decking outside the sleepout, staring into the dark yard. The night was cold and she shivered. She didn't like the sleepout and didn't want to sleep. The room was Barry Puce's, a damp creosote-smelling timber rectangle, like a Swedish sauna gone cold. Tacked to the walls were posters of Paul Newman and Jackie Stewart; there was a shelf of sporting trophies, and hanging from the ceiling was an Airfix F-111. She thought of Barry assembling the model, fingers sticky, breathing in the heady acrid tang of glue. The room would always be his. Half the wardrobe and half the chest of drawers still held his clothes: white shirts; Fair Isle pullovers; denim jeans, and trousers made of corduroy, khaki, linen; singlets; Y-fronts; argyle socks. The thought of sleeping in his bed frightened Skip. She pictured Barry returning at any moment.

Over a wicker chair beside the bed, Auntie Noreen had laid out Skip's uniform for the morning: brown beret with badge, brown blouse, brown tie, brown V-necked jumper, brown skirt, long brown socks. Skip had immediately associated the uniform with the still-uncovered shit pit. The smell hovered over the garden like fog.

If she were a character in a book, thought Skip, the present chapter might be titled 'In a Brown Study'. Chapters in books were often called that, almost as often as they were called 'Food for Thought'. What a brown study was, she wasn't sure; Sherlock Holmes had a study in scarlet, but a brown one sounded nowhere near as good. It sounded damp. It sounded sad. She was sick of feeling sad. She knew, or half knew, that her dreams of running away were only that, dreams – but how real they seemed! Always the pattern was the same: the leap of possibility, like sunlight through clouds; then disappointment as the vision faded. If only Marlo could have believed too! Tonight they could have made plans that would make tomorrow all right, even if Skip still caught the school bus, and Marlo headed off to Puce Hardware.

The yard stretched perhaps a hundred feet behind the house. The shit pit, surrounded by its clutter of planks and tools, lay at a diagonal to Skip's left; to her right, shadowy in darkness, stood the shed. At the yard's end the ground sloped upwards; the fence, behind fruit trees, looked alarmingly high, but wasn't high enough to block out the lights from the house around the corner: three yellow-gold oblongs turned on their sides, agleam against the dark walls and rendered fuzzy by the leaves. The weather had turned with the fall of evening. The trees creaked in the wind.

Skip thought about Karen Jane. Had they put her in a padded cell? Did they really do that? Maybe Skip didn't have to blame herself. Karen Jane had been locked away before. She spoke about it casually ('When I was in the funny farm …'), as if there were kudos in her madness, evidence of sensitivity and talent. If only she had never met Caper. That, too, was Skip's fault.

One Sunday on Glenelg Beach, some years earlier, Karen Jane had lolled in sunglasses, smoking, smearing herself with Coppertone, leafing idly through *Go-Set*. Bored, Skip wandered the beach in her bathers ('Only paddling, mind,' said Karen Jane); Marlo, whose scholarship exam drew near, had insisted on staying home, for all that her mother called her a bore, a prude, and a pain in the arse.

Sometimes Skip wished she could call her mother hateful things: fat, old, ugly. But Karen Jane was beautiful: slender but curvy, skin smooth as honey, hair a curtain-like blonde cascade, like Mary's from Peter, Paul and Mary.

The sky was unclouded, one of those Australian skies that arc over the earth like a vast inverted porcelain bowl with perfectly even pale blue glaze. Skip stared at the horizon. How fascinating it was, that distant line where blue met blue! Reason told her the line wasn't real, that no seam joined sea and sky, but she could never quite believe it.

Skip plucked off her bikini top (stupid thing) and stepped into the tide. The beach behind her faded: that baby squealing, that transistor radio, that couple arguing, all receded. Wet sand pressed between her toes and foam curled, not quite coldly, around her ankles. Shallows lapped her calves, then she waded thigh-deep; a wave swept in, making her stagger back, aware of the heft behind its seeming gentleness. Flinging herself into the oncoming water, cleaving it with steely arms, she thought she would see the horizon fixed firmly, growing ever nearer; instead there were only green ramparts, silver spray, and blurry droplets glinting in her eyes.

Soon she was tired, desperately tired. She turned, treading water. Shimmery hills rose and fell. The beach was far off, a storybook tableau: long bright sands, jetty, hot-dog stand, stick figures in colourful costumes. Waves lapped in all directions; now there were no more glimpses of the beach between the shifting hills, and she was no longer sure which way was back and which out to sea. She waved a hand. Could anybody see her? She imagined herself imprisoned within castle walls, a circle impregnable as if it were made of stone.

Time distends strangely when you are about to die. Hours passed in her watery prison; each dip beneath the surface was an eternity, and she felt herself plunging down, down. When she bobbed up again she saw herself, as if from far above, tiny against the swell and lost for ever; then all at once she was scooped up into an embrace. Wildly she resisted, as if this new presence had come to drag her under, but she was too weak to hold out for long, and gave in to the strong chest and confident, sleek arms.

Feeling hot sand beneath her back, she opened her eyes. A shadow passed over her and a face came into focus: a man's, deeply tanned, with a droopy black moustache. She turned her head and saw people all around, jabbering in excited voices. 'Push down on his chest!' said one. 'Give him mouth to mouth!' said another.

Skip sat up indignantly, coughing, as Karen Jane descended upon them, Mary-hair flying. 'Helen, you stupid girl,' she said in a choking voice, while murmurs broke out among the onlookers.

'Say, he's a girl!' said the man with the moustache. His accent was strange: American, no mistaking it. Karen Jane had crushed Skip to her with all a mother's ardour; now, seeing the stranger, she let her daughter slump back and, with a delighted smile, turned her attention to the girl's saviour.

The lifeguard's hippie-length hair, ropy from the sea, flowed from underneath his tight cap. Beneath the droopy moustache stretched a dazzling grin. His arms and torso were well muscled, with thick fur that spread in wide wings across the pectorals before plunging in a tapering line towards a pair of tight red briefs beneath which swelled a prodigious lump.

'My apartment's just up from here,' he said to Karen Jane. (Apartment? Nobody said *apartment*, not in real life.) 'I'm done for the day. I guess you folks could use a Coke, huh?' He held out his hand. 'Kendall Caper.'

'You're a Yank?' said Karen Jane, and tickled his palm.

Caper lived in a sprawling single-storey mansion, one street back from the beach, which had fallen on hard times and been divided into flats. Lush gardens, a barely held-back jungle, lapped at the wide, listing verandas.

That night, Skip fell asleep on the sofa while Caper played Karen Jane an LP called *Surrealistic Pillow*. Once Skip stirred to see Karen Jane and Caper propped side by side against the wall like rag dolls. Both had cigarettes in their hands, fat, shaggy roll-ups. There was a funny smell.

'When the war's over, I can go home,' Caper was saying.

'San Fran?' said Karen Jane.

After that, she spent many nights away. When some weeks had passed, she drove Skip and Marlo to Caper's place one sunny afternoon and said, as if it were the most inconsequential of matters, that they were all going to live there now. Caper, in jeans cut off at the knees and nothing else, stood grinning in the doorway as they arrived. In his hand he held a can of Foster's; he swigged from it lustily before he bestirred himself, mooched forward and kissed Karen Jane long enough for the girls to be embarrassed.

Karen Jane looked eagerly to the future. The present, she told the girls, was a mere prelude to the glories that awaited them when the war ended (it had to end soon) and Caper took them to San Fran.

In Glenelg, Skip spent many an hour on the beach, coming to know it in all its moods: mornings when haze hung white over the sea; nights when kids dug fire pits in the sand and the sky was brilliant with a million stars; afternoons when the moored boats knocked and sloshed and it seemed the water would rise up over the Esplanade and spill in a grey flood down Jetty Road. Good old stinky, fishy Glenelg, with its shrieking gulls and back-to-front name! Marlo, who knew everything, said Glenelg was a palindrome, which Skip, who knew nothing, thought must be a cross between a paradox and an aerodrome.

Adelaide's last remaining tram service tethered the shabby beachside suburb to the city. On weekday afternoons, Skip could be seen at the stop on Jetty Road, waiting for Marlo to return from another day at Adelaide Ladies' College. Their course home would be a winding one, peering into shop windows, stopping for a chat at

Mr Cominetti's fish shop, browsing in the public library (for Marlo, the Brontës; for Skip, Biggles) or seeking out Caper on his boat. Skip grew used to Caper: to his shaggy hair and moustache, to his tie-dyed T-shirts, to his broad lopsided grin and the way he tousled her hair. He was amiable, like a friendly dog. Everybody liked Kendall Caper. Karen Jane, after too many men, had come at last into a safe harbour, or so Skip liked to tell herself.

Behind her now, laughter carolled from the kitchen, where Sandy Campbell still held court. Faintly, different sounds came from the neighbouring house: a piano, and voices raised in song. Curious, Skip made her way to the fence, and scrambled up into a pear tree. From the branches, she had an unimpeded view.

The house, surprisingly, was large and modern, the bright oblong windows punctuating a wing shaped like a shoebox. At the far end, unfurling beyond it like a poked-out tongue, stood a brick patio, while a parapet at gutter height with overlapping palm fronds bore testimony to a roof terrace. Tonight both were empty, but many a shadowy figure moved behind the curtains. The branch Skip sat on stretched across the fence. She edged towards the end, dropped in a flurry of legs and arms, then picked her way through a patch of silverbeet, stepped over a line of garden stakes, and hurried towards the house.

The music sounded clearly, a male voice riding with prissy elegance over rippling chords. Skip found a gap in the curtains. Inside, the place looked like a house on TV, with colourful swirling pictures on the walls, wickerwork chairs and sofas, low glass tables, and a white baby grand at which a plump, balding gentleman pressed the keys with a contemplative air. Surrounding him were perhaps thirty people, some standing, drinks in hand, some leaning against bookcases, some lounging over the furniture.

Two figures flanked the pianist: on one side was the singer, a tall, heavy-jawed young man in a purple suit with a yellow, huge-knotted necktie; on the other a small gypsy-like woman with a nut-brown face beneath a cap of black hair. When the young man fell silent, she picked up the melody. Her voice was less assured than his, almost screeching, but from the solemn attention of the listeners she might have been a diva in her prime. She wore a white blouse with many ruffles, a red miniskirt, black stockings and gleaming stiletto heels. Golden hoops hung from her ears, bangles circled her wrists, and on her fingers were many rings. She turned to the young man with a smile and their voices blended.

The song, Skip realised, was in a foreign language. From war movies she had seen she judged it to be German, though neither 'Achtung' nor 'Sieg Heil', 'Schnell, schnell' nor 'Jawohl, mein Kapitän' featured in the lyrics, so far as she could tell.

The duet ended on a dying fall. With sorrowing expressions, the singers cast down their eyes while the pianist hunched forward, double chin ballooning as he touched the final chord. The singers moved together; they embraced, as if stirred deeply by their song; applause rang out, and the pianist began a new, jaunty tune, requiring no voices.

Wind skirled. Skip told herself she should go back, but something kept her there, watching. It was then that she noticed the boy. Ignoring the grown-ups, he sat cross-legged on the carpet, facing the window. In his hand was a colourful tube that he held to one eye: a kaleidoscope. He turned it. The boy, aged perhaps twelve or thirteen, was coppery in complexion with dark, springy curls. Lowering the kaleidoscope, he looked directly at Skip.

Quickly she retreated, and was about to run away when a glass door slid open and two figures appeared on the patio. She flattened herself against the wall.

'Whew! Hot in there.' It was the gypsy woman.

'Enjoying our little *Schubertiade*?' Her companion, her fellow performer, swept back luxuriant hair. His accent, Skip thought, sounded peculiar: fruity, strangely precise.

'*Licht und Liebe*,' said the lady. 'Love is a sweet light. But here am I, abandoned and unloved –'

'Not when you've got Vladislav, surely.'

'Do you know why I married him? He was the only boy in Crater Lakes who'd heard of Dvořák.'

'Hmm. And are you telling me he's since forgotten?'

'Naughty boy! Give me a cigarette.'

The young man reached into his jacket. 'Looks like rain.'

'It always rains in Crater Lakes. But you don't mind your exile so much now, do you?' The gypsy's voice was husky, caressing. She reached up for the young man's lapels. How small she looked beside him: a child, a doll. 'I've always liked a six-footer.'

'Do you think they'll go for our plan?'

'It's been a long time,' said the woman. 'Years. But sometimes things are better if you wait.'

'And what are you waiting for – to play Ophelia?'

'Lady Macbeth might be more my line.'

What were they on about? Skip squirmed. The couple, she feared, were about to kiss. But while they kissed, she could scramble over the fence. She edged her way along the wall. She was just a few yards away from them. If they looked around they would see her. Ditto if she ran to the fence.

Howling, basso profondo, burst upon the night. If a monstrous piece of earth-moving equipment had appeared beside the house, motor roaring, metal jaws gnashing, it could not have frightened her more. For an instant Skip stood frozen, mouth open, gaping at the hound that hurtled towards her, baying for blood.

Crashing back through silverbeets she could hear the dog inches behind her, collar clanking, paws pounding, breath snorting. Looming before her was the five-foot fence, grey in moonlight. A bewildered crowd – glimpsed once, in a wild look back – had spilled onto the patio, and the kaleidoscope boy, surging forward, called to the dog, 'Get him, Baskerville!' and 'Baskerville, go!'

Fear propelled Skip over the fence. She lunged at it, ploughed her palms into the tops of the palings and swung up even as hot jaws snapped at her sneakers. She kicked, flailed, fell with a thud to the other side, and rolled down the grassy slope.

Still the dog bayed, scrabbling at the fence like a plague of rats; then the palings shook as the boy, with a cry, dropped over the side. At once, Skip was on her feet again. The boy clutched her arm. She slapped him away. Rain gusted on the air. Tears filled her eyes: shame, rage, horror. Blinded, she hurled herself down the long yard, arms working like pistons, feet pounding the grass, until suddenly there was no grass, nothing under her feet at all.

The splash filled the night like an explosion.

In her shock, Skip barely registered the stench that consumed her. Viscous liquid soaked through her clothes. She rose up, spluttering, spitting out foulness. Her pursuer danced above her, a demonic sprite, pointing and cackling.

Light fell across the yard; then came the kookaburra call of Auntie Noreen, asking the boy what the bloody hell he thought he was doing, and he cackled again. Now Auntie Noreen, Uncle Doug and Sandy Campbell were there too, gaping with astonishment into the shit pit. Rain pocked Skip's drenched head and the foul water that surrounded her.

Auntie Noreen howled, 'Is that Baby Helen? Helen, you look like a drowned rat!'

'A sewer rat!' cried Sandy Campbell.

'Poor little mite.' Uncle Doug shook his head.

Then, like the boy, all three of them were laughing.

# Chapter Three

One blustery afternoon some weeks earlier, Skip had been on her way to the tram stop in Glenelg when a man she had never seen before approached her with a friendly, purposeful air. He was tall, erect of carriage, and dressed immaculately: hat like a TV detective's, detergent-advertisement shirt, dark suit devoid of creases, shiny shoes like enormous black beetles.

'Afternoon, li'l miss,' he said, and raised the hat. His voice was like Caper's, if less exuberant. 'Don't suppose I could talk to you for a minute? Perhaps you and I could have a little chat.'

Skip half expected him to offer gum. 'I've been warned about men like you. You're a child molester.' She wasn't scared. She would kick him where it hurt.

'What's your name?' he said. 'Skip, isn't it?'

A pulse leaped in her neck. She narrowed her eyes. 'How do you know that?'

'That name might be a boy's. But you're a girl.'

She wondered whether to deny it.

'Been living here long?' the man asked. 'Like it, do you?' Now he really did offer her gum, and Skip wasn't sure if he was asking whether she liked gum or liked living where she did. She took the gum, though she supposed she should not. More than this man's voice was familiar: the curve of the jaw, the set of the eyes.

'One of the Wells sisters, aren't you? You call your mom by her first name. But what do you call the man who lives with her?' Skip was sure he knew already: he was toying with her, and she wondered why. Frowning, she would have walked away, but the man gripped her arm. She gasped. In the same moment she was frightened, excited, confused. He reached into his jacket. Would he bring forth a revolver? Would he hold her for ransom?

He produced a photograph. 'Look.'

The picture showed a clean-cut young man in collar and tie, with a dark short back and sides and a grin which, no denying it, she recognised. A moment passed before she realised that this was Caper, another Caper from another life. She looked again at the man who held the photograph.

'You're his brother.' Her voice was hoarse.

Still holding her arm, he brought his face close to hers. 'Do you have any idea who Kendall Caper is? You don't, do you?'

'What are you talking about?' Skip kicked the man in the shins, but she was wearing sneakers and did no damage. She writhed, broke free and ran. When she looked back, Caper's brother had vanished.

Skip reached the stop as a tram was drawing in. Passengers fanned out from the squeaking doors. Seeing Marlo, she called to her, waving her hands and leaping up and down.

'What's with you?' said Marlo, puzzled.

'Can't I be happy to see you?' Skip was breathless. She said nothing about Caper's brother. The encounter felt barely real, and indeed hardly could have been: Caper had never spoken of a brother; his past consisted only of the magical name San Fran, where you must be sure to wear flowers in your hair.

34

Two days later she was walking home from school when a white sedan crawled along the kerb beside her. She eyed it suspiciously; the passenger door swung open and Caper's brother leaned across from the driver's side and said in that syrupy voice, 'I'll give you a ride.'

What force compelled her into the car? They moved off, shadows of trees passing across the windscreen, as Caper's brother said, 'I didn't introduce myself properly the first time. I'm Richard Wrightman.'

'Wrightman? Not Caper?'

'You have a sister. You wouldn't like it if you lost her. That's how I feel about my brother. I've lost him, and long to get him back. You didn't say anything about our meeting the other day, did you? I'm hoping to surprise my brother. Yes sir, a merry chase he's led me these last few years. A clue here, a lead there, and most have been false. But not this time. Dad and Mom back in Frisco have been frantic. Think how happy they'll be when they hear the news! Now, you'll have to show me which way to go.'

Skip gulped. Oh, she was a fool! Why, why had she got into this car?

'I'm not kidnapping you! Show me where you live.'

'Will you let me out, please?'

Richard Wrightman laughed. 'Now, what would that achieve? I know I'm in the right place. I've been to Bogotá. I've been to Bangkok. I've been to Brisbane. Not much longer now.'

They had reached a stoplight. Skip threw open the door, flung herself into the street and, not looking behind her, ran all the way back to the school gates. She plunged inside, and hid out in the bike sheds until the sky was nearly dark, when she ventured home.

As she trailed to school the next morning, Qantas bag slung across her shoulder, she fancied that the white sedan crept after her down the street. Several times she glimpsed it from the corner of her eye, but each time she turned it was gone. In class she felt jumpy, as if at any moment a knock might come at the door, and the headmaster with an imperative beckoning finger would call her from the room.

'Helen Wells? This gentleman wants to talk to you,' he would say, and emerging from behind him would be Caper's brother, grin at the ready, detective's hat clasped against his chest.

On the weekend she stayed indoors, not wanting to stir from the room above the garage she shared with Marlo. Listlessly she lay on her bed and read about Superboy and Lana Lang. On Saturday evening it was raining lightly. Saturday meant the pictures. Every week they went to the Ozone, but Skip, for once, was reluctant to go. Music blasted from Caper's apartment. The Norfolk pine beside the garage creaked in the wind like a sailing ship at sea.

'Skip, what is it?' Marlo said at last.

'What what is?' said Skip, and snatched back the comic Marlo had plucked away from her.

'Something's wrong. It's been wrong for days.'

'How do you know? You're always at school.'

'I'm here now,' said Marlo.

Skip looked at her sister doubtfully, as if she might disappear at any moment. She turned away. 'There's a man. He's Caper's brother.'

'Man? What man?'

'He followed me after school. In a white sedan.'

Alarmed, Marlo grabbed her sister's shoulders. 'Who is this man? What did he do to you?'

'Nothing. Only asked questions – about Caper.'

'And you answered him? Oh, Skip!'

'I don't understand!' Skip wailed. 'What have I done?' But already the burden of guilt was upon her.

Marlo's next words made Skip's throat bulge as if she were about to vomit. 'I heard Karen Jane and Caper talking. They were frightened. He's not just dodging the draft. It's worse. He's hiding out –'

'What? What are you talking about?'

'He's a deserter. From the navy. If this man finds him –'

'It's his brother!'

'Are you sure? How long ago was this?'

'Days.'

'We have to tell him,' said Marlo.

But Skip had delayed too long. As in a film or a dream where one scene dissolves effortlessly into another, they raced to the top of the concrete stairs that led down from the garage block, only to be halted by the sight below. There were shouts, and a crash, the screen door banged, and two police officers led Caper from the apartment. Cuffs circled his wrists and he was struggling, cursing, as they hustled him off in the rain.

Under the Norfolk pine stood Richard Wrightman. Stepping out from its shadows, he turned his face ceremonially, like a mask, towards the girls, who swayed at the top of the steps. Marlo looked away from Skip and said only, 'You should have told me,' while Karen Jane stood on the veranda, hugging herself, and the police car drove away.

The next morning, the *Sunday Mail* reported that Kenneth Wrightman, twenty-six, who had deserted from the US Navy in Sydney, had been apprehended by police in the Adelaide suburb of Glenelg, where he had hidden out under an assumed name. More details emerged over the following days: Wrightman, renegade younger son of a wealthy San Francisco family, had been in and out of trouble for years – marijuana, grand and petty larceny, receiving stolen goods. The navy had been his last chance. He would now be sent back to America to face charges. Glenelg neighbours were quoted saying that 'Ken Caper', as they called him, had always seemed a dubious character. He played his music (if you could call it music) too loudly. They were sure he used drugs.

Two days later, Karen Jane took an overdose of painkillers. Marlo found her slumped on the sofa in the living room, unmoving, silvery saliva running from her mouth. The ambulance men came and took her away. They never brought her back.

\* \* \*

On the grassy rise just down from Puce's Bend, Skip stood, shivering a little, Qantas bag shrugged over one shoulder. A curl of puddle, cat-shaped, glistened beneath the rise; the paddock across the road was a quivering emerald sea. The sky was the colour of tin.

She wanted the bus to come and she didn't. She thought about running off, finding somewhere to hide. But not in this cold. She would have to get it over with, this first day. No one would notice her, she told herself. Not one girl among many.

Breakfast had been a torment.

'Very smart,' brayed Auntie Noreen, as Skip sidled into the kitchen. 'I been telling Marlene, it's important to make an impression your first day. But then' – she winked – 'Baby Helen knows how to make her mark, don't she?'

Skip tilted the milk bottle over her bowl, face burning, as Auntie Noreen, slathering margarine into a crumpet's pock holes, evoked like a fond family anecdote the sight of her niece slipping and sliding as old Dougie pulled her out of the shit pit. 'And her white eyes, blinking in her black face! Sandy reckoned she looked like an abo – bloody well smelled like one, I'll tell you!'

As she stood at the bus stop, Skip's hands were cold as marble. She stuffed them into her bomber jacket, jumped to keep warm, lost her footing, thudded into wet grass, and slid down the rise.

'What you do that for?' came a voice.

The boy stood foursquare on the muddy road, on the other side of the puddle. A shabby rucksack dangled from his fist. Let him mention the shit pit. Let him. She would knock his teeth down his throat.

'You should be careful,' he said, and she asked why. He stamped, and water doused her.

'Bastard!' She jumped the puddle and hurled herself on him. Kicking, pummelling each other, they rolled about on the road. He was bigger than Skip, and heavier; swiftly he pinned her down, but she wrenched an arm free and swung savage punches at his head.

He was ecstatic. 'Give up? You give up?'

Skip punched him again; both were so engrossed in their battle that neither was aware of the approaching yellow bus until it was almost upon them.

Brakes squealed, a horn blasted; then a door rattled open, and an ample-breasted, ample-hipped lady in a tight-skirted black uniform burst into the road. Furious, she stood over the combatants as they scrambled to their feet. 'Honza Novak! What the hell are you doing?'

Skip stood breathing heavily beside the boy. Honza Novak, she thought. Pavel's brother?

'Fighting a girl!' The lady's eyes blazed. She shook him by the shoulders. 'Stupid boy, what are you thinking of? Wait till Mr Rigby hears about this!' She grabbed the boy's rucksack from the ground and thrust it into his arms. 'Now get on that bus!'

Cheers, applause and stomping broke out as Honza, like a conquering hero, mounted the steps.

To Skip, the lady was all benevolence. 'You all right, dear? You're new on our run, aren't you? That Honza Novak's going to get what's coming to him! But you're all muddy – better go inside and change, eh?'

And face Auntie Noreen? Never! Skip wriggled away, brushed down her bomber jacket, followed Honza into the idling bus, and hunkered, wet and cold, into an empty seat.

Honza was sitting just behind her, on the long bench at the back. Boys tussled for places, squashing together, punching each other in biceps and thighs, every so often forcing one of their number to the floor. 'Quiet back there!' and 'Calm down, yous brats!' the driver lady called, but the boys were too busy yelling, 'You'll go down, mate!' and 'Fight! Fight!' to listen.

The high was huge. Skip's yellow bus was one of many that disgorged noisy passengers into a broad asphalted car park; pupils evidently came here from all over the district. The main building, set back behind wide lawns, was an imposing two-storey edifice, its many-windowed wings pinned together by a boxy central rectangle with a wide, arched entrance.

On the bus, the driver had instructed Skip to present herself at 'the office'. Making her way to the building, she was conscious of stares turned in her direction. Inside, at a counter in a dim corridor with linoleum on the floor, a birdlike lady in twin rows of pearls hovered over a card index, flicking with red talons, and chirped, 'Helen Puce, isn't it – Noreen's little girl?'

'Wells. I'm not related to Auntie Noreen.'

'Your timetable.' Unconcerned, the lady handed her a mauve sheet that smelled of methylated spirits. A talon pointed. 'That's your home group. Here's your classes for the week, and all the rooms. Don't suppose you brought your phys ed gear? Or your apron for home ec?'

Skip's home group met in one of the science labs, a long room with fixed, high benches, stools instead of chairs, and posters ranged around the walls depicting the solar system, a cross-sectioned volcano, and human bodies variously eviscerated, flayed or X-rayed. Skip hauled herself onto a free stool just as a balding young man in a lab coat rose from the front desk, clapped his hands for silence, and bade the class good morning.

'Good *mor*-ning *Mis*-ter Some-thing-or-other.'

Window monitors used long poles to pull down transoms from the tops of high windows; board monitors swept blackboards with windscreen-wiper arms; lunch monitors distributed brown paper bags on which pupils were required to record their lunch orders.

Four boys barged in late, laughing: a piggy-faced fat fellow with blazing red curls; a swarthy Greek type with a wispy dark moustache; a hatchet-faced blond boy, gangly as a marionette; and Honza Novak, who shambled after them. Skip's heart sank. She smoothed her timetable, which already resembled a battered treasure map. First years had no choices, no options; she would be with Honza Novak all day, every day, as they traipsed from class to class, separating only into boys' and girls' groups for craft (woodwork for boys, home ec for girls) and phys ed.

Mr Something-or-other hushed the boys angrily. Then, after further demands for quiet, he launched into a roll call.

Adamson, Janine? Present.

Baker, Nathan? Present.

Bunny, Wayne? Where's Wayne Bunny? Wayne Bunny could not be found.

The roll resumed. Cunliffe, Kylie?

'Cunt lips,' came a boy's whisper from the next bench, followed by a wail from (presumably) Kylie Cunliffe, a well-developed girl for her age, who beat the whisperer – Honza's piggy friend – savagely about the temples with a ruler until Mr Something-or-other restored order. Whether he had heard what the boy said, Skip could not be sure.

An elbow nudged her. 'Happens every day,' said the girl beside her, a dainty creature with blonde ringlets, icy eyes, and skin so pale it was almost translucent. 'You're new,' she added accusingly, and Skip could not deny it.

Fidler, Jason.

Gruber, Kevin.

Guppy, Joanne.

The piggy boy, with a cry of 'Yo!' – which brought him another reprimand – answered to Lumsden, Brenton.

'Lum's Den!' said the girl beside Skip. 'What sort of animal is a *lum*, do you think?' When Mr Something-or-other called 'Sutton, Lucy', the girl responded proudly, back straight, hands folded neatly on the scored bench.

Skip started as a monitor slapped a lunch bag on top of her timetable. NAME, the bag demanded, then HOME GROUP, followed by check boxes for PIE, PASTIE (extra boxes permitted W/SAUCE), CHIKO ROLL, and SANDWICH: CHEESE, HAM, PICKLE. Prices were printed beside each item: 8c, 10c, 12c.

She was scrabbling for a pen when she realised she had no money. A two-dollar note in the pocket of her jeans had perished in the shit pit; Auntie Noreen had given her no more. She pushed the bag away. 'I never eat lunch,' she told Lucy Sutton, and regretted it at once. Now she would never be able to have lunch at school.

Mr Something-or-other had reached the end of his list (Wigley, Gary; Wilkinson, Leonie) and passed to other matters – bike sheds, a sports day – before he realised what he had forgotten. 'And don't we have a new girl in class today?' He shuffled papers. 'Helen Wells, where's Helen Wells?'

Helen Wells raised her hand and declared with attempted casualness that everybody called her Skip. Faces swivelled towards her. 'Eh, Skip!' cried Brenton Lumsden, and clicked his tongue, while the lean boy, the Greek boy and Honza Novak brought their heads close to his, and crooned, like a barbershop quartet, the theme tune to *Skippy the Bush Kangaroo*.

'Now you've done it,' said Lucy Sutton.

The hooter sounded for the day's first class. Skip looked at her timetable: Maths – Central 12. She hated maths, and this was a double lesson. Glumly, to the accompaniment of Skippy mouth-clickings (did kangaroos really make a noise like that?), she followed the others to a hot upstairs room where a turbanned Indian fellow tried and failed to teach long division in a chaos of catcalls, guffaws and paper jets. To most of the class, but especially to Brenton Lumsden, everything the Indian said was hilarious. His name, Skip gathered, was Mr Singh, but the Lumsden gang addressed him as 'Harry', shooting hands skywards and crying, 'Harry! Harry!' with mock eagerness each time he asked a question.

'His first name's Harinder,' explained Lucy Sutton, who sat with Skip and three other girls around a table topped with white vinyl.

'They call him Harry the Hindu. Or sometimes Harry Krishna.'

This was not his only name. Every time Mr Singh turned to the blackboard, chants of 'O Buddha-Buddha … O Buddha-Buddha' broke out around the room. Kylie Cunliffe led the way, slipping to her fat knees and salaaming.

Lucy Sutton spent most of the lesson drawing hearts and arrows on the back of her folder, and whispering and giggling with the three other girls, a pair of spotty brunettes and a redhead whose large green eyes gave her a look of perpetual surprise.

With an imperative air, one of the brunettes leaned towards Skip. 'Do you like Johnny Farnham?' It seemed there was no choice.

Much discussion, much glancing and pointing, centred on the Lum's Den, Brenton Lumsden's gang. Soon Skip knew them all. The hatchet-faced boy was Shaun Kenny; the Greek one, Andreas Haskas, aka Greaso. With Honza Novak they surrounded Lummo in an admiring arc, taking their cues from him in everything, ever eager to do his bidding. Brenton Lumsden was the king of their class, and no doubt of their year, too. Perhaps of the whole school. Of the whole town. She wished she were back in Glenelg.

Dealing with recess was easy, or so Skip had decided at her last school after Marlo left. Rule one: walk. Walk round and round purposefully as if heading somewhere. Never linger. Rule two: keep to crowded parts of the yard, close to buildings, entrances, shelter sheds and playing fields. Rule three (this was paramount): no toilets. School toilets are places of danger, torment, humiliation and shame. In a sane world, schools would be constructed without toilets. Rule four: hold in view, but under no circumstances approach, teachers on yard duty. In a yard full of snot-nosed brats, you need teachers around, but never risk being made to pick up litter or run messages. And never be seen as an object of pity. A firm stride, that's what's needed: head forward, eyes sliding quickly away from any gaze.

Her first recess went well: nobody spoke to her; she spoke to nobody; she kept well away from the Lum's Den and maintained a steady, rapid pace for twenty minutes. Her circuit was soon established: all the way around Central and the asphalt yard behind it; around the art block; around the gym; past the tinny, echoing shelter shed; down the path towards the outlying portables, but only as far as the first row; there she veered sharply as if remembering something, and tracked back along the edge of the oval, watching out for flying footballs.

The next lesson was English, and the teacher was late. Trying to avoid Lucy Sutton's table, Skip instead found herself sitting next to Kylie Cunliffe. Just behind them were the Lum's Den. Fearlessly, Kylie turned to the boys. Sitting astride her chair, she plumped her chin onto crossed arms and demanded of Honza, as if it were the most ordinary question, 'Would you bum off Brooker for an apple?'

The boy blinked. 'No.'

'Would you bum off Brooker for an orange?'

'No.' He grinned foolishly.

'Would you bum off Brooker for a banana?' And so on through the greengrocer's shop. Honza always said no, until finally, apparently beaten down by these denials, Kylie cried, 'I give up! What *would* you bum off Brooker for?'

The reply came explosively: 'Nothing!' – at which she leaped up in triumph, big breasts wobbling like twin jellies, and Honza sank back, abashed, while his three mates cuffed him about the head and whooped, 'Poofter! He'd bum off Brooker for nothing!'

A shout rang out, 'Shut up, cretins!'

Silence fell suddenly.

Skip recognised Mr Brooker. The tall young man had exchanged the purple suit of the *Schubertiade* for jeans, a denim jacket and tie-dyed top. Around his neck and wrists he wore beads, and his thick dark hair swooped down from his forehead in sculptural waves. In one hand he clutched a sheaf of papers, which he flapped frequently, like a fan, as he paraded before his pupils, discoursing in detail on their imbecility, illiteracy, and incapacity for all but the most degraded pleasures.

The reason for this, Skip picked up, was the compositions Mr Brooker had just marked, in which not one pupil (not one!) had demonstrated more than the most rudimentary understanding of some mouldy old sonnet. Imperiously he swept between tables, flinging at the hapless authors the crumpled pieces of work on which he had scribbled copiously in red.

Kylie watched him, dreamy-eyed. 'I don't reckon he's really a poofter, do you?' she whispered to Skip.

Finally, like a wind-up toy running down, Mr Brooker lost momentum. He couldn't be bothered with them today, he declared. They would spend the lesson reading aloud. There were groans.

Skip, who had no book, had to look on with Kylie. Mr Brooker slung his long frame into a chair at the front, jutted out his legs, tilted back the chair as if deliberately to expose his lumpy crotch (Skip saw Kylie's interest quicken), crossed his hands behind his head, and, with exquisite languor, directed first one, then another pupil to read. One boy stuttered; one girl stumbled over words with more than two syllables; Kylie never turned the pages on time. Skip was soon bored, and barely listened as the resentful monotone of Andreas Haskas trundled out:

*'Say – what is dead cats good for, Huck?'*
*'Good for? Cure warts with.'*
*'No! Is that so? I know something that's better.'*
*'I bet you don't. What is it?'*
*'Why, spunk-water ...'*

The uproar was immediate. Kylie gaped at Skip. Mr Brooker, who seemed to have fallen asleep, started upright, and was shouting halfheartedly when crackling erupted from a loudspeaker overhead and a prissy secretarial voice instructed Honza Novak to report to the headmaster's office.

Honza looked bewildered, and not until Mr Brooker cried, 'Cretin! What are you waiting for?' did the boy leave the room at last. In the doorway, he jabbed fuck-sign fingers in Skip's direction, and she remembered the driver lady, who must really have reported him.

When he returned, his face was flushed and he limped; slipping gingerly back into his seat, he whispered intently as his mates leaned towards him.

'But what did he *do*?' Kylie wondered, and Skip, to her disgust, heard admiration in the girl's voice.

The Lum's Den emerged from their huddle and turned, all of them, to look at Skip. Brenton Lumsden pointed at her, fingers poised like a pistol that he pretended to fire, mimicking the sound from spitty lips.

Lunchtime.

Skip trudged back to home group. The monitors, let out early from the last lesson, were ready with the plastic crate known as the lunch basket. One by one they read out names from the brown paper bags that were now plump, splotched with grease, and reddish and soggy if a check had been placed in the box marked W/SAUCE. Some bags the monitors pitched above the crowd like footballs; some were batted through the air by many hands, while hapless owners struggled to claim them. Within moments, all around the grounds – on lawns, under trees, in the shelter shed, up and down the Central steps – pupils clustered with their pies, pasties and Chiko Rolls; later, they would jostle at the canteen window for Mars Bars, Cherry Ripes, Smith's Crisps, Twisties, Kitchener buns, Amscol icy poles. Coins would clink into the Coke machine; *clunk* into the silver tray would fall Cokes, Fantas, Leeds in sleek returnable bottles.

Skip wanted to run away and hide. To have no lunch was bad enough. To have others realise it would be worse. Peeling off from the others, her destination lay behind the shelter shed: a last, low outpost of school buildings before the oval stretched away to a distant chain-link fence. She had glimpsed the place at recess, a colony of drably functional outbuildings: a gardener's hut made of green timber; a galvanised-iron shed; and a low limestone wall that curtained off the incinerator and three huge silver bins. She glanced behind her. Nobody was watching. She slipped into the two-foot gap between the incinerator and the shelter-shed wall. The green hut, flush against silver metal, blocked the passage at the other end, but halfway down the fence a space opened out where the limestone curtain ended. Incinerator smells caught in her throat, a bitter ashy dampness. Stray planks, lengths of piping, and bricks in teetering piles cluttered the passage. She leaned against the shelter shed, hearing the hubbub through the wall.

Then came different voices, closer, harsher: 'You're weak, Novak!' 'Am not!' 'Yair, wanna prove it?' They came from around the limestone corner.

Skip groaned silently. She had walked into the Lum's Den.

Retreating, she blundered into a pile of bricks, which clanged against the pipes with the sudden startling heft of a church organ. She fell forward, grazing her palms, and staggered upright as a hand tapped her shoulder.

'Well, well. So the mountain comes to Mohammed. Or is it the other way round? Fucked if I know.'

Skip drew in her breath. She turned. Brenton Lumsden had a fag in one hand and in the other a pastie, half out of its bag. Sauce smeared his lower lip and his tight brown pullover. Skip's eyes darted up and down the passage. At the other end stood Shaun Kenny, sneering; Andreas Haskas appeared behind him. Next to Brenton Lumsden stood Honza Novak.

47

The fat boy devoured the last of his pastie, balled up the bag and flung it to the ground. He licked his fingers. 'See here,' he said after a moment, 'you got our mate into trouble, you did. Why'd you do that, Skippy?'

Skip, pretending a boldness she didn't feel, started forward as if to push her way past, but Brenton Lumsden set plump hands on his hips like Henry VIII and stood his ground. 'We don't like squealers,' he said. 'You're not going to squeal on us again, eh, Skippy? I reckon a binning's in order.'

He grabbed Honza by the collar, thrust him towards her, then stood back, smirking, as his henchmen closed in. Skip swung her fists. It was no good. One boy punched her, another pushed her, and she fell, jarring her hip. Honza Novak seized her feet. Shaun Kenny grabbed her hands. As she swung into the air, her vision zigzagged over shadows, sky, planks, pipes, galvanised iron, dirt, grass, concrete, Honza Novak grinning, Shaun Kenny biting his lip, and Andreas Haskas, silver circle upraised, like a waiter removing with a flourish a cloche from a dramatic dish.

They flung her headfirst into a bin.

Skip gagged. Stench filled her nostrils. Something sharp stuck into her forearm; something sticky seeped across her neck. She tried to push herself out, but when she pressed down with her hands they only sank deeper into a mulch of grass clippings, banana skins, balled-up lunch bags, ripped-off wrappings, cigarette butts and half-eaten sandwiches.

First the shit pit, now this! Skip hated Crater Lakes.

She braced herself on the edge of the bin. Grip the rim, that's the idea. Haul yourself up. Her first attempt failed and she slipped back. She despised herself. Why must she be so small, so female? One day, she told herself, I'll kill Brenton Lumsden.

Skip had resumed her struggles when a battering filled her ears – the sound of hands, feet, clambering up beside her. Somebody grabbed her shoulders. What now? Were they going to force her deeper into the filth? She kicked and thrashed; the hands only gripped her shoulders more firmly, but then she felt them pull her up. Gracelessly she rode over the bin's high edge and tumbled to the ground.

Beside her stood a bashful Honza Novak. He signalled to her to be quiet, and whispered, 'Said I was going to the bog.'

'What?' Skip spat out the word. Her brown skirt had ridden up on her thighs and she slapped it down angrily. She wanted to wear jeans. She only ever wanted to wear jeans.

'Come to see if you was all right,' said Honza.

She punched him, hard, in the stomach and ran: ran and ran, not back towards the school buildings but across the oval, dodging footballs, fights, games of tag. Cries rang after her: 'What happened to her?' and 'Get a load of that!'

When she made it to the boundary her left hip ached and she was gasping for breath, but she hurled herself at the chain-link fence, scaled it, and dropped to the ground below.

'Streuth! Who dragged you through a hedge backwards?' Doug Puce goggled at his niece. Hunched over rickety scales, he had measured out carpet tacks in a spiky heap; his customer, a seamy-naped fellow in saggy overalls, turned, elbow on counter, and blinked at the new arrival.

Skip caught her breath. 'Where's Marlo?'

'Out back.' Uncle Doug jerked a thumb and Skip, without pause, ducked under the flap in the counter and vanished through a curtain of plastic streamers as he called, 'Eh, love, shouldn't you be at school?'

'Skip!' In the back room, Marlo rose from a cluttered desk. 'What's happened?'

'Nothing! I fell in a bin.'

'Just slipped?'

'Uh-huh.' Skip smiled like Stan Laurel, slapped her head, and sent debris flying: cut grass, ash, a sticky wrapper. All the way down Volcano Street she had imagined pouring out her sufferings to her sister, calling down curses on the Lum's Den. Suddenly she knew she would say nothing.

In a corner of the room was a sink. Wrenching the tap into wailing life, she doused her hair and her bent neck. The water thrilled her: so clean, so cold. She shrugged off the bomber jacket and wet that too. Red slime (an icy pole, squashed?) spread and dispersed.

'You've run off, haven't you?' Marlo said accusingly.

'Lunchtime. Aren't you having lunch?'

Marlo gestured around her. All across the desk and the floor surrounding it were papers, folders, suspension files. 'Do you know how long this lot's going to take? So much for Auntie Noreen keeping an eye on things! Uncle Doug's been shoving things any old place, waiting for some mug (that's me) to sort it all out. I'm going to have to ring half our suppliers and ask if we've paid them – that, or sit back and wait for the bailiffs.'

'I could help,' Skip said brightly. She slung herself into a chair and made it swivel. The desk opposite Marlo's was larger, almost twice the size, and entirely clear but for a chocolate-brown telephone, a none-too-clean ashtray, and an inverted V of plastic embossed with the legend MR D. PUCE, GENERAL MANAGER. Filling the remaining space was an easy chair in caramel-coloured vinyl, a filing cabinet, and shelves heaped with bathroom-fittings catalogues, old copies of *Pix*, and paperback books by Harold Robbins and Alistair MacLean. A Mobil calendar hung on a wall; in the window, pulled back dustily, were floral curtains that looked as if they might crumble at a touch.

'Lunch?' Pavel stood in the doorway. Skip was glad that he expressed no surprise to see her there. Test-tube head frothing, he advanced on Marlo and grabbed her hand. 'Come on! Old man Puce can hold the fort for a while.'

Relenting, Marlo allowed herself to be tugged out of the office, Skip pulling one hand, Pavel the other. Out the back, on a strip of driveway, Pavel's Land Rover glimmered greenly. Skip scrambled into the front seat.

'Piggy in the middle.' Pavel flicked a finger in her hair.

They swung into the street, narrowly avoiding a Ford station wagon. As the day had advanced, the sky had grown brighter, the clouds turning from black to greyish-white.

'Chicken and chips? I'm buying.' Pavel drew up at Chickenland. The enormous fibreglass chicken on the roof loomed above him like a science-fiction monster as he vanished through glass sliding doors. Skip thought how much he resembled Honza: a larger edition. But his character could hardly have been more different. Pavel was that rare thing, a boy who wasn't a bastard. She had thought at first that he was stupid. But he was really just kind.

'Is he always so happy?' she asked Marlo.

'First thing Monday morning! I don't know how he stands it. Uncle Doug's on at him all day – fetch this, carry that, shift those shovels, unpack those crates, drive these sacks to the other side of town. And *he's* got his feet up half the time. If I were Pavel, I'd tell him to take a running jump.'

'Won't you tell him anyway?'

'It's not that simple.'

'Why not?'

Two young mothers passed by on the pavement, pushing strollers. Lightly, Marlo touched her sister's shoulder. 'Skip, I'm sorry. I've been horrible to you. I don't mean to be. I'm worried – hell, I'm scared out of my wits. You know we can't count on Karen Jane coming round?'

'She always comes round,' Skip said.

'She's worse this time. The social worker said so. I don't know what will happen. None of us can know. But we may just have to make the best of things, you and me – here in Crater Lakes.'

Dread blocked Skip's throat. With twitching fingers she picked at the brown leathery seat, wondering how she could make the best of Brenton Lumsden. And Honza.

'Poor Skip! It isn't too awful, is it?'

'School? It's great.'

'Mission accomplished! Here, hold the provisions.' Pavel, returning to the Land Rover, thrust into Skip's hands a family-size bottle of Coca-Cola and a hot, heavy plastic bag. Inside were three foil cartons with white cardboard lids, white plastic knives and forks, plastic beakers, and a large damp-looking parcel wrapped in white paper. Steam rose deliciously. All at once she was ravenous.

They slid off down Volcano Street. Marlo made polite offers to pay Pavel back, but he shook his head. Her first day at Puce's! This was a celebration. 'Sun's coming out again,' he said. 'We can sit in Crater Gardens.'

The gardens flanking the town hall were laid out immaculately, if somewhat fussily, with neat plantings of roses, bluebells and begonias edging the inside of the low stone wall, and cool arbours of non-native trees.

Skip kept up and Marlo hung back as Pavel led them down an asphalt path. A metal fountain with cavorting dolphins and mermaids looked admirably ancient under streaks of verdigris. Further on was a wishing well, with a cupola raised above it on twin painted struts; around the hatlike dome ran the words LIONS CLUB OF CRATER LAKES.

The gardens were bigger than they looked from Volcano Street, bending in an L-shape behind the town hall and the two buildings beside it, the institute and the theatre. Marking off a large area was a picket fence surmounted by a thick, almost tropical, wall of foliage. A gate led into a shadowy path; from below came a watery, insistent thrumming.

They sat on a park bench, Skip between Marlo and Pavel. With growing eagerness she passed around the foil containers, the beakers, the plastic cutlery; she ripped open the damp parcel and stuffed a handful of chips into her mouth. Soft crumbly salty vinegary warmth slid down her throat, and she said with her mouth full, 'I'll keep these on my lap, shall I? Then you can both reach.' She tore off the cardboard from her foil box. A prodigious chicken thigh swam in dark gravy; peas glistened, green as grass. Good old Pav!

She asked him if he had always lived in the Lakes.

'Born and bred. Mum, too. Years ago, her dad was mayor.'

'And you're working in Puce Hardware,' said Marlo – her first words since they had left the Land Rover. Her sister, Skip decided, didn't much like good old Pav.

If he noticed, he didn't let it show. Coca-Cola foamed like champagne as he bit off the bottle cap. He licked the neck of the bottle, laughed, and glugged the black liquid into the beakers. As they ate, he listed the attractions of Crater Lakes. Skip, to her mild surprise, realised that Pavel Novak wasn't ashamed of the town where he had been born, and felt no need to apologise for it, ridicule it, or claim that he would soon leave. They must see the lakes, of course: the blue, the green, the brown. The blue one was grey all through winter but changed in spring to brilliant blue, and no one knew why. He spoke of swamps, sinkholes, underground tunnels. The climb to the top of Mount Crater – what a view! You could see the coast thirty miles away.

First, though, the cave. After they had eaten, he led them through the gate in the picket fence. Palms and ferns lined a tarred path that curved downwards in a spiral. The roar Skip had heard from above grew louder as they descended. The temperature seemed to rise; mist danced on the air. Skip strode ahead, arms swinging, enjoying the sound of her shoes on the path as the gradient propelled her on. Walls of rock, moist and primeval-looking, shelved above a deep depression in the earth; a narrow but intense rivulet cascaded down them resoundingly, sending steamy curlicues into the air.

She turned back to Pavel. 'But where's the cave?'

They were still just halfway down. The spiral tightened; the last curve brought them to a viewing deck, a rectangle banded with a fence of painted pipes, like a stage-set fragment of an ocean liner. Water splattered Skip's face. She gripped a blistered railing. 'It's so loud,' she cried. Here was the cave: dark chambers opened behind the curtaining water, and she wondered how far back they went and where they led.

'Where does the water come from?' she asked Pavel.

'From the lakes, they reckon.' A pool below them surged and foamed, buffeted by the impact from above. 'Then it runs off again. There are underground rivers all along this coast.'

Skip marvelled at this surprising information. Dull, sensible South Australia was not all it seemed. Volcanoes had once shaken this green corner of the state; riven with fissures, faults, subterranean channels, the earth spoke of strangeness. This hole in the ground was a prehistoric pit. The park above, with its rows of roses, the town hall with its tick-ticking clock, were the merest imposition on a timeless land.

Marlo said suddenly, 'I don't like it here.' Something in her voice was wild, almost pleading, and Skip turned to her sharply. Marlo looked helpless, lost, and with an aching heart Skip vowed that somehow, in some way, she would make things better for them both. She must.

She took her sister's arm and gripped it tightly.

# Chapter Four

'I got a good one, I got a good one!'

The words exploded on a gust of beery breath. Sandy Campbell slammed down his bottle, wiped his mouth with his hand, and tilted his chair precariously away from the table. The others turned towards him: Auntie Noreen eager for mirth; Uncle Doug with a weak smile; Marlo cold-eyed; Skip not ungrateful. It was Sunday evening. A week had passed since the sisters' arrival in Crater Lakes. A moment earlier, their aunt had been informing Sandy Campbell that Baby Helen wasn't Miss Butter-Wouldn't-Melt – no, not a bit of it! Bunking off school, eh? Fighting with boys. Old Noreen heard everything.

'Get this, then.' Sandy Campbell, who only wanted to tell the good one, crossed his furry, barbecued forearms over his barrel chest and began. 'There's this bloke, see, and he's driving up the Birdsville Track. There he is, way out in the sticks, burling along in his old red FJ, like you do, sinking a few stubbies, splattering a few echidnas, knocking a roo or two six ways from Sunday ... when he reckons he needs a piss.'

'Eh, language!' Auntie Noreen gestured to the girls.

'Needs a *piss*,' repeated Sandy Campbell, 'so he pulls up, like you do, on the side of the Birdsville Track, clunks open the car door, steps out (whew! fucking hot up here!), flops his dick out. There he is, having a good old piss, like you do – *sss-sss, sss-sss* – when, what do you know, he sees he's stepped into quicksand. "Fucking oath," the bloke reckons, "I'm sinking!"

'Already he's up to his ankles. Well, he tugs his feet, tugs and tugs and tries to get out, but does it do him any good? Not fucking likely. Before he knows it, he's up to his calves. "Fuck me, I'm a goner," the bloke reckons, but lo and *be*-hold! Just then he hears an engine – *brmm, brmm* – and here's a pink Torana, burling along the Birdsville Track. Looks like his lucky day.

'The bloke waves and waves, shouts and shouts; pink Torana pulls up next to the FJ; bloke in the Torana leans out, looks at the bloke in the quicksand, and reckons, "Fucking shit! What's happened to you?" "Mate, I'm sinking!" says the bloke in the quicksand. "Can you pull me out?" That's when a twinkle comes in the other bloke's eye and he reckons' – Sandy Campbell's voice grew high and fluting – '"Ooh, duckie, only if you give me a kiss." So, as you'd expect, the bloke in the quicksand reckons, "Poofter!" and tells him to fuck off. Pink Torana drives away.' Sandy Campbell took a swig of beer. Gingery whorls of hair protruded, thick as couch grass, from the V of his open-necked shirt. Rolls of belly oozed over his belt.

'By now the bloke's up to his waist. He's sinking fast. "Fuck me dead, I've cashed in me chips," he reckons, but lo and *be*-hold! Just then he hears an engine – *brmm, brmm* – and here's a mauve Monaro, burling along the Birdsville Track. So the bloke waves and waves, yells and yells; mauve Monaro pulls up next to the FJ, and the bloke in the Monaro winds down his window, leans out and reckons, "Shitting fuck! What's happened to you?" "Mate, can't you see I'm sinking? Pull me out, for fuck's sake!" Well, the bloke in the Monaro puts a little pout into his lips, a twinkle comes into his eye, and he reckons, "Ooh, duckie, only if you give me a cuddle." So, as you'd expect, the bloke reckons, "Poofter!" and tells him to fuck off. Mauve Monaro drives away.'

For the third act, Sandy Campbell rose from his chair, lit a fresh ciggy, and paced around the table, heavy boots shaking the floor. Auntie Noreen's bulk wobbled as if she knew the punchline and could barely hold back laughter.

'The bloke's just about done for. He's up to his neck. "Time to meet me fucking maker," he reckons, but lo and *be*-hold! Just then he hears an engine – *brmm, brmm* – and here's a black Kingswood burling along the Birdsville Track. Going like a bat out of hell it is, clouds of dust behind, but it's the bloke's last chance; he screams at the top of his lungs, and bloody hell, he's in luck. Kingswood pulls up, bloke gets out, comes and stands over the bloke in the quicksand and reckons, "Jeez, you're in a fucking pickle."

'Well, as you can imagine, the bloke's really packing shit by now, so he yells, "Mate, pull me out, for fuck's sake! I'll give you a kiss, I'll give you a cuddle, I'll let you ram it up me fucking bumhole, just pull me out!" And the other bloke looks down at him – just this head, that's all that's left, sticking up from the quicksand – and a scowl comes over his face, and he stamps on the top of the bloke's head' – Sandy Campbell, with a clumping boot, mimed the action: *squelch!* – 'and reckons, "Poofter!"'

Auntie Noreen's laughter was uproarious.

Skip and Marlo rolled their eyes. They were used to dinner at their aunt's by now. Whether Sandy Campbell made it worse or better was a moot point. Without him, their aunt dominated the table, stuffing down food while holding forth upon the government ('a mob of bloody galahs'), the economy ('this country rides on the sheep's back'), and the youth of today ('don't know your arse from your elbow, that's your trouble'). With Sandy Campbell, she presented a different side: girlish, flirtatious, delighted alike by his mock grace before the meal

('Two-four-six-eight – bog in, don't wait'), his bellowed jokes (many concerning poofters), and the disquisitions he sandwiched between them on dog racing, hot rods, two-up games (good); war protestors, abos, pop singers (bad); and his dead wife, whom he described variously as beautiful, a cow, or – if he was drunk enough – a fucking bitch. This was his third visit since the girls arrived. Only coach trips to Adelaide kept him away.

Marlo rose, scraping back her chair. 'We'd better go, Skip.'

'Go?' cried Auntie Noreen. 'Yous haven't had your cherry cobbler.'

'There'll be snacks at Novaks'.'

'Novaks'!' said Sandy Campbell. 'Some wog muck that bloke cooks? What yous want to go round there for?'

'Cul-cha! Sunday swah-ray,' brayed Auntie Noreen. 'I've a mind not to let them go, but I suppose they've got to see for themselves what a stuck-up cow Deirdre Novak is. No later than ten, though – Baby Helen's got school in the morning, and as for you, Miss High-and-Mighty, I'm not having you yawning your way through a day at Puce Hardware.'

'Give over, love,' said Doug Puce – his first contribution that evening. 'They're just going next door.'

'Yair, and when's that cow ever invited us?' Auntie Noreen looked warningly at the girls. 'I'll tell yous one thing: I remember Deirdre Gull before she married that wog. Thought she was a cut above the rest of us, and what does she do? Throws herself away on a dirty reffo, and still puts on her airs and graces! God give me strength. She's a Lakes girl through and through, and don't yous believe no different.'

'We won't, Aunt.' Marlo tugged her sister to the door.

Skip was torn. She hardly wanted to stay at Auntie Noreen's (though the cherry cobbler was tempting) but dreaded Mrs Novak's. All through the school week she had avoided Honza. In class, she watched contemptuously as he sniggered with the Lum's Den, dead-legged Shaun Kenny, traded fuck-signs with Andreas Haskas, and gagged with laughter at Brenton Lumsden's jokes.

Now she said to Marlo, 'I thought you hated Pavel.'

'This isn't about Pavel. We can't be rude to Mrs Novak.'

They walked in the middle of the dirt road. Marlo's eyes had gleamed when she showed Skip the white card, scrawled with loopy handwriting, that invited them to what Mrs Novak called Sunday in the Sanctum. Sanctum! Skip thought of the singers last week, warbling away in German. And one of them, to make matters worse, had been Mr Brooker!

Numerous cars jammed the Novak driveway and lay becalmed at angles across the lawn. From the front, the house was dark; music and voices drifted from the back. Marlo rang the doorbell several times before, at Skip's suggestion, they followed the path around the side. Cypresses rose rustlingly. White concrete walls glimmered in the moonlight.

'Big place, isn't it?' said Skip.

'Pavel said they had it remodelled. Somewhere under all this is a house like Auntie Noreen's.'

They had almost reached the rear when loud barking broke out, and a meaty monster burst from the trees. Skip had forgotten Baskerville.

'Run!' She slapped Marlo's arm.

The night was warm. Guests spilled across the terrace; faces turned, startled, as the girls dived among them, pursued by the mighty beast.

'Baskerville!' a voice screeched, and the dog scrabbled to a halt and stood panting, as if expecting a treat. Skip was impressed. The screech belonged to the gypsy woman she had seen the week before, who now scurried, shouting and waving, towards the new arrivals. 'The Wells sisters!' she cried, and thrust forward a hand with long lacquered nails. 'I'm Deirdre Novak.'

The little woman had about her the air of a hyperactive elf. Tonight a bejewelled silver band crowned her jet-black bob of hair;

beads clattered at her neck and bangles at her wrists. Her dress was alarmingly brief, a simple shift printed with interlinked purple rings against a bright orange background. She wore black stockings and teetered on spiky heels, in which she still stood some inches short of Marlo.

She looked Marlo admiringly up and down. 'Marlene' – Mar-*lay*-nah – 'I declare, you're even prettier than that son of mine said! Welcome to the Sanctum. You're going to be a big hit in Crater Lakes, young lady.' And clutching Marlo's arm, Mrs Novak led her away.

Looking around the Sanctum – what *was* a sanctum? – Skip felt both boredom and alarm. The guests, straggling between the terrace and the long bright room behind, were dreary, the women mostly mutton dressed as lamb like Mrs Novak, or dowdy in a would-be intellectual way; the men, some with combovers, some with thick sideburns, variously resembled golfers, fishermen or TV evangelists. One wore a medallion over a white turtleneck; another sported a black beard intended, no doubt, to suggest a beatnik, though Skip thought he looked like Rolf Harris. Mr Singh, in his saffron-yellow turban, and his skinny wife in her matching sari provided a more authentic exotic touch. How embarrassing, to see teachers outside school! Leaning against the baby grand was Mr Brooker, gesticulating at a toothy lady in pearls. Skip hoped they weren't about to sing.

'And what can we get our youngest guest?'

Skip turned as a man addressed her in a thick foreign accent. He was the pianist she had seen last Sunday, a hulking mound of a man, bald on top, with soft grey eyes, who carried trays of canapés in both plump hands and wore over his paunch an apron bearing the legend CHIEF COOK AND BOTTLE WASHER.

'Lemonade?' he went on. 'I'd say gin and tonic, which you might well need, but I don't think it's allowed for ten-year-olds.' He found a place for the canapés on an already laden table: nuts, crisps, crackers, cubes of cheese on sticks.

'I'm twelve,' said Skip. 'Are you Honza's father?'

'Helen Puce, isn't it? Honza's still not home. Been out with that Lumsden boy all afternoon. Typical!'

Skip tried not to look relieved. 'I'm Wells. Like H. G. But really I'm Skip,' she added, as Mr Novak presented her with a brimming tumbler.

'You're in Honza's class? I hope you're a better pupil. Both my sons, such terrible pupils! In Czechoslovakia, I study to be an engineer. Here, I am a lowly clerk. But didn't I hope better for my sons? Pavel should have gone to university, done something with his life, and what happens? Stupid boy! Ends up in a hardware shop.'

Skip was about to ask where Pavel was when she saw him on the other side of the room, serving drinks. Did he mind being a waiter? As always, he looked happy enough, but then a glass smashed in a far corner and he jumped a little and reeled around. Mr Novak hurried off to help.

Left alone, Skip applied herself to the canapés, not without gusto, until a lady – Rhonda Sweetapple from the Greyhound? – looked at her snoogishly. She felt as if she were at school and it was recess. Time for a circuit. She slipped off to explore the house. Behind the Sanctum stretched long darkened corridors, branching in two directions, with a skylight in the ceiling at the point where they met. She peered into a bedroom. Everything smelled new. The kitchen, silvery in moonlight, might have belonged to a restaurant. Copper pans of many sizes hung from hooks above a wide range. Open shelves displayed big jars of preserves and little jars of spices. Skip opened a jar of something and smelled it. She wrinkled her nose. Wine bottles lay in a crisscrossing rack. Yellow-gold candelabra, spaced evenly, thrust up in a line down the middle of a long table that appeared to be made of railway sleepers.

Skip felt sad as she made her way back to the Sanctum. The Novak house hinted at a permanence she had never known. But perhaps the impression was false. After all, it was just a house. And it was in Crater Lakes.

In the Sanctum, Mrs Novak huddled beside Marlo on a sofa, muttering intensely as if confiding sisterly secrets. Marlo looked tolerant, even indulgent. A picture on the wall, an abstract swirl, churned above their heads like a mushroom cloud.

Snatches of conversation drifted in and out of Skip's awareness.

'... So I asked the cretins' (Mr Brooker's voice was loud) 'which ones liked opera. Groans, of course, from the usual suspects. "Well, looks like some of us will be off to the library to do revision while the rest of us hear this opera," I said. "Pity. Because this opera is *Jesus Christ Superstar –*"'

'... You've heard she's writing a novel, I suppose?'

'Deirdre? Painting and ceramics, now writing – whatever next?'

'The story, I gather, concerns a young girl's awakening one burning summer in the Tuscan hills –'

'... Yairs, so the boys hired a van and went all over England, John O'Groats to Land's End –'

'Me, I say you should see Australia first –'

'... What *is* this about Deirdre's big announcement tonight? She's been dropping hints like confetti.'

'Howard Brooker's in on it, of course.'

'Mr Stick-His-Oar-Into-Everything? No doubt –'

'... But Howard, what's this Webber bloke trying to say? I've heard it's blasphemy, pure and simple.'

'Of course, there's no resurrection in *Superstar* ...'

Skip was nerving herself for a second raid on the canapés when a spoon clinked a glass. The Sanctum fell silent. She craned her neck; the clinking had come from Mr Novak, but he gestured at once to his wife, who stepped into a clear space beneath the chandelier that illumined the long room.

Under bright light, Mrs Novak looked older than she had seemed at first. Her face, which had seen a lot of sun, was withered, and her neck speckled and reddish, ridged with tendons that stood out like wires. Smiling, she waited for the applause to die down, then began, speaking with seeming casualness, though Skip sensed the emotion behind the words. Tonight meant a lot to Deirdre Novak. And so, no doubt, did Howard Brooker.

'Thank you, my good friends. Some of you know that this is a special night. But if you're still wondering what it's all about, it's time to tell you. Lord knows we do our best here in Crater Lakes. It's all of you' – she stretched out her arms and the bangles clattered – 'who provide this town with what culture it has. We're lucky. There's Mr Heinz's art club.' She gestured to Rolf Harris. 'There's Mrs Boucher's pottery class.' A plump matron blushed. 'We've the book club. We've the library. We've these evenings in the Sanctum. But something's missing. It's been missing a long time.

'The Crater Lakes Players was once a thriving concern. What happened to the Players? One of our triumphs, and we let it lapse. We were wrong, wrong!' The admission, it seemed, was a significant one for her. 'We need a local drama society. Oh yes, we've talked about this before, dreamed of it. But we needed someone, a man of vision, to turn our dreams into reality. Well, that man's here. He's come amongst us only this year, but already he's a force to be reckoned with. You know who I'm talking about. Howard Brooker, tell us about your vision.'

Mr Brooker's vision! Was it time to go back to Auntie Noreen's? Her English teacher, Skip had decided, was a bighead and a bore.

Fresh applause broke out as he joined his hostess in the middle of the room. Another man might have been embarrassed by the fulsome introduction, but Mr Brooker took it as a matter of course. He wore a green corduroy jacket over a floral shirt, crotch-hugging jeans with a chunky belt buckle, and elaborate reddish cowboy boots. He blew out smoke in a long stream.

'Deirdre's right,' he declared ringingly, as if challenging anyone to disagree. 'A town this size needs a good drama company. That's why Deirdre and I have decided to launch the New Crater Lakes Players.'

The cheers were loud. A lady cried, 'Bravo!'

'Oh, I know there've been a few attempts at reviving amateur drama here in the Lakes. I've heard' – his tone was bantering – 'there was a nice production of *Salad Days* a few years back, and of course the high's put on a show or two – *Oliver!* last year, *Bye Bye Birdie* the year before – but we're talking about a much more ambitious scheme.

'People say you can't be ambitious with amateurs, you have to pander, you have to patronise. I've never believed that. It's my conviction that first-class drama, acted boldly, must find its audience. Deirdre's shown me the scrapbooks for the Crater Lakes Players, who last performed over twenty years ago. She hasn't looked at them in all that time. Not keen to revive old memories. I understand. She's always been one to look forward, to embrace the future. Well, so am I. But it's the past that shows us the way to the future. And those who forget the past will never surpass it. Shall we do better? I think we shall.

'We've laid out the scrapbooks on the baby grand. Have a look, my friends, and marvel at what was achieved: *Man and Superman, King Lear, Oedipus Rex*. The New Players will carry on that tradition. We've booked the King Edward VII Theatre for the third week in November. We'll be holding auditions this week, then rehearsing every Tuesday night, Thursday night and Sunday afternoon here in the Sanctum for the next six weeks.

'I suppose you're wondering what we're going to perform – and I can tell you that no, it won't be *Salad Days, Oliver!* or *Bye Bye Birdie*.' (Urbane laughter.) 'Drama, real drama, should challenge and confront, not comfort and coddle. The New Players must start where the Players left off. That's why the first production of the new group will be the last of the old: one of the most powerful and demanding plays in the modern repertoire, a groundbreaking classic about the prejudice and small-mindedness of a provincial town ...'

While Mr Brooker poured out his rhetoric, Skip edged her way back through the crowd. Where was Marlo? Now Mr Brooker was going on about somebody called Henry Gibson, the man who had written the play – excitedly, he called Henry Gibson a genius, a revolutionary, but all the time it sounded as though Mr Brooker was saying what a genius Howard Brooker was for appreciating Henry Gibson, who was too difficult for everybody else. Too boring, more like it. Skip could bet he was as boring as Mr Brooker.

Skip thought about making for the back fence and finding her way home but then remembered what had happened last week. In a corner of the Sanctum was a staircase, a dark metal spiral that corkscrewed into the ceiling. When applause rose again and Mr Brooker bowed like Sir Laurence Olivier taking a curtain call, she spirited herself up the stairs and emerged on the roof terrace, a broad expanse lined with garden furniture and droopy potted ferns.

Freedom! For a time, at least. She stepped towards the parapet. The garden shone purple-grey beneath an unclouded moon; the sky was a dark blanket, scattered with glitter. She stretched out her arms.

A voice came. 'Reckon you can fly, do you?'

Skip whirled around. In the shadows some feet away was Honza.

'When did you get back?' she said coolly.

'Mrs Lumsden run me home. Her car really smells. Ain't got no husband to clean it out, poor cow.' As usual, the boy was scruffy, the tails of his plaid shirt hanging over his jeans. From a pocket of the shirt he drew out a pack of Marlboros and a box of Redheads. 'You smoke?'

'Yair, I smoke.' What was this, a peace offering? Skip hung back, reluctant to take her place beside him. He flipped open the Marlboros, pulled up a fag and extended it towards her; then he struck a Redhead, bringing it to her face. Drawing in the smoke, she did her best not to cough. Both squatted, as if to use the furniture would be weak, even shaming.

'Do anything good today, then?' Skip asked, as if she cared.

'Smoked out back. Kicked the footy round. Chess.'

'Lummo plays chess?'

'Well, kind of. I got him in checkmate and he upset the board.'

Skip wondered how to tell Honza what she thought of him. Imagine: to talk about Lummo and not even mention how Lummo had treated her! She saw herself springing up, grinding her fag underfoot, telling Honza to fuck off.

The boy blew smoke rings and looked up at the moon. 'Good night for stalking,' he said. 'Ever go stalking?'

'What's stalking?'

'You go out late. When you're meant to be asleep.' He seemed puzzled that she didn't know this. 'Everything's different in the dark, like another planet. Pav and Baz, they used to do it. They went all the way into Volcano Street. You go looking for the ghost of Crater Lakes, see.'

'What ghost?' Skip scoffed.

'Big as a house. With fangs dripping blood.'

'Bull.' Screwing up her forehead, she did her best to smoke like Robert Mitchum in a movie she had seen at the Ozone. She wasn't very good at it. But neither was Honza. 'Pav and Barry Puce?' she said after a moment. 'They were mates?'

'Baz used to scrape on our bedroom window. "Night stalker, come … Night stalker, quick!" – that's what he'd whisper. I wanted to go too. Buggers never let me. I'd lie awake, wishing I'd followed them. They'd be gone for hours.'

Wind creaked in the trees. The patio below had been quiet with the Sanctum doors closed. But now came voices, speaking low. Skip squinted down. Two figures stood in the darkness. Honza looked as if he was about to say something; hushing him, crouching, Skip pressed her face between the parapet's pillars, straining to hear the soft words.

'I can't convince you? You're perfect for Petra.'

'Me? I'm no actress.'

'You don't know till you try.'

'Mr Brooker, I know it means a lot to you. But I couldn't commit myself to the Players.'

'You're a tough cookie, Miss Wells.'

'Marlo, if you like.'

'And I'm Howard. I get enough "Mr Brooker" at school.' He scuffed a boot against the paving, sipped from his glass, and went on, 'You and I are much alike, aren't we? Both in bondage. I'm bonded – that's the word they use – to the Education Department of South Australia. They paid for me to study and so, for two years, I've been where they've sent me. Last year Renmark. This year Crater Lakes. Still, could have been worse – Oodnadatta, Coober Pedy. Exile, all the same. And you, Marlo, have been exiled too.'

'You seem to know a lot about me.'

'No secrets here! In a few months my bondage will end. I'll go travelling. London. Paris. Decadent Berlin and the Côte d'Azur. You'll get out too. I can't see Marlo Wells stuck in Crater Lakes. But while you're here, make the best of it. Join the Players.'

'We're not alike, Howard. You finish your two years and you're gone. What'll I have after two years at Puce Hardware? I wanted to study too. And I can't.'

Skip was alarmed. Nothing Marlo said was unfamiliar to her, but something in her sister's tone, in the way she said *Howard*, made her seem like a stranger.

She crushed out her cigarette. She hated cigarettes.

Mr Brooker moved in front of Marlo, angling his long body as if at any moment he might press himself against her, lumpy crotch and all. 'You realise, don't you, that all you have to do is *sit* those exams?

They're public exams. You don't have to do them at Adelaide Ladies' College. Any school in the state will do.'

'I can't go to school. Puce Hardware, remember?'

'You're a clever girl. What were you taking – English, French, Latin? I'll coach you, and what I don't know I can get my colleagues to help with. You got yourself a scholarship to that snooty college, didn't you? You'll get one to uni. A few months and it's goodbye, Crater Lakes!'

Marlo stepped away from him. 'Why help me?'

'At the high, I've got class after class of cretins. You wouldn't believe the idiots I'm supposed to teach. White trash, they'd call them in the States. I spend my days shouting at them. Then I meet the one person in Crater Lakes who wants an education, and she's denied it. I swear to you, I'll see you through those exams.'

'You'll be busy with the Players.'

'Not every night. Tomorrow's Monday. Are you free?'

Marlo hesitated, but only for a moment. 'One thing: Auntie Noreen mustn't hear of this. Let her think I'm rehearsing the play. She'll ridicule that but won't really care. Studying, that's different. She'll try to stop it.'

'Our secret. You have my word.' He might have said more, plunging, horribly, into still deeper intimacies, but to Skip's relief Mrs Novak intervened. Crying that charades were about to begin, she grabbed Mr Brooker's arm and led him indoors. As he went, he called back to Marlo, 'You *will* be Petra, won't you?'

Marlo hugged herself and did a little twirl. Then she was gone too.

Skip stared into empty space. Should she feel angry? Guilt had consumed her ever since their banishment to Crater Lakes. Of course Marlo blamed her. Now Marlo could have her revenge. What could be simpler? Goodbye, Crater Lakes. She would leave Skip behind.

Skip glanced at Honza. The boy lay belly-down, resting his head on his crossed arms. Was he asleep? Disgusted, Skip scrambled into a crouch beside him, welded her fists together and swung them like an axe between his shoulder blades. He jerked up, gasping.

Her eyes were hot. 'I hate you, Honza Novak! Who do you think you are? You're too afraid of Lummo even to look at me at school. You treat me like shit and then, when it's convenient for you, expect me to be your mate. You're lower than a snake's arse.'

If one thing maddened Skip more than what she was saying, it was the way Honza received it. All he did was look at her, blink, and say, 'Want to go stalking? We could do it later tonight, when everyone's asleep.'

'That you, lovey?'

Skip, on her way to bed, was leaving the bathroom when Auntie Noreen called her. Reluctantly, she presented herself at the living-room doorway. In darkness but for the television, her aunt sat alone, surrounded by Kit-Kat wrappers. Sunday night had sunk to its dregs. On Channel Eight, a cheery but earnest American proselytised on behalf of the Christian Television Association.

'Sit with your auntie for a minute, eh?' Auntie Noreen patted the sofa beside her. 'Jeez, I thought that Campbell bugger was never going to go. Quite a handful, he is. Yous should have seen him when he was a lad! All the sheilas wanted to ride in his Land Rover. Bastard, he was.'

Skip could believe that. Bastard then, bastard now. What she couldn't believe was that any girl would want to ride in his Land Rover – ever. Had Auntie Noreen? The thought was creepy. And Auntie Noreen was creepy, sitting in the dark with her TV and her Kit-Kats. Creepy, but sad. Dutifully, Skip perched on the sofa. She wished she had the guts to go.

'Had a rough time, ain't yous?' Auntie Noreen said.

Skip decided not to agree. To admit weakness of any kind seemed an unwise move. Never let anyone know you're weak. They'll pick on you worse than ever. She kicked her foot against the frilly base of the sofa. It was a horrible sofa. Everything in Auntie Noreen's house was horrible.

'That sister of mine's led us a merry dance, eh?' her aunt went on. 'Always a wild one, little Kazza. What larks we used to have when she was just a tot. And so pretty, everybody said so. Our mum kicked the bucket and I was mum to her. Well, tried to be. Maybe I didn't do so well. What did I know? When Mum died, I was no older than you is now. Eh, and Kazza was marked out for trouble. I knew she'd never do well at that school. Fags behind the shelter shed, sneaking off with the boys, drinking beer. "I'm bored," she used to say. "So bored!"

'Happy as Larry she was when she left school. There she was the next day, bright-eyed and bushy-tailed, behind the counter at Puce Hardware. Huh! That didn't last for long. Three weeks, and she was off with a travelling salesman from Wagga Wagga who flashed his Irish eyes at her and promised her the moon. Dermot somebody, his name was. Derro, more like it. Not even good-looking. Forty if he was a day, with a beer gut big as a basketball. Slapped Kazza round when he got sick of her. Christ, I'd like to have got my hands on him, the dirty bastard! Don't think old Noreen didn't try to make her come home. Me little Kazza was underage and all. No, don't think I took it lying down. But what can you do?'

Skip was only half listening. Often enough, Karen Jane had told stories of her past lovers. To Skip, all this took place in a land of shadows. If one of the lovers had been Marlo's father and one of them had been Skip's, one of them a bastard and one of them a good bloke, it made no difference. Sometimes Skip wished she had known her father. But what was the point? If only you could *choose* your father. Perhaps, she thought, we all have a secret father, a real father, not just a man who stuck his thingy in our mother, and one day we will meet him. She knew that was silly. But the longing, when it possessed her, was real all the same.

Auntie Noreen squeezed her hand. 'Tired, aren't you, lovey? Poor little thing! It's a tough time in your life. You're becoming a woman. Oh, it won't be easy. Never is. I suppose you think you know all about it – you and your sister, with her Greer Garson! Take it from me, there are things Greer Garson don't know about. Don't think that cow's ever had a hubby and kids, eh? Then she don't know bugger-all. That's what a woman's life is all about.'

Did Auntie Noreen even believe this? Tears had appeared in her little eyes and Skip shifted restlessly. Her aunt had been drinking, of course: beer after beer with Sandy Campbell.

'I'm glad you're with us, Baby Helen,' she was saying. 'Might be a bit dull for you, I know. But yous are safe here. Remember that, eh? Down here in the Lakes, at least yous girls is safe.'

Credits rolled on the Christian Television Association broadcast. What next? Weather. God Save the Queen. Goodnight and close. Gently, or as gently as she could, Skip pulled herself from Auntie Noreen's grip. From the mantelpiece, Barry Puce stared at them impassively. And Auntie Noreen stared back at him. She looked at her son in his soldier's uniform and, Skip was certain, struggled not to cry.

'Night stalker, come ...'

At first Skip didn't hear the voice; nor did she register the soft, ratlike scratching at the flyscreen. She stirred slowly. She had dreamed she was in a green, wet place. From all around came a drip-drip of water; voices taunted her, but where they came from she couldn't be sure. Her heart pounded like a bass drum: *boom, boom.* Light shone from somewhere, but dimly, slithering over fantastical fleshy forms. She heard a crack: a gunshot, far away. All she knew was two things: she was frightened, and far from home.

'Night stalker, come ... Night stalker, quick!'

Fully awake now, she sat up sharply. A torch beam flashed on the Airfix F-111 above Barry Puce's bed, then dazzled her eyes. Squinting, she saw behind the beam a face. Grinning stupidly, it stared at her through the window. 'What are you doing?' she asked.

'We're stalking,' said Honza. 'Remember?'

'You're mad. I never said I'd go.'

'But you will, won't you?'

'It's the middle of the night. Everyone's asleep.'

'That's the point!'

'Go away.'

For a moment, Honza was silent. His head bobbed down beneath the windowsill, and Skip heard no sounds of him moving on the decking. She pulled the covers around her ears, but a clucking reached her: *Brkk-brkk ... brkk-brkk ... brrrrkk-brkk*. It stopped, then started again.

'I'm not chicken!' she declared, too loudly. On the floor beside her bed was a glass of water. She stepped out of bed and seized it, strode to the window, and flung its contents through the flyscreen.

'Missed,' said Honza. 'Hurry up, it'll be light by the time you're ready.'

'I'm going back to bed,' said Skip, but even as she said it she found herself tugging her jeans over her pyjamas. She pulled on socks. She stuffed her feet into sneakers. She was no chicken. She would never be a chicken. She bundled on her jacket. She wrenched open the door. 'Happy now?'

'Shh!' Honza held a finger to his lips. He sprang down lithely from the decking, led her across the garden and unlatched the gate. Like spirits, they slid into the night.

Puce's Bend soon lay behind them. They passed between paddocks; fence posts listed, the wire strung between them thrumming faintly in a midnight breeze. Grass, inky black, shivered and swayed. Branches creaked.

'Bet you never done this before,' said Honza.

'Why d'you reckon that?'

Skip remembered a night last summer. Karen Jane had been rhapsodising again about San Fran, about how their lives would change entirely from the moment they arrived in that place to which they had never been, which became in her descriptions the Land of Oz, *Adventure Island* and the Woodstock Festival all rolled into one. Suddenly, she could not say why, Skip felt the sickening certainty that they would never go there – never, not even if the place was real. 'It's all dreams!' she cried. She was sick of Karen Jane's dreams that never came true. Her mother gazed at her, hollow-eyed. She told Skip she was a stupid, ungrateful girl and Skip told Karen Jane she hated her; then she ran out of the flat and along the beach until she could run no more. She slumped in the sand and stared out to sea. It frightened her – its blackness, its immensity – but she watched and watched. The sounds it made, its suckings, its sighings, were words she did not understand but felt compelled to learn. Where would she be, she wondered, in ten years, in twenty, in fifty, in a lifetime? It was too much to imagine, impossible, yet all that was certain was that time would pass and pass. Her mind drifted, and her body too, floating on the blackness, until Marlo found her and shook her awake. Karen Jane had been too stoned to come.

'So it's into town and back?' Skip said now.

'Volcano Street. Up and down.'

'What sort of game is that?'

But it was exciting. Was there really a ghost of Crater Lakes? How Skip wished there were! In the dark, with the torch making fuzzy luminous tunnels, ordinary sights of the day appeared touched by strange magic. Eerily the beam played over tussocky verges, potholes, twisted trees.

They talked about whether ghosts existed. 'Don't reckon so,' said Skip. 'They'd have proved it by now.'

'Who'd have proved it?'

'Scientists.'

'They don't know shit. There was this farmhand on the Kenny place, back in the old days, got his head chopped off in the combine harvester. Every year, on the night this bloke died, you could see him in that paddock, under the big old bluegum – just a body, no head.'

'Bull.' Honza, Skip knew, was trying to frighten her.

'He held the head under his arm.'

'Bull.'

Paved streets were upon them now. No cars passed; in the space between Sunday night and Monday morning, the town slept as if beneath a spell: drawn blinds, darkened windows. Behind a fence, a dog let out a mournful howl; afterwards, the stillness was deeper.

They walked in the middle of the road. Honza turned off the torch. Streetlights were dim and set far apart, each one offering only a urinous yellow trickle. Skip looked into carports as if shapes might lurk there. Leathery bushes rose like sentinels in grassy front yards.

'Frightened now?' Honza whispered.

'Course not.'

'What if we get caught?'

'Who'd catch us?'

'The ghost of Crater Lakes!'

'As if …' Skip laughed.

Honza seemed affronted. 'There's this movie I saw on TV one night. Dad reckoned I weren't allowed to watch it, but Pav stayed up so I snuck out and watched it with him. There's this bloke, see, he has this waxwork museum. He's, like, a genius at making waxworks that look like real people. Then there's this fire, and the bloke gets all burned up.'

'Vincent Price,' said Skip. 'I've seen that movie.'

She had never forgotten it: not the wax figures ablaze, not the boiling, bubbling vats of wax, not the hideous burned face of the sculptor when finally it is revealed. She adored Vincent Price. In a Price movie there was a secret, and the secret, she sensed, was that the one most haunted was Vincent Price, even if he was the monster others feared.

'Remember after the fire?' said Honza. 'His face is all scars and his hands are claws. The bloke can't make waxworks, not proper ones any more. So he gets real people, pretty girls and stuff, and has boiling wax poured all over them.'

'Remember when the wax mask cracks off his face?'

'Remember when he falls in the vat?'

'Best bloody movie I ever saw,' said Skip.

'Well, he went stalking, didn't he? All twisted over in a sort of cloak. Hood over his face. He'd knock you out, and when you woke up you'd be tied down, and he'd have hot wax ready to pour all over you. What if there's a bloke like that?'

Skip shook her head sadly. 'Is there a wax museum in Crater Lakes?'

The sawmill massed before them: grand silent sheds of corrugated iron by the railway line, grey-white in the darkness. Honza said they should cut through. Veering off the road, he waved to Skip to follow. No fences, no gates stopped them from passing between high metal walls.

'Turn on the torch again,' said Skip, as shadows encroached.

'Scaredy-cat.'

'It's pitch black, idiot.'

The yellow beam was wavering, thin. They followed a concrete drive. Beyond a garage was a sawdust-smelling yard, with twin forklift trucks standing before the entrance as if on guard; caught in torchlight, the paintwork yielded up a sickly glow. Filling the yard was pallet after pallet of stacked pine planks. Each stack was the same: a cube, twice Skip's height.

'Tim-*ber*!' cried Honza, pretending to be a lumberjack. 'This is what the Lakes is about, Dad reckons.'

'Doesn't he work at the town hall?'

'In the office. Sometimes he stays back real late.'

'Keen, is he?' Or not keen, Skip thought, on Deirdre Novak.

'What about your dad?' said Honza.

'Haven't got one.'

'Did he die? How did he die?' Honza seemed to think the answer should be funny. Suddenly Skip was sick of him. Stalking was silly, a kids' game. But what did she expect? There was no wax museum in Crater Lakes and never would be. This was a town where nothing happened. She wondered if she could find her way home by herself. She looked around the piny yard. Between each pallet was a space a foot wide; the pale stacks rose like an ancient monument, some crumbly archaeological find uncovered in a desert – a set of tombs perhaps, or a strange priestly construction for calculating the movements of the stars.

There was a yowl. She jumped, and Honza laughed. 'Pussycats,' he said. 'Hah! If I left you by yourself, you'd be screaming.'

'I don't scream. When did I ever scream?'

'Girls scream. In that movie –'

'What if I left *you*?' Skip started forward. Briefly she jumped into the torch's beam, fingers curled monster-style, tongue poking out, then plunged out of sight between the pallets.

Crabwise, grateful for her smallness, she slipped down corridors of cut pine. Splintery ragged ends of planks scraped her like rough hands. Honza's beam scissored through the blackness. She pressed into the wood and barely breathed, willing her heart to stop beating.

'Where are you?' Honza called.

Then: 'Come on, where've you gone?'

Then: 'Stop messing about.'

His voice was still little more than a whisper, but Skip heard the fear in it. Honza was walking around trying to find her; each time he spoke, his words came from a different direction. Cautiously she made her way between pungent woody walls, then emerged into the yard behind him. She crept forward, ready to disappear back into the pallets if he turned. Quiet as a ghost, she scudded towards him, then jumped onto his back.

Honza screamed. The torch clattered down and the beam blinked out. Blackness surrounded them as they scuffled.

Laughing, Skip cried, 'Only me!'

He flung her away from him. 'Stupid girl. What was I thinking of, stalking with a girl?'

Skip kicked him. 'You take that back!'

'Fuck off.' The boy dropped to his hands and knees, looking for the torch. Thick clouds made the moon a mere candle that seemed at times to flicker out entirely. 'Bugger, we'll never make it home tonight.'

They did, but not for hours. The walk home was confusing, creepy and boring all at once, and both were thoroughly tired and cranky by the time they reached Puce's Bend. Back in her room, Skip dropped into bed and fell asleep instantly, knowing that morning – and school – would come too soon.

# Chapter Five

Everything in Crater Lakes was old.

That wasn't really true, of course: Coles New World was a new world, with soup cans and soap powders in Warholesque banks; Coca-Cola Bottlers had built a plant in town; the new block at the high was what the Education Department referred to with pride as an open space unit. But half close your eyes on Volcano Street and time slipped back: gone was Chickenland with its fibreglass chicken rearing hugely over the parking lot; gone that XR Falcon, that Torana HB among the battered Yank tanks and utility trucks that looked as if they lodged in barns with hay and horseshit, when not running into town. Life was black and white: it was 1939, and those men with short back and sides, lining up at the betting shop, were jug-eared boys anxious to enlist. There were places in the Lakes where time seemed calcified, ready to crack: at the Federal, where Sandy Campbell, shitfaced, leaned at the bar and told the one about the Dago, the Kraut and the Aussie; at the bake sale in aid of Crater East Primary, where leathery ladies with plastic teeth shrieked ecstatically over lamingtons; in the dingy clutter of Hill's Newsagency, where that *Advertiser,* framed on the wall, which said the Yanks had landed on the moon, might have been some bloke's idea of a laugh. Nowhere was this impression stronger than in the library that occupied the ground floor of the Crater Lakes Institute. Skip had taken to going there every Saturday morning while she waited for Marlo to finish work at midday.

The Institute Library was like a church: the stone arch of the entrance, the double doors, the dark bookcases that suggested pews grown weirdly tall. In the Juvenile section, by a window looking out on Volcano Street, Skip perched on a rickety wooden chair. Books in plastic covers glimmered from the walls of shelves around her and across a central table. The table displayed, laid out like offerings, sometimes standing half-open, the worthy books a grown-up might approve: *The Humpy in the Hills* by John Gunn, *Ash Road* by Ivan Southall, *Storm Boy* by Colin Thiele. In the shelves – sardine-squashed, faded, dog-eared, broken-spined – were books that made grown-ups shake their heads: Trixie Belden, Biggles, Bobbsey Twins, Billy Bunter, Chalet School, Nancy Drew, Famous Five, Hardy Boys, Jennings, Malory Towers, Rover Boys, Secret Seven, Tom Swift; the Island, Castle, Valley, Sea, Mountain, Ship, Circus, River of Adventure.

Of most interest to Skip were the papers in yellowing stacks beneath the window. The institute allowed no Yank rubbish, no Superman or Batman, but English children's weeklies were another matter. This particular morning, Skip had followed a Trigan Empire adventure in *Look and Learn*, eagerly riffling through the musty pile for the next week's issue, and the next and the next. When the last episode was missing she was dashed, but then she turned to ragged copies of *Lion*, a comic for boys, and was soon contented again, reading one page-long strip after another about Mowser, a cat who lived in a castle, and his enemy, James the butler. Always James was trying to get the better of Mowser, the 'tatty old furbag', as he called him, throwing him outside or denying him food; always Mowser got the better of James, ending up with a roast chicken, or a plate of kippers and cream. There was something comforting in the Mowser cycle. It wasn't that good triumphed over evil – Mowser was greedy, selfish and cunning, James treated abysmally by his employers, Lord and Lady Crummy, and often blamed for Mowser's crimes – but Mowser was Mowser, James was James, and neither ever altered.

Light fell, warm and honeyed, through the tall window. The best thing about the institute was its quietness. The very dust seemed fixed in the air, drifting down perpetually. Through a corner gap in the wall of shelves, Skip could look across the waxy floor to the desk where the lady librarian presided over this dreamy torpor. From time to time the lady murmured with another lady who came in to change books; with soft precision she applied the date stamp, entered names of borrowed books on cards, and jingled with the cashbox as she collected subscriptions or fines. When another child entered the Juvenile corner, Skip stiffened; the corner was hers, her little kingdom. Lucy Sutton had appeared last Saturday, with her red-lipsticked mother, and Skip withdrew to the reference section, praying that Lucy would fail to spot her. To Skip's delight, Lucy had not, intent as she was on deliberating with Mrs Sutton over *I Own the Racecourse!* by Patricia Wrightson or *A Sapphire for September* by H. F. Brinsmead, even calling over the lady librarian to contribute her opinion. The lady left no doubt as to her view of Lucy. 'Such a well-brought-up child,' she remarked to Mrs Sutton, in a whisper loud enough for Skip to hear.

Skip had fallen into a doze when a hand shook her shoulder. It was Marlo. 'Twelve already?' Skip blinked and rubbed her eyes.

'Pavel's still clearing up. I've slipped out.'

'Why?'

'To make sure you turn up on time.'

'Picnic? Count me in. Where did you say it was?'

'Some wretched swimming hole. He's been on about it all week: I have to come, I'll love it, the weather will be great, first really warm day since winter … God! No way am I going with him unless you come too.'

Skip felt contrary. 'What if I won't?'

Marlo grabbed her by the collar. 'You're coming!'

A sharp *ahem!* issued from the lady librarian. Quickly, Skip gathered up the one book and three 'periodicals' (as comics were known at the institute) permitted to holders of a Juvenile subscription. Approaching the front desk, she nervously checked the book. On her first visit to the institute she had tried to take out *Odhams Wonder-World of Knowledge in Colour,* a book Marlo (who had paid for her subscription) would surely find impressive, only to have the lady glower at her, hold the heavy volume open at the flyleaf and point to the sticker declaring: REFERENCE ONLY. Skip had tossed her head defiantly, pretending not to care. But the humiliation still burned.

Today the lady just pursed her lips, lemon-sucking style, as if to communicate her certainty that Wells, Helen was not, and never would be, a well-brought-up child.

Marlo waited impatiently. 'Now remember,' she muttered, as she steered Skip into the street, 'whatever you do, don't leave me alone with him.'

'The Lakes!'

The world was rising. They had passed the big houses where the quality lived, high above the Housing Trust fray, and the town cemetery, field after field of stony slabs and crosses tumbling down a hillside as if a battle had been fought there once. Imagine it: but there had been no civil war in South Australia, and the Aborigines, like ghosts it seemed, had merely melted into the past.

The Land Rover rounded an arc of road. On one side, scrubby slopes plunged towards water; on the other, farmland rolled richly away. On this sunny day, the lakes, in their volcanic craters, were dazzling jewels of water, glittering out of lush drapings of gums and willows. Skip, in the back, swayed dangerously on the picnic basket. Wind rushed in her hair.

Marlo twisted in her seat. 'Off that box! Off!'

'I'm flying!' Skip flung out her arms.

'I've told you – Pavel, tell her.'

Skip poked out her tongue but thudded dutifully to the flatbed's floor. Beside the basket lay Pavel's swimming togs in a rolled-up towel; a red-yellow-black tartan rug, folded roughly; *Tom Swift and the Asteroid Pirates*, two *Lion*s and an *Eagle*; and Baskerville, who seemed quite benevolent when dozing, as now. She petted his floppy ears; he thumped his tail. She liked him: a stupid dog, but the sort of dog you would be glad to have as a friend.

A watchtower, like the one on the mag the J. Dubs flogged door to door, surmounted the dead volcano. Skip wanted to climb that tower, but there could be no stopping now. Spinning off from their orbit of the lakes, they hurtled through the green landscape. They might have been in England, as seen on TV, bound for a country house weekend where someone, it was good to know, was certain to be murdered.

She asked Pavel where they were going.

'Dansie's Pond. It's way out. Sort of a special place.'

Special? There were implications in this: a special place, just for me and Marlo. But if Skip felt guilty, she was also triumphant; Saturday afternoon, which had stretched before her like the Simpson Desert, was desert no more. If Pavel was disappointed that Skip had come too, he was doing his best not to show it.

They saw no other cars, and had driven well out of town before they encountered anyone else on the road. At first Skip saw only a dark mass, and looked on curiously as Pavel decelerated, gliding up beside a solitary shape hunched over a motorcycle, his face averted from them. Throbbingly the Land Rover came to rest, and Pavel called, 'Black Jack! What's up?'

A grunt came in reply. The motorcyclist had long dark curly hair and wore a plaid flannel shirt untucked over baggy jeans. His machine, a Harley-Davidson, was an ancient spindly thing, its black paint flaking and speckled red with rust in many places. Adding to its ungainly appearance was a sidecar, like an enormous bulging pipe bowl, brimming with groceries from Coles New World.

Pavel hopped down from the Land Rover. 'Old thing conked out at last? Let's have a look.'

Turning, the motorcyclist revealed broad flaring nostrils and skin of purplish brown. Skip remembered him from their first day, the only Aborigine she had seen in Crater Lakes. He held a wrench and his shirt was streaked with grease. Beneath heavy brows, his eyes were black as olives against their yellowish whites. Muttering, he waved Pavel away.

'Come on, mate. I can help.'

'I don't think he wants help,' said Marlo.

'He gets a bit funny.' Pavel would have touched the black man's arm, but the wrench swung back. It flashed, catching the sun. Baskerville bounded down from the flatbed, barking, but Pavel backed away and grabbed the dog's collar. 'All right, boy. It's all right,' he said, and ordered him back to the Land Rover.

Only when Pavel had revved away did the Aborigine lower the wrench. Fascinated, Skip stared back at him. Standing on the pale pebbly verge of the tarmac, he had about him a loneliness that seemed suddenly unbearable.

'Who is that man?' asked Marlo.

'They call him Black Jack,' said Pavel. 'His name's Jack and he's black. Everyone reckons he's not all there. Kids tease him, but he can take care of himself.'

'He works for Sandy Campbell?' Skip said, remembering Jack unloading the bus.

'Sometimes. He picks up odd jobs. Tootles round on that old Harley, up to this and that. Used to do a bit of work for us, until he went a bit funny one arvo in front of Old Ma Puce.'

'Funny how?' said Marlo.

Pavel, the loyal employee, seemed reluctant to say. 'You know! Wouldn't treat her like she was Queen Noreen.' He shrugged. 'Black Jack's okay. Lives at the old Dansie house.'

'Dansie?' said Skip. 'Like Dansie's Pond?'

'Out that way. Wreck of a place it is. Them Dansies used to be real rich. Owned every sheep in these parts, yonks ago. Owned the pines. Owned the mill. King and queen of Crater Lakes, they reckoned the Dansies was. Then things fell apart. Lost their dough. Son went to the bad. Black Jack worked on the property, see. But he was more like part of the family.'

'Is there a family now?' asked Skip.

Pavel shook his head. 'Black Jack's all that's left.'

Again, like a wave breaking over her, Skip felt the loneliness, as if it belonged to her, not to the black man on the tarmac's edge. She twisted back around, but the road had curved and he had vanished.

'Black Jack's okay,' Pavel said again. 'He'll probably still be there on our way back, diddling about with that piece of junk. Silly bugger. Serve him right. Maybe he'll let me help him then.'

Trees enclosed them, and the bright day was shadowed. Skip, sitting cross-legged, shut her eyes as sunny streaks flashed across her face. Behind her eyelids was a black cave, shimmering erratically with bursts of red. The Land Rover juddered down the country road, thrumming its ponderous rhythm through her spine. Baskerville let out a snorting snore.

'There we go,' said Pavel. 'The haunted house.'

'What?' Skip snapped open her eyes in time to glimpse the wreck of a place, set far back from the road: a sagging dark veranda, a blind eye of window, a chimneystack listing above a high gable. Trees, in tangled profusion, obscured it swiftly; the green landscape swallowed it, as if it had never been. 'That's where the Aborigine lives?' she said.

'All on his lonesome. Except for the termites. And the rats. And the bats. Unless you believe in the ghost of Crater Lakes.'

They turned off the road onto a potholed track, overhung with grey branches. Sunlight pulsed ahead of them in a pale powdery column and they trundled into it, coming to rest in a cool resinous clearing among mingled willows, gums and ferns, and pines liberated from plantation discipline.

'Dansie's Pond,' said Pavel, and cut the motor, leaving a silence thick as treacle. Skip, half standing, stared around her. Edging the clearing was a rocky platform, shelving above a luminous circle in which the sky, a pale-blue sheen, shone back as if from a perfect mirror. She looked for ripples and could see none. The water was held as in a tilted bowl, with rocks rising higher on the opposite bank, anticlockwise in reddish sandy ascent. Everywhere, high and low, hung curtaining trees.

Pavel clunked shut the driver's door, whirled the dusty blanket from the back, and tossed it over his shoulder in crumpled folds. Skip, keen to help, took the wicker basket, pleased to feel how heavy it was. Staggering, she followed him to a grassy space in the shade; from behind, torso half-emblazoned in the drape of tartan, he had about him the look of a brave Scot, marching into battle for Bonnie Prince Charlie.

'Here, I reckon.' He flicked out the blanket in a confident sweep, and presided, enchanter-like, as it billowed to the ground, a magic carpet spent from flight. Grunting, Skip slammed down the basket.

Pavel winked at her. 'Look at Basky.'

With a puzzled air, the big dog patrolled the watery edge, here and there stretching his muzzle towards the sky, collared neck narrowing, haunches clenched like a fist. Droopy-eared, he looked back at Pavel. Could this be water? If not water, what? Pavel tossed a stone; it burst the blue mirror with a startled *hrropp!* and Baskerville sprang back. Birds squawked skywards from concealing leaves.

Skip watched the spreading ripples. The reddish rocky walls skirled with dull fire. 'Must be great here in summer.'

Pavel shook his head. 'Dangerous. Come November, the water drops too low. Swim first?'

The question was for Marlo, who had moved towards the blanket, on which she descended gently, as if to a divan, drawing her knees into a blunt arrowhead beneath her blue skirt. In one hand she clutched a small maroon book, like a hymnal; with a settled air, she opened it. Skip had seen the book, some dreary thing Brooker had prescribed for Marlo's exams. She wondered how Marlo could stand Brooker. Skip looked at him and thought only one thing: what a whacker. But for Marlo, of course, it was different. He was her ticket out of Crater Lakes. Sadness plunged in Skip's chest at the thought, and she hoped that at least Brooker meant no more than that to Marlo. What if Marlo loved him? No, surely not! A girl who read Germaine? But Skip was worried. She missed Marlo. Funny, how you could miss somebody when they were still here with you.

Pavel had grabbed his trunks and towel and gone discreetly into the trees to change. Baskerville, meanwhile, floundered into the pond, splashing through quicksilver slippings of light: ears, muzzle, paddling paws. Like all big dogs, he possessed a certain grave dignity.

Marlo said suddenly, 'Uncle Doug thinks I love him.'

Skip turned, puzzled.

Her sister's face was a pale mask. 'Not Uncle Doug – Pavel. Has he said anything to you?'

'When does Pavel ever talk to me?'

'Not Pavel. Uncle Doug. He closed the office door, paced back and forth, cleared his throat three times, leaned over my desk, pressed my wrist with one skinny hand and looked into my eyes like a doctor delivering bad news. Have you felt his fingers? They're rough.'

'This was this morning?' Skip asked. Something alarmed her in the way her sister spoke: the words seemed to hover three feet above her head, a cloud dispersing on the air in gossamer skeins.

The voice dropped as Marlo slipped, with cruel accuracy, into the broad back-of-beyond tones of Uncle Doug. '"I know it's been a big shake-up for yous, coming to the Lakes. Yous might feel a bit funny. Yous might lose your way ... I seen the way yous been looking at young Pav."' Marlo hooted, a high screech that should never have come from her lips. '"Just don't get too hung up on him, love. He's only a year younger than our Baz, remember."'

'Stop it.' Skip hated Marlo talking this way. Marlo, perfect Marlo, should never sound like a hick. But before she could launch herself on her sister, ready to pummel her, water exploded behind her and sprayed across them both. Reeling around, she saw a sleek ottery head bobbing up from the convulsive pond. Marvelling, she gazed at Pavel. He laughed, treading water, teeth huge as a horse's in his brown Slavic face.

'The Jump.' A hand whipped out of the water, pointing. Twelve feet above the pond was a boxy outcrop, the highest point of the fiery walls.

All Skip wanted was to be in the water too. She wrenched off sneakers, socks, jeans and shirt, everything but underpants and boyish white singlet, and plummeted in from the nearest point: down, down, through swirling depths. Rushing filled her ears; cool fleshy tendrils brushed her wrists and ankles as if about to bind them; darkness pushed up from below, a soupy brown shading into black suggesting underwater chasms, tunnels, caves that would lure divers in, as if on promise of treasure, never to release them again. Breath tore from her lungs; she steeled her arms, fighting her way back. As she broke the surface, in sudden spearing light, it seemed to her there were two worlds, the green world and the golden, and she had burst from one to the other like Thunderbird 4, blasting out of water into sunny sky.

Pavel slid towards her and murmured, close to her ear, 'Will she really not come in?'

'When Marlo's made up her mind, she won't be moved.'

'Like a tree? She's seeing that teacher.' His face was glum.

'He's teaching her,' Skip said quickly. 'That's all …' That's all! It was everything – to Marlo, at any rate; but the hurt, bewildered look in Pavel's eyes made Skip long to reassure him. Cold scythed through her, and she knew that Marlo had to fall in love with Pavel. Wouldn't that solve everything? Then Marlo would stay in the Lakes! But this was no way to think. Already Skip had begun to believe they might be in the Lakes for a long time. No: of course they wouldn't. Karen Jane would come and get them soon.

'I want to dive off that rock too,' Skip said, striking out for the bank, where Baskerville shook himself in a streaky rainbow cascade.

'Race you!' Pavel was upon her at once, the hard curve of his hollowed belly almost cupping her back as they scrambled from the water, then floundered over rock, grass, sand and slipping stones. Pavel would win: he was bigger, and shouldered Skip aside when she almost overtook him.

'Bastard!' she cried, but didn't mean it, pounding in dripping underwear after the brown knobbly back, the floral board shorts that stuck, unflapping, to his sinewy thighs. Their path twisted, slid in sharp obliques, vaulted over boulders and clumps of scrub, crashed through leathery leaves, before propelling them abruptly onto the rocky overhang, where Pavel, with a jubilant 'Bombs away!', capered, cartwheeling, through empty air. The splash echoed around the rocky walls.

Skip swayed on the edge. She had wanted to follow him, but now that she was here could only stare into the foaming water, eyes squinting in the sun that seemed much brighter here than below. How far away the water was, how far away and strange; and strangest of all was the centre of those radiating waves, that dazzled eye into which Pavel had disappeared, and from which, it seemed, he would not return. A pained cry writhed up from her lungs, only to swerve, as the otter head erupted through the watery sheen, into a half-laughed 'Bastard!'

Skip plunged from estranging sun into a rapture of gasping, grappling, and wild high laughter as she pursued Pavel through flickering silver-green. He jack-in-the-boxed from the depths, pushed down her resisting head; she struggled to duck him in turn, but Pavel was a slithery eel, always escaping. Let him. Let him laugh at her, flinging back his horsy head. Skip felt entirely happy, and her happiness only grew as they clambered out of the water and raced around the rim for a second bombing run. This time she skidded first onto the Jump, and leaped shrieking into the blue before Pavel could push her.

'Some days are perfect,' said Pavel.

Hours had passed at the pond, or so it seemed to Skip, as she huddled on the tartan rug, long-tailed shirt wrapped around her like a robe. Delicious sour sweetness filled her mouth; Chickenland chicken never tasted like this. Charcoal and caramel crackled on the skin; the flesh parted from the bone like clotted cream. Pavel, or Mr Novak, had excelled himself. She peered into the picnic basket: crumbed veal, red and black grapes, purplish sticky chutney, an enormous crusty loaf of homemade bread, and a massive dark fruitcake, rich with raisins and glacé cherries. Wax paper, peeled back, revealed three types of cheese: a sweaty flaxen brick of cheddar, a red-lacquered Gloucester, a crushed collapsing brie. Even Marlo's mood had lifted. Baskerville, at the clearing's edge, yawped and snuffled over a meaty bone.

And yet, Skip began to feel, something ominous beat beneath the day. What was Pavel saying now? Something about Baz. 'Yair, yair ... used to come here with Baz. He'd drive us out here, the year he got his licence. I can still see Baz chucking bombies off the Jump.'

Skip could not quite believe her cousin was real. Every day she saw his clothes, his books, his Paul Newman and Jackie Stewart posters, his Airfix F-111 that revolved above the bed, but still Barry Puce might have been made up, like God or Moriarty or the Milkybar Kid.

Now Marlo mused on Barry too; *Cousin Barry,* she called him, as if he were a character in a book and so was she. In Skip's chest something strained and flopped, like an injured bird struggling to rise. Too many questions. Why did Marlo care about the answers? Was she starting to like Pavel? Or was she only making fun of him? That, thought Skip, would be unkind.

In any case, Skip too was curious about this cousin whose room she shared. On and on the questions came. What would Cousin Barry do when the army was done with him? Would he come back to the Lakes? Would he work at Puce Hardware? How long now until they let him go? Obscurely, she felt the day's enchantments slipping, and then heard them smash when Pavel said, 'I've a birthday coming up. Never know, I might be saying howdy-do to Baz again soon.'

Sunny spangles played through the leaves and spun across the water like coins catching the light. Skip said quickly, 'But you wouldn't go, would you?'

'Got to do your bit.' His voice was almost cheery.

'The war's wrong, everybody knows that.'

'They're fighting the commies.'

'You could be a – what do they call it, Marlo?' Skip urged.

'Conscientious objector.'

Pavel shook his head. 'Cowards, I call them. Dad says we've got to stop the commies whatever we do.'

'You'd let yourself be an agent of American imperialism? Marlo, tell him.'

'What can I tell him? His father's in Australia because he fled the communists.'

Pavel nodded, and earnestly evoked Mr Novak's flight from the Soviets who rolled into Prague in 1948. Skip listened impatiently. Czechoslovakia? Another planet! Dimly she imagined, in black and white, a lean swarthy young man with test-tube hair like Pavel's clambering over barbed-wire fences, dodging bullets, flattening himself against walls as soldiers in regimented rows marched by; she could not connect this young man with big-bellied, kindly, bland Mr Novak, who cooked in an apron saying CHIEF COOK AND BOTTLE WASHER and handed around the drinks on Sanctum Sundays.

She cried, 'But Barry's life is ruined!'

Pavel blinked. 'He'll come home, proud to have done his bit.'

'He'll die!' Skip was shrieking now. She had sprung to her feet, upsetting her plate and a glass of Coca-Cola. 'Your precious mate will take a bullet in the back in some stinking, steamy jungle!' she cried. 'He'll sink into the swamp and rot! Will you be happy then? Will you think he's done his duty? You're stupid. You're stupid and I hate you!'

Pavel gaped. Marlo reached out, but Skip shook off the restraining arm, turned and ran.

She had flailed far into the bush before she paused to wonder where she was going. Shame burned in her face. Already she saw herself trudging back, slump-shouldered, rehearsing muttered apologies: 'Sorry, Pavel. Sorry, Marlo. Didn't mean it. You know I didn't mean it.' But she did, she did. She had thought Pavel was special, but he was just as stupid as Honza.

Angrily, Skip brushed tears from her eyes and pushed on. Woods stretched thickly away from the pond. She tugged a thin branch off a bluegum and swished it like a whip against the mulchy ground. Moments later, hearing a familiar breathy loping, she turned to see Baskerville. He looked up at her, brow furrowing, pale pink tongue lolling, dripping saliva. 'Your master's stupid,' she told him. 'Do you know your master's stupid?'

The dog stiffened, snarling. Had he understood? But his gaze snapped away from her; the collar jangled on his neck and with a low *bow-wow-wow* he was off, crashing through the undergrowth after a sinuous ginger flash.

'Baskerville! Come back!' she cried and set off after him, ducking low branches, slapping away leaves. The dog quickly vanished into the trees. She followed his barking but soon became confused. Among thicker, darker bush, sound echoed oddly; noises might have come from several directions at once, and she turned, then turned again.

The barking ceased. Baskerville could be anywhere, and so could the cat. Skip imagined reeking yellow fangs clamping shut on Mowser, the priceless puss: a spurt of blood, a crack of spine. The thought made her desperate. If Baskerville committed so vile an act, she couldn't stand it, she would hate him for ever and ever. She looked around again. Ahead of her, glimmers of sunlight picked out a long, unbroken slope of ivy; so dense was the growth that she did not at first realise she was looking at a fence, a high fence sagging under its green burden.

Scratching and a low growl sounded close by, and she took a few steps forward. Baskerville, head down, nuzzled at the ivy like a bloodhound on a scent. Relieved, Skip moved towards him, but then he slipped through a hole in the fence. She followed him through.

She found herself in an overgrown garden. Far off, beyond tangled apple trees, choked paths and knee-high grass, and flanked by tumbledown outbuildings, lay the house they had passed earlier on the road. The old Dansie house. Now she approached it from the back. Ivy had overwhelmed it almost as thoroughly as it had the fence, but here and there the weathered timber walls could still be seen. Sunlight glinted on surviving glass. The veranda looked like the entrance to a cave.

She felt something nudge her thigh. Baskerville. She curled her fingers in his collar and let him lead her onwards. Wading through the high grass she imagined they were small and growing smaller. She remembered Marlo reading to her from the book about Alice; that, she thought sadly, had been a long time ago. They passed what looked like a dairy, open to the weather; they passed sprawling stables. A door sagged open, half off its hinges, revealing a car raised on blocks; an old car, like a hearse, greenish black. How long had it been abandoned?

They had paused under the deep cracking canopy of an elm, six feet from the veranda, when Skip saw Mowser again, an orange swish, bounding up the steps. Baskerville snarled. 'Don't,' said Skip, but rather than racing after the cat, the big dog shrank back as if abashed. She screwed up her eyes. Ivy trailed from the gutters like ragged curtains and the shadows on the veranda were deep, but she made out a couple of wicker chairs, then a small circular table, then Mowser, belly slung low, leaping up onto the table, and hands that reached from the darkness, cradling him, swinging him into the air.

The hands, long and slim, were pale as a ghost's.

Skip's pulse roared in her ears. The ghost must have seen her walking towards him with Baskerville. With a powerful sense of eyes watching her, staring from the darkness, she found herself stepping out from under the elm. Whether Baskerville remained behind her, she could not be sure. She said to the ghost, 'I'm sorry ...' Sorry for what? Some force compelled her forward.

But she had taken only one more step when an ululation rent the air, and a dark figure leaped out of the grass. In her terrified scramble she barely had time to register Black Jack, face contorted in rage, wrench still in hand. She ran, too frightened to look back to see whether he was following. All the way back up the long yard she seemed to hear him crash behind her, and when she tripped over a branch, almost falling, she felt the sickening certainty that in an instant he would be upon her, pinning her down, wrench swinging back in a glittering arc. Wildly she sought out the hole in the fence, shoulder butting against rotted wood, like an insect crashing at a windowpane, before finally she found her way through.

On the other side of the fence she lay gasping. Angrily she told herself she must get up, get up, until she realised she could hear no sounds of pursuit. Could she be sure? She felt as if she had started awake from a nightmare. Perhaps she had; she knew the scene would haunt her, the weird entrancing vision of the white hands slipping out of darkness, and the black face, lips curled back in a scream, rearing up against the bright day.

Slowly, clumsily, Skip moved away from the fence. Her face was scratched and her shirt was torn. Hearing a flurry in a patch of ferns, she turned in fear. But it was Baskerville. She ran to him, hugged him. 'Stupid dog. Oh, you stupid dog.' Sunlight in fuzzy columns burned between the trees.

Now which was the way? They walked and walked: *swish, swish* between ferns and scratchy leaves. It all looked the same and Skip feared they were going in circles. There was something drug-like in the warmth and smell of sap. She knew they were close to the clearing only when a voice called her name, and she flailed out of the bush and into her sister's arms. Skip almost burst into tears, but relief turned into laughter instead: a crazed pealing, too loud, too long.

Marlo thrust her away. 'Come on. We're going. *Now*, Skip.'

'What?' Words tumbled through Skip's mind – a haunted house, a ghost, that black man tried to kill me – but to say them aloud was impossible when Marlo, like a furious schoolmistress, was hustling her back towards the Land Rover. Colour rode high in Marlo's face and when Skip asked her what was wrong, she only spat, 'I told you not to leave me!'

On the drive home, Pavel was flushed and silent. Marlo held her book open on her lap but did not appear to be reading it. More than once Skip tried to imagine the scene at the pond – Pavel, eyes ardent, declaring his love; Marlo recoiling in horror – but her thoughts kept sliding back to the old Dansie house. As she recalled what she had seen there, she found she no longer wished to speak about it. The story, like a secret, was one she would not tell.

# Chapter Six

Marlo strode back and forth. 'There's no end of hypocrisy both at home and at school,' she said. 'At home you must hold your tongue, and at school you have to stand up and lie to the children.'

A young man with a receding chin offered, 'To lie?'

'Yes!' Marlo glanced at the shabby paperback she held open in one hand. 'Do you think we don't have to teach many and many a thing we don't believe ourselves?'

A shy clergyman, too late: 'Y-yes! We know that well enough.'

'If only I could afford it, I'd start a school myself,' rejoined Marlo, picking up after this stumble, 'and things should be very different there.'

'Hmm. Pause.' Mr Brooker sprang up from his canvas folding chair and paced forward, his back stooped, fingers interlaced beneath his chin; players parted to let him by. 'Think, here, of those first faint soundings of a motif Beethoven might develop across a symphony – those goblin footfalls crossing the universe in the sublime Fifth, *par exemple*. Take it down, Marlo.'

'Petra's passionate. You said so.'

'Passionate, but suppressed. Thwarted. A virgin, of course. Imagine a young girl's thighs chafing as she lies at night in her lonely bed.'

Marlo flushed, and Mr Brooker plunged on. 'An innocent? Not in her heart. Only small-town life – that dreary day-to-day crushing of the spirit in the drab provinces – prevents Petra from breaking free. Think: who might Petra be in the modern age?'

'Ah … Miss Elizabeth Taylor?' Mr Singh suggested.

'Miss Mary Quant?' attempted Mrs Singh, who was skinny and dark and wore her saffron sari.

'Germaine Greer!' yelped Mrs Novak.

Mr Brooker nodded excitedly. If the others were embarrassed by his speech, they concealed it, and even managed not to react when he came to a halt before Marlo, gripped her shoulders, and murmured loudly enough for all to hear, 'Play Petra as a sexual volcano, perpetually on the brink of eruption.'

Skip sat cross-legged on top of the grand piano, leafing through the scrapbooks of the old Players, still laid out to inspire their successors. She had accompanied Marlo to the Sanctum only to avoid another night of Channel Eight with Auntie Noreen, but Henry Gibson seemed a poor swap for *Homicide*. All the characters had silly names and nothing happened except a lot of talk which Mr Brooker interrupted every minute. He had, Skip gathered, assigned himself the main role, an inspector of drains or something equally dreary. Mrs Novak played his wife and Marlo his daughter.

The three scrapbooks – stout, musty, brittle – each contained a mixture of black and white photographs, press cuttings, playbills, programmes, ticket stubs, and drawings of sets and costumes in brownish ink. Productions opened and closed with the turning pages: *Man and Superman, Antony and Cleopatra, Oedipus Rex, King Lear, Journey's End*. The same faces occurred again and again. Who was this balding middle-aged man with prissy lips, sporting here a bow tie, there a toga, here a soldier's khaki? This plump girl with wing spectacles, smiling shyly – could that be Rhonda Sweetapple? The skinny birdlike little thing was Mrs Novak, it had to be. Skip saw something of Pavel in her, of Honza too – wiry, tight-coiled, a pent-up eagerness that longed to burst free. But that thought reminded her of Mr Brooker's sexual volcano, perpetually on the brink of eruption. How she hated Mr Brooker!

One figure appeared in shot after shot, a tall, slender fellow with dark hair and a square jaw who looked heroic in whatever costume he assumed. For all his height, he seemed young: very young. Frequently he directed his gaze at the camera, and Skip saw in his eyes a thrilling flash of fire, something playful, something dangerous. She turned a page and a photo fell out, a stiff eight-by-ten. It wasn't a Players picture; instead it showed a boy on a tennis court, leaping up, body twisted, racquet whipped back ready to strike the ball. The picture looked old-fashioned and so did the boy: hair too short, shorts too long. Skip recognised him, though. He was the hero from the Players. The big knuckly hands, the tight torso, the muscular, strangely animal thighs made Skip feel oddly sad, as if the tennis player called to her across the gulf of time. But what could he be saying? One day, she thought, we will all be people in old photographs, a little ridiculous and decidedly strange even if we don't have wing spectacles or bow ties.

'And how's Skip Wells?' Mr Novak appeared at the piano. He wore his CHIEF COOK AND BOTTLE WASHER apron and smelled of garlic and wine. 'Your sister's good. Last time the Players did *An Enemy of the People*, my wife played that part.' In his tone Skip detected a certain forced cheeriness. 'Of course,' he added, as if he meant more than he was letting on, 'she wasn't my wife then.'

'Why aren't you in the play?' asked Skip.

'Me? I just do refreshments.' Perching on the piano stool, he essayed laggardly chords while Mr Brooker, in the middle of the room, expatiated on the meanings of the play. The rehearsal space was a clearing in the Sanctum. The players, twenty or so in number, reclined on easy chairs and couches ranged around it in a rough semicircle and coloured variously beige, orange, purple and chocolate brown. Older folks sat stiffly; younger ones slouched, some hugging cushions. Rain brushed the windows and the lights were too bright.

'He wanted me to be in it,' Skip said. 'Morten, that was the name. One of the kids. Right age, right hair, he said. I don't think he likes me since I said no.'

'Rash! He's your teacher. Aren't you scared he'll fail you?'

'Funny name for a girl, isn't it – Morten?'

'Morten's a boy. He wanted Honza to be Eylif.'

'Eye-what?' said Skip.

'The other son. My poor boy ran a mile. Now where is he? Off with those rowdy friends again, I suppose. I'm sorry he's not here to play with you.'

'We don't *play*,' Skip snapped before she could stop herself.

'Of course not. All grown up.' Mr Novak ceased his plangent chords. 'Would you like some lemonade? Just promise you won't put the glass on the piano.'

Pavel hovered at the back of the room. During Marlo's scene, he had watched her intently; now he circulated with drinks and bowls of nuts. At a gesture from his father, he brought some lemonade for Skip and repeated, with an automatic air, the admonition not to put the glass on the piano.

Mr Novak looked mournful. 'And yet why not?' he said and sighed. 'All these years, all these guests! Rings, scratches, burns. This piano has suffered abuse worse than one little girl could inflict.'

The lemonade was delicious, and Skip, who had only ever drunk Leed and Woody's, asked him if it contained real lemons. Mr Novak, it emerged, had squeezed them himself. She looked at him fondly. Would Pavel and Honza look like him when they were old? He was bald and fat with wiry eyebrows and dark craterous pores gaping in his nose and cheeks. He smelled of pipe tobacco.

'Hell,' said Pavel, 'there's more of it.'

Rehearsals were proceeding with Mr Brooker taking centre stage. As actor or director, his manner was the same: pacing, stalking, declaiming with outflung hands, dropping suddenly to a stage whisper. Unlike the others, he did not consult his book; he had his part to perfection.

'Now,' he cried, 'let them go on accusing me of fads and crack-brained notions! But they'll not dare to. Ha-ha!' (A flourished hand.) 'I know they won't.'

There was more in this vein, about his writing, his pamphlets, his great discovery, the truth he must deliver to a shocked town. Other players serviced his monologue as chorus and prompts.

'Father, do tell us what it is,' Marlo pleaded.

'What do you mean, doctor?' demanded Mr Singh.

'My dear Thomas …' began Mrs Novak worriedly.

Triumphantly, Mr Brooker declared that the spa town's baths were pestiferous. Putrefying organic matter infected the water, rendering the health resort a health hazard. The baths must close. Shocked cries greeted this announcement. The economy, the economy!

'What a ham,' said Pavel, as Mr Brooker called another halt.

'Our first review.' His father's eyes twinkled. 'And Miss Wells? How does she see her teacher's talents?'

Skip drained her lemonade and wished she had more. 'Last week in class he read us this horror story. Real gruesome it was. This bloke killed another bloke and buried him under the floorboards. But the first bloke could still hear his heart beating. So this bloke, the first bloke, went nuts.'

'I may have heard that story,' said Mr Novak.

'Well, old Brooker really turned it on. He started in a whisper. He whimpered. Snivelled. Gibbered. Sometimes he went real fast, sometimes slow. By the end he was screaming, "It was the beating of his hideous heart!"'

'And you enjoyed this performance?' said Mr Novak.

Skip picked at a sneaker. 'Might have. If somebody else had done it.'

'He's a ham,' Pavel said again, with a haughty sniff, and returned resentfully to the refreshments table.

'Poor boy, he was desperate to play alongside your sister,' said Mr Novak. 'But Howard cast Mr Singh.'

'I didn't know there were Indians in Sweden.'

'Norway. Howard felt Mr Singh added a certain international flavour. I gather he's going for an unconventional staging. Emphasise universal themes and all that.' Wearily, Mr Novak rose from the piano. The kitchen called. Then he noticed the photograph of the tennis player lying, curled a little, across the scored ebony. His voice seemed strained, perhaps surprised, perhaps alarmed, as he asked Skip where she had found the picture.

'In the album. It was there loose.'

'It's my wife's. I'd better put it away.'

He reached for the picture and Skip felt an impulse to snatch it back. She had put down her glass on the piano. 'Who is that boy?' she asked.

Mr Novak touched her glass, shifting it a little on the polished wood. His hand was pudgy, the back thickly furred. 'A long story. The bright hope of Crater Lakes. Roger Dansie, his name was.'

'Dansie? Like that family that lived in the haunted house?'

Mr Novak looked at her sharply. 'He was one of them, yes. The last one.'

'He looks like a star – a real one, I mean.'

'We hoped he would be. He went to London to study with the Old Vic Theatre School. I liked him. When I first arrived in Crater Lakes, just a reffo boy as they called me then, I was weak and thin and coughed all the time. This young man was kind to me.'

'What happened to him?' Skip eyed the picture possessively.

Mr Novak held it against his chest. 'Long story. Sad story. You might say he came to grief in foreign parts. But that's a common fate, isn't it? The same might be said of me.' He smiled. But it wasn't really a smile.

Mr Brooker, clapping his hands, settled down the cast for a speech – one he appeared to have rehearsed well – on his director's 'vision' for the play. With many a murmur, many a whistle, many a smacking of lips, they learned that it was to be set on a space station in AD 3000, and to be performed in silver spacesuits. The costume department (several ladies tittered) had a task and a half before them over the coming weeks; the set designers, too.

Rain beat steadily behind the curtains.

Most of life consists of being bored. Boredom, like a ground bass, underscores all we do. What we call growing up is largely a matter of learning to accept boredom. Those we call the well-adjusted, the mature, are those able to endure boredom with the least complaint, even to pretend it isn't boredom at all. This enables them to work in offices or factories, get married, raise kids, work on cars in driveways, crack a few coldies, smoke fags endlessly, watch Ernie Sigley, and listen to Slim Whitman – or so thought Skip Wells, aged almost thirteen, who like all young people was capable of neither such endurance nor such self-deception. Time hangs heavily for those who feel intensely. A school term is a prison sentence; even an afternoon can stretch interminably. Of all the dull times a young person encounters, few compare with Sunday afternoon in a country town.

Skip sat with her back against the wall of the abandoned service station at Puce's Bend, that daily accusation to Uncle Doug that neither as an entrepreneur nor as a man could he hold a candle to Willard Hartley Puce. Grass, thick as spinifex, pushed up between cracks in the forecourt; Skip ripped it out, stalk by stalk, and shredded the stalks into flakes like parsley. In the vacant lot, discarded stoves, engines and refrigerators teetered around the blowhole's rim. She was hiding. If she went into the house, Auntie Noreen would find jobs for her to do. Tidy your room. Fold the laundry. Have those dishes been done? She scooped up little stones and pinged them, one after the other, at one of the two rust-pocked Golden Fleece pumps. The quiet was narcotic. Slowly the day burned away towards evening, when a pall, like sickness, would descend over everything, the ashy awareness of time wasted, and school in the morning.

Honza Novak mooched along the road towards Puce's Bend. Skip had avoided him since the night they went stalking. Now she quickly concealed herself behind the service station wall, and peeped through a broken window as he scrambled up on top of an old fridge. What a dirty, dishevelled boy he was! With his dark complexion, his coiling coppery hair, he might have been a gypsy, a ragged stranger, posed like a portent against the sky. Faintly, wind flurried over the paddocks. The sun was a lemony pallor, seeping through clouds.

Hatred welled in Skip's throat like bile. She knew what Honza was doing: waiting for Lummo. She had seen them the Sunday before, kicking a footy, firing catapults, tumbling into the long grass, pummelling each other in fights that seemed sometimes real and sometimes play.

She still had her stones. Honza, ten feet distant, was facing away from her. Sharply, she swung back her wrist and hurled a stone through the smashed glass. It clipped his shoulder. He turned around, but already she was the Invisible Girl, hidden under the window ledge.

When she looked up again, Honza still sat on his white plinth, rubbing his shoulder, looking around him confusedly. When he slumped back, she aimed a second shot. He cried out. She had clipped his left ear.

Delighted, she sifted through her stones, choosing a big one for the third assault. Three strikes and you're out: this time she would knock him off his perch. She bobbed up to pitch, just as he twisted around again.

'You!' Honza launched himself off the fridge and pounded in her direction, darting around the side of the wall as she skidded into the forecourt. She hid behind a petrol pump.

Honza, cautious now, emerged through the doorway. Skip leaped out, screamed a wordless war cry, and lobbed the stone at his cheek. She missed. He rushed at her. She pelted towards the blowhole but tripped on tussocky grass, and at once he was upon her. They grappled for a moment on the edge of the blowhole, then rolled and tumbled down its steep walls.

When they reached the bottom, they remained locked together. Skip, winded, lay breathing in gasps. Honza pinned her down; his frothing head was jammed beneath her chin. Guttural hiccoughs erupted from his throat. The boy was laughing.

'What's so funny?' She was outraged. 'Get *off*.'

'Bloody good fighter, you are. For a girl.'

She glared at him suspiciously. Could Honza be her friend? Maybe. When Lummo wasn't around. With little grace they disentangled themselves and sat cross-legged at a wary distance, both sullen-mouthed, both covered in dirt.

'I come down here a bit,' said Honza. 'You find things.'

'What things?' Skip tried to sound hostile.

'Bike pump. Better than mine. Somebody chucked out a chess set once.'

'Great. You can play with Lummo. So where is he, this mate of yours?' Skip added acidly.

Honza shrugged. 'I reckon he's not coming. He can't always come.'

'That bugger? I thought he did what he liked.'

'Nah. His mum's real strict.'

Brenton Lumsden, a mummy's boy? The sun spilled, reddening, down the blowhole's bleak walls. Tracks wound between the debris like mountain trails; breezes skirled the grass at the rim.

'This is like being on another planet.'

'Shipwrecked,' said Honza. 'Like Robinson Crusoe.'

'Space-wrecked. And there's two of us.'

'Crusoe had Friday. Say, I'll be Crusoe –'

'I'm not being Friday!'

'You will. You're littler – and a girl.'

'We're both Crusoe.'

'You're stupid. There's only one Crusoe!'

'We're battling for the island.'

'For the planet.'

Skip jumped up. They faced each other like gunfighters.

That was how the blowhole game began, a thrilling contest in which they grappled, aimed punches, pursued each other, and hid around the back of heaped-up stoves, upended twin tubs and burned-out forty-four-gallon drums, zapping each other with imaginary ray guns. Both died more than once, disintegrated in sizzling blasts.

Honza declared that the fridge on the eastern slope was a space capsule, their only link to the home world, and they battled for possession of it, scaling the blowhole's slippery sides as if competing to plant the conqueror's flag on Everest. Skip clambered up, slipped back; then clambered up again, almost to the top, only for Honza to pounce on her, sending her rolling back before he scrambled up to claim the prize.

He was leaping in triumph when a voice boomed out, 'Novak! What the bloody hell you doing?'

Lummo loomed on the blowhole's brink. Squatting on his Fanta-orange Dragster, the boy stared through the high handlebars first at Honza, then down at Skip, like an avenging Zeus, poised to give judgement.

This was the scene Skip saw now, in dumb show against the gathering twilight: Honza grinning, shaking his head; Lummo gesturing down at Skip as if he could barely believe this treachery; Honza, hand up like a stop sign, repelling the accusation; Lummo pushing him in the chest and Honza flailing backwards; Lummo, bike clattering behind him, squelching his bulk on to Honza's chest, swinging back a fist.

'Stop it!' Skip shouted. 'Bastard, stop it!'

Furious, she scrabbled up the blowhole's side again, but by the time she reached the top, Honza lay moaning, clutching his jaw, and the best Dragster bike in Crater Lakes had soared regally away. Spooling in an arc around Puce's Bend, Lummo stabbed two fingers savagely in the air.

Skip returned the gesture. 'Fuck you too!'

'You shouldn't have done that,' Honza muttered. Frowning, he hauled himself upright, and before Skip could say more he broke from her, a desperate exile, pelting off in the direction of home.

Did he hate her? She couldn't tell. Watching him go, she thought again of a gypsy boy, running darkly against the purple sky.

'Skippy's got a boyfriend!'

Skip had guessed there would be trouble at school. But not how much. First thing Monday morning, when she stepped off the bus, girls surrounded her, giggling, shrieking, jabbing fingers into her ribs, arms and back. Bewildered, she pushed through the chorus of harpies, hating them, wanting to kill them. Honza was surrounded by his own group of boys, whooping, slapping cupped palms on upraised forearms, thrusting fingers back and forth between circled lips.

At the lockers, it all broke out again.

'Who's Novak's girlfriend?'

'Helen Wells is a slag!'

'Skippy done it with Novak – down a blowhole!' Kylie Cunliffe led the charge, grabbing Skip's hand, smooching mock kisses halfway up her arm.

Skip's face burned as she took her place in home group. On the blackboard, someone had drawn a huge heart, pierced by an arrow.

In the right atrium were the initials 'H. W.'; in the left ventricle, 'H. N.' When she glared at Lummo he turned away – telling her, it seemed, that she wasn't worth bothering with; but, as if he had commanded it, the taunts began again, the sniggering, the sneers, the obscene gibes, growing in volume until Mr Something-or-other arrived, too late, and called the class to order.

All morning, the kids smouldered with scandal. 'In a blowhole!' wailed Lucy Sutton, appalled, when Skip, turning confusedly, looked for a place to sit in maths; Joanne Guppy, a dull-eyed girl, pizza-faced with acne, more than once mouthed taunts at Skip; every time he caught her eye, Wayne Bunny jerked a fist in the air, whack-off style, as if to say he knew what she had done with his mate and that maybe, just maybe, she could do it with him, too. The Lum's Den shunned Honza, and Honza and Skip shunned each other, as if both were ashamed.

It was after lunch, though, that the real trouble began. What was the gust that set the fire ablaze? Skip never knew. The class was lined up outside the art block, waiting for the teacher, when Andreas Haskas pushed Honza in the chest, knocking him down, and cried, 'You're weak, Novak!' That was all it took. As Honza tried to get up, Shaun Kenny and Lummo were there too, piling on him like a rugby scrum. Other boys in the class, and many of the girls, surrounded them in a pack, chanting, 'Fight! Fight!' in feverish ecstasy.

Skip had no time to think before she threw herself into the fray. Never mind that she was small: surprise was on her side. She crunched an arm around Lummo's neck. He gagged, and Honza took the opportunity to push him off. Suddenly there were fights in all directions: Lummo, Novak, Haskas, Kenny, Wells. Onlookers gasped, hooted, howled, as Honza knocked down Haskas, Skip booted Kenny in the arse, and Honza wrenched Lummo's arm up behind his back. Then the cry, like a hurled knife, slashing across the asphalt: 'Children! What do you think you're doing? Stop it at once!'

The headmaster! Silence fell.

Mr Brian Rigby was a large man, large in all respects, a one-time army major who took great pride in his war service, which, as all his colleagues and pupils knew, had taken him to Tobruk, El Alamein, New Guinea and Borneo. In youth (this, too, was widely known) he had been a keen boxer, and all his mates had said – meaning it as a compliment, one of the highest payable to a man – that he was built like a brick shithouse. His burly chest swelled as he strode forward. Pinprick eyes glowered in his brick-red face.

The five fighters stood before him, grazed and dusty, as the hero of El Alamein boomed that he had never, in all his born days, witnessed so disgusting an exhibition. 'Each of you,' he declared, 'wears the uniform of my school. And no pupil of my school will act in this manner. Understood?' A hank of Mr Rigby's grey-white hair had been trained in a combover across his bald skull; it flapped now in time with his words. None dared to smirk.

Later, in his office, Mr Rigby caned each of the boys. Skip sat in the corridor outside, kicking her legs back and forth with feigned indifference as sharp cracks sounded through the closed door. Fixed to the wall opposite her was a wide plaque headed HONOUR ROLL; inscribed on it in twin columns, gleaming goldenly against dark varnish, were the names of which the high was proud.

1908 – P. TELFORD.

1909 – D. JACOB.

1910 – W. JONES.

Her eyes ran down the list, on which, she knew, H. WELLS could never feature. One name appeared to have been scratched out; shakier lettering, in the pale rectangle that remained, declared: 1948 – NO AWARD.

The boys emerged from the office: Lummo, with cheeks like fire; Andreas Haskas grinning; Shaun Kenny snivelling, wiping his nose; Honza unsteady on his feet but defiant. As he passed Skip, he winked.

What would it feel like, Mr Rigby's cane? First she told herself she didn't care. Then she told herself she wanted to know. Of one thing she was certain: she would never cry. Never. When she entered the office, the headmaster was sitting behind his desk, and the cane, with its hooked head, leaned in the corner. Before the desk was an empty chair. Skip went to sit in it and he yelled at her to stand. Light, in pale strips, glared through the venetians behind his head.

'There is behaviour we expect in boys,' he began, 'which in the female of the species is grossly inappropriate. For the male, a little roughhousing is only natural – regrettable if it interferes with discipline, but a useful letting-off of that steam which naturally arises with his burgeoning strength, and indeed must do so if that strength is to develop normally and in time be channelled into the useful pursuits of manual labour, sport, or the bearing of arms. I speak, Miss Wells, of boys. You, by contrast, are a girl. In a few years, you'll be a young lady. But not a very nice young lady, if some of the stories I've heard are true. There are names for young ladies like you. Slapper. Slattern. Slut ....' Skip saw in his eyes a hunted look, as if he were contemplating 'bitch' or 'whore' and thought it best not to go quite that far. 'Think long and hard, Miss Wells. What do you want in your future? Do you want a husband and children?'

What had that to do with anything? Hatred burned in Skip's heart. She told herself she must not be weak: not one sign. Stupid man! If only he would cane her – cane her, and be done with it!

'Young lady, I asked you a question.'

Skip shrugged. 'Don't know.'

'Don't know – *sir*!' Mr Rigby thumped his desk.

She said nothing. Did he think she was in the army? She'd be damned if she'd call him sir.

He went on, 'Do you consider your behaviour ladylike?'

Her cheeks burned. She looked up at the ceiling, and shifted her weight from one foot to the other. An itch had started in her side, and she scratched it. 'Why don't you just cane me?'

Mr Rigby looked as if his head might explode. It was all purple: face, ears, neck, and the bald dome that showed beneath his combover. Her parents, he said, would be informed of her behaviour and could devise a fitting punishment. At once, almost brayingly, she returned that she had no parents. He was not amused. His fist slammed the desk, and he shouted at her to shut up, shut up. Wretched girl! Hadn't she achieved enough for one day?

Before she turned to go, Skip asked him, 'Have you read *The Female Eunuch?*'

At home time, Skip was hauling her books into her bag when a hand grabbed her wrist. Honza drew her behind a bank of lockers.

She tried to break free. 'I'll miss the bus!'

'Come to the shop. We'll ride home with Pav.'

She wrenched her wrist from Honza's grip but didn't move away. Locker doors clanged shut. Shouts, laughter, clattering footsteps ricocheted down the corridor. Afternoon light slanted, greenish-white, across the scuffed linoleum. Slowly the noise retreated. Silence fell.

Still wondering if she could trust him, Skip followed Honza out of the school by the back way, clambering over the chain-link fence.

'You should have left Lummo to me,' he said in a tone of calm reason as they shambled towards Volcano Street.

She sneered. 'He'd have beaten you to a pulp.'

'Would not. Me and Lummo fight all the time. For a laugh.'

'Not this time. Why's he such a bastard?'

Honza trailed in the gutter, kicking stones. 'Know what he did once?'

'What?'

'There was this mother cat with kittens. It was under one of them portables at school. Lummo dragged the cat out by the scruff of the neck. Everybody cheered him on. And you know what he did then?

Cat's head in one hand, back paws in the other – he tugged it, real hard, and broke its spine. *Crack!* – just like that. Sheilas screamed. Lummo was grinning like anything. So he chucked the cat on the ground and it tried to crawl back under the portable, pulling itself on its front paws, while the back ones dragged behind. The kittens were meowing, helpless, while the mother died. Mr Rigby found them later and drowned them.'

Skip was speechless for some time. She thought of the cat and the kittens and Brenton Lumsden and felt as if she had plunged again into the shit pit. But this time, she would never get out. The shit pit was the world.

'And you?' she said flatly at last.

'What?'

'You cheered him on, didn't you?'

When Honza looked up, there were tears in his eyes. 'I hate that bastard. I fucking hate him.'

Oleanders glimmered in the sun.

Honza said, a little later, 'Skip? How long you been in the Lakes?'

'Dunno. Few weeks now.'

'And you've lost me all me mates.'

She ripped at oleander leaves. 'With mates like that ...' No need to say more. Among Honza's many talents, she was beginning to see, was the ability to accept, with neither wonderment nor regret, each new situation in which he found himself.

He attempted a grin. 'Blowhole was good, eh?'

'Yair.' It had been sort of fun.

They turned into Volcano Street. A dirty semi lumbered out of the drive of a discount carpet warehouse. In the distance, the huge fibreglass chicken stood like a sentinel over Chickenland.

Honza screwed up his mouth. 'That girlfriend business ...'

At the same moment, Skip began, 'That boyfriend business ...'

Both had reddened.

'They're *sick*.' Skip's words were vehement.

Two boys in school uniform whirled by on bikes, hooting as they passed. Honza did the fingers. So did Skip.

After that they were always together. School had become an obstacle course. Everywhere were dangers: in phys ed with its hurtling missiles (ball, bat, javelin), its charging shoulders, its feet thrust out to trip, its slithery showers abuzz with naked tauntings; art, aglitter with scissors and knives; maths with its compasses; science with its gas taps and Bunsen burners. There were no safe times – not recess, not lunchtime – and no safe places: not by the gates, morning and evening, when the hordes entered and left; not by the bike sheds, where crimes of all kinds were committed in galvanised-iron shadows; not in the toilets, where assassins waited to drag their victims into reeking dank cubicles. Girls tugged Skip's hair, pinched her, pushed her, spat on her. Kylie Cunliffe snatched Skip's ruler and, next to the name SKIP WELLS, added: IS A MOLE. Honza often found himself in Mr Rigby's office, hauled up for fighting.

'It's so unfair,' said Skip. 'What did we do?'

'Nothing,' said Honza. 'It's all that bastard Lummo.'

But did either mind so much? They defended one another, saved one another. They fought back when they could. In woodwork, Honza whacked a plank of pine into Shaun Kenny's nose. Blood went everywhere – like a massacre, everyone said. In home ec, while the teacher was out of the room, Skip pounded a shrieking Kylie Cunliffe with a dozen eggs: every one in the carton. Mr Rigby almost did cane her that day. In maths, during a chaos of paper planes, pinging bra straps, and hysterical chantings of 'O Buddha-Buddha', Skip and Honza crawled between the desks and set off firecrackers under the Lum's Den. Each afternoon when the school day ended, they felt like victors: Henry V at Agincourt, Wellington at Trafalgar, Brian Rigby at El Alamein.

They gave up the school bus. Honza rode his bike to school, though it was a long way, and Skip, determined to join him, salvaged a bike from the blowhole. Hardly a match for Honza's purple Dragster, the bike was too big for her, its mudguards crumpled, its paintwork pitted, but with new tyres, the seat adjusted, and liberal applications of Uncle Doug's oilcan, it was not quite good as new but good enough: a boy's Raleigh, fire-engine red, and faster than it looked.

Each morning they left home early, whirling down rackety roads like brats in Enid Blyton books bound for adventure. Sometimes they competed with each other, racing, standing on pedals, look-no-hands, skidding in circles to the peril of their tyres and calling to the other to keep up, keep up. Other times they rode quietly side by side. Those were the best times. Magpies cackled up in weird morning ecstasies, and sunlight, golden with spring, spilled across the broad green paddocks.

Honza taught Skip to smoke. He laughed at her when she coughed, and she punched him, but soon she could do the drawback as if she had been at it all her life. 'Natural as breathing,' said Honza, and Skip agreed. At the far end of the school oval, by the back fence, was a gnarled old bluegum that became their special hideout. As the days grew warmer, they spent many hours high among the thick khaki leaves, often hours when they should have been in lessons, leaning back against that scratchy trunk, side by side on brittle boughs, Marlboros in hand.

Childhood is a green world. When that world lies behind us, it becomes a riddle whose answer we once knew, then forgot, remembering only a question that nags at us to resolve it. Skip and Honza were children playing. They climbed trees. They peered into windows. They slid down slippery dips and clambered on jungle gyms. They had adventures without leaving Puce's Bend: Wild West shootouts, magic quests. Everything could be transformed. If the blowhole was another planet, the abandoned service station was a war-torn city.

A grove of trees was the Amazon jungle. One Sunday, they climbed the watchtower over the lakes. From the top, panting, they looked across the waters in their jagged calderas; across the town with its bungalows and wide streets; across pines and paddocks towards the green horizon, as the land with its limestone and volcanic soil rolled away towards the Southern Ocean. It was beautiful. The world was beautiful.

Skip stretched out her arms. 'I wish I could fly,' she said, but she knew she could. She really could.

They were not always in motion. For long afternoons, they sprawled on their bellies on the floor of the bedroom Honza shared with Pavel, playing chess, reading comics, listening too loudly to the top forty countdown on 5AD until Mrs Novak told them to turn that rubbish down. They came up with schemes for revenge on Lummo. They ridiculed Mr Rigby. They talked about the great things they would do one day: Honza would fly in a rocket ship to Mars; Skip would find the philosopher's stone, like Sylvester Turville in *Lion*.

Everything was plans and schemes. What they never said was: 'When I grow up ...' Time, that spring, was held for them in suspension. Both knew, with dazzled half-knowledge, that something was about to end. Their days in the green world were almost over. They were playing in gardens that were about to close. Soon they would leave and the gates would shut, never – not for them – to be opened again.

# Chapter Seven

There is a plangency in the fall of evening, as light seeps from the sky and darkness comes. Dusk, always poignant, is particularly so on Saturdays in South Australia in a country town. For hours the main drag has been dead, since the shops closed at midday. Kids are away somewhere, in playgrounds, in backyards; housewives are at home, with their magazines, their movie matinees, deep in their weekend torpor; husbands have gone to the football or the races or squint into greasy engine innards on their concrete driveways or in sheds. Families here and there have had barbecues. Some have gone to the beach. Some have taken the car out to charge up the batteries. The middle of town is silent, belonging to no one, but soon it will fill again, and noise – hoots, cries, jukebox C&W – will pour from the doors of ancient pubs with verandas frosted in iron lace. Later, when the dark is full, yahoos driving up and down the street ('chucking a mainy') will find the place all headlights, horns blasting, grinning blokes and their tarted-up sheilas lurching across the pavement as if it were the deck of a ship in a storm. But all this is to come. For now, the sky is a reddish purplish grey. What is it about that quality of light?

It was one such Saturday evening, a little too late for kids to be out, when Skip and Honza, after a long ride, fetched up at Crater Gardens. They leaned their bikes against the low wall. Inevitably, they descended to the inner gardens where Pavel had once taken Skip and Marlo. The place was deserted. On the viewing deck, watching the water crash down and down, Skip told Honza about a movie she had seen once, where these blokes and this girl went on a journey to the centre of the earth.

'There was dinosaurs and everything,' she said, in the lazy slurring voice she had developed, not quite consciously, for talking to her mate. 'And man-eating plants. And a whole ocean, under the ground. And guess how they got there? Volcano. Down the top.'

Honza was excited, as she had known he would be, and they planned how one day they would make their own journey to the centre of the earth.

'We'd better get home,' Skip said at last. The cave was eerie in the fading light. Shadows cut blackly into the rocky walls above, and the waterfall sounded like the steamy roar of some monster underground.

Turning, Honza slapped her arm. 'Race you.'

Their sneakers echoed in the silence like shots as they slapped their way up the asphalt spiral. First Skip took the lead, then Honza; then together, pushing and elbowing each other, they rounded the last of the steep rise, battered through the gate, and collapsed, Skip on the path, and Honza against the side of the wishing well. The gate banged back and forth.

When Skip had regained her breath, she joined Honza. The wishing well was shabby, hardly a credit to the Lions Club of Crater Lakes, who claimed it in lettering emblazoned around the cupola. Cladding the sides were irregular stony slabs like crazy paving; some were cracked, some gone, exposing concrete beneath. The plaque bolted to the side, recording the gift of the well to the town, seemed to speak of a time lost to history.

UNVEILED BY THE RIGHT WORSHIPFUL
THE MAYOR OF CRATER LAKES
ARCH L. GULL, ESQ.
22 MAY, 1949

Honza pointed to the words. 'My gramps.'

Mrs Novak, Skip recalled, had once been Deirdre Gull. She wondered if the gramps was still alive, but Honza gave the answer before she could speak. 'Kicked the bucket yonks ago. Before Pav was born.'

'That long?' Skip had no more to say. Grandfathers were strange to her and not quite real. After all, even her father was a mystery to her, a myth, not a man, one of many such myths in Karen Jane's past and not, to her sorrow, even the same myth as Marlo's. The thought of fathers filled Skip with bafflement, even contempt; grandfathers could only be worse. Dimly she pictured a wheezing figure, tugging at her shirttails with long, gnarled fingers. She nuzzled closer to her best mate. Solemnly they hung their heads over the well. Through the brackish water glimmered faint flashes of silver and copper.

'How much dosh you reckon's there?' said Skip.

'Tons. People chuck it down all the time.'

'Fifty? A hundred? What's it all for?'

'Lions Club, ain't it? Charity.'

'Every so often some bloke must come along and clear it all out.' Honza shrugged. 'Suppose so.'

Skip assumed a thoughtful air. Leaves rustled in the quiet gardens as she offered, like a scientist formulating a theory, 'How does he clear it? That water's, what, six foot deep?'

'Has some pole thing, I suppose. With a scoop on it.'

'But there's a grille.' The grid of metal, a foot underwater, was bolted to the sides.

'And a lock. That grille lifts up.' Eagerly, before Skip could try, Honza rolled back his sleeves, plunged his hands into the water and tugged at the grille. He bit his lower lip and tugged again. Veins stood out in his forearms like cords. For a moment he looked older; he might have been Pavel. 'Bloody thing's loose. Rusted near clean through.'

'Reckon you could rip it off, then, muscle man?'

'Might do. Could saw through it easy.'

Skip thought of the hacksaws at Puce Hardware. 'The well would still be filled with water, though.'

'Something drains it,' said Honza. 'They drain it, then fill it again. But how do they drain it? All the water would have to go somewhere, wouldn't it?'

'There's a tap on that wall.' Skip pointed to the near wall of the town hall.

'That's for the gardener.' A hose lay coiled beside it. 'They must fill the well from there. That's the inflow – but the outflow, where's that go?'

'Buggered if I know.' Skip had begun to get bored. She shouldn't have brought up the wishing well. Why talk about a wishing well when you could talk about journeys to the centre of the earth?

'Imagine if we could empty that well!' Honza was saying. 'There's a job for the night stalkers. We'll come at midnight. Old Doug must have a hacksaw we could flog, huh?'

Skip nodded, inspired again.

'We'll bring a couple of bags for the dosh.'

Honza circled the well. On the side near the cave entrance, a hunch of pipe was visible where cladding had fallen away. Pondering, he looked at the well, then at the gate that led to the cave. A thick wall of trees and bushes rose darkly above the picket fence. He swung open the gate and stepped inside. Skip heard thrashing and swishing as he searched around in the foliage.

'Got it!' he called, after a moment.

Skip joined him. He held back heavy leaves. Arcing upwards from the black soil was a low tap, bronze and discoloured. Beneath the tap ran a terracotta drain, half-filled with dirt and leaves.

'It must be for the well,' she said, impressed.

Honza turned the tap, applying all his strength. For a time it seemed nothing would happen; then gouts of sludgy, greenish liquid vomited forth and swept the dirt and leaves down the terracotta channel. His face shone with excitement. 'Go back to the well, eh? See if it's going down.'

She did as he said. At first there was no movement, but as she watched, tremors rippled the surface. They could rob the wishing well: they really could. That was when she grew frightened. Skip had thought this just another game, a wild scheme never to be put into practice. She liked stories, fantasies. This was too real. 'All right,' she snapped. 'You've proved it. Turn it off.'

'No fear. Do you know what we could do with a hundred bucks?' Honza, dancing around her, chanted like a mad thing, 'Night stalker, come … Night stalker, quick!'

'We can't! It's stealing.' Firmly Skip strode towards the tap and shut it off. It was rusted stiffly, and she gasped as she strained to turn it.

Honza looked on, face twisted in contempt. 'Should have known! Lummo would have jumped at the chance.' He turned away from her, disgusted. 'Going round with a girl! What was I thinking of?'

Skip was enraged. 'You take that back!'

The fight was brief but intense. With her first lunge, Skip brought Honza down; she sat astride him, pummelling him, until he roared and flipped her off. She fell heavily; then they were grappling, rolling across the grass, until a portly man, passing through the park, saw them and lumbered towards them, yelling, "Ey, stop it! 'Ey, yous kids!' They scrambled up and raced back to their bikes.

They rode home in silence. Several times Skip pushed ahead, though her broken-down bicycle had no lamp and the night had come in cloudy. Each time Honza managed to catch her up. They had rounded Puce's Bend when he arced forward and skidded to a halt in front of her, blocking her path.

'Know what?' he said, grinning.

'What?' Her voice was hostile. Was Honza still her mate?

'You still fight good. For a girl.' He laughed, a strained laugh, plunged down on a pedal and rode away. Left alone, she thought the night that closed around her was darker than before, darker and colder.

Skip was through with Honza. That week she rode to school alone, leaving early in the morning to be sure to avoid him. In class, she sat apart from him. She spent recess and lunch in the school library, staring with pretended intentness at pages that blurred before her eyes. Twice he tried to approach her – once catching her alone at the lockers, once leaping out at her from around a corner. She didn't jump. 'Go back to Lummo!' she called, and hurried away. But Honza had not rejoined the Lum's Den. On Tuesday, Mr Rigby caned him for fighting Andreas Haskas. Skip looked at him ruefully as he limped back into class. Honza had guts. Maybe, just maybe, they should still have been mates.

She got into trouble herself on Wednesday. It was the worst trouble she had ever been in. After lunch they had maths – bad enough at any time, but worse when Mr Singh was sick and Mr Rigby took the class. He glared at Skip as she slouched in late. The purple was already rising in his face. Angrily he chalked fractions on the board and spun around to bark at Jason Fidler. Skip wished she had been on time. The only free seat was next to a big pudding-faced girl called Maggie Polomka, who several times jabbed her in the thigh with a succession of sharp objects. Skip bore it for as long as she could: Maggie Polomka, known among the boys as 'Mag the Slag', was a spaz, everybody knew that. But when ruler, pencil and pen were succeeded by compass, Skip burst to her feet, chair crashing behind her, punched Mag the Slag in the chops and yelled at her to fucking well cut it out.

Later it seemed to Skip that there had been no time, not an instant, between the blow she struck and the blow that struck her. There must have been, of course: moments when Mr Rigby whipped around from the board and Skip stood aghast and Mag the Slag wailed and Mr Rigby thundered down the aisle, combover flapping, beefy arm swinging back.

The blow came like lightning. With a cry, Skip sprawled across the gibbering Maggie, only to be jerked upright again as Mr Rigby grasped her collar and marched her to the door. 'Wait at my office!' He flung her from the room. 'If you think you're a boy, I'll beat you like a boy!'

The door crashed closed behind her. The corridor, with its linoleum wastes, seemed to narrow in her gaze, then widen. Startled, she brushed away tears. She felt her cheek where the blow had connected: it throbbed. From the class came sounds of uproar, and Mr Rigby's bullish attempts to quell it. Would the bastard really do it this time – beat her like a boy? She had taken only three steps towards his office before revulsion shuddered through her frame. Fuck Rigby. Fuck him. She broke into a run, and burst out into the bright afternoon. The grounds were deserted. No one stopped her as she raced for the bike racks, grabbed her bike, and tore away from the school.

Her progress had slowed by the time she reached Puce's Bend. On fleeing the school, she had barely thought about what might happen next. She imagined a car drawing up beside her, a window rolling down, and Rigby fixing her in an artillery-sight gaze. But no cars came this way. Perhaps tonight the telephone would jangle, and Auntie Noreen would listen in mounting fury before slamming down the receiver and crying, 'Helen Wells!'

Perhaps Skip could never go to school again.

Suddenly all she wanted to do was lie down. She was sad. She was tired. She would sneak into the sleepout, she decided. It was

Wednesday: Auntie Noreen would be watching telly. The old bag adored Wednesday, the one weekday when Channel Eight started up early. Every Wednesday after lunch, Noreen Puce was ready, Twisties, Mars Bars and Custard Creams at hand, for *Woman's World*, *Motel* and a nice movie matinee. More than once in her dinner-table musings she had expressed the wish that television would go all day, every day. Was she to endure for ever the meagre rations of Channel Eight, which most days had nothing on until half-past five? Even the ABC (and nobody watched that rubbish) was just test pattern and music till the kiddies got home.

Skip, ducking down, was walking her bike past the front fence when a bright orange Ford Falcon crunched around Puce's Bend and halted beside her.

'Helen!' Struggling out of the car was a purple-haired creature dressed in what looked like frilly pink curtains. Lips rimmed in red parted, rictus-style, revealing gleaming white plastic. 'It's Baby Helen, isn't it?'

Skip was shaking her head, vehement in denial, when Auntie Noreen cackled from the front porch, 'Valmai! Quick, before *Motel* starts,' and before she knew it, she found herself being propelled into the living room, where her aunt had laid out an elaborate afternoon tea.

'Good to see you, Valmai,' Auntie Noreen said in a cheery voice as she tugged Skip down beside her on the creaking sofa. 'You've met Mrs Lumsden, ain't you, Baby Helen? Me old cobber from way back. New perm, Valmai?'

Valmai Lumsden, who had squeezed herself into the best armchair, was almost as huge as Auntie Noreen, and every bit as ancient, but disported herself as if she were much thinner, younger and more attractive. Girlishly she patted the rock-hard perm and, while Auntie Noreen poured the tea, launched into a discourse in which the phrases 'my colouring' and 'my skin' featured often. Finally, over 'Love Is

Blue', the theme song from *Motel*, Valmai Lumsden observed, 'You're home early, Helen.'

Skip thought quickly. 'Maths this arvo was cancelled. Mr Singh's sick.'

'The Paki? Probably shirking it.'

'He's Indian.'

'They're all Pakis,' Auntie Noreen said sagely, as if in her years at Puce Hardware she had employed many a dusky denizen of the subcontinent and found them all shiftless and dishonest. Would Valmai like some lemon cake?

Valmai liked the look of them pink lamingtons.

'You always did like a lamington, Val.'

'But them chocolate fingers look delightful, too.'

Deliberations continued – so much to sample! – between, above and around the goings-on at the motel. The ladies didn't so much watch television as wallow in it, like a hot bath, as if its blue-grey flicker, its voices, its eruptions of music were a sustaining medium for their cooings and purrings. 'Don't reckon that blouse does her any favours,' one might say, gesturing to the screen. 'Saw a lovely blouse at Arlene's,' the other might reply. Next might come: 'Haven't seen Arlene for yonks, have you?' or 'Vanilla slice, Valmai?' or 'They reckon in *TV Week*' – referring to the screen again. Skip squirmed. Miserably she nibbled at a chocolate finger. Her role, she realised, was dutiful niece: evidence, like the scrim that hung in the window, the floral swirls of the carpet, the generous but prissy tea table, of Noreen Puce's well-ordered life.

'Doing well at school, Helen?' said Mrs Lumsden, as if she were interested, while a girl onscreen displayed, in a mouth as wide as the Grand Canyon, the Colgate Ring of Confidence. 'You're in my Brenton's class, ain't you?'

'Such a well-behaved boy,' said Auntie Noreen.

'I see a bright future for my Brenton,' said Mrs Lumsden.

A voice shouted about specials on steak, chops and liver at Coles New World, and Mrs Lumsden, pointing to the picture on the mantelpiece, observed to Auntie Noreen that Your Barry was at least doing his bit. Skip bit her tongue, and wondered what 'at least' meant. Could anything about Barry be less than perfect? Could there be anything for which he had to atone? She glanced towards the hall where the telephone crouched menacingly. Surely Mr Rigby would ring soon?

Mrs Lumsden lit an Alpine ('My health,' she explained) and Auntie Noreen, between bites of the last lamington, launched into a disquisition on My Baz, and how proud she was of the bit he was doing. Restless, Skip noticed an envelope pushed, as if for concealment, along with a crushed Jaffas box and several Minties wrappers, between the sofa arm and the cushion. Furtively she picked at it, and had dislodged it a little when two things happened at once: the telephone rang, and the handwriting leaped out with sudden clarity.

'Karen Jane!' Skip jumped to her feet, quite spoiling the climax of *Motel*, while Auntie Noreen tried to snatch back the purloined letter. Startled, Mrs Lumsden looked between them.

Backed against the tea table, Skip crushed the letter like an icon to her chest, while Auntie Noreen, bouncing absurdly, struggling to rise from her sofa wallowings, roared, 'Private mail … private mail is not for little girls!'

'It's to us. To me and Marlo!' Skip had had time to read the address.

Still the telephone rang and rang.

'Marlo and I – Mar-*leen* and I.' Noreen Puce, risen now, lunged towards Skip. A fat hand clutched a skinny shoulder; fat fingers prised, gouged. Skip pressed the letter tighter against her chest. 'I *am* sorry about this, Valmai,' Auntie Noreen was saying. 'You know how girls get. If it's not Johnny Farnham, it's some other nonsense they've got themselves worked up about.'

'And the other one seems so quiet,' mused Mrs Lumsden.

'Different dads. Still, even that one's going the way of her mother. Some of the things I found in her room! That Greer Garson book full of smut, for a start. That woman's poor mum must be so ashamed.'

Sagely, the permed head nodded. 'This one on the rag yet?'

'Not long now, I reckon. Can tell, can't you?'

Horrified, Skip kicked Auntie Noreen in the shin, wrenched her shoulder free, and plunged off down the hall, as her aunt, all pretence of gentility lost, screeched, 'Helen Wells! Come back here this instant, you fucking little bitch!'

Auntie Noreen, when she had to, could move with fearful speed. Footsteps boomed and floorboards squelched, almost snapping, as her huge rubbery legs juddered after her niece. 'You give me that letter, Helen Wells, or I'll beat you black and blue!'

Skip flung herself into the bathroom, just in time. 'Shut up!' she yelled. 'Shut up, shut up!' She clunked the bathroom lock in place and leaned against the door, slithering down, feeling the remorseless blows through her spine as the fist pounded and pounded.

'It's nonsense, Helen! You don't really reckon yous're going to America? That mad cow couldn't get you to Gepps Cross Abattoir. She's got no money, no job, and no one's going to give her one. She's off in Cloud Cuckoo Land, like she always was. I didn't want yous to see that, lovey!'

Skip blocked her ears. Let words rain around her: she refused to listen. The telephone, which had briefly ceased its clamour, started up again: let it ring itself off its cradle, let it dance across the hall table and drop and smash to the floor. Hateful phrases stabbed in her mind like daggers: *Helen Wells, you fucking little bitch ... This one on the rag yet? ... Different dads ...* She hated Auntie Noreen. Hated Valmai Lumsden. Hated everything and everyone. The chill of the bathroom floor seeped like wetness through the back of her skirt.

The pounding had stopped. Auntie Noreen was on the telephone. Dry-eyed, face burning, Skip uncrumpled the envelope. It had been opened crudely, with a finger under the flap, and the letter hastily stuffed back. She drew it forth and smoothed it over her knees. Twice, three times, her eyes slithered over Karen Jane's girlish rounded handwriting, trying to take it in.

*Darlings!*

*I hope you're both well and enjoying life at your aunt's. Fresh country air, that's what you need! Don't mind Noreen. She can be an old bitch and she's stuck in Consciousness II just like Charles A. Reich reckons (GREAT book), but she means well. She needs love. Everybody needs love. I'll be out soon. That's what I'm writing to let you know. Can't wait to escape! (Don't really mean escape of course!! – they'll have to let me out for good behaviour.) Imagine, the three of us together again! I've got it all worked out. The agents (CIA) who came for Caper are on my trail.\* We can't stay in SA, but when did we ever want to?! We're off to SF, Caper or no Caper! In here I've had time to reflect. I feel I've got it in me to be great, and so have you. We'll all be great – I've a feeling I've got it in me to be a poet, a real one, like Edna St Vincent Millay. Watch out, world!!*

*I'll be coming to get you, just as soon as I can. There's NOTHING wrong with me. These doctors (CIA) want to keep me here. But they won't, they can't. I so look forward to the wonderful times ahead. (San Fran – be sure to wear flowers in your hair!!)*

*All my love, KJ xxx*

\* SUBVERSIVES *must be stopped.* FASCISTS *want the* WAR *to go on 4* EVER.

Skip let the letter fall. If there were parts of it she didn't understand, she didn't care. With Karen Jane, there were always parts you didn't understand. But the main point was clear. They were letting her out. Skip's heart soared. Could it be? No more Crater Lakes!

In the hall, the telephone crashed into its cradle and Auntie Noreen stomped back, thunder in her thighs, screaming, 'You little liar!' and 'What do you think you're playing at?' and 'Both you bitches, you're crazy as Kazza!'

*Bam! Bam!* came the doom knell through the door ('Just wait till my Dougie gets home! He'll rip this door off its hinges'); then Valmai Lumsden was there too, urging *Nor, Nor* – horrible how she said it – to calm down, let me make you a fresh pot, nothing some silly brat did could be worth this fuss; while Skip, cold on the bathroom floor, silvered in the light from the window slats, thought only of her old life with Karen Jane, picturing it as paradise, one from which she had been expelled, but one that soon would receive her again.

Yet what could Skip know? What could she believe? Caper, the draft dodger, had been captured at last, Karen Jane was in the funny farm, Marlo sat at a desk in Puce Hardware, and Auntie Noreen filled the sky, omnipresent as God. They would never make it to San Fran. They would never make it to Gepps Cross. Skip held on to Glenelg Beach: the Norfolk pines, the sand like spangled stars, St Vincent's Gulf promising that everything, for all the cleavings of time, was connected after all. Look at this place, this provincial hellhole they've stuck you in. The same moon shines in America as here. Walk on a beach in South Australia, arsehole of the world, and stick your fingers in the tide: the great pulsing field of the sea touches every shore in the world. I'm touching India. I'm touching Egypt. I'm touching Antarctic ice and the green mouth of the Amazon.

Skip remained in the bathroom long enough for Auntie Noreen to retire, led away by Valmai Lumsden with many a soothing *Nor, Nor.* Long enough for her left side (curled against the door) to go numb. Long enough for the frosted slats to glimmer less brightly, the matching bath, sink and toilet darkening from pinky-mauve to deep purple. From down the hall, beneath the orchestral swoonings of the movie matinee starring Dana Andrews and Susan Hayward, came Noreen Puce's anguished sobs, Valmai Lumsden's caramel cooings.

Finally stirring, Skip felt as if she were waking from a dream. She swayed upright, grabbed the side of the bath, and sat down quickly on the purple ledge, nursing pins and needles. If only she could escape! But maybe she could. She eyed the window above the sink. When she could stand again, she quickly removed several window slats from their metal frames, laying them on the cistern tank. Behind the slats was a flyscreen; she was fumbling for the catches that held it in place when Auntie Noreen renewed her assault, shouldering the bathroom door and crying out execrations at her evil, crazed niece.

Suddenly all was chaos. The door throbbed like a drum skin; then, with a crack, a crunch, a clatter, the lock was on the floor. Skip tore at the flyscreen; it fell from the frame, and she jumped up on the sink and hurled herself into the gap just as Auntie Noreen crashed through the door. Wild words – 'You little bitch!' and 'Come back here!' and 'No, you don't!' – splattered from the raging mouth; a hand grabbed Skip's ankle. She bucked, writhed. Slats shattered, cascading glassily on porcelain and tiles. With a kick, Skip was free and dropped to the grass outside.

But where could she run? There was nowhere to go.

Still, she pelted into the road just as Honza Novak came spinning by on his bike and almost knocked her down. She gripped his handlebars and he grinned at her, delighted. 'You're crazy.' He shook his head. 'Crazy.'

'We're doing it.'

'Doing what?' he said.

'The wishing well. Every last cent.'

'Helen!' Noreen shrilled from the porch. 'Back here this instant – this instant, I say!'

Skip's mouth curved up in a smile. She hummed, twirled a little, even waved at her red-faced aunt. Now that she knew she would soon be escaping, she felt invincible. Why be afraid? Let Noreen Puce do her worst. Skip was almost sorry for the pathetic old cow.

Soon, thought Skip, we'll be gone, gone. Me and Marlo. Whether they would head for Adelaide, South Australia, or San Francisco, California, she didn't yet know. She hadn't thought that far ahead. But she knew they would never stay in Crater Lakes. Never, never.

Tossing her head, Skip sauntered back to the house.

# Chapter Eight

'Nah. Never make it.'

'Why not? I'm going.'

'Yair? A kid on your own?'

'I won't be. Marlo, she'll come.'

'And leave Brooker? You'll be back first day. What about that bloke that drives the bus? Won't he tell your auntie?'

'We'll hitch!' Skip's voice rose. She should have said nothing. Let Honza think the raid was for fun, just another game. But her plan was hazy even to her. The money, that was what mattered. The money, and then, somehow, escape.

Night pressed around them like dark velvet. Sporadically, streetlamps made glowing pools. Already Skip knew they had chosen badly. Saturday night had slipped into that hinterland when it is Sunday morning by the clock but Saturday refuses to end. They had made their way down side streets, keeping to shadows; they shot across Volcano Street, then down the path beside the town hall. Horns and faded revelling sounded from the street, but in Crater Gardens all was still. They rested their bikes against the sandstone wall.

'Can't see,' said Skip. 'Where's the torch?'

Honza pressed it into her hand. 'Just a flash or two. When we need it.'

A car passed, radio loud. Skip wished they had waited. On any other night, Volcano Street would be dead by now. But the preparations had all been made: that morning she had stolen the hacksaw from Puce Hardware; Honza, dropping by Crater Gardens at dusk, had turned on the hidden tap. All through dinner (chops, mashed swede, Birds Eye peas), all through an evening hunkered in the sleepout, Skip thought of water sinking tremulously in the well. When Honza hissed his summons – 'Night stalker, come … Night stalker, quick!' – she was wide awake and waiting.

Her punishment, at least, had finally come to an end. Chores, chores and more chores, straight in after school, early to bed – how the days had dragged! Auntie Noreen's reproachful looks had been bad enough. Worse was her relentless braying. 'Don't think you're having any telly tonight, missy!' – as if Skip wanted to watch *Division 4.* 'Done that vacuuming yet, missy?' – as if Skip were a slave who deserved to be whipped. Uncle Doug had been useless, glancing shame-faced at her when he thought she wasn't looking; all this embarrassed him, his manner seemed to say, but he could do nothing to stop it. Even Marlo treated her coldly, disgusted, it seemed, that her sister could squander so heedlessly the blessing of schooling. Skip tried to explain: 'It's Rigby, he's a bastard, he's …' But Marlo wouldn't listen. Never had Skip felt so alone.

She flashed the torch. Purple leaves, branches: the foliage wall. A grey gleam: the path. Crazy paving, vertical: the well's stone-clad side. They peered over the edge. She exulted. Empty! The water had all drained out. The torchlight, cut by shadows of the obstructing grille, played across the well's curving sides of blackish oily green, and flashed up glitterings from silver-copper depths. The Treasure of the Sierra Madre dazzled their eyes.

134

Honza nudged Skip and she flipped off the torch. 'Hacksaw.' He might have been a surgeon. *Scalpel. Forceps.*

'Let me.' Skip drew the saw from her Qantas bag. Leaning into the well, she gripped the grille, which was at once rough with rust and soft with slime. Back and forth she zigzagged the blade. The metallic raspings were deafening in the night.

Honza, beside her, could barely keep still. He sighed loudly, wrung his hands, bounced up and down on the balls of his feet. He didn't care why Skip wanted the treasure. He didn't believe she would leave the Lakes. The adventure was all that mattered. 'You'll break the blade! Give me a go.'

Skip resisted as he grappled for the saw. She gasped as it fell from her hand; fortunately, it didn't fall through the grille. Light, just a little, flickered over the dark scene; the clouds were shifting above them, like a curtain drawing back to reveal the moon.

Skip let Honza grab the saw. All right, she decided. Let the boy be the boy. He sawed, sawed. Here. And here. And here. He worked his way round the well, while Skip crossed her arms and tapped a foot impatiently.

'Bugger.' The blade broke. But Honza thought he had done enough. Determined, he threaded his fingers through the grille. He tugged hard. Cords strained in his neck and he hunched forward, breathless. 'Help me.'

Their fingers mingled. There was a series of rapid clicks, then a loud snap, and they collapsed backwards, the grille falling over them like a cage. Skip gasped, winded. Disgusted, she pushed away the grille. It stank. Honza sprang up and punched her arm. 'Your bit.'

'Bit?' she said.

He gestured to the well. 'Six foot deep. Whoever goes down is going to need a hand up. You're lightest.'

Sometimes Skip wished she were as big as a mountain. Reluctantly she scrambled up to sit on the stony brim. Darkness pressed between her dangling legs. Uneasily she looked below and questions flashed into her mind: 'You won't leave me?' and 'This isn't a setup?' and 'You'll help me get back out?' But she knew enough not to ask them aloud.

'Bombs away.' She pinched her nose as if the well still brimmed with water, plummeted forward, and landed with a crunch on the coins. She slipped and grabbed for the wall, then snatched away her hand as oozing soft blackness sank coldly beneath her palm.

'Stinks down here.' Her voice sounded hollow.

'Stinks up here.' Honza shifted darkly in a circle of moonlight. He raised an arm. 'Watch out.'

Something thudded down beside her: his rucksack. She sank to her haunches. Hurriedly she tugged at the fastenings and pushed back the flap. She scooped stiff hands into the coins. How deep they were: how deep, how cold. They clinked from her fingers in an icy surf, and clattered heavily into the hessian bag. Her heart thrilled. After all those issues of *Lion*, after all those Tom Swifts, after all those Saturday nights at the Ozone, here was adventure, real at last. No longer Skip Wells, she was a safecracker, ear against a bank vault, feeling for the click of a combination; a cat burglar (black mask, black jumpsuit) spiriting away diamonds across pitching rooftops; a pirate, parrot on shoulder, sinking a shovel into the place marked X on a dog-eared, crumbling map.

'Hurry up,' called Honza.

'I'm going as fast as I can.' For a time it seemed that more coins slid down the sides of the rucksack than went into it, but at last it was full.

Neither Skip nor Honza had considered how to lift a laden bag from the well. On the first try, half the coins tumbled out. Skip cursed as the avalanche slid around her, hard and chill. Adventure! This was adventure? Her back ached, her hands were numb, and the stench in the well had grown worse, a dank fetor that wrapped itself around her like octopus arms. Clumsily she bundled more coins into the rucksack, secured the straps tightly, and raised it, gasping, above her head.

'Christ!' Her arms throbbed like tensile wires. 'How in hell will we get this home?'

Gritted teeth obscured Honza's answer. 'Slowly.' Or was it: 'Search me'? He leaned so far over the edge that she feared he would fall in. Relieved of her burden, Skip slumped against the wall, then sprang away at once, feeling the slime squelch against her back. Above, the rucksack thudded to the ground beside Honza.

The Qantas bag next. Floppy vinyl slapped her head. Now she was a boxer, punch-drunk, reeling into the ring but certain, in jangling seconds, to take the knockout blow. Groaning, she bent over, heaving up more of the rattling coins that seemed never to diminish, like sand on a shore. Rattle, crash. Rattle, crash. Honza said something, but his words were lost. She steeled herself. Adamantine, that's what she must be. Marlo had taught her that word, Skip thought proudly. Adam-Ant-I-Am. I'm escaping, she told herself, I'm running away, but where she was running and why had become, in this reeking darkness, a question as mysterious as the meaning of life or why Karen Jane had to be a crazy bitch and not a proper mother like other people's mothers. They wouldn't really let her out, would they? She was nuts. Rattle, crash. Rattle, crash. Skip was a machine, if machines could ache, if machines could shiver, if machines could sob in disgust, horror and sadness – but that sound … What was that sound?

A whoop. A shout. Footsteps thundering nearer, nearer.

Skip froze. The cops!

Where was Honza? The moonlight was brighter, and glinted on the coins, the Qantas bag, the slick encircling walls, but no face, no figure, was visible to her above the narrow well mouth. 'Honza?' she called faintly, then louder; she heard him – was it Honza? – call out, then more yells: 'Get him!' and 'Come on!' and a wild war whoop all strangely distant from down in the well, and the dull sickening meat slap of punches connecting. The cops? It couldn't be. Skip scrabbled at the well's sides, but her hands found no purchase in the slithery dark. She cried out, 'Honza! Honza!' but heard only echoes in return. They swirled around her, growing faint. Then there was silence from above.

Now a shout. Now a snigger. 'Bugger it, you've knocked him out. Kick him.'

*Thop! Thop!* 'Ain't moving.'

She recognised the voices. Shaun Kenny. Andreas Haskas. And the silhouette of Brenton Lumsden was leaning over the well.

Lummo let out a long whistle. 'Well, well! And what have we here?' he said, like a *Play School* presenter introducing a surprising but delightful segment. He turned and called back, 'Haskas! Leave him.' (The *thop!* had been repeated.) 'Get the hose. Seems the well's run dry.' Lummo's laugh was high, too high – a girly giggle.

'Bag's fucking heavy.' Kenny, with the rucksack?

'Leave that!' cried Skip, and all the Lum's Den laughed. Now the three of them appeared above the well, shoulders jostling; she heard the hiss of the hose, and could only stare up, gaping, as the cold shock hit her. Flung back, splayed against the well wall, she convulsed as if from a thousand volts.

'Cool off, Skippy! We don't like thieves in Crater Lakes.'

The spray slammed and slammed her; she twisted to avoid it, but all she could do was stumble in circles, pursued by the pitiless jet of water. She collapsed, coins jabbing her knees and hands; she gulped; she struggled to breathe, and barely registered when the spray ceased.

Shouts broke out above. There was the thud of retreating feet, then all Skip could hear was the writhing of the hose, muffled now, soaking a patch of lawn above, then dying out as the water dribbled to a stop. Now there was silence, but for the boom of Skip's heart in her ears, the intolerable unending throb of her pulse. Shivering, she plucked at her shirt, her jeans. What had happened? Had Honza, coming round, seen off the Lum's Den? Something had frightened them away. But where was Honza now? Had he turned off the hose?

She filled the silence with his name.

She filled it again.

She looked up, blinking. The moon was a blinding glare.

She heard a footstep, a breath.

The form that now appeared over the well's rounded edge was neither Honza's, Lummo's nor any boy's; the figure was tall, a man's, but its head was strangely hidden – cowled, that was the word, like Vincent Price at midnight, stalking his victims for the wax museum.

Something in Skip's chest crashed like a body through a rotted floor. This was a dream made real: as if a story she had heard but never believed, a story bizarre and arabesque, had been revealed as prosaic truth, propelling her into a dimension she could neither understand nor explain.

A hand reached down, a man's hand in a leather glove, extending from a sleek black sleeve. The words Skip heard were whispered – 'Quickly. Come' – and sounded posh, too posh by far for Crater Lakes.

For a moment she shrank away, but she knew she had no choice. Vincent Price would have her. The thought came as the hand engulfed hers: *He's murdered the boys, now he'll murder me.* But he tugged her hand and she let him. There was no resisting fate. With his help, she scrambled free of the well, then collapsed in a heap on the grass. Bewildered, she looked up at the man above her. Gloves. Cowl. Cape. Or an overcoat, perhaps, with a hood. All black, in any case, black as night. She tried to see his face but he turned, as if the sight of her pained him, and began to walk away. She stared in dumb surprise. He was leaving? No wax museum? No murder? Without another word, the stranger slipped across the lawn, coattails billowing, to be swallowed by darkness.

Trembling, Skip rose. She clasped the edge of the well to help her stand.

Honza lay some feet away, moaning. She went to him, shook him. His rucksack had gone and there was no sign of the Lum's Den. All was quiet. Saturday night on Volcano Street had reached its end at last. Wondering if the cowled mysterious stranger had been a figment of her imagination, if he had really stood over the well and held out his hand to her, Skip gazed solemnly in the direction he had gone, as if she might still see him there, his tall form dark and strange against the moonlight. But there was no one. Nothing.

'Vincent Price.' She said the name like a prayer.

# Chapter Nine

Something was drumming, *k-plak-plak-plak*, like a bundle of sticks being dropped, picked up, then dropped again. The shuddered face stared back from the glass, eyes-nostrils-mouth black pits in snow. I've escaped, Skip said to the dark window. For how long now had they driven through the night? Bush, like a river, rushed past the headlamps. From above, from the truck's high cab, it looked, in its streaky pallor, like the bitter foamings of a dying world. Everywhere darkness. Everywhere death. *K-plak-plak-plak*. Geiger counter clicking off the end of time. Country music jangled from the eight-track: Buck Owens, that philosopher, who had to do only one thing and that was act naturally. The driver laughed, as if this were a joke. Skip pulled her eyes from her reflection. How many hours had they been on the road? Never, until now, had she looked at the driver. *K-plak-plak-plak*. Something under the dashboard scratched, thumped, skittered, like rats inside a wall. The cowl had slipped. That smile was no smile. That hand on the wheel was a skeleton's hand.

In states between sleeping and waking, time can shimmer, part, and meet itself again like raindrops on a window, slipping down and down. Dreams and dreamy sick half-impressions make nights endless, or so it seems to the sleeper-waker, shifting on furrowed sheets. Peace, if it comes, is fleeting, and forgotten at once when the night ride resumes, a wearying progress – no progress at all – through room after room of a decaying palace. The mind, in some outpost of reason, knows that night must end, that somewhere there is morning, like a town reached at last after too long a journey, with its smells of breakfast, its eye-pinching light through the updrawn blind. But the waker-sleeper travels on, no hard floors underfoot, the ghost condemned to haunt the empty halls. All night Skip shuddered through the labyrinth.

'What is it? Are you sick?' The voice seemed muffled, as if through cloth.

Skip's eyelids flickered. Marlo, by the window, stood turned towards her; the blind cord swayed. Brightness burned obliquely through the glass.

'Something in here smells.'

'I don't know.' As if this were an answer.

'You've missed breakfast. Will you stay in bed all day?'

'You didn't say.'

Marlo moved above her. Hair still wet. So clean. 'You're filthy.'

'You should have said, Marlo.'

'Said what?'

'Said I was right. Rigby isn't good. He's bad. Auntie Noreen isn't good. She's bad. Why would you believe them instead of me? I'm the one you love.'

'You're burning.' Cool fingers touched Skip's forehead.

'Vincent Price. He was there.'

'Oh, Skip! You're really sick, aren't you?'

Then Marlo was gone; Skip had wanted her to pull down the blind. Sunlight throbbed on the Swedish sauna floor. Already it licked the dishevelled bedclothes, not so much creeping as advancing in sudden leaps each time Skip shut her eyes for an instant. Something in her struggled but she made no move, only sank deeper into the seamy sheets.

How had she got home? She wished she could believe that everything the night before had been a dream: the well, the coins, the jetting icy water, the cowled figure that had vanished into the dark. Why should all that be real, more real than a jolting semi-trailer with a skeleton at the wheel? The dashboard rats made sounds she really heard. The palace in decay was a place she had been. All of it was real and all of it illusion: like the journey home with an incoherent Honza, walking their bikes for much of the way; like the hot swirl that possessed her as she floundered into the sleepout, tearing at her clothes, urgent for sleep that it seemed would never come, not in that undaunted night.

A voice: 'Stuck together with his sticky fingers all that summer with his sticky fingers wouldn't let his father stick his sticky fly above the jungle after the sleepout went up used to sit by him here all that summer sick with scarlet fever sticky sticky fly always close to his mother said to Valmai yes said to Valmai just hasn't found the right girl yet Baz hasn't but good boy close to his mother marry a nice girl when he comes back if there's ever hardy har a nice girl in the lake to watch it watch it flat on his back a boy needs his privates see har har judging by his sheets on washday hardy har not that I'm a stickybeak watch it fly after his tonsils come out used to sit by him a nice girl in the lake on her back with his sticky fingers boom boom ...' And Skip thought of a girl adrift on water, tangled up in reeds, and a plane, grey-green, thrumming over the jungle, sides still sticky with Airfix glue, and in the plane a boy called Private C who burned with fever as bombs fell on the green sea below, the private sea where the green girl drifted.

The girl sank in that private sea. Brightness on the bedclothes grew sharper, sharper. Draw the blind: the blind, draw it. But down she went, down the wishing well to the centre of the earth, where slime dank as dinosaurs slithered from the walls, and Vincent Price was waiting, dark-shrouded, foreboding.

She started awake. 'He's real.'

Noreen Puce, wedged in wicker, creaked and cracked. On the low table before her was a tray: teapot, fruitcake, bikkies, chocs; a modest morning tea, offered in good faith to Baby Helen, and if Baby Helen – well, couldn't let it go to waste. Blearily, Skip watched as her aunt, anal mouth oozing chocolate cake, waved at the Airfix F-111, at Barry's sporting trophies, at the open wardrobe which disclosed a glimpse of his jackets, shirts, trousers. Oh yes, he was a good boy, our Baz, and as Auntie Noreen again addressed the subject of the girl he might marry, a nice girl here in the Lakes, the appalling notion filled Skip that the girl her aunt had in mind was Marlo. Why not? It was ideal! They could run Puce Hardware together when old Dougie retired.

Among Noreen Puce's better characteristics was a buoyant forgetfulness. In the sunny sleepout, on the cusp of afternoon, she might never have considered Baby Helen to be a nasty little tearaway. The niece was sick; the aunt must minister. With her purple-puckered lips flecked with brown, with her Sunday roast in the oven, Auntie Noreen had not a worry in the world except, perhaps, the problem of raising herself, as she soon must, from the wicker chair. Comfy it was, comfy indeed, but her rump had got stuck in it more than once before now, and those creakings, those crackings, were ominous as fate.

And what, she wondered aloud, was that smell in here?

Footsteps sounded on the decking outside. A head appeared around the door, then darted back, but not before Auntie Noreen had seen it. 'Eh!'

Honza shuffled into the sleepout. 'Come to see how she was.' What a sight he looked: ripped shirt, panda-black shiner, swollen lip.

'And what have you been up to?' Queen Noreen fixed him with an accusing stare. From her wicker throne, the monarch in the muu-muu reduced him to an abasement he had never, Skip was certain, displayed before Rigby. 'And your mum lets you go out like that?' Honza was a disgrace. Auntie Noreen expected no reply; indeed, she seemed glad that the boy presented so shabby an appearance. Let Deirdre Novak's fecklessness be exposed for all to see.

She went on, 'Your mum's still putting on that play, I suppose? I remember them plays she used to be in, yonks back. Bloody rubbish, too: *Hamlet, Prince of Renmark*; *Man and Superman*, and Superman weren't in it! The snores were louder than the talking on stage.' She shook her head, her venom for the son subsumed, it seemed, by venom for the mother.

Honza (Skip could tell) wondered if he could go now.

'Aunt.' Marlo had come back. 'There's a man. Wants to see you.'

'What man? If it's one of them J. Dubs, you can tell him to bugger off. I'm not having no bloody religious fanatics disturbing me Sunday rest.'

'It's a policeman.'

Noreen Puce blanched. 'Me shop!'

'Shop's fine, Mrs P.' The police constable had followed Marlo. Stepping into the sleepout, he appeared remarkably callow; a boy, gangling and gawky, with an air of shame that extended, it seemed, to the very fact of being young and male. Acne blistered redly on his cheeks, and his Adam's apple bulged almost obscenely from his stalky neck. In too-large bony hands he cupped his cap, and squashed behind it was something else, something red and shiny. Skip eyed it uncertainly; so did Honza.

Queen Noreen, like a judge in court, questioned the constable. The Adam's apple bobbed absurdly – bob-bob, bob-bob, like the red red robin in that maddening cheery song. His name (she introduced him to the girls) was Constable Bonner, Mark Bonner, but Noreen Puce, remembering him as a toddler, could, of course, only call him Marky.

'And how are you, Marky?'

Marky was fine.

'Like it down the cop shop, eh?'

Marky liked it.

'What's that? Yous had a letter from Baz?'

Marky and Baz had been good mates. Real good mates.

'See his plane,' Noreen went on, 'still there above the bed? Remember when he made that plane? Sticky fingers that day!'

Marky knew. Marky had been there.

'Well, Marky, what's all this about, then? Raffling a chook for the Cops' Benevolent Fund?'

Marky shook his head sadly.

'No chook! Marky, if you been standing here magging away when me window's smashed in and half me stock's gone up the Khyber, I'll ... I'll have your flyballs for marbles, lad!'

The boy's colour deepened. Had Mrs P. alluded to his private parts? Queen Noreen only cooed, 'Marky, you're such a tease!' and not until she had subsided into smiling silence did Constable Bonner – stammering, acne pulsing fit to burst – set forth his theme: last night's robbery in Crater Gardens.

How glad Skip was she was sick! She could be flushed, trembling, and it seemed quite in order. Honza twisted his hands; she wished he would stop. Marlo looked confused, and her confusion grew as the red-red-robin Adam's apple heaved up words in a vomitous rush: words about the wishing well and water running away and evil acts with a hacksaw blade and evidence of a scuffle and bike tracks in the lawn, and this, this – big hands descended from the uniformed chest – this, I have to report, was found at the scene of the crime.

Scene of the crime: Marky's eyes grew wide, as if he could not quite believe he had used the phrase, while Skip, slipping down in the bed, wondered how she could explain this Qantas bag that he uncrushed and held up, all the time (she was certain) fighting off the temptation to call it 'Exhibit A'. But there was no time to think of alibis. Auntie Noreen had already spotted the name, in black felt pen against the bag's white lining: HELEN WELLS.

Honza, by the door, almost broke into a run, but fear gripped him and he only scuffed a heel, grinning stupidly at Constable Bonner. Marlo's eyes met Skip's, horrified, amazed. From somewhere, Skip imagined, came a cattle-truck rattle: the sleepout had always looked like rolling stock; she had wished more than once that it would bear her away, across the far paddocks, never to return. But it was going nowhere. A spell had fallen upon the players, freezing them into attitudes variously expressing accusation, guilt, shame.

Noreen Puce broke it. 'Deary me, Marky, you had me going!' She gestured to the bed. 'Baby Helen, a master criminal? I don't reckon, do you? Laid up all weekend. Bad dose of flu. But even if she was full of beans I hardly reckon a little filly like this would be jumping down wishing wells in the middle of the night! Sugar and spice and all things nice, eh? And as for this old bag – this Qantas bag, I means, not meself, Marky! – it was pinched last week. Terrible, what goes on at that school. Yous blokes at the cop shop ought to be patrolling there. Up and down the corridors. Round and round the grounds. That's what cops do in America. Saw it on telly. Big-city schools filled with wops and blackies, what do you expect? Here's your bag back, Helen.' And the fond aunt tossed it to the bed with girlish nonchalance. 'I'll tell you this, Marky' – she leaned forward, eyes narrowed; a sausage finger poked the air – 'you find what bugger stole poor Helen's bag and you'll find what bugger robbed your wishing well. That high school's a hotbed of crime, make no mistake. Little buggers! Might as well be Yanks.'

Whether P. C. Bonner was satisfied or merely browbeaten by her logic was difficult to determine. He pushed out his lower lip, nodded sagely, and might even have thanked her for assisting him in his investigations had she not interrupted, asking him jauntily to stay for her Sunday roast. 'How's about it, Marky? Crack a few coldies with Doug, eh?'

The constable shook his head with regret. 'On duty and all.'

'Who'd have thought it, Marky? You all grown up and responsible. And I remember when you was just a little nipper, running round me yard with Baz. No pants on. Little winky poking out under your singlet.'

Little winky! The lawman, Skip realised, was defeated; he turned to go, then gestured to the F-111 that swayed in a breeze above Barry's bed, and observed, his voice thick, 'Don't suppose Bazza's been in one of them. Slogging through the jungle, he is, not flying up above. You know, Mrs P., sometimes I think of him and ask myself: why Bazza? Why not me?'

'His number come up, love.' Noreen Puce softened. 'You're fine young men, the pair of you, serving your country in different ways. Some have to fight the foreign scum, to keep Australia free. Some have to stay home and keep our own scum in line. Like them buggers I told you about, eh?'

Marky Bonner conceded this with a philosophical air. 'I'll see myself out, Mrs P.,' he said.

Moments passed and his footsteps faded down the path. Skip looked at Marlo: Marlo looked at Skip. Honza, a grinning fool, seemed to think the danger was over. The side gate clunked.

Queen Noreen attempted to rise. One-two … one-two-three … Grimacing, she strained against the tight wicker. The drama of Marky's visit had wedged the great lady all the more firmly into her ill-advised throne. Her face flushed. Leg-o'-mutton arms flapped like fleshy sails as she reared forward, shaking the floor. The chair lifted, protruding like a bustle from her mighty rump, but she burst out, oblivious, 'Robbing the wishing well! Stealing from charity! You'd better have some explanation, Helen Wells!'

Skip's brain spun like a car's wheels in quicksand, and all she could do was whimper out useless denials as Auntie Noreen massed over her, electric with rage, then turned sharply and pointed. Heaped in a corner, revealed by the displaced chair, were the filthy clothes, smeared with slime, that Skip had discarded the night before – the smell, traced to its source!

Terrified, Honza slunk towards the door, but Noreen Puce would not let him go. A hideous bent-over thing, half-woman, half-chair, face bright enough to burn, she lunged at him, shrieking, 'This is your doing, Honza Novak!' and grabbed his shoulders and shook him, hard. 'Dirty little wog – you come round here, perving on me niece through her window (don't think old Noreen don't know!), luring her into a life of crime and God knows what else. Jesus, I don't expect much of yous Novak brats – reffo for a dad, slag for a mum – but this time you gone too far, and you better count yourself lucky I don't shop you. Because I'll tell you one thing, young feller-me-lad: if I sees you hanging round me niece again, that's what I'll do. Know what that means? Reform school, and about bloody time – cold showers, beatings, and some big boy's stiffy up your bumhole every night! Don't think you can put the blame on Baby Helen. No niece of mine's going down. Everybody will believe it was just you, and it'll serve you right for sniffing round good Australian girls instead of sticking to your greasy wog sluts. Got that? Got that?'

There was more in this vein, and neither Skip's protests ('It's not his fault!') nor Marlo's efforts to calm her aunt ('Aunt, please! You're hurting him') were anything but futile. On and on the waves of execration came – much of it directed more at Deirdre Novak than at her son – cresting each time with an urgent 'Got that? Got that?'

So violently did Noreen Puce shake the hapless Honza that all he could do was grunt through clashing teeth, until, in rising rage, she flung him from her. The boy crashed to the floor, scrambled up, and rushed out the door; through all this, Marlo stood white-faced against the wall, while Skip struggled to rise from her bed. Could she have followed Honza, she would have: run alongside him, scaled the fence with him, escaped Auntie Noreen's and never come back.

Auntie Noreen was straining, straining; shit-a-brick noises erupted from her throat as she struggled to free herself from the wicker bustle. '*Nrrghh …! Nrrghh …!* Marlene, help me …' But Marlo had no need to act, for in desperation her aunt twisted, wrenched, and the chair clattered free. Her face scarlet, Noreen Puce plunged towards the door.

But she stopped on the threshold and turned back, eyes ablaze. Her words came slowly, levelly. 'I'll say one thing, and say it clear. Neither of yous girls goes round Novaks' again. Ever. Got it?'

Skip could not speak. Her head throbbed.

Marlo gasped. 'The play!'

'Play! Yair, and making eyes at Pav all day. Or is it that poofter teacher from the school? Don't think I don't know what you get up to. Remember, Marlene, you're under my roof. You're working in me shop. I pays your bloody wages, and if I want to turn you and your thieving sister out on the streets, I bloody well will and who's to tell me no? Nobody. You're stopping indoors, the pair of you, till you learn how to behave. School and work! School and work, then home. Dougie can drive yous both. One bit of trouble from either of yous, and I'll dob in Deirdre Novak's brat before you can say Jack Robinson. Don't look at me like that, Helen. I mean it. You're a stupid, ignorant girl and I'm just doing what's good for you. If you weren't sick I'd drag you out of that bed this minute and beat you black and blue.'

'You bitch,' Skip said. 'Fucking old bitch.'

Did Auntie Noreen hear this as she lumbered from the sleepout? If she did, she only added Skip's words – weariedly, resignedly – to the teetering evidence that her mad sister's kiddies were rotten to the core. The wicker chair, on its side, still lay where it had fallen.

Miserably, Skip sank into her pillow. Marlo stared at her with something between sadness and horror. Skip knew what she had done. Marlo, dragged out of school, forced to work in a hardware shop, had found hope in Howard Brooker. Without him, she would never pass her exams. She would never escape. Skip turned from Marlo's gaze. If her sister had said 'I hate you' she would not have been surprised. She hated herself.

But Marlo, without a word, slipped away after Auntie Noreen.

# Chapter Ten

Summer a-coming. Not long now.

Morning shadows stretch from the bluegums that rim the school fence. Brightness glares off the yellow buses as they swing into the grounds. One day, give it a few weeks, smoky haze will shimmer over the tarmac; flies will buzz like bees while the skies stand arrested, day on day, in unbroken pale blue. But for Skip Wells, aged almost thirteen, the world is grey.

'See you this arvo, love,' says Uncle Doug, as she hauls up her Qantas bag from the littered floor of his van. He winks at her, clicks his mouth. 'Cheer up. Snot so bad.'

Snot so bad! Skip slams the van door. Slopes through the gates. The school-in-the-morning hubbub claws at her mind like scrabbling gulls. How many weeks of this torment remain? One is too many. Drag along this path, up these steps, down this corridor, open this locker, stuff in your things and crash it shut. Ignore taunts, stares. Fuck off, Maggie Polomka. Fuck off, Shaun Kenny – one step towards me and I'll fucking deck you. Tough little bitch: that's what they're saying.

Monday morning. Stiffly she sits in the gas-tap home group, in turbanned maths, in Brooker's English class, and sneers at Honza

Novak if he turns around to look at her. No more Honza. No more anybody. Never, never.

Some slut says, 'Skippy's broken up with her boyfriend.'

Some whacker says, 'Boyfriend? Fucking lez, she is.'

But something's going on. Big announcement.

'... That's right, a time capsule,' says Howard Brooker.

Light slants like balm across the yellow-white tables, scored and scuffed already, which replaced only recently the inkwelled desks that had borne in their scarifications a generation's legacy.

'Time capsule?' Brenton Lumsden looks affronted.

'Like *Doctor Who*?' squeals Wayne Bunny, whose voice is breaking.

Kylie Cunliffe snorts. 'Will we go into the future?'

'Ten-nine-eight-seven-six-five-four-three-two-one-zero – blast off!' yells Andreas Haskas, spit spraying in a glittering semicircle, fist, clenched whacker-style, surging skywards.

'All right, all right.' Brooker does his best to calm the class. See those hands, palms down, pressing something invisible? Shoosh. Shoosh. What's he on about now? One hundred years, one whole hundred years since the Lakes was proclaimed a town. This calls, doesn't it, for something special? Mark the occasion. Make it memorable. Stake a flag in the flux of time. The capsule, stuffed to the brim with pictures, objects, letters, is to be buried in Crater Gardens by the town hall, to be dug up by your great-great in another hundred years.

Now anybody clued up, watching this man-boy with his hippie sideburns, poofter shirt, medallion, hipster jeans with their big shiny belt buckle, might sense his degradation, his shame as he stands before these imbeciles, spooling out these platitudes as if every phrase that drivels off his lips doesn't make him want to throw up. 'No, no, we're not going to the future,' Brooker says cheerfully, 'but the time capsule is.' (Have his eyes – what a ham! – widened a little? What does he expect, intakes of breath?) The clued-up might guess, too, that sometimes in bed at night Brooker feels himself drowning and starts up, gasping, struggling for breath; that old uni mates are in London right now, pulling pints in pubs, pulling birds in discotheques, or trolling around on the Grand Tour in a beat-up V Dub campervan. This causes Brooker pain. Among the books in his boarding house bedroom is a tatty *Lost Illusions*, relic of some dreary course at Flinders University, with the passage underscored: 'Neither distinctions nor dignities will seek out the talent that is running to seed in a provincial town ...' And he had once thought Adelaide was the provincial town!

'Yes,' Brooker says brightly, 'imagine if you could read a letter from your great-great. Our task' – he claps his hands, suggesting resolve, a can-do spirit, not a moment to waste – 'is to write those letters for our great-greats to marvel over one day (sooner than you think!) when we're all dust and ash, in their world of bubble cars and personal helipads and package tours to Venus. And that, class, is our project for this week.'

Brooker divides them into groups to discuss it.

'I reckon it's stupid,' says Mag the Slag, whose blondish hair looks this morning as if a tub of margarine has been melted over it.

Their letters, Brooker enthuses, should have a theme. Here he comes now, working the room, bending over this and that yellow-white table, interrogating: 'What about you, Maggie?' (Flabby cheeks redden.) 'Think of your life – what, in your life, would fascinate your great-great ...'

'Sir! Sir! Mr Brooker?' Lucy Sutton offers her inspiration: music. She will consecrate to eternity (with pictures, clippings; even, if the envelope will allow, a 45-rpm single or two) the talents of Johnny Farnham, Jeff Phillips and Ronnie Burns.

'Excellent, Lucy.'

Lucy Sutton beams.

Brooker draws Skip aside after the lesson is over. Leave me alone, she thinks. Don't even look at me. Is he going to tell her how surly she's become? (As if she didn't know!) How she sits hollow-eyed in class, lower lip protruding, cheek pulped into an upheld fist?

'Helen,' he begins, 'I'm concerned about your sister.'

Skip shrugs, both relieved and wary. 'Marlo can't come,' she says without expression. 'Can't any more.'

'I don't understand why your aunt won't see reason. Marlene's Petra was shaping up so well. And her exams!' His hand, as if sincerely, lands on Skip's shoulder. 'Your sister has talent. Real talent. Perhaps I could talk to your aunt.'

'Or a brick wall.' Skip pulls away from the hand.

Her time capsule letter weighs heavy on her mind. Who will read it in a hundred years? She has to write something, but the thought of Brooker reading it, red-penning it, handing it back for her to copy out fair, freezes inspiration. Through class after class she does fuck-all while Lucy Sutton, whose letter, exceeding all others in splendour, will be accompanied by a collage, scissors out Johnny, Jeff and Ronnie from back issues of *TV Week*.

Only on the night before they have to hand in their drafts does Skip stir herself. In a ragged *Eagle*, courtesy of the comics pile at the Institute Library, is a 'Futurescope' feature called 'Standing Room Only'. In 1967 the entire population of the world, notes Lyall Watson, PhD, BSc (Hons), FZS, could stand heel-to-toe on the Isle of Wight. But two babies are born every second: 172,800 each day. By 2000 AD there will be twice as many people in the world; by 2200, one hundred times. How will humanity feed itself? First, Watson says blithely (this is a thought experiment, after all), we must eliminate all land wildlife, and use the land for farming. Second, harvest the seas: algae, don't you know, is a rich source of protein. (All sea wildlife, too, will have to be 'removed'.) But still the population grows. Food, food! is the cry. Where will it come from? Elementary, my dear Watson. More sunlight, that's what we need! By 2400, enormous space mirrors, orbiting the earth, bring perpetual daylight and melt the polar ice. Sea levels rise. Temperatures soar. Oceans boil and evaporate away. Now all food is synthesised in laboratories. The whole planet is roofed over. All space is used for human habitation: one million million million human beings, thronging through air-conditioned corridors under a dome that spans the earth. Such is the world of AD 3000.

Skip copies Dr Watson's words exactly.

Afterwards she feels sick, and feels sick again the next day when Brooker hands back her work in class. Says the flare of red biro: C minus. Impersonal. Far-fetched. Brooker has altered Dr Watson's punctuation, and here and there a phrase.

Pupils must copy out their corrected work, to be sealed by afternoon's end in stiff card envelopes, each with the author's name on the front, like letters to themselves. The room (Skip thinks) is hot. Her stomach churns, clenches. She sits by the window. A fly buzzes, butts against the glass, and buzzes again. Again: Two babies are born every second, 172,800 a day, like adding the entire population of Great Britain to the world each year. So says Watson; so says Skip. Sluggishly her hand moves across the page. She tugs at her collar. Hot, hot. Sick, yes: isn't it sickening, these babies, babies, babies? Millions, and for what? More Brenton Lumsdens. More Kylie Cunliffes. More Maggie Polomkas. Why won't this hateful reproduction stop?

On the wall, the clock is ticking. Skip's hand moves faster, flying over the page, and before she knows it she has written down thoughts that have no origin in the pages of *Eagle*. She writes about babies and what they become. She names names: Brenton Lumsden. Yes, she's written it in Bic biro: B-R-E-N-T-O-N ... More! K-Y-L-I-E ... The feeling of power thrills her. On and on the Bic skitters like a deranged insect. Bugger Dr Watson. She writes about what she hates, and what she hates most is Noreen Puce, the meanest woman in the world. Frenzied now, Skip piles on details of Auntie Noreen's vileness. Frizzy perm. Little piggy eyes. Blubbery arms. Huge fat tits. Fat belly. Fat arse. Fat fingers, like sausages about to burst, stuffing Kit-Kats Smith's Crisps Arnott's Custard Creams all day into her arsehole mouth. Hate! Hate! Up, up, goes Skip's temperature (are the oceans, she wonders, already boiling away?), but what does it matter when she has skewered Noreen Puce, fixed her on paper for the future to know her in each obscene detail?

Sweat beads on Skip's forehead as she writes. She flicks it away. When will the bell ring? Ten minutes. Heart pounding – this feeling can't end – she turns to Barry Puce, the cousin she has never met, who naturally must be as vile as Auntie Noreen because he is after all (repellent phrase) the fruit of her loins. Inventing freely now (the historian has the last word), she attributes to Barry halitosis, cheesy feet, rotten-egg farts and a carnal interest in dogs that terrified Baskerville, the neighbouring hound, before Barry was packed off to Nam, where he machine-gunned many a peasant farmer, coshed old women with his rifle butt, skewered babies on his bayonet, and left behind him a trail of abused Fidos and Rovers; but he was sure, any day now, to be captured by the Viet Cong and tortured and mutilated before – ears lopped, eyes squished in – being turned out to wander through a minefield. Boom!

The bell. Brooker, raising his voice, says, 'All right, seal your envelopes. Is your name on the front? Make sure your name's on the front. Now drop it in here.' Down the aisle he comes, sack at the ready. Drop, drop, go the messages to the future, soon to be borne away to the town hall where they will be secured inside the silver-milkcan time machine. Skip shudders with pleasure. She lets her message drop. Exultant, she has stood up, impatient to leave the class, when she hears a scream behind her: Kylie Cunliffe. Why is Kylie screaming?

'Bleeding! She's bleeding!' Kylie points, her expression one of horrified glee. Everyone turns and stares; there are gasps and whispers. Someone giggles. Boys stand on desks to see and Brooker drops the sack as Skip, nonplussed, looks down, aware only now of the hot viscous liquid that trickles down her leg and has stained the back of her skirt. Strangled horror bursts in her throat, an animal howl, and she runs to the door and down the corridor as if the crowd, like hunting dogs, are pursuing her.

Brooker calls, 'Helen … Helen Wells!'

Her name, like a reprimand, rings behind her. But Helen Wells has gone. She has seen Brooker's face. She disgusts him. She disgusts herself. This happened (exactly this) to a girl at Glenelg Tech, a reffo girl, a total spastic, with a squinty eye and a nose that ran with snot. Back then Skip, baying with the others, had vowed this would never be her. Now it was: Skip Wells, no better than a dirty reffo with nits in her hair and stinking of piss.

Bikes gleam in bike racks. Here's Honza's, and Skip, of course, knows the combo of his lock. Away, away, with the shame that will destroy her searing like a brand.

Three times she changes direction: stop, skid, go another way. Crater Gardens: she could fling herself down the waterfall. No, she will go out of town: leave the Lakes, ride until she can ride no more, and a truck comes, and she thumbs a lift, and sings along to Buck Owens on the eight-track all the way to – where? Everywhere is ruined if Skip Wells is there. Go to Puce Hardware. Do it, Skip Wells. Throw yourself on Marlo like an accusation. You forgot me, Marlo. And look what happened. You've killed me. Look at my blood.

No. Marlo wouldn't care; she would only turn away.

Blue fills the sky. By the road, scattered on rich green, are buttercups, daisies, dandelions. All around her is the mocking spring, this spring that pounces in the year's last third, potent already with a summer heat that presses down mercilessly, month on month, even in these southern corners of the continent. The birds mock her, cackling as she passes. Kookaburras. Galahs. But no one, nothing, stops Skip Wells. Let the reffo go. Blood scalds her thighs.

At Puce's Bend stands a Greyhound bus. Skip lets Honza's bike fall by the verge. Perhaps she will faint now; she wishes she would – anything, to be free of the burden of being Skip Wells. But something is strange: from the house comes a pulse, beating softly on the bright air. She moves towards it.

So: Sandy Campbell is here. Front door unlocked. She flits down the passage. In the sitting room are cake-crumbed plates, teacups sticky with sugar. Television dark – no *Motel* today. On the radiogram, a record spins silently, its playing time passed. *K-chuck. K-chuck.* 'Cara Mia' by Slim Whitman, an Auntie Noreen favourite. But where's Auntie Noreen? Where's Sandy Campbell? The pulse keeps drumming: rattling teacups, rippling under wallpaper, heaving up lumps in the floral carpet. Understanding now, Skip heads deeper into the house.

Thud. Thud. The door to the master bedroom stands ajar. Skip pushes it open further. Whitely, light pulses through net curtains and collects and shines in the mirrored wardrobe doors: collects, shines and flings back unreally the figures on the bed, who are all too real. Thud. The headboard, pink quilting on plywood, knocks the wall. Thud. That pink lampshade rocks. Thud. The bedspread, pink and peeled back in crumples, reveals on pink polyester sheets the sweaty straining form that plunges, plunges, a surfer riding a wave of white jelly, then ends at last with a grunt that sounds like a drunkard throwing up.

Skip watches. Nothing, she thinks, will hurt her again. She has triumphed. They are even, the world and Skip Wells. That is why she laughs, though she should flee or shrink in revulsion as Sandy Campbell pushes himself off the bed and lumbers towards her, doubled in the mirror, eyes wide as he confronts, as if in a dream, this girl who should be anywhere but here. Look at him, belly swinging, thick with damp fur, and the billy club below, purple-headed, marbled with veins, dripping its drippings on the pink carpet. And Auntie Noreen on the bed, round-eyed, a white whale wrapped in polyester.

Sandy Campbell grins: that lopsided grin! He comes closer and Skip tells herself she will not let him scare her. One barbecued forearm flattens against the wall. His dick, still half-stiff, butts her skirt.

'Eh, heard a good one the other day.' His voice cracks the mirrors, shatters the light. 'There's this little girl, see, and her name's Fuckarada.'

Fuckarada! What sort of name is that?

'It's a wog name,' says Sandy Campbell, as if Skip has spoken. Unashamed, even proud in his nakedness, he remains directly before her. From time to time he moves a little, prodding at her obscenely. 'And this little girl,' he says, 'she's a real goer. Just like her mum. Makes eyes at all the blokes. So her mum's boyfriend sees Fuckarada and reckons, "Jeez, I wouldn't mind a bash at that. Bet she's nice and tight." Well, one day Fuckarada's mum goes to the shops. "Fuck," reckons Fuckarada's mum. "Haven't got a babysitter." Well, the bloke sees his chance: "I'll look after Fuckarada." "Jeez, thanks," reckons Fuckarada's mum, and goes out.

'So the bloke rubs his hands together. "What are we going to do, little Fuckarada?" Fuckarada reckons, "Reckon I'll go to bed." "Bed?" reckons the bloke. "It's the fucking arvo." "Aw, but I really want to go to bed," Fuckarada reckons with a cheeky little grin. Bloke reckons, "So, Fuckarada, shall I come and tuck yous in?" Fuckarada reckons, "If you like."

'So there he is in Fuckarada's bedroom. There's Fuckarada slipping off her shoes and socks and little frilly panties, slipping into her nightie and into the sheets. Well, the bloke ain't half got a stiffy by now. Big as a fucking baseball bat. Fuckarada's in bed. Bloke pulls the curtains. Fuckarada reckons, "Perhaps we could play a game." Bloke reckons, "Yair? What sort of game?" Fuckarada reckons, "What if you put your stiffy up me twat?" "You reckon?" says the bloke. "Aw, I suppose I could try it."

'Well, he shoves it in a few times, and reckons it's bloody good, nice and tight, not like her sloppy old mum, when the little girl reckons,

"Aw, you're no good. Harder!" "Harder?" reckons the bloke. So he fucks her harder. But now the girl reckons, "Harder! Harder!" So he's really going at it, hammer and tongs. "Harder!" yells Fuckarada. "Fuck me harder." And he's fucking and fucking, sweat dripping off, breath like bellows, heart thumping like it's fit to burst, and just then the girl's mum comes back from the shops and reckons, "Where's Fuckarada?" So she yells, "Fuckarada! Fuckarada!" And the bloke yells back, "Harder? I'm fucking her as hard as I bloody well can!"'

Laughter wheezes from Sandy Campbell's mouth. Spit splatters Skip's face and she wipes it away. She'll go. She has the power. What can Sandy Campbell, with his belly and his billy club, do to her now? In the bed, the great mound that is Noreen Puce is wobbling, wobbling, but whether with mirth, shame, sorrow or anger, Skip cannot say. For a fleeting moment she wishes she could bridge the gulf between them. Say what you like: they are women, she and her aunt, and should be on the same side. Sandy Campbell is a bastard.

The doorbell rings. What is to be done?

Auntie Noreen fumbles for her dressing gown. Sandy Campbell retrieves his Y-fronts, furry arse-crack opening as he bends, balls from behind pendulous as a dog's. Skip is the one who goes to the door, smiles, and thanks the boy. Squinting, head on one side, she watches him go, standing up on his pushbike, treading down the pedals. Time has stopped. The telegram hangs in her hand. It might have dropped to the floor if not for Auntie Noreen, appearing beside her, huddled in pink, eyeing Skip's hand, gasping, and, it seems, knowing everything before the envelope is open. The telegram, barely read, flutters to the floor.

'Never.' Her voice is cold. 'Never. Never.'

# Chapter Eleven

The F-111 turned above the bed: turned, tugged against the suspending string, then turned back again. Moonlight flickered on the green-grey fuselage. What had the F-111 been doing? Killing kids today, like LBJ? Little Hiroshimas for the jungle gooks. DDT clouds descending over green. If you could squeeze the world into a ball, that ball would be this fiery thing in the boyish flat chest of Skip Wells, burning her heart and lungs. It froze her, this burning. She was all ice and fire. How could she rise from this Barry Puce bed when the heart in her chest was too tight to beat, when the world-in-a-ball would not let her breathe?

The evening had been endless. With the telegram, the count of time was knocked back to zero. The world before? Nothing. Bloodied thighs, headboard rhythm, Fuckarada; all were stages of a rocket fallen away. Everything was the telegram: Auntie Noreen keening on the carpet, dressing gown open over one enormous breast; Sandy Campbell standing at the hall table in Y-fronts, strangely in command as he phoned Puce Hardware; Skip numb in the still-open door, picking up the yellow slip her aunt had let fall, staring at it once, twice, three times between looking out at Puce's Bend, where the telegram boy, as if eternally, rode away.

Naturally, the scene was succeeded by others, like slides in a projector clunking into place: Uncle Doug like a schoolboy in crisis, perched on the sofa beside Auntie Noreen, not quite daring to take his wife in his arms; Valmai Lumsden proffering a casserole, shaking her head and tut-tutting as if Your Baz had been a naughty boy; Marky Bonner on a kitchen chair, swallowing and swallowing his Adam's apple as Sandy Campbell bit the cap from a bottle and said, 'Here, mate. Get that down your neck.'

Strange, how death travels! Barry Puce was all over town. How he had died, where he had died, if the body would be flown home and when – all this remained unknown. Only one thing mattered: Our Baz was a saint and martyr. Here comes the clergyman, collar dazzling white, murmurously assuring the sobbing woman-jelly that Barry has gone to a far, far better, that the Lord in His wisdom – oh, what does He do? Watch the fall of every sparrow? Here comes Pavel, tongue-tied, with Marlo hovering behind him, willing him to leave. Here comes Brian Rigby, recalling one of the finest lads ever, ever to pass through the portals of Crater Lakes High. Here comes everybody, the mayor, the doctor, the president of the Lions Club, every dutiful citizen flocking to the court of Queen Noreen. And all the time, as the light declines, and Barry Puce's picture glimmers on the mantelpiece, and Sandy Campbell's brown bottles line up on the sink, and Valmai Lumsden's casserole sits beside them uneaten, and Noreen Puce sobs, and Doug Puce, brown wizened whippet of a man, looks just a little more downcast than usual, Skip feels the world-ball hardening in her chest, and something is blackening, like inkstains creeping over pink polyester, soon to consume it entirely.

The evening ends at last. No nighty-nights, no TV shutdown with God Save the Queen, but somehow the lights in the house are dark, Queen Noreen is quiet, and Skip, in jeans and bomber jacket, lies on the dead boy's bed, pinned down by the world-ball and watching the wind, like air currents on high, buffeting the F-111 back and forth. For too long, for all the dazzled hours of the telegram, the keening, the here-comes-everybody, she has felt the world-ball grow and thought it numbness, but now she knows differently. It is guilt.

My fault. I killed Barry Puce.

'Night stalker, come ...' But the words never would. Nights when Honza hunkered beneath the window spun away through blackness like an exploded moon. Skip sat up: her feet, in sneakers already, connected with the floor. The plan possessed her mind, fixed as the telegram and easier to read. The time capsule letter had gone to the town hall, ready for the burial that would take place in the morning. Skip must go to the town hall too.

The moon that night had a hollow, pained look. Honza's bike was gone from the verge; she dared not take her own from the shed, risk the creak of opening doors. She walked. Why shouldn't she? She had all night, and this time all she needed to steal was a single creamy envelope.

Crater Lakes lay like a town in a story, suspended in sleep for a hundred years. Perhaps it had been: a hundred years ago, nothing; now this town with its Lions Club and Chickenland and Coles New World. But had it ever been awake all this while? What, in truth, are any of us but sleepwalkers, going through motions dictated by time? Parents. Place of birth. (And some places are cursed.) The heft of history, pressing down like a coffin lid. Nothing else moved as Skip, like a ghost, slid through Crater Gardens. A hole, covered in canvas, had been dug already to receive the milkcan time machine.

Shimmery under the moon, the town hall rose above her. She had pictured herself smashing windows, forcing locks, but her criminal act was easy: a window on the first floor, open just a crack; a tree by the window, a branch brushing glass. She shinned up the tree.

She edged along the branch. The window sash protested faintly as she pushed it open.

In a dark office she made out typewriters under covers, filing cabinets, and a duplicator with a spindly stiff handle. Padding over the floor, she kicked a wastepaper basket. The sound it made was a gong, mournful in the silence. She winced. Where was the milkcan? She didn't dare turn on a light. Bluish pallor flickered through the windows; faintly she heard the waterfall from the cave, falling unregarded against the night. She creaked through a door. She found herself in a hallway; a staircase stretched downwards, a hefty Victorian affair of deep carpets, slippery polished banisters, upthrusting carved newel posts. That milkcan, it had to be heavy. They would keep it downstairs.

She descended. She knew her quest was stupid: to take back the letter would undo nothing. Time would not turn back; death would still be death, and the aunt she could not love, though she knew it was only human to love her now, would still feel her agonies for all that one letter-writer might say (and mean it): I didn't mean it. Who would read the letter? No one, not for a hundred years, if ever. But Skip knew that the letter, festering secretly, would poison her life.

Below, the light was dim. She wished she had a torch. She missed her footing on the last stair and lurched forward, tiles slapping coldly under her sneakers. Along one wall ran a counter. Portraits, in heavy frames, glowered down from the walls. Was that Mayor Gull, Honza's gramps? Flowers on a table underneath him gave off a sickly scent.

Milkcan, where was the milkcan?

She had moved towards the back of the staircase when a loud *crack* sounded in the silence. From beneath a door seeped a pool of light. Skip stood, breathing. She crept forward, pressed her ear against the door. Silly. She was being silly. Someone had left a light on. Old buildings go *crack* at night.

The milkcan lurked in the darkness under the stairs. Skip crouched before it. The lid had been screwed on firmly, but she twisted hard, gritting her teeth, and the secrets of time were hers. Eagerly she pulled out the contents. Envelopes flurried about her on the floor. So many. Too many. She patted her jacket. Marlboros: two left. Redheads: ten? She struck one, then another, and riffled through envelopes until flame lapped her fingers. Look at these names, bound for the future, as if the future cared: Cunliffe, Kylie. Gruber, Kevin. Polomka, Margaret.

One envelope leaped out, twice as thick as the rest: Sutton, Lucy. With some satisfaction Skip might have destroyed Lucy's A-plus effort, Johnny, Jeff, Ronnie and all, but she forgot her spite when she saw the envelope underneath: Wells, Skip. She flicked out her match. For a moment she almost believed she had saved something more than a sleeve of card and the paper inside. Yes, now that her letter to the future could never be sent, time would be rewound like a tape on a reel-to-reel. Imagine tomorrow: good old Auntie Noreen, the same old bitch again. And Barry, one day soon, is coming home.

So Skip imagined, just for a few precious seconds.

She closed her eyes and pressed the envelope against her chest. Through the stiff paper she felt her heart, the drumbeat of time. That a door had opened behind her, that light fell across her back in a yellow plane, that a hand, reaching out, was about to touch her shoulder, she had no idea until there came another *crack!* – the floorboards, it had to be – close enough this time to make her whip around, gasp, and scramble up.

In the darkness, nothing was certain, neither the figure, big and lowering, and what it would do next, nor Skip's direction as she blundered confusedly back and forth, and broke at last for the door. The figure called out something, she didn't know what, as it pursued her into the night. All that filled her mind was a name: Vincent Price. He had come to take her to the House of Wax.

She raced across the lawns. How close was he? At the kerb outside the gardens was a purple Valiant. Swinging behind it, she gripped the handle of the back door. It opened, and without another thought she plunged inside and pulled it shut with a sharp clunk. Crumpled on the seat was a dusty blanket; she huddled on the floor, tugged the blanket over herself and lay unmoving as footsteps, moments later, echoed along the pavement. Had Vincent Price gone away?

Skip tried to think. She must take her chance, check the coast was clear, slip out of the car and run home; soon enough she could be miles from here, back in the sleepout as if nothing had happened, staring up at the F-111. Yes, do it: take action.

She could not move. The blanket pressed down on her, heavy as time, and fear of Vincent Price manacled her in place. If he could be in the town hall he could be anywhere. Had he watched her all this time? She lay frozen under the blanket until footsteps sounded from the street again, and voices; the car doors opened and shut, springs jogged at the weight, and two men (from their voices) took their places in the front seat. Someone turned the ignition, the engine thrummed to life, and the car moved away from the kerb.

Skip knew the driver's voice all too well: a foreigner's, thick, deliberate, as if it issued from a mouth filled with mush. Damn: despite the dark, she should have known this car. It swung around a corner.

'You're taking risks,' said Mr Novak.

'Maybe,' said the passenger. 'They'll find me out in time.'

'You sound as if you want them to. And they will. All you have to do is carry on as you are, wandering the streets at midnight, pressing your nose against windows, sitting with your old friend in the town hall looking at pictures from the filing cabinets. What would you say you wanted?'

'You hid in a barn on the border, didn't you? Night after night before you could cross. But you crossed in the end. You laughed once, Vlad, when I said I envied you. But I did. There's why.'

'Don't.' Mr Novak sighed. 'I had to do it and I did. What does Aldous Huxley say? Adventures are only exciting at second hand. Lived through, they're just a slice of life like the rest.'

Skip, at that moment, was sure this was false. But Mr Novak always sounded dismissive when he talked about his past, as if Czechoslovakia and his youth and his escape were part of a world that had grown unreal to him.

The passenger spoke again. His accent was odd too: British, like an RAF pilot's in a film, yet with Australian undertones. He was saying something about Huxley. 'Deirdre was mad for him, our last year at the high.'

'You read him for her? So did I.'

The two men laughed, but their laughter was brief, even sad. A window juddered above the back seat.

'There was an intruder,' said Mr Novak. 'In the council offices.'

'Burglar?' The passenger didn't sound particularly interested; the world, he seemed to imply, was full of crime. Only to be expected. 'I burgled Mayor Gull's office once. Did you know that?'

'I did. He'd confiscated *Point Counter Point*. Filth, he said.'

'Disappointing, from that point of view.'

So, Skip thought, it had been Mr Novak who emerged from the door behind her. Was Mr Novak Vincent Price? Every instinct told her no: of course not, it was the passenger. He was speaking again, something about Crater Lakes long ago, when all the people who were old now had been young and he drove up and down Volcano Street every Friday and Saturday night.

'Strange,' he said. 'We talk about the future, but it's only ever a story we tell. We're in the loop of the present, going round and round. Up and down Volcano Street. Up and down, up and down.'

The car came to a stop, its engine idling. The driver's door opened. Mr Novak, to judge by the noises, seemed to be dragging open an awkward gate. He returned, drove forward a little, alighted, shut

the gate again, then carried on down a potholed track. Jolt, jolt: Skip
was relieved when the car slowed again and the engine thunked into
silence. The two men opened their doors, then slammed them shut.
She heard their footsteps crunch away down a path.

Cautiously she peeled back the blanket, crept fingers up a fabric
wall, and peered over the rampart of the front seat. She could make
out enough to recognise where they were: the overgrown lawn, the
decayed drive, the dark forms of the men vanishing into blackness
as they climbed the veranda steps. She heard a door swing shut.
Impelled as if by fate, she eased open a door and slipped towards
the old Dansie house. In her hand she still carried the envelope from
the milkcan.

Her heart was huge in her throat. Creeping up the steps, she heard
each rustle and snap as a gunshot in the silence. She paused on the
brink of the veranda. Light shone in a thin, jagged line between the
drawn curtains. All else was black as she tiptoed forward. Voices
sounded faintly from inside. Distractedly she stuffed the envelope
into the back pocket of her jeans. She put an eye to the glass.

Behind the curtains was a huge old-fashioned drawing room, a
place of overstuffed chairs, high shelves tight with leathery books,
dusty-looking seas of ornate carpets. Mr Novak, portly and smiling,
stood before the fireplace, hands clasped behind his back. And
Vincent Price? Skip's gaze, roving the room, found him at a corner
table. Bending, his back to the window, he was mixing drinks; a
moment later he turned, bearing two tumblers. Skip drew in her
breath. His face was long and pale, and his hair shone darkly with
oil in the style of years before. He really was Vincent Price! How tall
he was – how tall, how handsome, this phantom from the movies
of a television childhood.

The two men clicked their glasses together and drank. Though
the night was warm, flames leaped on the stony hearth. Mr Novak
was saying something; Skip strained to hear the words, but made

out only the anxious, almost pleading tone that contrasted with the bonhomie of a moment earlier. Vincent Price paced the floor, as if revolving an argument in his mind that he found hard to express. Above the mantelpiece, a mirror shone dully, framed elaborately in dark gold. Mr Novak, as if the house belonged to him, indicated a chair; sit, he seemed to say. But Vincent Price kept pacing. He downed his drink in a single gulp.

Skip, longing to hear their words, was about to press her ear to the glass when she saw a bright flash reflected in the window. What could it be? She stiffened and looked behind her, but could see nothing there. Moonlight, perhaps, shifting on leaves in the overgrown garden. But then a thought gripped her. The fire in the hearth. Who had made up the fire? Not Mr Novak or Vincent Price. There hadn't been enough time before she crept up to the window.

She knew what would happen next. A torch flared to life, catching her in its beam. She cried out, crashing into something – bucket? broom? chair? – and went sprawling, then picked herself up as the woodcarved face of Black Jack swooped close, spectral in torchlight, and his hand reached out to grab her. She flung herself off the veranda. Commotion broke out behind her as Black Jack yelled and the torch beam wavered wildly; his shouts were quickly joined by the querying voices of the others.

Skip ran. Night enfolded her. She clambered over the gate outside the property and fled down the road. Hearing Mr Novak's car start up, she dived into the bushes and crouched down as it tore past. Black Jack thrashed among the foliage, mumbling and emitting strange, high-pitched whistles, his torch beam cutting erratically through the darkness. At any moment he might seize her, thrash her. That searching beam, she felt certain, would never relent; but the Aborigine retreated eventually, and the car returned to the house. Skip heard Mr Novak speaking on the veranda. What was he saying? False alarm. Another false alarm. Black Jack, in reply, made discontented sounds – he might have been gnashing his teeth – but at last both went inside, and all was quiet.

Dawn flickered in the sky by the time Skip got home. Uneasily she examined herself for scratches, bruises. A red line ran down her cheek. On her forearm, like a brand, was a raw bruised circle where Black Jack had grabbed her. Only after a moment did she remember why she had ventured out that night. The time capsule letter! Her hand darted to the back pocket of her jeans. The letter was gone.

# Chapter Twelve

In the calendar of Crater Lakes, no event was more important than the Show: the Crater Lakes Agricultural, Pastoral and Horticultural Society Exhibition, to give it its official title. Come the last week of October, with the season rounding the turn towards summer and the end of the school year firmly in view, the broad acres of the Crater Lakes showgrounds resounded to the clamour of an Oriental bazaar. No rooms were to be had in the town's hotels; no campsite or caravan park had space to spare. From Thursday afternoon, with its mayoral 'I declare ...', to the climactic fireworks at midnight on Saturday, the Show was the culmination of a year's glories and the promise of more to come.

For the wealthy pastoralist, the town councillor, the stock and station agent, this climax of the year brought many a satisfaction: proudly, hat tilted back, paunch thrust forward, cigar loose between pudgy fingers, a fellow might watch the crowds and remark, as he had remarked every year since the war, that the Lakes was really going ahead. What other country town had showgrounds that were a patch on ours? Dansie Grandstand was – as a Yank visitor once described it, to general amusement – a fine set of bleachers. The Arch

L. Gull Memorial Hall, where the Show Ball rounded things off in (as the local paper always put it) 'glittering' style, was, so Mayor Gull's successor had said when he opened it, a noble neoclassical structure in Crater Lakes limestone.

All this was by the bye. For the kiddies, the shopgirls, the spotty apprentices, the Show was sideshows: shooting gallery, coconut shy, Ferris wheel, ghost train, an octopus with eggcup cars whirling at the ends of mighty mechanical arms. Popcorn. Candyfloss. Maze of mirrors. Turning metal clowns with gaping mouths.

This year it rained.

Thursday was drizzly. The mayor, in his speech, made witty asides about 'our Lakes weather' and (glancing skywards) the heavens, which he hoped would, unlike the Show, soon be closed. On Friday, though, they opened further; wind drove rain in waves across the green acres, walkways turned to mud, and the Ferris wheel shook dangerously against a steel-grey sky.

But on Channel Eight that night, the news was good. A young reporter, filmed that afternoon, stood in scarf and trench coat in front of the showground gates. 'The Show's a washout,' she said. 'But still they come.' The camera pulled back. Ladies battled with brollies; kids on half-holidays squealed and stamped in puddles, and one made rabbit ears behind his mate's sou'wester as the reporter edged back into view and carried on gamely, 'There's just one question on everybody's lips – tomorrow's weather! The bureau reckons a change is on the way …'

Sure enough, overnight the rain eased. Saturday dawned bright, if blustery; by mid-morning, clouds had lifted like scrim drawing back and the sky was pale blue. The day would be beautiful; everybody said so.

Skip was both glad and sorry. She had little thought of the Show. Friday had been the day of Barry Puce's memorial service. The rain, drumming on stretched umbrellas, washing across the chapel roof, had seemed unending and she hated it – hated it as much as Auntie Noreen's wailing, Marlo's solemn grown-up elegance, and her own crushing guilt. Funerals (if this could be called a funeral) should happen on bright hard days. Rain made it all too much. The bright hard day had come too late.

That Saturday, Auntie Noreen was bright and hard too. She was up early. Sizzling filled the kitchen: bangers, fried eggs, bursting juicy tomatoes, crisping strips of fatty bacon. 'Good *mor*-ning,' she cawed to the girls, and clattered down laden plates before them. Cheerily she leafed through *TV Week*, hoping there might be some nice films coming up, and showed her nieces the latest news on Johnny Farnham. Who'd have thought, the King of Pop was starring in a musical – live on stage in Melbourne! What wouldn't yous girls give to be there? After Uncle Doug and Marlo had set off for Puce Hardware, she smiled at Skip. 'We'll have a nice morning together, won't we, Helen?' she insisted, with a resolve Skip could not help but find dismaying.

They spent the nice morning sorting through Barry's things. In the sleepout, the curtains opened fully to admit the bright sun, Auntie Noreen piled into sacks and cardboard boxes the coats, jackets, jumpers, shirts, trousers, Y-fronts and socks that had filled so much of the wardrobe and chest of drawers. Many times she proffered the same few sentences: 'I'll get Doug to run these down to Goodwill ...', 'Baz looked nice in this ...' and 'Some young lad will be grateful for that ...'

Skip thought of the memorial service. How empty it had seemed: no body, no casket. Her cousin might have vanished from the world as if he had been a ghost all along. The letter from his commanding officer said Barry had died a hero, saving his mates from the Viet Cong. 'I'll bet you say that about all the boys,' Skip said when she read it. But only to herself.

Auntie Noreen had set her the task of packing up Barry's sports stuff (football, basketball, cricket bat), his few toys and fewer books.

Down came the posters, leaving sticky residue. Goodbye, Paul Newman. Goodbye, Jackie Stewart. Auntie Noreen had spoken of 'storage'; as they proceeded, though, she decided on a bonfire. Burn it, she declared. Burn it.

'You're sure?' said Skip. 'Goodwill bags too?'

'Am I going to see some young hoon prancing down Volcano Street in my Baz's jumper? I'd rip it off his back!' Auntie Noreen blew her nose on a hanky embroidered with a 'B'. She had been sitting on the bed (springs almost scraping the floor) and now struggled to her feet. The face she turned to Skip was grim. The nice morning had gone on too long; she was tired; it was lunchtime; the Viet Cong had killed her son.

'We'll burn it all,' she said, her voice thick. 'Now help me.' She reached for a sack, then spotted the F-111 over the bed and lunged as if convulsed with sudden wild hatred. Skip gasped as the hook tore from the ceiling, then cried out, with real grief, when the plane crashed to the floor, shattering a wing. She could still have saved it, scooped up the bits, glued them together, but a heavy foot came down and there was a crunch.

'You didn't have to do that.' Skip's face was pale. She stepped back, then back again, as Auntie Noreen sank down, sobbing, on the sleepout floor. The stricken woman wailed. She cursed.

Skip thought: Embrace her. Say you love her.

Skip thought: Ring Uncle Doug. Stupid bastard, why did he leave her today of all days?

Skip thought: What are you crying for, you old bitch? You wanted Barry to Do His Bit and he did. Well, that was his bit: to die. To die for the Yanks and their crazy war.

Auntie Noreen gaped at Skip. The eyes in the big round face were wide. 'Bugger. I've let go. I've bloody well let go.'

The puddle spread out from beneath her muu-muu.

\* \* \*

Skip fled.

Of course she shouldn't have: shouldn't have shown her disgust on her face, shouldn't have cackled, shouldn't have escaped. But loathing had churned up in her like lava as she imagined Auntie Noreen's embrace, the shared tears, the gibberings of 'You're a good girl, Helen …' She could picture all this as clearly as if it had occurred. But the good girl who would let it happen was not Helen Wells.

She floundered to a halt at last. How wearying it is to know all the things we should have done. Somehow or other, life would go on. Auntie Noreen would rise from the pool of piss, squelch to the bathroom, peel sopping knickers down lumpy thighs; later, she might haul Barry's stuff to the incinerator and stand with a stoical face as she watched it burn, Y-fronts, Jackie Stewart, cricket bat and all. Did it matter? Did anything matter?

Skip ambled on. Green paddocks. Blue sky. Saturday arvo. Grey branches hung above her and she reached up, snapped off a stick. She tossed it, as if to a dog. Time would be more bearable if you could snap it like that. Snap. Toss. This is my time, a stick in my hand. I've thrown that bit away. Gone.

The pink Valiant drew up beside her. 'Off to the Show?'

Skip stood frozen on the passenger side. Mr Novak, one hand on the wheel, leaned across the seat. His face, twisted towards her, looked like a mask hanging upside down. Dread throbbed in her chest. Empty paddocks lay all around.

The door clicked open. Gulping, Skip knew she could not resist. She slid into the shadowy interior. On the back seat, Baskerville thumped his tail. She turned towards him. 'Hello, boy.'

'How's school?' Mr Novak's voice was gentle.

Skip turned back and stared ahead, watching the road as though she were the driver; Mr Novak smiled in her direction as if he were any ordinary neighbour and she any ordinary neighbour's child. They spoke, but said nothing. Poor Barry. Terrible. Yes, a shock. The funeral? Funerals were sad. Something in the dashboard rattled, and Skip wondered if she ought to say, 'What's that?' or 'You'll have to get that seen to.' People said that sort of thing, didn't they – normal people? But Mr Novak was speaking. And what, he asked her, was she looking forward to most? She did not at first realise he was talking about the Show. What should she say: haunted house? Maze of mirrors? A fearful vision came to her of Vincent Price stalking her, tracking her through silver corridors.

Did she know, Mr Novak went on, that he would be at the Show himself, running cartoons for the kiddies in a room at the back of the Arch L. Gull Memorial Hall? Perhaps she'd like to look in for a while. Or was Skip Wells too old for Bugs Bunny ('What's up, doc?'), Porky Pig ('Be-de-be-deep-deep, that's all, folks!' – did Mr Novak, in his Czech accent, really say that?), Roadrunner ('Meep! Meep!') and Kyot. Poor Kyot! Did she think he'd ever catch that pesky bird?

Yes. Yes, she did. He'll rip it apart today.

The Ferris wheel, emerging over a line of trees, made a colourful clockface against the sky. Screams sounded distantly. Skip could think of only one thing: the pink Valiant, purple in the night, crunching up the drive of the old Dansie house, with the men talking quietly in the front, unaware of the stowaway in the back. What had Vincent Price said? 'They'll find me out in time.' And yet he seemed not to believe in time at all. 'We talk about the future,' he had said, 'but it's only ever a story we tell. We're in the loop of the present, going round and round. Up and down Volcano Street. Up and down, up and down.'

Mr Novak said now, 'You're not as thick with my son as you used to be.' His tone was neutral, not accusing at all.

'I suppose,' said Skip.

'Suppose? Did something happen?'

She shook her head and tried to think of something else to say – anything, to hold back what she feared must come next: I know it was you, Skip, outside the old Dansie house.

The Valiant slowed as they reached the showground gates. Noise filled the air: cars, voices, bicycle bells, music. Mr Novak looked at Skip fondly, and said that perhaps she ought to hop out here. It would take him a while to park. Relieved, confused, she thanked him for the ride.

He nodded. She had walked a few steps from the car when he called her back. He reached into his jacket and then extended towards her a dusty crumpled rectangle of paper. 'Yours, I believe. You dropped it.'

The time capsule envelope was creased, dirty, and the seal was broken. Appalled, she looked up at Mr Novak again, but already the Valiant was nosing away, joining the queue of cars for the parking lot.

The letter burned in her hand. As she stood in line for the ticket booths, she tore it into bits, and crushed the confetti in the dirt beneath her feet. Impatiently she shoved her coins across the counter and fled into the Show.

She wandered blindly. Elbows stabbed her, broad backs blocked her way, but she pushed through where she could. Canvas aisles channelled her past flowers, food, art. Here, the roses. First prize: Mrs E. Sutton. Ladies in hats and gloves and pearls cooed admiringly. Here, the lamingtons. First prize: Mrs V. Lumsden. And here, posing for a photographer, the lady herself, plastic teeth beaming. And over here? Stinky enormous cheeses. And there? Fine specimens of Australian flora, some in watercolour, some in oils – some of them (this was much remarked upon) the work of armless artists who held their brushes with their mouths or feet. 'Mar-vellous what those poor people can do, isn't it?' shrieked one stringy farmer's wife to another, who nodded sagely.

In the animal sheds, where fluorescent lights, yards long, glared hollowly under galvanised iron, Skip inhaled the bristly reek of straw, combined in a heady cocktail with the brown damp animal smell and its undertow of shit. Look at that merino with its curling horns. Look at that pony with its furry flares. Look at that fat sow, just like Auntie Noreen. First prize: Mrs N. Puce.

The sow on its straw, stricken in fatness, teats protruding pinkly from its belly, seemed suddenly obscene, and Skip hurried from the sheds. She was lonely. She was frightened. She was hungry too. She had spent all her money on the admission charge. Children trailed by, laughing.

There was nothing to do. She trudged through a display of Massey Ferguson tractors. Rubber and oil could smell as bad as shit. At the back of the Arch L. Gull Memorial Hall a sign announced: CARTOON FUN TIME. She turned away briskly, but not before a figure emerged and hailed her: 'Wait!'

She didn't want to, but the crowds were thick, the hand gripped her arm, and the familiar face grinned into hers. Skip had not spoken to Honza since Auntie Noreen banished him from the sleepout. But Honza seemed to have forgotten all about her aunt's threats. 'Guess what?' he said. 'Just blagged five dollars off of Dad.'

'Congratulations,' Skip said sourly.

'Been on the Ferris wheel yet?' said Honza.

How dense could one boy be? If he cared or noticed that tragedy had engulfed her, he chose not to mention it. Why would he? The sun shone, music played, and crumpled in his pocket was a five-dollar note. Laughing, he led her towards the sideshows, and Skip (she had to admit it) was glad to follow. Bunting fluttered over the crowded alleys and tinny music mingled on the air, rolling out the barrel by the old mill stream, last night in dreamland in a gilded cage.

Their first ride was the Octopus. Whirling on its vigorous arms, one moment crushed against Honza, the next sliding away, Skip was exhilarated in spite of herself. The crowds, the tents, the sheds, the cars, the green paddocks whizzed dizzyingly by below, and she wanted to be dizzy, laughing as they tumbled like drunkards out of the car. 'Again!' cried Honza, and would have bought them a second turn, but Skip urged him on: too much to see.

Too much to do: a world of toffee apples, kewpie dolls, painted chipped horses and moving metal clowns, the sugary aroma of candyfloss and donuts, and revolving over it all, like the wheel of time, the Ferris wheel. The man who operated it had only one ear; where the other should have been was a thrilling dark hole in bonelike skin. A lady in a high wig, hoop earrings and a long red dress paraded outside the fortune teller's tent, drumming up custom. A man who might have been the Wizard of Oz, with cane and top hat, a fob chain gleaming across his straining girth, stumped back and forth across a platform under a banner proclaiming: MARVEL OF MARVELS. Skip let Honza lead the way. He had the money, of course, but more than that she wanted him to lead, wanted somebody else to be in charge.

They had just jumped down from the dodgem cars when three faces appeared before them: Lummo, with his ballooning chins; Shaun Kenny, acne red-raw; Andreas Haskas licking a toffee apple, tongue protruding redly.

'Well, well!' Lummo began. 'What have we here?'

Shaun Kenny began, 'One Czech wog –'

Andreas Haskas finished, '– and his mole mate.' (Lick.)

'Come on, Honza.' Skip tried to pass, but Kenny pushed her in the chest. She staggered. Lummo pushed her further back, and Haskas jabbed his toffee apple into Honza's face like a burning brand.

'What you see in this one, Novak? Flat and ugly – get it?'

'Where's your cousin, Skippy? Dug him up yet?'

'Get fucked.' Honza broke away, dragging Skip behind him. Both were surprised when the Lum's Den let them go. They expected pursuit, a murderous game of hide and seek among the sideshow labyrinths. But the three boys passed on, guffawing; there was, after all, everything to do, and Lummo, for now, only flung back a single taunt: 'We'll be watching you!' He poked a fat finger into the air, and Skip realised that he was plastered. Blotto. What would Valmai Lumsden think if she could see her precious son?

Shambling off, the boy made a metallic rattle; the pockets of his long shorts bulged and sagged. Skip had heard that sound before, that chunky hard susurrus, deep in a slimy well in the dark: coins in bulk, shifting, shifting. Her face flared scarlet. 'I could kill those bastards.'

'Hah! Don't reckon you could.'

She punched Honza's bicep. 'Could so!'

He rubbed his arm. 'They're in the money. You know they've got the dosh from the wishing well? Lummo was bragging in the boys' toilets on Thursday. He reckons they'll spend it all today.'

'That copper had my bag,' Skip said, confused.

'Not mine. Lummo buggered off with my rucksack that night.' Honza gestured around them. 'I reckon he's hid it at the Show. Stands to reason, don't it? Couldn't carry it all around with him. Couldn't keep it at home. That fat bastard's stashed it somewhere.'

'And every so often he fills his pockets?'

'Want to go on the Ferris wheel?'

The Ferris wheel was the best thing at the Show. Round and round it went, up and down, high and low, like life, like fortune. Girls were meant to scream as it turned skywards; Skip watched silent and unblinking, lightly gripping the chipped metal rail that locked them in place. From on high, two worlds were laid out clearly below them: on one side, flowers, pigs, tractors – dreary, worthy, officially approved; on the other, sideshows with their bright illicit alleys. In the sky, the music was thinner, frailer. Skip had never been in an aeroplane but imagined it would be like this. Everybody loves Ferris wheels. Everybody loves aeroplanes. Everybody wants to be Superman, swooping over a world of toys.

Gazing down into the alleys, Skip pointed. 'Look!'

'Where?' Honza had been humming.

The Lum's Den, emerging from the crowd, had veered towards the back of the tents. Lummo led the way. Weaving between caravans and cars, he appeared furtive, steering clear of sideshow folk on breaks who sprawled on patches of grass, or leaned, smoking, against bonnets of cars. All the cars were old.

Shakily, the Ferris wheel swung down.

'They're up to no good, I'll bet,' said Skip.

Honza shrugged. Perhaps he wanted to pretend for now that no Lum's Den existed. On Monday, at school, he would know all too well that it did.

The wheel surged up again. 'Where did they go?'

'Maybe Lummo needed a piss.'

'The rucksack.' Conviction burned in Skip like fire. Honza must be right: Lummo had the rucksack hidden somewhere at the Show. She and Honza must steal it back. Impatiently now, she waited as the wheel brought them down, then up again, and was relieved when the ride was over.

They plunged back into the fray. 'Ghost train next!' Honza was insistent.

So was Skip. 'Lum's Den!' But no Lum's Den was in view.

Hovering blackly over the far end of the alleys was a house of canvas and lath, its high walls emblazoned with skeletons, monsters and sheeted ghosts. All afternoon, screams had issued from within. Reluctantly, Skip followed Honza to the tall house. A burly man with slack jowls, sullen behind levers, snaffled their coins; a pale youth with spidery, many-jointed fingers clamped them into a podlike car. Unimpressed, Skip looked around the flapping canvas veranda with its painted ghouls. Other cars, becalmed between rides, whirred and knocked on slithery tracks.

Rockingly, the car conveyed them into blackness. The ghost train was a roller-coaster of an unambitious sort, weaving its way upstairs and down through a darkened primitive stage set filled with skeletons, cobwebs, giant spiders, bats, corpses rising perpetually in coffins, House of Wax scenes of murders and executions, and a bolt-necked monster of a gangrenous green that lumbered forward, arms outstretched. Accompanying it all were recorded screams, cackles, sudden bursts of organ music, and sounds of thunder that shook the flimsy corridors. To these horrors Skip remained impassive; Honza, beside her, was stoical too, only jumping, not crying out, when draping bony fingers brushed his head.

They were rounding a corner past a pointy-hatted witch – a green-painted mannequin with Shylock nose and bicycle-reflector eyes – when the witch swayed, as if pushed from behind, and toppled onto the track. Crushingly, the car swept the mannequin along.

Honza twisted to look back. 'Somebody's there. On the ledge.'

Thumping footsteps sounded over the music. They heard a scuffle; and a cry, too close to their ears, made them gasp. Something – a boot, perhaps – struck the side of their car, then all the cars shuddered to a halt. Time itself might have been running down. There was silence. No music, no thunder.

Somebody laughed. A panel opened, exposing the corridor to searing daylight. Bewildered, Skip and Honza climbed out of the car and walked, as if to salvation, towards the light; other kids trailed raggedly behind. The burly man bellowed, 'Come on, come on,' and the spider-fingered youth pushed past them grimly, footsteps shaking the plywood floor.

Not until they stood with the crowd on the lawn outside, staring back at the evacuated house, did Skip and Honza realise what had happened. Yelling, the youth emerged with two ghosts struggling in his grip: one, a cursing Andreas Haskas; the other, a cowering Shaun Kenny. Lummo, grinning, slouched behind them. The burly man, to cheers from the crowd, slapped the back of Lummo's head, then swore as the fat boy kicked him in the shins. Laughing, the

Lum's Den made their escape, fists in the air like sporting heroes.

A little girl next to Skip said, 'They was them ones in the maze.'

Skip said, 'The maze of mirrors?'

The girl nodded, pigtails waggling. 'Mirrors got broke. Fatty couldn't find his way out. So he smashed his way out.'

Skip grabbed Honza's arm. 'Let's follow them.'

'They're drunk.' He sounded awe-struck. 'Totally pissed.'

'You've only just realised?' Sometimes Skip felt older than Honza.

Their task was clear. That afternoon, they would avenge themselves on the Lum's Den. They would bide their time, but they would do it. No matter what it took. For a while their enemies vanished, but soon they were back: Lummo at the shooting gallery, firing askew ('Eh, watch it, son!'); Kenny, to guffaws, swinging back the hammer on the try-your-strength machine ('Bad luck, boyo! Better luck next time'); Haskas clambering up on a fence, making a wild leap for an Octopus car just as the cars were about to whirl.

'Go for it, Greaso!' Lummo cried, even as the operator swept forward and tossed Haskas back over the fence like a sack. The boy lay in the dust, shouting abuse, until Lummo and Kenny bent down to haul him up, when the abuse turned to screams. Crowds watched, enthralled, as Haskas was surrounded by sideshow folk, who pushed and prodded him until one little man declared, as if in triumph, 'The bugger's broke his arm!' Gently, they bore away the shrieking boy.

'Let's get more dosh,' said Honza, and made Skip follow him to Cartoon Fun Time where, at the end of a fuzzy beam of light, a flea in a Mexican hat spotted Elmer Fudd's dog and yammered out that there was food around the corner, food around the corner for me. On the floor, little kids variously wailed, laughed, punched each other, or curled up on cushions, asleep.

Skip hung back while Honza begged his father for just a few more dollars. Mr Novak sighed and reached for his wallet. He winked at Skip. 'Having a good time?' She shrugged. Twice that afternoon she had thought of telling Honza what she knew about his father: once on the Ferris wheel, before they spotted the Lum's Den; once as they squatted between tents, eating candyfloss. But both times something had held her back. Her thoughts, the revelations she might make, had seemed no more solid than the sugary nothingness on the stick in her hand.

Mr Novak threaded a new film through the projector. Light, juddering into brightness, caught his foreign face and cut it into jagged, shadowy planes. He was a strange man. A stranger. Like Vincent Price.

On their way back to the sideshows, Skip and Honza passed a lady in a violent floral frock who tugged a boy by the ear. Skip had to look a second time at the villain: Shaun Kenny. Twisting away from his mother, he threw up on the grass. Mrs Kenny looked away with lemon-sucking lips.

'Guess what?' said Skip. 'That means Lummo's alone.'

The afternoon had drawn towards dusk, and the painted colours on canvas and plasterboard took on an unearthly glow. Rows of bulbs, suspended like grapes, winked on above the alleys, where the crowds remained unthinned and their fervour rose with the empurpling sky.

They found Lummo at the Ferris wheel. The wheel was becalmed and a queue waited, impatient and complaining, as the fat boy on the creaky wooden platform demanded a turn on the ride. The man without an ear said no. 'You're drunk, boyo. You're disorderly.'

'I can pay!' Lummo plunged a hand into a bulging pocket. A seam gave way and the Treasure of the Sierra Madre, like a sudden nightmare pants-wetting, clattered down his trouser leg. He was on his knees, scrabbling for the bullion, when the man with no ear kicked him in the arse, sending him tumbling down the steps. 'I'll get you!' Lummo spat, and forced his way through a group of kids. Squealing girls parted to let him by; a boy tripped him, and he sprawled again, but picked himself up and plunged into the gap between Marvel of Marvels and the fortune teller's tent.

'He's off to his hideout,' said Skip. 'I'll bet he is.'

On the platform outside Marvel of Marvels, now lit brilliantly, a bearded lady sashayed in a many-tasselled bikini while the Wizard of Oz barked through a megaphone, inviting all the ladies and gentlemen and little chickadees to roll up, roll up for the strangest critters in creation: half-man, half-goat! Man with no limbs! Smallest boy in the world!

'Let's get him.' Skip followed Lummo into the gap. She couldn't see him ahead; he must have turned a corner. Honza came after her, but it seemed without enthusiasm. Briefly, she wondered why.

Behind the tents was another, wider grassy corridor where the caravans of sideshow folk backed on to the alley. Skip peered around the corner in time to see Lummo propel himself forward, as if he too were about to chuck, then lunge into the back of Marvel of Marvels. He was gone. Puzzled, Skip looked at Honza.

'Through here.' He led her along the canvas wall and lifted a flap. Wooden steps led up to the freak-show stage from the rear. They quickly drew back as the bearded lady swished by them in a sweaty cloud and vanished into a caravan across the way. But where, Skip wondered, was Lummo?

Honza pointed. Beneath the stage was a dark space, like the cavity under a house. Skip leaned down and in the gloom saw Lummo lying on his side, turned away from them, holding his belly. He groaned. On one side of him lay Honza's rucksack, open and empty; on the other was a flagon of cider. Sacks, rags, ropes, boxes and discarded planks and beams littered the grass around him.

Skip slapped him. 'You knew this was their hideout, didn't you?'

'Don't hit me. Why should I know?'

'You're one of them. I'll bet they use it every year.'

Above them, the Wizard of Oz had repaired to the front of the stage, pacing before a drawn curtain. They heard his footsteps creaking and his voice, distorted oddly, speaking again of marvels and miracles, this time to a paying crowd enticed into the tent. Reddish lights flashed through cracks in the boards.

'Scat! Scat!' A Munchkin in shorts, braces and bow tie, labouring down the steps, flicked pudgy hands at Skip and Honza as if at unwanted cats. Breathlessly, the Munchkin climbed into the caravan and emerged, moments later, leading a man in a rooster suit with an enormous floppy comb. The rooster swigged from a bottle, jabbing it with difficulty into his beak, before the Munchkin sprang up and batted it away. The bottle fell; acrid-smelling brown liquid fizzed into the grass.

'Bugger you,' slurred the rooster, but allowed himself to be prodded up the steps, just as the curtain pulled back above and applause broke out.

In that moment the plan emerged fully in Skip's mind. It was irresistible. 'Quick,' she urged Honza, and crawled into the space beneath the stage. First things first: rag, sack, rope. Footsteps thumped above and light made zebra stripes through the boards as she tore back Lummo's hair, stuffed a rag into his mouth, and bundled his lolling head, like a cabbage, into the sack. Honza gasped. Lummo protested a little, but was too sluggish to resist as Skip, fighting her revulsion, tugged off the drunken boy's shoes, socks, shorts, shirt and, last – no flinching now – his Y-fronts too. An awe-struck Honza, comprehending, wrenched Lummo's arms behind his back and bound the wrists with rope.

The rooster had finished his strutting, his flapping, his drunken cacophonies of 'Cock-a-doodle-doo!' as Skip, with Honza's aid, rolled the naked Lummo into the grassy corridor. Just then the Munchkin, resignedly following the giant fowl, thumped down the steps again, ready to summon the next act.

Rooster and Munchkin disappeared into the caravan. Skip and Honza exchanged a thumbs-up. Honza slammed shut the caravan door and stood against it, bracing himself as little fists hammered within. Triumph! They forced Lummo to his feet and prodded him, swaying, up the steps.

In the tent, the Wizard of Oz announced the next atrocity of nature; the curtains pulled aside again, and blundering into the light came the obese pale naked form of Brenton Lumsden. Cries broke out; the Wizard, shocked, tried to hide his confusion, while a writhing Lummo, shocked into alertness by the noise, wrenched his hands free and tore the bag off his head. The laughter was tumultuous.

'Got him,' Skip whispered to herself, only wishing she could see the horror, the disgust, the appalled fascination on the jeering faces. She reeled around to Honza. 'Got him!' she cried, and both raised fists in the air.

By the time Lummo had been hustled from the stage, they were long gone, rushing off into the gathering night. They held hands. Honza had snatched the bottle of cider. He hugged it against his chest.

# Chapter Thirteen

Imagine being Marlo Wells. Probably you wouldn't go out with Pavel Novak. What could he offer, especially now, when you would soon sit your exams? He wasn't the most attractive boy; he was gangly, his teeth were horsy, and his high-templed head, with its springy curls, really did look like a test tube bubbling over. He had done badly at school; he was unambitious and, no doubt, not very smart. Your scholarship was almost in the bag (you'd sit those exams – Auntie Noreen couldn't stop you); in a few months you'd be gone, spirited away, and where would he be? Shouldering boxes in the back of Puce Hardware, now and for all time. And if you'd met another man, one who didn't wear a blue apron at work, who could stage a play and have a 'vision' for it, who opened up the world of knowledge for you like Aladdin's cave, what time could you give to a blundering country boy who drove you down the main drag in his Land Rover and said, quite sincerely, 'The Lakes is really going ahead'? No, you wouldn't go out with Pavel Novak.

But if, on that Saturday of the Show, you had worked back late, typing invoices until your fingers ached, and knew he was out there beyond the office door, hanging around to keep you company, because that was the kind of boy he was, perhaps your feelings might soften a little.

The shop had shut at midday; it was now after five.

'Give it a rest, eh?' Pavel said at last, and Marlo looked up gratefully. He had taken off his apron and leaned against the doorjamb in his jeans and a Rolling Stones T-shirt. Muscle balled tightly in his crooked left arm.

'I can't go home,' she said, before she could help it. 'I can't stand it. Everything's so horrible.' She stood, with a scrape of chair, and went to the window.

'Hey.' He came to her. Would he put his arm around her? He was thinking about it, she could tell. But all he did was gulp, sniff a little, and say as if he meant it, 'It's all right.'

'He was your friend. You didn't cry at the service.'

'It wasn't real. I just kept thinking about the body and where it might be. Did they even find him? Is he lying in the jungle somewhere, rotting away? They said he was on patrol. That could mean anything.'

Marlo hugged herself as if she were cold. Sunshine streamed between the dusty curtains. 'Funny to think of a boy our age going to war. Once I asked Uncle Doug what he did in the war, and he just sort of clammed up. Auntie Noreen said he was in New Guinea. He must have killed men, seen men killed, seen guts spilled on the jungle floor. He's buried all that so deep he can't even find it. Poor Uncle Doug. He's a dead man walking.'

She felt the warmth from Pavel's arm, so close to hers. 'How about the Show?' he said softly. 'Whole town's there.'

'Yes. Let's.' Marlo swung back from the window. Quickly she began putting away the files that cascaded in cardboard waves across her desk, while a smiling Pavel, who had slumped into her chair, drummed his fingers with mock impatience. The cup of Nescafé he had made her an hour ago sat before him, undrunk. Turning in haste, she knocked it. Dark liquid soaked his lap.

Marlo gasped. 'I'm so sorry.'

His smile didn't drop. He raised the cup as if in a toast. 'Guess I'll have to scoot home and change first.'

Pavel remained in good spirits as they hurtled in the Land Rover out of town. All was quiet but for distant sounds of the Show, buffeted on the wind: loudspeakers, carnival tunes, birdcall flurryings of an excited crowd.

'Tracks get laid down in our heads so fast,' Marlo said, as houses gave way to green paddocks. 'Round and round we go, Puce's Bend to Volcano Street and back, and it seems we've been doing it all our lives.'

'I have been. It's all I've ever known.'

'Don't you want to go away?'

'Dunno. Is there all that much, out in the world?'

'There's everything.' What could she say? London, Paris, decadent Berlin and the Côte d'Azur – would the names mean a thing to him? Perhaps there *was* only Crater Lakes, and all else was illusion. But no. For so long Marlo had thought: I'll go away like Germaine and not look back. My life is rising like a Saturn V rocket, shedding stages as it shoots up through the sky. Those years in Glenelg have crashed and burned and so, soon enough, will these months in Crater Lakes. But uneasily Marlo knew that life, for almost everyone, could never be a rocket. It could never leave the earth.

'Your father lived in Prague.' She looked at Pavel.

'I'm not even sure I could find that on the map.' Gooseflesh stood out on his arms beneath the frayed sleeves of his Rolling Stones T-shirt. The stain, black in the middle, brownish at the edges, covered the bottom of the T-shirt and his denim thighs. Marlo felt her cheeks grow hot.

Parked outside the Novak house was a red Morris Minor. 'Brooker's car,' Pavel said in a sour voice. 'He's driving Mum to the Show Ball.'

He jumped down to the drive with a stony crunch. 'Coming in? Only take a minute.'

'I'll wait in the Land Rover,' Marlo said. She felt confused, a little ashamed, as he vanished into the house. White walls glimmered in the early evening sun and she thought of Spain, as seen at the Ozone, Glenelg. Turning, she looked across empty paddocks. Would they all be covered with houses one day? There were so many people in the world. Too many.

Marlo remembered a time when she was small and Skip was a baby. They had lived with Karen Jane in dirty rooms in North Adelaide with a garage mechanic who reeked of beer and fags. On many a drunken night he smashed Karen Jane to the floor. In the mornings he was all tenderness, declaring that he had been mad, that he didn't know what had come over him, that he hated himself and would do anything to make it up to her. Marlo had seen her mother draw him towards her, stroke his hair, and tell him to hush, hush, it was all right. On his birthday, she cooked him a special dinner, but Jimmy – that was his name – didn't come home. He had promised! Karen Jane refused to give in. She would go and get him. Brutally, she dragged Marlo out of bed, flung a coat over the little girl's shoulders and buckled her shoes. The baby had woken up and began to howl. 'Shut up, shut up.' Karen Jane wrung her hands helplessly, then grabbed the swaddled form and thrust it into Marlo's arms. Yes, they would all go. Let Jimmy see, let all his drunken mates see, what he'd been neglecting! The smell of a burned roast lingered in the air. On the table between the dinner plates was a little box wrapped in paper: cufflinks, Jimmy's present – as if he would ever wear them! Karen Jane snatched up the box and laughed. Marlo clutched Skip tightly. Helplessly, she followed their mother down the stairs.

In the leagues club, Jimmy looked first startled to see them, then angry. He had been leaning at the bar, slurring out some anecdote to his sozzled cronies, when blearily he took in mother and daughters:

Karen Jane accusing, Marlo whimpering, the baby howling. Swaying, pint glass in hand, he slurred, 'Whadya doing, woman?' Karen Jane said nothing, only flung the little box to the floor at his feet and blathered out a tuneless 'Happy birthday to you …' He laughed then, and his mates laughed; all around the clubroom men were laughing, flinging back sunbeaten necks, baring brown teeth and baying like dingoes.

Brown teeth seemed to swallow the world. Marlo remembered everything as brown: the bar, the beer in a hundred glasses, the linoleum, the walls, the stained baize on the snooker table, the weak drizzling light. Then Karen Jane was screaming as if the force of her despair could shatter this brownness that threatened to destroy her. None of what happened next seemed real: not the manager storming out of his office, yelling at the barman to call the cops; not Jimmy's glass smashing on the floor and Jimmy swinging in a rage towards Karen Jane, calling her 'woman', commanding her to shut up, shut the fuck up; not the fist whipping back, then slamming into her again and again.

The police arrived to find Jimmy hunched, sobbing, over a motionless form. Karen Jane woke in a prison cell. But of course it wasn't a prison; it was a madhouse. Ever afterwards, Marlo remembered her mother that night, a small frail figure in the middle of a brown floor, men parting around her in a wide circle as she turned and turned, screaming, hands outstretched, and Marlo asked herself: What is she reaching for?

Wind rippled in shifting waves across the green paddocks. Marlo knew why she had stayed outside. She didn't want to see Howard, that's why. No doubt she had been a fool about him, a silly girl with a crush. She had thought her life could change and already it was set in stone. She was tired. But no wonder. She was the girl who worked in Puce Hardware. Damn Crater Lakes! Damn them all. Restlessness filled her, and she followed Pavel into the house.

Never before had Marlo entered the Novak house by the front door; she had always gone round the back to the Sanctum. A cool corridor enfolded her, a place of soft carpets, vases with flowers, pictures on the walls. Through an arch she saw a large kitchen with flagstones, varnished timber, copper pans. She imagined herself walking through to the Sanctum, where Howard and Mrs Novak would be chatting, perhaps with tea, perhaps with wine, about the future of the Players. She would say, like a grown-up, 'Hi, Howard. Hi, Deirdre.'

Where was Pavel? Absurdly, she thought: I'll hold his hand. Hold his hand as I say, 'Hi, Howard.' She wished she could afford modern, carefree clothes. She had bought her own clothes for as long as she could remember, and everything she owned looked like her school uniform. She couldn't bear to look like Karen Jane. No tie-dyed T-shirts, no pink hot pants, no paisley caftans. But everything was different without Karen Jane. Her mother was gone, gone, gone.

The corridor had a crossroads. In the ceiling above it was a skylight, aglow with whitish blue. She turned to the left. Soft music sounded: Mozart, maybe. Some horn concerto. Pavel wouldn't play that. She heard a laugh and a gasp of breath. What impulse pushed her forward?

A door stood ajar. 'Pavel?' said Marlo.

Mrs Novak had been careless. No doubt she thought she would be alone in the house all day. Never could she have imagined Marlo Wells creeping to the bedroom door, looking through the crack, then pushing the door suddenly wider.

Mozart grew more loud. The room was furnished with the same careful taste as the rest of the house: the beige, the white, the pictures on the walls. Light pressed behind drawn curtains, giving a golden sheen to the figures on the bed.

Howard was the first to see her. Marlo screamed.

* * *

'But if there was a T-Rex –'

'And an allosaurus. No, a T-Rex and a –'

'One of them flying ones –'

'A pterodactyl! If there was a T-Rex –'

'I'm confused. You talk bullshit, Honza Novak.'

Honza sniggered. 'Know what?'

Pause. 'What?'

'You're mad and I'm not.'

Skip sniggered too. It was the funniest thing she had ever heard. Honza punched her thigh.

'Some Enchanted Evening' coiled around them in sugary swoops: Glenn Miller, thirty years too late, with a band shrunk to a quarter of the size. In the Arch L. Gull Memorial Hall, Skip and Honza huddled by the back wall near the podium, knees drawn up, half in shadow, watching the dancers turning and turning. Midnight must be close now. Neither had been home. Neither wanted to go. Dinner had been donuts, hot chips, and more candyfloss for dessert. Both felt a little sick.

'They're all so old,' said Skip.

Foxtrotting by came Mr Rigby, huge-shouldered and barrel-chested in a yellow checked sports jacket; his partner was one of the ladies from the school office, who appeared more than a little apprehensive as the headmaster compelled her this way and that with manly firmness. Crowding the floor was many another local identity: Mrs Lumsden, puffed up on her flower-show win, confidently leading a hapless Mr Singh; Mrs Kenny, in her violent flowers, doing a turn with a local dentist; Mrs Sutton with the mayor; Mr Hill, the newsagent, who had foregone his habitual cardigan for the tux he pulled out each year from mothballs, dancing now with the lady librarian.

'Some Enchanted Evening' ended; there was a polite smattering of applause and on the podium a real estate agent, glistening with Brylcreem, claimed the microphone with a whistle of feedback to

197

declare the results of the Arch L. Gull Memorial Raffle. Drumrolls preceded each announcement. Third prize (good on yer, Len): a ten-dollar book voucher from Hill's Newsagency. Second prize (you can keep it for Chrissie): a frozen turkey from Diamond's Meat Emporium. First prize (and of course we're sorry, very very sorry Doug and Noreen can't be here tonight): a Victa power mower from Puce Hardware.

The Show Ball! Even in the Lakes there were events more lively: school socials where kids smuggled in grog; woolshed dances with oafish farmers eyeing up the sheilas and, later, chundering out the back; lock-ins at the Federal after the coppers had given the wink; teenage revels when the oldies were away, in which lounge rooms normally given over to Channel Eight, Nescafé and Dad in the Jason recliner were rendered exotic with coloured hankies draped over the lampshades, Led Zeppelin booming from the stereo, and the air sweet with thick illicit smoke. The Show Ball, by contrast, was the enactment of a ritual. The sideshows might be rowdy, but in the Arch L. Gull Memorial Hall the finest citizens of Crater Lakes – the respectable businessmen, the prominent landowners, the essential professionals – gathered with their wives in communal display. Without them, no land would be legally owned, no sheep or cattle slaughtered, plantations would be barren of Monterey pines, no Monaro would gun its way down Volcano Street, Channel Eight would sputter into darkness, weddings would go unlicensed, foreskins uncircumcised, and middle-aged mouths unfilled with plastic teeth.

The hall was hot. Gentlemen had stripped off jackets, rolled back shirtsleeves; ladies, not so much mutton dressed as lamb as mutton dressed as mutton, fanned themselves with copies of the *Crater Lakes Times*. Only the lights – a mirrorball, installed controversially the year before, spangled muted Milky Ways through the smoky haze – gave the evening a fugitive glamour. Everyone was waiting for the fireworks at midnight.

Bert Noblet's Rhythm Stompers, since 1945 the finest ensemble between Crater Lakes and Tailem Bend, launched into 'Woodchopper's Ball'. Some of the older folk chose to sit this one out, but many a jug-eared farmer's son, short back and sides newly clipped, led his girl on to the floor – and weaving between them came Pavel and Marlo.

Honza nudged Skip. 'There they are again.'

Marlo had said she would not go to the Show. How had Pavel persuaded her? Before the ball, Skip had seen them at the sideshows, where Marlo seemed distracted, standing by vacantly while Pavel, at the shooting gallery, won her a stuffed koala. Now he danced frenetically, arms jerking, while Marlo barely moved. She looked ashamed, appalled. Skip's merriment had subsided. She watched her sister sadly, then with sudden fear. When Pavel reached for Marlo's hand, she broke from him as if he had insulted her, and charged off the floor.

Skip scrambled to her feet. Pushing between bulky figures, she skirted the dance floor towards her sister. Marlo leaned, breathing heavily, against the refreshments table, while the ladies behind it eyed her with alarm, certain now – they had always suspected it – that young Miss Wells was not quite-quite.

'Hey, Marlo,' said Skip.

'You should be home in bed.'

'And miss the crackers?' She tugged her sister's arm. 'What's Pav done? He's upset you again, hasn't he? He don't mean it. Not Pav. Let's go outside. They'll have the crackers soon.'

'Stop saying crackers. What are you, five years old?' Marlo stared back towards the dance floor; 'Woodchopper's Ball' had slipped, without a break, into 'In the Mood'. Following Marlo's gaze, Skip saw, at the centre of the throng, a woman in a red mini-dress with a dark cap of hair jitterbugging with a long-haired young man in a purple velvet suit.

'How could she?' Marlo's voice was thick.

Pleadingly, Skip looked at Pavel, who had been hanging back, abashed. Moving like a man condemned, he reached for Marlo. With a cry, she flung him off and charged between the dancers. Skip, too loudly, called her sister's name. Faces turned: drunks opened bleary eyes; sleepy kids perked up; respectable ladies, fearing this evening had gone on too long, were about to find out how right they were as that Wells girl – you *do* know who her mother was? – pushed aside one protesting couple, then another.

Obliviously, the band played on, but the dancers had stopped. Stock still. All, that is, except the pair in the middle. Reaching them, Marlo pushed Mrs Novak out of Howard Brooker's arms. Mrs Novak reeled back.

Mirrorball light flickered like stars across Howard Brooker as he turned, startled, to see Marlo before him. Only two things moved. One was the mirrorball; it must flash its meaningless signal until the universe wound down. The other was Marlo, swinging back her hand. Concentrated in the slap was all her rage since her exile in Crater Lakes began.

Deirdre Novak crumpled.

At once all was commotion: Howard Brooker rushing to comfort Mrs Novak; Skip and Pavel grabbing Marlo's arms; the crowd buzzing; Bert Noblet's Rhythm Stompers collapsing into tunelessness. In the end, Pavel led Marlo away. Skip wanted to follow her sister, to escape with her into the night, but the crowd was too thick, and the pair soon vanished.

Honza appeared beside Skip. His words were like a blow, every bit as hard as Marlo's. 'Your sister's nuts.'

'Don't say that.' Not that. Never.

'She's round the twist.'

Stupid boy, did he have to grin like that? Skip pushed him and he sprawled. Hands reached to restrain her. She flung them off and burst through the crowd, just as Bert Noblet, attempting a swift recovery, bawled into the squealing mike that the moment we'd all been waiting for had arrived. 'Cracker time!'

Did he have to say crackers?

Outside, the air was warm, almost sticky. Hordes spilled from the Arch L. Gull Memorial Hall. Skip slipped off to the side, turning her back on the fools with their crackers. Only five-year-olds talked about crackers. Shoulders hunched, muttering to herself, she was heading for the parking lot, wanting to conceal herself between the massed metallic ranks of Chryslers, Holdens, Ford Falcons, when two dark legs like pillars blocked her way. Whistling, that of a bomb before it bursts, filled the air; with a thunderclap, the sky flowered into brilliance, just as she looked into a familiar face lit weirdly in green and gold, then heard, over the next loud ascending whistle, the words: 'I'm not going to hurt you, Skip. You know I'd never hurt you.'

'I can't go home again,' she said.

'Then we're alike – refugees, both of us.'

'Hey, Dad.' Honza was behind them. Skip looked between man and boy, boy and man. Honza offered her his usual foolish grin, as if he thought she'd been joking when she pushed him away. Nor did he seem surprised when his father, sadly perhaps, told him that it was time he should know the truth as well.

'Want to watch?' said Pavel.

Marlo shook her head. In a dream she had let herself be led to the Land Rover. She shivered, although Pavel's arm lay around her shoulders. He helped her into the passenger seat and she slumped back, gulping in air. Vaguely she had been aware of Mrs Novak calling after them – 'Pavel! Pavel!' – and Pavel not turning back, leaving his mother to Mr Brooker.

Bright eruptions filled the sky as they drove out of the parking lot. They turned down Volcano Street. On Show Saturday, the main drag was quiet, almost deserted. Marlo wondered how Pavel could stand her. 'You must hate me. I'm so stupid. And there I was, thinking I was special.'

'You are special. I always knew that.'

'Just a stupid girl with a crush on a teacher.'

'Brooker's a bastard,' Pavel said hotly. 'Dad should fight him. If he had any guts, he would.'

'Your father knows?' said Marlo.

'Sure does. She's done this kind of thing before.'

Streets passed, passed; between the flaring rockets, night pressed around them like purple velvet. Where could they go? Home was impossible. Home did not exist. They were strangers in the land.

Their destination was inevitable.

Marlo perched in the Land Rover while Pavel, at the glass doors, fumbled with his keys. The courtyard looked larger than during the day, a concrete wasteland under jaundiced streetlight. Black windows gleamed like pools that would leap with sudden light at the impact of a stone.

Pavel opened a jangling door and Marlo carefully, as if it might be dangerous, left the Land Rover at last. She followed him inside. 'We'd better not turn on the front lights,' he was saying.

In darkness, Puce Hardware was a cave of looming half-seen shapes: rakes, brooms, coiling serpentine garden hoses, curving bottles and cans that winked in fugitive light. The hardware smell seemed stronger: linoleum, bristly dry wood, acrid chemical pungencies of glue, paint, varnish. Marlo stumbled into a bank of boxes.

'Give me your hand.' Pavel's palm was warm. Unerringly he lifted the flap in the counter and tugged her through the rustling curtain of streamers into the office. He flipped on the desklamp; in the burnished glow, the room looked surprisingly comfortable with its faded floral curtains tied back in soft folds, its chocolate-brown telephone like a sleepy tortoise.

'Drink? Doug's got his secret stash,' said Pavel, and he bent down behind the big desk, opened a drawer, and produced a bottle of Bell's.

'Can we really stay here?' said Marlo.

'In Puce Hardware? Best range of camping gear in the Lakes. Ground sheets. Sleeping bags.'

'Why do I get the feeling you've done this before?'

Pavel poured Bell's into enamel mugs. He sat on the edge of Uncle Doug's desk; Marlo took the room's single easy chair. Stuffing burst from the chair's splitting arm like wool freshly shorn; she pulled out a skein. The room smelled of vinyl, smoke, musty paper. With the desklamp behind him, Pavel's hair leaped with orange fire. Soft-eyed, he gazed at her.

'I've never drunk whisky.' She took the mug.

'It's good. After the first taste.'

The burn in her throat was thrilling. Through the curtains came the muffled swish of cars. Show Saturday was over at last. Above the door, a clock ticked, loud against the quietness like a time bomb counting down.

A shudder passed through Marlo. It wasn't just the whisky. 'I've lost my koala.' Tears caught in her throat. 'That's the sort of thing I do, you see. You know, my koala, the one you won. I've left it at the ball. I can see it there, with its silly little snub nose and the ribbon round its neck, sitting in a corner on a foldout chair. Paws outstretched. Waiting. For me.' She covered her face. 'Christ, I'm so ashamed. How could I make such a fool of myself?'

'Hey.' Pavel slipped off the desk and kneeled before her. 'How many times do I make a fool of myself? Every bloody time I open my mouth.'

'I thought Howard was queer.' Angrily, Marlo brushed away her tears. 'In the beginning, I mean. I told myself we'd be friends, the best of friends. The play was just the beginning. He talked about London, New York, Berlin. I thought I'd go too. How sophisticated our lives would be! We'd be liberated. Artists. Radicals. We'd both have affairs and laugh about them. That's what I dreamed about. Stupid girl. And now I've ruined everything.'

'He's just a teacher.' Pavel gripped her hands.

'Why are you so kind to me?' said Marlo. 'I'm a bitch. And I'll go crazy, like my mother.'

'You're beautiful,' he said.

Tick, went the time bomb. Tick. Tick.

What would Germaine do? Marlo didn't know. Which one it was who drew forward first, neither could have said. The kiss, when it happened, was long and deep. Marvelling, Marlo reached up, gripping Pavel's frothing head. She slipped out of the chair. His arms enfolded her tightly. She sank and sank into a dark enthralling warmth.

She laughed. 'You *have* done this before, haven't you?'

They spread the sleeping bags on the office floor.

Skip had no questions. There had been too many questions. Answers would come; she only had to wait. Scrubby vegetation slid by the car, flashing green-grey in the sweeping pallid headlights. Honza snored lightly on the back seat.

Mr Novak spoke of the past. His voice was gentle. Once, he said, he lived with his father, mother and three brothers in Bohemia in a town called Pardoo-bitzer. He spoke of the cobbled town square, and the big gloomy church, and crazy goggle-eyed Uncle Yarn whose head grew bright red and swelled enough to burst when he drank too much becherovka; he spoke of train journeys into Prague in winter, three hours in a steamy compartment, sweeping a woolly sleeve across the window to look at the white world passing. In Australia, Mr Novak had always missed the snow. Soon it would be Christmas. Oh, for a Czech Christmas! The sharp frozen journey to midnight mass. Long stripy socks pinned expectantly over the hearth. The carp in the bathtub, flicking blackly back and forth, until Uncle Yarn in red festive braces came stomp-a-stomp down the hall, clashing together long knives that sounded like a swordfight in an old film.

The Valiant swung around the curve of the lakes. Honza stirred but did not wake. The boy had fallen asleep almost immediately after clambering into the car. Sometimes, thought Skip, he is much younger than me.

Mr Novak said he had wanted, when he grew up, to be an engineer and live in Prague. But even as a boy he knew his plans were idle. We think we are free but are constrained on every side: we do only what history lets us do. He spoke of the war, the occupation, and the bleak years afterwards when Czechoslovakia, abandoned first to Hitler, was abandoned again to Stalin. But what, after all, was Czechoslovakia, this cobbled-together country, this tattered rag of the Austro-Hungarian empire? You turned. You ran. You did not look back. Czechoslovakia was barbed wire and machine guns. But in dreams Vlad Novak walked the streets of Prague again: the golden city, castle on high, with the Vltava below, tumbling green and deep beneath its medieval bridges. The river dazzles and the castle flashes as the sun sinks behind far-off hills. Do not imagine it is always winter there. What wouldn't he give to run again through a cornfield in Bohemia in the tender burgeoning summer?

Vladislav Novak had been a student in Prague when the Russian tanks rolled in, a thin young man with, yes, hair like a frothing test tube who smoked too much and bit his nails to the quick. In time, his escape would seem unreal to him, a story he had heard about another man. Many times that other man had thought he would be killed. Russians with machine guns patrolled the border. Did he kill one? More than one? Maybe he did. When he made it to the refugee centre in West Germany, he was starved and half-mad. He wondered when they had decided to send him to Australia. Was he told? Did he agree? But here he was and a lifetime had passed. Never again would he see the golden city.

The rhythm of the car made Skip sleepy too. What happened next unfolded as in a dream, with a dream's inevitability. Mr Novak's voice had become quieter as his story went on. When they turned off the road he fell silent.

The Valiant drew to a halt. A grassy verge lay silver under the moon. Before them, the veranda sagged wide like a ruined dark mouth. Skip heard the squeal of a door opening, as if in response to the crunch of tyres. She looked at Mr Novak and he smiled as if to say: Go. You must. The figure that awaited her stood, half-revealed, on the edge of darkness and light. Of course Skip had seen him before: Vincent Price. But that was not his name.

'You know who he is, don't you?'

Skip thought of a picture she had seen, a boy on a tennis court, heartbreaking in his youthful vigour, racquet ready to slam back a serve in a world lost in time. He was the leading light of the Players, the name scratched out from the honour roll at the high: 1948 – NO AWARD.

Roger Dansie. Ghost of Crater Lakes.

# Chapter Fourteen

Marlo looked at Pavel for a long time. She had watched him while he slept; now he had woken but remained silent, gazing at her. How deep his eyes were, how dark! His lips were lovely, too. With a smile, she tousled his curly head. 'Puce Hardware is a rotten place to sleep.'

'I'll never make you sleep here again.'

'Maybe I'll have to.' She kissed him playfully. Sunlight pressed between the curtains, sparkling on curling covers of *Pix* and the green chipped filing cabinets that had stood guard all night beside the camping gear.

Marlo stretched; her dark hair tumbled into her eyes. She wore Pavel's shirt from the night before, buttons undone. He pulled her down again. Some time passed before she broke free.

Today, she decided, must be a great day. 'Let's not go home. I can't bear it. Not yet.'

'We don't have to,' said Pavel.

'Remember our picnic? That day at the swimming hole. It should have been perfect and I ruined everything. If only we could have that day again.'

'Why not? It's warm. It's the weekend.' Pavel was on his feet at once, tugging on his dishevelled clothes; he had already, some time earlier, stripped the shirt from Marlo's back. He bundled together the camping gear and returned the whisky bottle to its hiding place. By the time Marlo appeared beside him, flicking back her hair in the mirror over the sink, he had washed out the enamel mugs.

Morning was almost over. Sun splashed Marlo's pale arms and her hair whipped back and forth in dark ropes as the Land Rover whirled away from Puce Hardware. Happily she watched Pavel. His stubbled chin gave him a raffish air. He had pushed back his shirtsleeves; muscles tautened in his veiny brown forearms as he spun the wheel, veering off Volcano Street.

Not until Puce's Bend was upon them did she realise he was driving the wrong way. They passed the abandoned service station. 'Hey!' she protested. 'What's the idea?'

'Picnic time, ain't it? There's tons of stuff back home. Quick raid and we'll be off.' They passed the blowhole and rounded the grassy corner.

Marlo waited apprehensively in the Land Rover while Pavel went into the Novak house. The white walls and picture windows flared in the sunlight. The house, to her relief, looked no more alive than Auntie Noreen's or the service station. Death might have descended on Puce's Bend.

Magpies cawed. The paddocks across the road smelled brisk and ripe. Marlo's fears subsided. So what if Deirdre Novak came charging out of the house, intent on vengeance for the night before? Nothing could touch Marlo Wells.

She remembered a time before Skip was born when Karen Jane had lived with an eccentric older man, a librarian, in the Adelaide Hills. To Marlo, the memory of his cottage would always be vivid: the rag mat in front of the big stony fireplace where she lay on cold days, leafing through *Pickwick* and *Alice* and *Mr Sponge's Sporting*

*Tour*, loving the pictures long before she could understand the words; the bed where she slept in an attic under the eaves; the overgrown garden with the swing that hung off-kilter from an enormous peeling bluegum. Karen Jane in those days was still a mere girl, but Marlo remembered her as more of a mother then than later: a matronly figure in a gingham shift, beating a mixing bowl in a shaft of morning light. In the afternoons they walked, hand in hand, down a bark-strewn unpaved road towards the closest shops, in a hamlet two miles away. Often not a single car would pass; the silence was deep, but for the wind in the leaves, the tickerings of insects, the high crazed cries of cockatoos and kookaburras; and Marlo, looking up at her beautiful young mother, golden in sunshine, felt a certainty that everything was all right: everything, she was sure, would always be all right. If only the librarian could have been Marlo's father. But he was Skip's. Marlo's father, she knew, had been some boy who drove a delivery van.

When Pavel came back, Marlo laughed, and he asked her what was funny. He was, of course! Struggling with that hamper, he looked like Norman Wisdom.

'Anyone home?' Marlo asked as Pavel gunned the motor.

'Quiet as a tomb. No Honza. No Dad.'

Pavel's face was calm, untroubled. He wasn't lying, not exactly, but thought it best to say nothing. Inside, he had raided first the pantry, then the fridge, then moved on to the wine rack, when Howard Brooker had ambled out to the kitchen in a pair of purple jockey shorts. Coppery hair fanned across his nipples and scudded down his torso in a wispy line. Scrawny! He scratched an armpit, murmured a greeting. Pavel, as if unconcerned, arranged his bounty in the hamper: fried chicken, mushroom casserole, Edam, Gouda, claret, homemade bread. Cutlery? Check. Plates? Check. Glasses and napkins. Not a haul like last time's, but not bad.

Brooker attempted, 'Who said you could take that?'

Brooker, the man of the house? 'I said.' Pavel stepped towards him and Brooker stepped back. Huh! The bastard was frightened. Pavel snorted. He could knock the bugger down.

Mrs Novak's voice rang down the hall. 'Howie? Are you coming back to bed?'

Howie! Pavel had pushed him in the chest.

Marlo's heart swelled as they approached Dansie's Pond. They had to play the scene again and play it right. Lemony light between the leaves. The heat. The sun-spangled water, held as in a chalice, a promise that had been kept. There could be no holding back. Strip off. Fling clothes into branches. Plunge with Pavel into glassy green. Cry out, exhilarated, as he thrashes after you, a friendly assailant. Spray dashes, dashes, mercury-bright. Then calm: calm. Round and round in a whir of green, sun red through closed eyelids. Bright, so bright. If this is eternity, all there is or can be, that will be enough.

He's here again. Revolve, lips together, in the still centre. Sun dazzles, dazzles. His tongue plunging deep and the strange column of flesh (I am desired: a man desires me) pressing against her under the water. Fingers on nipples, smoothly rough. Tug him to the bank. Laugh. Who would believe it? The boy next door turns out to be the one. He carries condoms in his wallet. He has done this before. But after last night, so has she.

Rug on the ground. Tartan. Red, yellow, black.

Later, half-dressed, they sprawled beside the picnic basket. The fried chicken had vanished, the mushroom casserole too. Idly they ate Edam, Gouda, and ripped off chunks of crusty bread. They talked about everything and nothing. Marlo had read *Lady Chatterley's Lover* and told Pavel the story.

'Reckon you'd better lend me that book,' he said.

'No,' she said, 'we'll just act it out.' Tipping up her claret glass, she felt the liquid sliding down her throat.

What made her say what she said next?

'I'm wondering about you. What will become of you.'

'Become?'

'You can't stay here.'

'In the Lakes?' Pavel wore only his jeans; his chest was bare and glistened, biscuit-brown. Fingers traced a seam of her crumpled dress. Go on, Marlo: take those fingers in your own.

'You and me,' he said, 'we're real different, ain't we?'

'Stay here and what will happen to you? You're smart, Pavel.'

'Me? I'm the bloke in that book of yours. The gamekeeper.'

'You're smart,' she said again. 'And here you are fetching and carrying for Uncle Doug. Bowing and scraping to Auntie Noreen. It can't go on. You've got to get away.'

I've made him sad, she thought. Say no more.

She said more. 'Look at the men in this town. Doug Puce. Sandy Campbell.'

'They're not all like that. There's Dad.'

'And what does he do? He had ambition once, but he got trapped in Crater Lakes. Look at him: a clerk at the town hall. I suppose he makes out bills for council rates. Collects parking fines. Issues fishing permits. And the rest of the time he's under Deirdre's thumb. That's no life for a man.'

Pavel looked out from the shade towards the sun. Reddish high walls cupped the bright pond like benevolent hands. His next words came to Marlo as if in a dream. At first, she could not believe he had spoken them at all. 'Don't worry, I'll be gone soon. Got me call-up papers, didn't I? Last week.'

Slowly, horror rose like bile in her throat. 'You can't go.'

'I have to.' His tone was firm. 'I can and will.'

She took a breath, then said, too calmly, 'You can't believe in this war.'

'It's what I have to do.'

'And Barry?' Stop, Marlo. Stop.

'It was good enough for Baz. He did his bit.'

Her next words were a whisper. 'You're stupid!'

'Don't call me that.' Pavel sprang up, spilling claret over the rug. Trees, thick and tangled, stretched away into green shadows. Jutting above the water, rockily defiant, was the Jump. He pounded up the scrubby track.

'Pavel!' Why call? Why, when you made him go?

His dive was clumsy, the splash cracking sharply as a stone against glass. Birds rose raucously into dazzling azure.

Marlo's tears were bitter. I'm a bitch, a crazy bitch.

Silence gathered again. And gathered. Unsteadily, she stood and moved to the edge of the pond. Brightness everywhere. Gold on green. The sky above, an infinity. Oh, Pavel! Stop playing this game. She couldn't say it aloud.

She didn't know why she followed him to the Jump. On the path she stumbled; grazed her shin as she clambered over boulders; pushed back coarse greyish sprays of leaves until she stood, swaying, on the brittle tongue of rock, taking in the pond from on high. See that line round the red walls? Summer a-coming. Level's gone down.

'Pavel?' Now she spoke aloud; sky and rock and water spiralled in her gaze as vertigo claimed her. Terrified, she stepped back. The world shuddered, scraping on its axis. She said Pavel's name again, cried it out this time. Mockingly, her cries rebounded from the rocks.

In that moment a stranger erupted from the trees. Marlo barely had time to see the tall sinewy man, casting off his shirt and throwing it behind him, before he crashed into the pond from the shore below. He might have been a vision: for a moment there, then gone. Only the churning water told her he was real.

Her heart was a tympani booming in her ears. She clutched her arms about her and shivered, consumed by love and fear as the stranger broke the surface, floundering with Pavel back to shore.

As her lover lay on his back, so far away, his breathing laboured, all she could do was watch, until at last he rose on his elbows, turned on his side, and spluttered water.

The stranger looked up at Marlo and smiled: a large man, a handsome man. His age was hard to tell. Heroes in old films looked that way: dark hair, square jaw, torso tight but pale, almost ghostly beside Pavel's brown skin.

'We were out walking and heard him dive. Dangerous, at this time of year.' The voice behind Marlo was kindly, and one she knew well.

Turning, she almost lost her footing, but a grip steadied her, and drew her away from the edge of the Jump. Dazedly, she let herself be embraced. 'I don't understand,' she said and pulled away.

'Let's go up to the house. Your sister's there,' Mr Novak said.

That was the beginning of the family of the heart.

There were seven of them at the old Dansie house: Mr Novak, who had long known the house's secret; Skip and Honza, Marlo and Pavel, outcasts of a kind who had found a place to go; and the two who had lived there all along. Black Jack, or Jack, was not retarded at all, and the man Skip had thought of as Vincent Price was no monster, madman or murderer.

When she first arrived, Roger Dansie led her down a corridor, waved a pale wrist and said, 'This room can be yours.' She marvelled, as if reality had given way to a story she longed to hear. The rooms with their wormy panelling, their shabby curtains and hangings, their watchful ancient portraits, had lost their original glamour long ago, yet magic lingered in every one. Jack, with Mr Novak, had tried over recent years to fix up the place, stripping wallpaper, painting, cleaning windows; with new inhabitants to help, these efforts were redoubled. Pavel was often to be seen up a ladder, scraper in hand, in a room littered with papery leaves, or on hands and knees, replacing rotted floorboards. Somehow, though, little really changed. A few small rooms were papered brightly, fresh paint mingled with the smells of mould, but it seemed to Skip that the shabbiness was forever creeping back, reversing any changes as soon as they had been made. She didn't mind.

Life at the old Dansie house during that heady strange November was like nothing she had experienced before. 'Know what a commune is?' Marlo asked her one day. They sat on the veranda, looking towards the outbuildings. 'That's what we've got here.' Skip stroked the big orange cat she called Mowser. Roger Dansie called him Purcell. 'We're a family,' said Marlo. 'All of us.'

In the evenings, Mr Novak cooked elaborate meals on the huge wood-fired range; nights were filled with laughter, wine (Skip, hating the taste, had lemonade instead), and the din of an old piano. Roger Dansie sang in a creamy tenor; Mr Novak played. Their songs were old, ballads from before time began, but to Skip the tunes did not seem corny as they did in the hands of Bert Noblet's Rhythm Stompers. Roger crooned 'Some Enchanted Evening', and she thought: That's tonight.

Their world was not enclosed. Every day Marlo and Pavel went to work at Puce Hardware, and Mr Novak to the town hall. Skip and Honza were still in school, but all that happened there – the bickering, the fights, the interminable lessons – seemed trivial when they knew that once the last bell rang they would disappear to their haunted house. Since the Show, they had lived in a world apart. After Lummo's humiliation, his gang had broken up. It might never have existed. Skip and Honza, to their amazement, were free.

Marlo, meanwhile, had defeated Auntie Noreen. That first Sunday evening, after Roger had saved him from the pond, Pavel drove the girls and his brother back to Puce's Bend to collect their things. While the boys repaired to the Novak house, Marlo, with Skip hovering, faced their aunt in her living room. Doug Puce, with the blank doleful face of a man responsible for nothing, who has never been responsible, had shown them in before retreating to his shed.

Auntie Noreen languished in darkness but for the flicker of the television screen. Wrappers littered the sofa and the carpet around it: Twisties, Mars Bars, Smith's Crisps; on a plate on the tea table lay a solitary lamington, its survival a small miracle. The room stank of sweat and stale air.

'You can't take Helen.' Auntie Noreen almost sobbed. 'Not Helen.'

Marlo was magnificent. 'Scandal travels quickly in a small town. We know what you've done. And if you don't want the world to know about you and a certain coach driver, you won't make a fuss.'

Auntie Noreen rallied, but feebly. Her voice was weak and her little eyes darted about her in fear. On the mantelpiece, Barry Puce still smiled politely in the killer's uniform that had killed him in the end.

'Oh, Marlene! You should be in the nuthouse like your mother. She's never coming back – you know that, Helen? I've talked to them doctors! No more crazy letters, I told them. It's not fair, upsetting them poor kiddies. There's no hope this time, they told me. She's gone right off the deep end. Now, Helen, your sister's going the same way. What rubbish has she been filling your head with? I suppose she's taking you to America too.'

'I'm taking her away from here,' said Marlo.

'And last night? Both of yous was out all night! I was frantic. Did yous even think about that?'

They had not. The television blared out a talent-quest diva's murderous assault on 'Try a Little Kindness' as Auntie Noreen grabbed the last lamington and stuffed it into her mouth. When she spoke again, cake crumbs spilling down her smelly muu-muu, she was almost crying.

'Out of my sight, Marlene,' she said. 'Go. You're old enough to leave school. Old enough to be a slut like your mother. Old enough to throw yourself at that poofter schoolteacher and God knows who else. I found them books in your room – Greer Garson, with filth on every page! Go to hell, Marlene, and see if I care. But you're not taking Baby Helen. I won't let you.'

'I'm taking her. You can't do a thing.'

'I loved your mum, would yous believe that? Loved her like she was me own daughter, not me little sis.' Tears sprang to Auntie Noreen's eyes. She snuffled loudly. 'Lovely, Kazza was, when she was Baby Helen's age. But Baby Helen won't end up like her. You're too far gone already, Marlene. I wash me hands of you. But not Baby Helen.'

Marlo stared back, unmoved. Uselessly, Auntie Noreen called for Uncle Doug. He didn't come.

'You won't do this, Marlene.' Sobbing freely now, Auntie Noreen sank into the sofa cushions. 'You won't. I'll find out where you've took her. I'll get Marky Bonner on you. You're crazy, every bit as crazy as your bloody bitch of a mum. You should be locked up – locked up, you hear?'

From the doorway, Skip looked back at their aunt and felt sorry for her. If only she could comfort her! We feel sympathy for evildoers, Skip realised, only when they are broken – and Noreen Puce, with her dead son, her foetid living room, her food, her fat, her mad sister, her loveless husband skulking in his shed, had been broken utterly. Marlo, impatient, pulled Skip away.

Applause thundered from the television: time for the scoring.

Skip was awed by the change in her sister.

'Are you doing what Germaine would do?' she asked her one evening as they walked in the woods behind the old Dansie house. Nearly a week had passed since they left Auntie Noreen's and nothing had happened: no Uncle Doug come to drive them home, no Marky Bonner brandishing a warrant. Auntie Noreen must have given up. They were free.

'There's Pav,' Marlo said. 'And my exams have gone to hell.'

Skip ventured, 'What's it like with Pav?'

'What's what like?' Marlo sounded amused, not embarrassed. That afternoon she had vanished with Pavel for a long drive in the country. Skip wanted to ask if they were 'doing it' but didn't dare. Should she envy her sister? She wasn't sure she did. Marlo and Pavel were different – they had to be – from Auntie Noreen and Sandy Campbell. But it was confusing. Honza, treading water one day in Dansie's Pond, had gestured to the bank where the lovers lay sunbathing and said, grinning, 'You and me next?' Skip squealed and ducked him viciously.

Marlo plucked pine needles. 'It's only for a while.'

Skip, puzzled, asked her what she meant, but Marlo would say no more. Baskerville chased Mowser through the gathering dark. Skip called the dog. As much as she admired her newly reckless sister, often she missed Marlo as she used to be. The little room they had shared in Glenelg. Saturdays at the Ozone. Walks on the beach, tossing stones into the waves. The days when they were younger, years younger.

For all their splendid days and nights at the old Dansie house, life was far from perfect for the family of the heart. Uncle Doug seemed not to mind what his employees got up to when they were not at work, but others minded very much. Vicious looks and whispers followed Marlo, Pavel, and all the members of the commune whenever they passed down Volcano Street. Mr Novak's masters at the town hall gave him notice. There were darker threats, too. One night a gang surrounded the house, howling and shrieking; they tried to break in, then rained rocks on the roof. Skip and Honza were sure they were kids from school, but in the dark they could see no faces. Pavel, charging around to scare the gang off, found Jack sprawled in the drive; a gash bled above his left eye, and he limped when Skip helped him stand.

'Who did it?' she demanded, ready to vow revenge.

'Oh, love!' the old man said and laughed. 'The whole town.'

Sometimes Skip came upon Roger Dansie standing motionless at a window. He would look down at her as if surprised she was there, this small strange girl who had appeared in his house. There was something stricken about him, but Skip never thought him broken like Auntie Noreen; flashes of life, bright enough to burn, were evident when he was singing, when he was swimming, when he ran across the yard, pursuing the cat he had called Purcell.

One day Skip asked Mr Novak, 'Will he hide out here for ever?'

Mr Novak, who had not been back to his wife's house since the Show Ball, was stirring a strong-smelling sauce. Solemnly he laid down his wooden spoon. 'I was working late at the town hall one night when I found Roger haunting the midnight streets. I suppose that was three or four years ago now. He fled from me, but I was patient. Months later I spied him again; this time Jack was driving him away in the Harley-Davidson sidecar. After that, of course, I knew the truth. Roger was frightened when I first confronted him. He thought I wanted to expose him. I would never do that, but I asked him your question, Skip. He says it's a matter of time. He wants to reveal himself to Crater Lakes again. More than once he's said it's time to come out of the shadows. I've walked the streets at night, he says; soon, I'll walk in the day. Oh, it's not so strange as you might think,' Mr Novak added, as if Skip had spoken. 'Poor Roger! He was so happy in this town as a boy. And so unhappy after he went away.'

Late afternoon brightness glinted on the wood, black metal and cracked white tiles of the big colonial kitchen. Skip, daring at last, said, 'What did he do? Tell me the truth, Mr Novak. Please.'

The big balding man had picked up his knife; he laid it down again, evidently moved, and gripped the benchtop. 'When I arrived in the Lakes,' he said, his voice distant, 'I worked as a gardener. Every Saturday I went to Mayor Gull's house at Puce's Bend. The house was different then, before Deirdre had it rebuilt: old and dark.

But it's where I met Roger. He was kind to me, the only person in the Lakes who was. You should have seen him then! So friendly. So handsome. Always joking, eyes shining. He asked me about Prague; he even knew where it was. I'd been unwell and he helped me in my garden work. One day in Volcano Street, a gang of high school boys surrounded me, calling me names. I was so thin back then they could have knocked me down with a finger. And they did. Roger swept down on his Harley –'

'Jack's?' said Skip. 'Jack's bike?'

'In those days it was red. Jack painted it black after Roger left it to him.'

'Left it? Roger's not dead.'

'Oh, but in a manner of speaking –' Mr Novak broke off. 'Here, chop these carrots. And don't cut yourself. Roger picked me up from beside the road, you see. After he'd chased off those boys. He was my friend then.'

'Tell me more.' To Skip, the need was urgent. But only slowly, over days and weeks, did she piece together the story of Roger Dansie. That November, much was never said. There were things she picked up as if by osmosis; things she saw at first imperfectly which only later came into clear view; and things, no doubt, she made up for herself. That is how we understand the past.

# Chapter Fifteen

Roger Dansie was famous in Crater Lakes. At seventeen he was a man in most respects, six feet tall with his chip-of-azure eyes and hero's jawline gleaming from the razor. He was school champion in swimming and tennis and star attraction of the Crater Lakes Players; local matrons, and not a few girls, jostled for his autograph after his remarkable turn as Stanhope in *Journey's End*. The Lakes had never seen the like. Picture him roaring down Volcano Street on his red Harley-Davidson, goggles flashing, gloved hands gunning the throttle. To ride in the sidecar was the ambition of every girl at the high. Few did so more than once; there was Deirdre Gull, of course, the mayor's daughter, but she was a special case.

The Dansies had been kings of Crater Lakes since settlement began. Lately, though, the family star had fallen. Roger's father had been a surly fellow whose sole delights were betting on horses, drinking, and thrashing Jack, the Aboriginal servant who more than once had saved his master from prison, brawls and car crashes. Nothing, it seemed, would tame Arthur Dansie. He squandered his fortune. He sold off land. Often at dawn, with red light spilling over the dewy outer paddocks, he paced his crumbling kingdom, stride purposeful, head down, as if he believed he could escape himself. His three older brothers had died in the Great War. Arthur used to say he should have died too.

News of Arthur's marriage had caused a sensation in the Lakes. The girl was a McKirtle, from the Melbourne suburb of Toorak, then and now one of Australia's most prestigious addresses. Dawn McKirtle was a lovely blonde fey thing who played the cello dramatically and dressed, disregarding both fashion and common sense, in flowing gowns of a type she termed 'Pre-Raphaelite'. She was a cousin of Mr Quentin Phelps, a schoolteacher who had arrived only recently at the high; Miss McKirtle had been visiting him in the Lakes when Arthur Dansie, in one of his many attempts at reform, spied her at a Presbyterian service.

The marriage at first appeared idyllic. The girl, townsfolk said, had tamed Arthur Dansie. Some said he worshipped her. No more did he tear into town for the six o'clock swill. The birth of his son was greeted with toasts all over the district. The Dansie dynasty would continue! And yet, as months and years passed, rumour had it that all was not as well as it had first seemed. Arthur Dansie still paced the paddocks at dawn, Jack had a broken arm, and a big new chunk of family land had been placed on the books with Elder's.

Dawn McKirtle, who looked younger than her years, had given up all hope of marriage before Arthur doffed his hat to her on the church porch that Sunday. 'Your bloom has lasted,' her Aunt Evadne used to say, 'but it can't much longer. Then where will you be?' Her niece could never have guessed the answer: Crater Lakes! A big shadowy house miles from town! When the first blissful days of marriage had passed, she began to wonder, only half fancifully, if Arthur Dansie possessed hypnotic powers.

Before her marriage, Dawn's life had been lived through poetry, art, theatre. In Toorak, she looked down from the iron-lace balcony and imagined herself as the Lady of Shalott. But Crater Lakes was another prison, and no saviour would come. Aunt Evadne, in spiteful spidery handwriting, informed her niece that she had made her bed and must lie in it. Quentin Phelps had been ardent for the marriage – he was such a snob, and the Dansies were top drawer; later, when his cousin reposed in him certain confidences which might have alarmed others, he dismissed them airily. Phelps was a prim, fastidious fellow who wrinkled his nose at the sordid things in life. The girl had always been highly strung.

Dawn Dansie despaired. Bruises like ink marked her pale skin. Soon Arthur's farm truck tore into town again. What did his mates say, down at the Federal? 'Hoo, boyo! Knew you'd be back.' She sat at home and read Tennyson and made Jack sit with her. Fascinated, she watched his velvety black hands poised uncertainly over the curving chair arms. 'You're the only one who loves me,' she declared, defying all shame. When Arthur found her in the drawing room with the abo, he whipped off his belt and thrashed them both.

Love has to go somewhere. Dawn Dansie's flowed into her son. 'Do what you like with me,' she told Arthur. 'But lay a finger on Roger and I'll kill you.' Her husband grumbled and let the brat alone. He was hers anyway: delicate, ethereal, hardly a fit heir for the king of Crater Lakes.

To the boy, his mother was from the first an object of wonder. He loved her as much as he hated and feared his father. How he revered her cello, her gowns, her hands with their delicate tracery of veins, blue beneath the pale unfreckled skin. What times they had: she would play a princess while he stood to attention at the bottom of the stairs, staring up amazed as she made her way down. Sunlight through the landing window danced on her jewels and they dazzled him. One day, he vowed, he would take her away. They would live a life in which their dreams became real. Naturally, the boy must perform for her in turn, striding through scene after scene from Shakespeare: Hamlet, Othello, Richard III. When he was alone, he would turn the pages of a musty *Complete Works*, conning famous speeches as if they were prayers. Jack had built a theatre in one of the barns: raised stage, footlights, red rep curtains that opened and closed. Each time Roger performed, his mother would applaud as if he were the greatest actor of the age.

One night she made her husband watch too. 'What is he, a boy or a girl?' Arthur Dansie raged, as his son pranced about in a tunic. He stormed out of the barn, and Dawn, as he did so, laughed and laughed, encouraging her son to laugh as well. Later that night, Arthur took out his anger on his crazy wife. The bitch had locked her bedroom door, but he smashed his way through. 'It's my house!' he cried, while Roger, cowering under the stairs, did his best to cover his ears. It did no good: he heard too much, terrible things that told him, once and for all, that his father was a monster, and his mother a saint and martyr.

Tactlessly, Dawn Dansie informed her few visitors – wives of local worthies, who felt obliged – that her little boy was the one light in her otherwise benighted existence. Driving away, the wives shook their heads. Hadn't they said that girl was peculiar? And the sight of her! Hair stringy, a hectic flush on her cheeks, dark half-moons under her nails. And that dirty abo! She makes him serve tea! Visitors grew fewer, then trailed off almost entirely. In business circles, word had it that Arthur was in hock up to his eyeballs.

Meanwhile, Dawn Dansie still dreamed of a better life. She decided to be frank with Quentin Phelps. Her cousin, after all, had his merits. At the high, he taught Shakespeare; as a young man, he had spent a year in London. And Aunt Evadne, his mother, had died recently, leaving him a small legacy.

'My son cannot remain here all his life,' Dawn Dansie said. Already, infancy lay behind him. Birthdays passed: seven, eight, nine. How quickly children grow! 'Crater Lakes? Such a stage is too small for him. Of course, I have taught him what I know of art and culture.'

Phelps nodded. They had listened to the boy recite Adam Lindsay Gordon; now he sat across the tea table, pouting at the carpet. A pretty boy. His hair was neatly brushed. He was always dressed immaculately.

'What I want for my son is a Continental tour. Imagine: La Scala. The Louvre. Covent Garden.' Dawn Dansie, as it happened, could imagine none of this: Melbourne, Crater Lakes, and the railway line that linked them marked the limits of her world. 'Naturally, we would need a guide,' she added, and lay back in her creaking chair, attempting a coquetry which even she must have realised was years too late (and, as it happened, sadly misdirected).

Phelps, twisting his pinkish lips, looked like Aunt Evadne. Gently he asked his cousin if she knew what was going on in Europe. Of course she didn't. She didn't read the papers. There was no wireless in the old Dansie house. Attempts to enlighten her would be useless, he knew. The world outside was unreal to her; he had always known this, but still the extent of her ignorance took his breath away. Take, for example, this moment now. Sunlight played through dusty curtains, and the stringy pale woman dressed as Ophelia asked her cousin why he, with all his gifts, had chosen to remain in Crater Lakes.

'My mother never told you? Well, well. It seems she *could* keep a secret.'

War broke out three months later. To Dawn Dansie, it meant only one thing: no Continental tour. She was crushed, and only nodded blankly when Arthur, one bright evening, told her he had enlisted. His voice, to her surprise, was tender; she could almost have believed he was still the man she had married. He asked her if she and 'the lad' would be all right, but it seemed he had convinced himself that they would. There were things, he said, that a man had to do.

As he left for the last time, clumping down the veranda in heavy boots, Dawn Dansie saw him briefly as the young man who had doffed his hat to her so many years earlier. Oh, but she had loved him! She loved him still; and when, as she knew it would, the news arrived of his death, she howled with a sorrow nothing could allay. Some weeks later, she dived into the swimming hole they called Dansie's Pond. It was high summer, and the water was low.

'Sad,' said the ladies of the Lakes. 'But a mercy.'

And merciful, all agreed, was the fate of the orphaned boy. Who was to look after him? Quentin Phelps, that's who – most popular teacher at Crater Lakes High! Quentin Phelps, coach of the Magpies, president of the Lions Club, personal friend of Mayor Arch L. Gull. Many times Mayor Gull had said that Mr Phelps brought a valuable perspective to their little community. Fine fellow, Phelps. A man of the world. A man of vision. A man who made things happen. A mover and a shaker, that was Quentin Phelps.

The boy's inheritance – the big, sagging house with its shabby outbuildings – was left in the care of Jack, who many said was a rum sort, even for an abo. When Phelps and Mayor Gull arrived to take the boy, Jack clutched him for too long, standing in the driveway, and sobbed in a manner both unseemly and disgusting, until Mayor Gull felt compelled to intervene, pushing the snivelling blackie into the dirt. The boy, overwrought, kicked the mayor in the shins, and resisted vigorously as the two men bundled him into the back of the Baby Austin. The boy, twisting around at once, gazed longingly through the kidney-shaped rear window.

'He's young,' said Quentin Phelps, unalarmed, slapping the wheel decisively as they turned out of the drive. 'There's still time to bring my influence to bear.'

Some said Phelps made Roger what he was. The boy was twelve when he came to the schoolteacher's neat modern house on Lakeview South. There was talk of sulks and tantrums. In his first year at the high, Roger was shy, withdrawn, applying no effort. His second showed little improvement, but more than once he lashed out at another boy and had to be punished. In his third year, few noticed him; he blended in among myriad lanky youths bound for futures in farming or forestry. But all the time he was a creature in a chrysalis. The fey McKirtle looks had faded; something of his handsome, manly father showed first in his face, then his body.

Quentin Phelps displayed remarkable patience. The boy might have been his own son. The townsfolk noticed how often the kindly schoolteacher took Roger out in the Baby Austin. Saturday morning at the servo: 'Where yous off to, then?' the bloke at the pump would ask, and Phelps, in the demotic manly manner he adopted for the lower orders, boomed, 'Picnic up the lakes!' or 'Fishing, ain't we? What do you call them rods, jutting out the back?' Roger Dansie used to box at the Boys' Club, with Phelps, his coach and mentor, cheering from the sidelines. Urged on by Phelps, the boy played football, cricket, tennis; Phelps also formed the Crater Lakes Players, some said wholly to show off Roger's gifts.

Ladies who lived in the better streets of the Lakes, tinkling teacups, wondered sometimes why Mr Phelps had never married. Wasn't he in the prime of life? Fine figure of a man, though he had been rejected for military service. Flat feet, wasn't it? Heart murmur, you say? Still, it wasn't as if he offered the boy no taste of family life. Mr Phelps spent many an evening at Mayor Gull's house, which meant the boy did too. Mrs Gull spoiled him rotten, they said. Many a time she stroked his cheek and told him that one day he would be a great man.

It was during Roger's third year at the high that Phyllis Gull died. Cancer, one of the viciously female kinds, carried her away in a matter of months. But what months they were. Poor Phyllis had been devoted to the boy, and he had loved her in his turn. He was different once she was gone. And that awkward, not-quite-pretty daughter of hers! Roger, from the first, had been a brother to young Deirdre; indeed, it was his kindness to the girl, according to some reports, that led Mayor Gull and Mr Phelps to club together and present him with his splendid sixteenth-birthday gift: the red Harley-Davidson. Roger's time had come.

In the Players, his rise had been swift. Quentin Phelps, though gifted with the common touch, had aspirations to art. Often he spoke of his year in London, hinting at a theatrical career which, alas, had been thwarted. Now, in the Lakes, he would fulfil his dreams. A smash hit with *The Admirable Crichton* (the King Edward VII Theatre had been packed for two nights) led to more ambitious fare: Pinero, Shaw, O'Neill, even the Bard himself! In his last years at the high, Roger Dansie played the lead in every production. His talents stirred the Lakes to fever pitch. Was a star in their midst? Quentin Phelps said so.

It was early in Roger's matriculation year that the Old Vic Theatre Company from London made its legendary tour of Australia and New Zealand. The war was over, and here, as if to prove it, were Sir Laurence Olivier and his movie-star wife, Vivien Leigh, bearing beauty and culture to the dominions. Everywhere they went the Oliviers were received like royalty, but never so much as in these distant backwaters of the British Empire. Their journey across Australia was a conqueror's progress: Perth, Adelaide, Melbourne, Sydney. For a continent starved of glamour, here was Hollywood and the British aristocracy rolled into one. Thousands lined the pavements just to watch the Oliviers pass.

Sir Laurence told reporters he was looking for new talent. In those drab years after the war, the vast continent of Australia possessed almost no legitimate theatre and barely a handful of professional actors. But there were amateurs. There were aspirants. Now, in each state capital the tour passed through, Australia's young performers could audition for one of the greatest and most powerful figures in world theatre. It was the chance of a lifetime. The prize was a ticket to London, and professional training at the Old Vic Theatre School.

For Roger Dansie, the day he auditioned for Olivier in Adelaide was, he would realise later, the climax of his life. Nothing could be greater. He had climbed to a pinnacle and, afterwards, could only slip inexorably. Yet the triumph, at the time, seemed no triumph at all. It was a drizzly afternoon in April. Traffic hummed along North Terrace; above, in a fussy drawing room of the South Australian Hotel, sunlight played across gilt and plush and panelling and thick green fonds of ferns and picked out the boy as if in a spotlight. At a desk six feet away, with a sandy-haired male secretary at his side, Sir Laurence sat expectantly, twinkly-eyed. Royalty's duties need all an actor's skills. How many products of Adelaide Ladies' College had they seen that afternoon? How many Mrs Worthingtons had pushed forward their daughters? But this was different. Country boy, eh? Was he really only seventeen?

The moment had come. Roger glowered and assumed a twisted gait. Everything rode on this. Quentin Phelps had told him as much, squeezing the boy's shoulder hard enough to hurt when the secretary called his name. Not any old commoner got to see Sir Larry; Mayor Gull had gone out on a limb, pulling strings with a crony at Government House.

Roger breathed deeply. Deirdre, thrilled at the news of his audition, had told him last night over a crackling trunk line that she knew he would succeed: she simply knew it. He was brilliant. He blinked; sunlight flashed in his eyes, and suddenly he was back in Jack's theatre in the barn, the theatre his father had smashed up years ago in a drunken rage. 'Now is the winter of our discontent ...' Roger had known the speech for as long as he could remember. Did he even consider that Sir Larry, that very evening, would proclaim it from the stage of the Theatre Royal? Olivier's Richard III was the star turn of the Old Vic tour.

The great man sat forward, back bowed, fist pressed against tautened mouth, as cadence after cadence rolled richly towards him. Was he insulted? Was he suppressing mirth? Impossible to tell. Afterwards, in a belated rush of shame, Roger feared as much; and yet, the audition over, Olivier spoke to him for a minute or so in a manner friendly enough, then murmured to the sandy-haired secretary, who gave the boy two tickets to the Theatre Royal. That night, six rows back in the stalls, Roger writhed in anguish. Between the acts he snapped when Phelps pressed him for more details about the audition. What, precisely, had Sir Larry said? Nothing: 'Last year at school, eh? What sports do you play?' Then it had been over. Yes, Roger admitted, Olivier had said he would be in touch; but that, no doubt, was mere politeness. Roger had acted in front of Olivier; now Oliver had acted in front of Roger. What more was there to be said?

The Oliviers were on their way to Melbourne when they detoured to inspect the South Australian stable, deep in the verdant southeast of the state, which had seen the nativity of their friend Robert Helpmann, greatest male dancer of his generation. The Lakes lay nearby. Was it coincidence that a special assembly had been called that afternoon at the high school? Was it by chance that reporters from the city papers, Mayor Gull in his robes of office, all his courtiers, and many a lady of the Lakes in her finery happened to crowd the hall? Not unless chance led Sir Larry, with the lovely Viv beside him, to ascend the podium and proclaim in that richest of voices that he had witnessed much remarkable talent in South Australia and had been given many decisions to make. Now he had made them. Crater Lakes schoolboy Roger Dansie was to be offered a place at the Old Vic Theatre School. Cameras flashed like a lightning storm. Roger gasped at Quentin Phelps, at Mayor Gull, at Deirdre. They had known. They had all known except him. The applause, the stamping and cheering, almost brought down the ceiling of the school hall. He ascended the podium in a daze. Never again would his life be the same. Henry V had called him to arms. Scarlett O'Hara kissed his cheek.

* * *

School years in Australia, where summer comes at Christmas, run to a different schedule from those in England. Roger, Quentin Phelps decided, must cut short his matriculation year. What could he learn in Australia when England beckoned? He would sail in August.

The months of waiting were the headiest of his life. He was the Laurence Olivier of Crater Lakes. But how to celebrate him before he went away? At school, his name was placed on the honour roll, months before it otherwise would have been: '1948 – R. DANSIE', the letters picked out in glittering gold. What other triumph remained to this darling of the gods? Only one thing would suffice: a last exhibition of Roger's talents.

Quentin Phelps planned it all. The Players (had they not, collectively, been blessed by Olivier?) must mount their most ambitious production yet. What play? No mere spectacle! No matinee-idol flim-flam! Let Roger show the gravitas of a great classical actor, the genius that had left Sir Larry awed and envious. What role better, Phelps decided, than Dr Stockmann in Ibsen's *An Enemy of the People*? Never mind that the play was gloomy! The after-show party would bring joy enough. The crowds that flocked to the King Edward VII Theatre that night were every bit as enthusiastic as those who had turned out for Sir Larry and Scarlett O'Hara in Adelaide.

And yet one person was unhappy. Deirdre Gull had loved Roger for years. How could he treat her like a sister when soon he would be gone? Only in *Romeo and Juliet*, with the whole town watching, had he taken her in his arms. Couldn't he see the longing in her eyes? Of course, she knew what the problem was: Roger respected her. She was the mayor's daughter. He needed a sign, that was all. 'I'll give myself to you, Roger.' Yes, she could hear herself saying that. 'Afterwards, I'll wait until you come back.' Because he must. Must. For her.

Deirdre's role in his last performance was a disappointingly meagre one. Petra! Never would she forgive Quentin Phelps. Playing

Cleopatra, with Roger as Antony, Deirdre would soon enough have made their kisses real. Instead, Roger had to be a country doctor obsessed with drains, and she his drab daughter.

On the night of the performance she arrived at the theatre early. Her declaration could not wait. Roger's last appearance in Crater Lakes must be fuelled by her love. In the foyer she pushed back swinging doors. She made her way down a linoleum aisle. Soon every one of these leathery seats would squeak and crack under human weight. Bellowing, whoops, the slap-slap of meaty hands would surge like a tide about these boxes, these mouldings, this chandelier that burned with brownish wattage and would fade into darkness when the curtain rose. She climbed the steps at the side of the stage; she lifted her chin to the dress circle. Where, she used to ask her mother, had King Edward VII sat? (Nowhere, her mother said. He was never here.) She pushed through the curtains. Behind them, the light was reddish. Her footsteps echoed on the barren stage. Quickly she descended into backstage passages.

Roger, as star, had the only solo dressing room. It was empty. Night gleamed behind a small window. His costume hung darkly on a rack. On the bench before the mirror, among the brushes, the powder puffs, the pots of cream, lay a book he had been reading: Huxley, *Time Must Have a Stop*. Deirdre had given him that. A shabby screen, papered with press cuttings, covered one corner. The room smelled damp; bluish mould crawled up the walls. Was she a fool? She stared at herself in the mirror: a small girl, nut-brown, not pretty. Her lips moved, whispering the words that would change everything: 'I'll give myself to you, Roger.'

She started, hearing footsteps. Did she dare? She could stop it now: 'Oh, just come to wish you luck, Rog.' But no. Soon the red rep curtains would part. They must take the stage as lovers.

Voices. The doorknob turned.

In a flash, Deirdre had hidden behind the screen. The door closed.

Mr Phelps was speaking to Roger in a voice low and intent. Deirdre peered through the crack where the screen's hinges folded. Oh, what had she done? What would Mr Phelps think if he found her here? What would Roger? Shame burned in her like fever. Surely they must hear her heart pounding. She strained to hear their words.

'I knew it would end.' (Mr Phelps. He sounded sad.) 'I'm just sorry it's come so quick.'

'Oh, Quentin!' (Quentin?) 'Nothing's over.'

'You'll be back? Sure. But you'll have changed. You'll meet people, have experiences.'

'I hope so.' Roger laughed. He turned to the mirror, and Mr Phelps clutched him from behind.

Deirdre felt first confusion, then astonishment, and finally horror. Could what she was seeing be true? Here was Mr Phelps – their teacher! – running his fingers through Roger's hair; Roger turning into his embrace; Mr Phelps shuddering, sinking to his knees, fumbling with Roger's belt buckle … Pleasure filled Roger's face as he stood against the dressing table, heels of his hands planted each side of him, arching his neck, head dropping back.

Deirdre screamed. Had she, in that moment, been able to think at all, she might have hoped her cry would shatter the scene like a pane of glass. Instead came the flurry of bodies springing apart, and Quentin Phelps calling out her name as she flung herself out of the dressing room.

In the corridor, she collided with her father. The mayor, who was to give an introductory speech, wore his robes and chains of office; gasping, his daughter clattered into his arms. She sobbed and sobbed. He tried to hush her. Backstage was busy; the auditorium was filling; and here, skidding dishevelled from the dressing rooms … Quentin? Roger? What was this about?

In seconds, the truth had burst on the air. Why should Deirdre feel shame? With her eyes blazing, the plain girl gathered all her small strength and flung back at the guilty parties their depravity in raw shrieked words her shocked father could barely believe she knew.

Afterwards, Deirdre's recollection of what happened next came in indistinct flashes, like a fever dream. Where was Roger? Where was Mr Phelps? Who pushed her into her father's car? Who drove the needle into her flesh? In the days that followed, she wandered her father's house like a spectre. Everywhere she heard voices murmuring: Deirdre, Deirdre. Did somebody laugh? Sweat beaded on her temples and pooled beneath her armpits. She dug desperate fists between her thighs. Frequently she broke down, calling for the boy she half believed was her lover: Roger, Roger. Oh, what had she done? Only Vlad, the reffo boy, could calm her. Slowly, the young gardener helped her understand: Roger Dansie was gone, and so was Mr Phelps.

Some said the Dansie business destroyed Mayor Gull. He had hoped the boy would marry his daughter; he had counted Phelps as a friend. Then there was the question of his own complicity. Phelps, or so rumour soon had it, concealed a dark past. Once a master at Geelong Grammar, he had, it seemed, left abruptly to sequester himself in the Lakes. Why? Obvious! He had been caught out in his perversion and the school, no doubt, forced him to resign – in return for covering up the scandal.

Citizens of Crater Lakes demanded an investigation: what other lads had Phelps lured into his clutches? Why, he had coached the Magpies. He had taught at the high. And the Boys' Club! At every turn, the picture grew blacker. 'The law must seek out that degenerate,' boomed hardware store owner Willard Hartley Puce across Mayor Gull's desk. 'Drag the bugger back to the Lakes in chains, I say, and try him in a court of law.' Much of the town would agree; but the mayor, who had clashed often with this prominent businessman, only shook his head and said, 'Wouldn't you rather have him drawn and quartered?'

It was a fatal response. Mr Puce had long suspected the mayor of liberal tendencies. Now horrible suspicions assailed him. Had Gull known about the pervert all along – tolerated him, indulged him, rather than hounding him out of town with a leper bell around his neck? If so, Mr Puce declared exultantly, Gull had committed the greatest folly of his career.

Mr Puce was right. Arch L. Gull's reign as mayor of Crater Lakes had begun in 1922 and seemed likely never to end. Now, in a matter of days, it crashed around his ears. He announced that, owing to his health, he would not stand at the next election. Soon afterwards he died, living just long enough (so Mr Puce crowed) to see his slut of a daughter marry a reffo.

The mayor's death brought relief of a sort for the townsfolk. The scandal was over. They could forget. Nobody would speak of the vileness that had been visited upon them. Life would carry on as if there had been no Roger Dansie.

Yet his story was far from its end. The young genius was very much alive and his scholarship to England remained in force. The horror that began at the King Edward VII Theatre was all the time mounting, biding its time like an angry volcano that swells in secret with its scalding burden until at last it erupts.

Spin the globe.

Half a world away. Look, London. Focus in: Earls Court, a shabby street with barren trees where autumn slides into winter. Our scene is a big house, part of a once-grand terrace, with stone steps leading to a portico fecund with trash and splashed liberally by the piss of passing drunks. Inside, up several flights of stairs at the back, Roger Dansie and Quentin Phelps share what is known in England as a bedsit: a single room, and a small one. It is cheerless. Damp presses behind the wallpaper, wind shudders the window that faces out on a back garden of thorns and brambles, and the gas fire burbles and plops and gutters out if coins are not fed often to its hungry meter. Saggy twin beds, a rickety chest of drawers, two squelchy armchairs with stained antimacassars and a mothball-smelling wardrobe complete the accommodation. In daytime, the light through the dirty window is brown. At night a single bulb, hanging from the high ceiling like a distant star, provides brownish light. The floor is brown linoleum. The lavatory lies two floors down and is freezing. Neighbours include a negro; a kindly old tart long past her best; several rowdy demobbed soldiers who still wear their uniforms; and two fellow Australians, a youngish would-be writer and his raw-voiced mistress whose drunken quarrels wake the house each night. The landlady, a whiskery Irish hag who should be ashamed of presiding over such squalor but is not, lumbers up the stairs for the rent each Sunday evening after attending mass.

Roger Dansie does not repine. He is jubilant. From here, he ventures each day on rattling tube trains (Piccadilly Line to Leicester Square, Northern Line to Waterloo) to the theatre on the south bank that gives its name to Olivier's company. Damaged in the Blitz, the Old Vic in 1948 remains closed as a playhouse; the company performs in the New Theatre over the river, leaving its shabby home to the students. Rubble, some of it fallen bricks and beams, some of it scenery from past productions, clutters the auditorium; classes take place in the foyer, the bars, and a big rehearsal room upstairs. Nobody minds. Students are proud to be here. Contained in this building is the spirit of British theatre; simply to walk in from the street is to feel the rush of a classic tradition. But the Old Vic is not all about tradition. The theatre school is radical in style, no stuffy bastion of anyone-for-tennis traditionalism like the Royal Academy of Dramatic Art. In the Old Vic, teachers speak excitedly of Stanislavsky. There are improvisation exercises, movement classes. Outside, the city lies in ruins; here, a glorious new era seems about to dawn: Roger Dansie's era. For Roger is a promising pupil – more than promising. This is no story of a puffed-up rube who comes to the metropolis only to be laughed at; from the first, there are murmurs of greatness. And Quentin Phelps, is he filled with regret? No. Postwar England shocks him, it is true – a drab place of ruins and ration cards, of pasty-faced shopgirls and spotty clerks hurrying by in threadbare raincoats – but what, he urges, is apocalypse but the start of something new?

Eagerly, Phelps shows his protégé the sights. Picture them, master and pupil, on a red London bus, or at the railings of Buckingham Palace, or walking on the Embankment as the dirty river rushes past, saved from reeking only by the cold. Australia – for all its blinding sunshine the truly grey place, the place of oppressive shame – is as far away as another country can be. Many evenings find our friends in a certain establishment in Soho, one Phelps remembers fondly from his visit years ago. Let the city gape with bomb sites like a mouth with carious teeth; here, time is suspended, as queens with cigarette holders cackle through skeins of smoke about Bette and Joan and the new young barman and close shaves in the gents' at Piccadilly Circus Underground, and eye up Roger and say, exchanging glances, *'She's* nice, isn't she?'

Winter seems endless, but then it ends. White evaporates from the streets and green returns to the trees outside their window. Grey skies turn blue. Warmth fills the air; there are irises in the overgrown garden. And Quentin Phelps thinks: My season has passed. The changes have come slowly: Roger is bored when Quentin proposes a visit to the Wallace Collection or the Strangers' Gallery at the Palace of Westminster. Roger has lines to learn: 'Quentin, let me read this.' Roger must practise his animal improvisation: 'I'm a lion. Let me be a lion.' (Quentin scoffs. Has he ever heard such nonsense? For days Roger has repaired to London Zoo, studying the lions, imitating their movements. Quentin never taught drama like this.) Roger stays out late, carousing with fellow students. Young men, and one young woman, call for Roger and seem puzzled, even alarmed, by the 'Australian friend' who shares their classmate's room: so shabby (for Quentin is shabby now), so old-maidish, so *old*. 'And what, Mr Phelps, do you *do*?' they ask. Do? Nothing! For the first month or so, he wrote to public schools: Eton, Harrow, Winchester. Only Harrow replied, and that was to decline his services.

Roger crosses less often to Quentin's bed; then not at all.

The quarrels began soon enough. Roger, to the envy of his fellow students, landed a part in an Old Vic production that would open early in his second year: Tony Lumpkin, Jack-the-lad troublemaker in *She Stoops to Conquer*. More than once, Quentin turned up at rehearsals; sitting far back in the New Theatre auditorium, he would sup on a bottle of whisky, applaud Roger's entrances, and rush up to his protégé between scenes and critique his performance. The director frowned. Fellow cast members laughed uneasily. The guiding light of the Crater Lakes Players was not wanted here. Gently, Roger tried to tell him so, to no avail. Next day, Quentin was there again, and this time he was belligerent, interrupting the dialogue, calling the director a blind fool. Three burly stagehands were needed to throw him out.

'Why did you do it?' Roger asked later.

'You really need to ask that? You've changed, Roger.'

And Phelps had not. In England he was an embarrassment, a provincial boor. Roger had swiftly eradicated his own accent; Phelps, by contrast, sounded ever more Australian. His slurring whine set teeth on edge. His pretensions to art and culture were pathetic: they might have impressed a boy in Crater Lakes, but hardly the worldly young man he had become.

'You've got to move out,' said Roger's newest friend.

Roger shook his head. 'I can't abandon Quentin.'

Quentin felt abandoned all the same. His jealousy over this new friend precipitated the crisis. Colin Manning-Symes was a personable young fellow with thick, extravagantly pink lips and floppy blond hair that he flung back frequently in a rousing laugh. When he invited

Roger for a weekend at his parents' place in Buckinghamshire, Phelps raged. He drank. And kept drinking. In due course he propelled himself through the streets, muttering under his breath, and hovered at last in public lavatories. How long had it been? Too long. Anyone would do. This drivelling old man with piss-stained flies. This spotty adolescent who cried, 'You're hurting me!' as Quentin fucked him against the wall. This drunken sailor (how Quentin had wanted him!) who knocked him to the floor, kicked him, took his wallet, and called him a dirty ponce.

Late on Sunday afternoon, Quentin waited for Roger's return. He sat in one of the armchairs, a hand on each fraying arm. Light came only from a pink tasselled lamp he had found in a junk shop the week before. Several times he heard noise on the stairs, and turned his head slowly; his neck hurt. He wore a grey silver-threaded smoking jacket and red spotted cravat that Roger had always, in the past, claimed to like. He had borrowed some powder, to cover a black eye, and pungent cologne from the old tart upstairs. An ashtray rested on one of the chair arms.

Night had fallen and Quentin had almost worked his way through a whole pack of Capstans when Roger finally opened the door. 'What are you sitting in the dark for?' he asked, and flipped on the overhead light.

Quentin winced. 'Nice weekend with Manning-Symes?'

'Hmm.' Roger leaned an umbrella in a corner. He flung down his suitcase, stripped off his coat.

'Get on well with the mater and pater?'

'Hmm.' He went to the window, flung it wide. 'The fug in here! I don't know how you stand it. Have you been sitting here smoking since I left?'

How late was it? Rain pattered on the unweeded garden. Quentin ground out another cigarette. The ashtray brimmed; his fingers were grey. 'Explored the estate, did we? Bit of motoring, what-what?'

'What are you talking about? They're not that sort.'

'Spot of shooting, perhaps? Bam!' Quentin stood now. With unsteady, pained steps, he made it to the wall. 'Go in for fox hunting, do they, down in Fuckinghamshire? Tally-ho, old bean! Or did he just suck your cock?'

'Quentin, I'm not listening. Stop it.'

'Don't want to tell me? Not like you to be a shy boy.'

Roger remained by the window, staring into wet darkness. Quentin plunged towards him, grabbed him, forced him to turn. 'That's right, recoil. You never used to, Rog.'

'You stink! And what have you done to your eye?'

'Oh! I stink, do I? You jumped-up little bastard.' Ashy fingers grabbed Roger's crotch. 'Christ, you're so green you can't even see through a mater-and-pater piece of shit like Manning-Symes. Does he say "actually" all the time? I'll bet he does. "Actually, I think the lavatory bowl is *ideal* for depositing a turd in, don't you, Mater?" He's only middle-class, you know! You probably think he's the royal family. Come on' – the fist tightened painfully – 'when do I get what little Actually gets?'

Roger pushed Phelps, who crumpled to the floor.

Despairingly, Roger surveyed the squalid room, the gas fire with its meter, the rickety single beds, the mouldering wallpaper, the brown stain that crept across the ceiling, and knew he could never stay. Long ago, in another world, his secret life with Phelps had filled him with welling power. No more. It disgusted him. But it was over. He would break away.

In that moment, for the last time in his life, Roger Dansie felt a marvellous lightness, as if he could fly through the open window, escape into the velvety dark and never return. It was time. For all his success, for all his new friends, Crater Lakes still reached out long tentacles, lashing him down. Now, at least, those tentacles must be cut. He had no more need of Quentin Phelps.

'Where are you going?' whined the stinking trembling thing as Roger grabbed coat, suitcase and umbrella, and marched, footsteps thudding, towards the door.

'Colin's digs are round the corner.'

'No!' Phelps flung himself after Roger. What happened next would always be a blur to Roger; it was the subject of much discussion in the trial that followed, and he could never describe exactly the sequence of events. But it was simple, it must have been: Phelps interspersing himself between Roger and the stairs, crying, pleading (others in the house claimed to have heard a commotion); the two men grappling; Phelps tumbling down the stairs and cracking his head; Roger thundering after him, calling, 'Quentin! Quentin!' with grief that gripped him so tightly he knew it would never let him go.

Roger lived through the trial as if through a dream. There wasn't evidence enough for murder, though the strong suspicion persisted that the death of Quentin Phelps had been more than mere accident. Endlessly, both prosecution and defence trawled through the facts, including the schoolteacher's prior convictions in Australia (a good half-dozen) for soliciting. 'Mr Phelps forced himself upon you. Naturally you defended yourself,' insisted Roger's counsel, but Roger's acting skills appeared to have deserted him.

Witnesses were no help. The Irish landlady expressed amazement, even horror, that she had let out a room to a pair of nancy boys ('I runs a respectable house, I do'); the old tart, who described her occupation as 'gentlewoman', said she had always thought those two fellows not quite-quite. The Australian writer and his mistress complained about the noise. Colin Manning-Symes blushingly denied all knowledge of the 'true nature' of the friendship between Mr Dansie and Mr Phelps. The verdict was manslaughter.

The case, of course, was in all the papers. Sir Laurence Olivier declined to comment.

Roger Dansie spent five years in Holloway Prison. Upon release he attempted fitfully to begin a new life. He was not penniless: the remnants of the Dansie fortune brought him a small income. For a time he travelled: France, Italy, Greece. For some years he lived in Tangier, plunging into a life of Arab boys and hashish. Later he drifted to New York, where he moved on the fringes of experimental theatre, but the heart had gone out of his acting. It was as if a spring inside him had snapped. Filling his mind was the old Dansie house: his home, his bitter heritage. The world lay all before him, but only one obscure provincial place called to Roger Dansie. He was not yet old; he was, when he made his decision, a man of barely thirty, but weary of the world. As a boy, he had dreamed of fame. He had not seen that he was famous already: famous in Crater Lakes. That was his portion; life had no more to offer. Let him return to the town where he had been born.

And so he went back to his tumbledown house, where Jack, all this time, had been awaiting him patiently.

# Chapter Sixteen

'What now, miss?'

Must the boy sound so belligerent? Marlo eyed him with a sad wonderment. He was Skip's age. How could so young a child get so fat? He had red swollen cheeks, no neck, and pendulous breasts visible beneath his school jumper; his buttocks and thighs might have burst at any moment from the brown polyester that barely contained them. She had heard that the boy had got into some sort of trouble; his mother, hoping to reform him, had inveigled Auntie Noreen into giving him an after-school job.

'Did you shift that potting mix?' said Marlo.

Brenton breathed. 'Them big sacks?'

'Out the back.' Marlo jerked a thumb. The boy grunted and mooched away. Skip said he had no friends. Once (Skip was vague on details) he had run his own gang; now, for some reason, all the kids laughed at him.

Marlo looked at the clock on the wall. Still half an hour! Wearily she applied herself to the big Remington she had never liked so much as Olly Olivetti.

Clack. Clack-clack. Now payable.

Tab. Tab. Dollar sign.

Heat beat on the tin roof. Summer here would be stifling. More than once Marlo had thought she would quit. But for what? She needed money. Better Puce Hardware than a Coles New World checkout.

'Bloke here to see you.' Uncle Doug stood in the doorway.

'What bloke?' said Marlo, too late, and had half risen from her desk when Howard Brooker stepped past her uncle. Colouring, she sank behind the Remington again; Uncle Doug slipped away as Howard, with a smile, planted himself in the easy chair and crossed one long leg over the other. Bemusedly he looked around at the Mobil calendar, the *Pix*, the Alistair MacLeans. He lit a Silk Cut and offered the pack to Marlo, who waved it away.

He blew out smoke. 'Saw young Brenton on my way in.'

'One of your more promising pupils?' Restless feelings churned in Marlo. Howard wore a wide tie, fire-engine red, and a canary-yellow shirt made of synthetic fibres. 'I'm worried he'll turn violent one day. Upend half the stock, sling gasoline around, strike a match.'

'He's a mummy's boy. We miss you, Marlo.'

'Who's we?' Marlo stuffed papers into a file. Uncle Doug had written on the battered cardboard in big slanting letters: CALTEX SERVO. She stood abruptly, making for the filing cabinet. Damn Howard. Her hair was a mess.

'The play can't work without you,' he said. 'Mrs Singh stepped into the breach, but she's no Petra. The part was made for you. Sure, it's only am dram. But I want to make an impact on this town before I go. This is my one chance.'

'You're going?' Marlo tried to sound indifferent.

'I've been offered a post in Adelaide – PAC.'

'Prince Alfred College? What about London, Paris, decadent Berlin and the Côte d'Azur?'

If Marlo's mockery angered him, Howard did not let on. 'Later. I've had enough of it here.'

244

'Mrs Novak can't be pleased.'

'Marlo, we were good friends, weren't we?' He caught her hand.

'You were my teacher. Of a sort.'

'You're still enrolled for those exams. You've got to sit them.' Marlo, at first, had neglected to snatch her hand away. Too late, she pulled free, and hoped that Howard did not feel encouraged. 'Of course,' he was saying, 'you'll need further coaching. Quit this rotten job. You can study in the school library. After classes I'll sit with you. We'll go through past papers; Mr Singh can help with maths. The play's in six days. Do it, and I'll see you matriculate.'

Marlo almost laughed. 'You're making a deal with me?'

Howard stood up. His face – and he *was* handsome – hovered above hers. 'Good one, isn't it? Mutual benefit.'

A voice came: 'Home time!' Pavel faltered when he saw Brooker.

The teacher, as he took his leave, whistled a little tune. Mozart? No, the Carpenters. 'And oh,' he said from the doorway, 'I meant it about quitting. You'll have a scholarship soon.'

Marlo's face was flushed.

'You're coming home?' Pavel seemed uncertain. Brooker, in these last weeks, seemed to have vanished like an illusion. But that was the illusion. Everything that had been before was still here now.

They drove in silence. Marlo wondered how Brooker could have changed things so quickly. Angrily, she told herself he had changed nothing, but she was lying to herself and knew it.

They had almost reached the old Dansie house when Pavel pulled up at the side of the road. A warm wind was blowing. Magpies carolled raucously out of waving grass, and he shook his head slowly and said, 'You love him, don't you – the teacher?'

'No.' Marlo turned and took his face in her hands. 'I've never loved him. I never will. But he makes me think about things I wish I wouldn't. Oh, Pavel! I can't just be the girl at Puce Hardware.'

'I know.' He pulled away gently. 'But everything's going to be all right. You'll leave the Lakes and so will I.'

'Not yet,' said Marlo. 'Nothing's happening yet.'

He drew a letter from his pocket and thrust it towards her. Uncrumpling it, Marlo knew at once what it was, but when she read it she inhaled sharply all the same. A week! Only one week more.

Clouds, long and ragged, travelled through the sky.

'How long have you known this?'

'Solves everything, eh?'

Clumsily, violently, she flung herself across him. So much had happened in these last weeks that Marlo had barely known what she felt, only that fate was propelling her forward. She heard Pavel's heart thumping, thumping, and knew it was the drumbeat of passing time. At last she drew back and stared tearfully into his dark eyes. 'You fool,' she whispered. 'I love you.'

'Easy to say that now.' His voice was sad, not angry. The old Dansie house hovered behind shifting trees, unreal, a picture from a story that was about to end. In years to come (Marlo saw it now) the life they had lived there would be distant as a dream. It might have been one already.

'Kiss me, Pavel. Maybe we won't always be together,' she said, shutting her eyes now. 'Life is long and contains so much. We're barely more than children. We'll grow up. We'll change. But what we've had will always be with us. We'll remember. Kiss me, you stupid boy.'

He did, and she felt herself tumbling down and down in warm darkness, and wanted never to stop. Uselessly, she knew that she didn't want to grow up: she didn't want to change. Let them fall unendingly.

The Land Rover's engine was still running.

'It's my duty,' said Pavel. 'But I don't want to go.'

\* \* \*

246

'Throwing stones?'

'Throwing stones.'

Often Roger Dansie appeared as if from nowhere. He sat down beside Skip. She tossed another pebble into Dansie's Pond, then wondered if this was rude to Roger; after all, it was his pond. She dangled her legs from the edge of the Jump. Below, ripples spread and dispersed. Why disturb the water anyway? It was better when it was still, like glass. She put the stones down beside her.

'You don't look happy,' Roger said.

The sun was setting and Skip squinted as she looked into his face. Ghosts should be old and scary; Roger was young, or appeared to be. His eyes were blue shards in a pale unwrinkled face. He wore a tweed jacket – stylish, if a little moth-eaten. The rocky walls around the pond were turning red.

'I don't like it,' Skip said.

'You're talking about your sister?' He knew.

'Why does she have to do that stupid play? Brooker's play!' To Skip, it was a betrayal. She had fought with Marlo, trailed her sister about the house for a whole evening begging her to see reason, to come to her senses. Didn't Marlo have Pavel? Howard Brooker was a creep of the first water. For Marlo even to be in the same room as him was, for Skip, madness. 'He's blackmailing her, I'll bet. It's about those exams, it must be: be in the play or I'll fail you.'

'I hardly think he could do that,' said Roger. 'It's a public examination. Strangers in Adelaide mark her work. But your sister's good in the part, you know. I've been helping her with her lines. Funny how much of that play I remember. I think I know it by heart.'

'I hate it. It's stupid.' Skip drew up her legs and hugged them to her chest. Mowser, or Purcell, swished towards them, meowing, and she stroked his orange back; his tail, magnificently stripy, prodded the air. 'A stupid play,' she went on, 'about a man inspecting drains.'

'Not quite!' Roger's look was wry. 'Dr Stockmann discovers a secret that nobody else wants to know. The infection in the water is the foulness underlying this respectable community. If the spa is a health hazard, the town is in dire straits. The baths must close. Businesses will lose money. Who wants to hear that? Besides, these bugs in the water, these bearers of disease, are too small to see. So they say the doctor is lying. It's easier that way. The town turns on him, casts him out. But he fights back. That's the thing about Dr Stockmann: he fights back.'

'I hadn't seen it like that,' said Skip, relenting a little.

'You haven't seen it at all. It's a story that could happen anywhere, but especially in a country town. You don't believe me? Oh, Henrik Ibsen knew all about Crater Lakes.'

'How could he? He was Danish.'

'Norwegian.' Mowser, or Purcell, butted his head against Roger's thigh. He swung the big cat into his lap. 'This furry pest wants his dinner soon.'

What was it, Skip wondered, that made her so happy to sit with Roger? He had killed a man and gone to jail. But with him she felt more peaceful than with anyone else.

Dark-eyed, he gazed into the darkening water. His voice was like that water, clear on the surface but deep, mysterious. Beneath the surface were writhing vines, entrapping caves. He must have been a great actor, Skip knew it.

'Ibsen,' he was saying, 'was born in a small timber port where the moan of sawmills filled the air.'

'There's a sawmill here,' said Skip.

'That's right. But here there are also fields and woods and lakes. When Ibsen was a boy in small-town Norway, he looked out on pillory, jail and madhouse, and saw nothing green. He always remembered the first time he crossed the Alps, making his way into southern Europe. In the brightness of Italy, he said, he felt he'd been released from darkness into light, escaping through a misty tunnel into sunshine. Most of his plays, the important ones, were written far from home. Yet he never left Norway in his mind.'

Roger spoke about Ibsen as if about a man he had known. How strange it was, Skip thought, that a writer, dead these many years, could carry on in the world that way – a sort of ghost, but not one that scared her. Roger said Ibsen was a poet and a revolutionary.

'And I thought he was just a boring old man.'

'You've a lot to learn, my dear. Oh, you're off, are you?' Purcell, or Mowser, squirmed in Roger's arms, then strutted away. 'That's right, find Jack. He'll give you your dinner.'

Gently, Roger drew Skip close to him; nuzzling against him, she ached with love. 'Ibsen,' he was saying, 'once defined his subject as the clash of ability and aspiration, of will and possibility – the difference, in other words, between what we want and what we get.'

'That's all he wrote about?' said Skip. 'Over and over?'

'But that's everything, don't you see? The comedy and the tragedy of life! What I love about him is his fearlessness. Ibsen was an adventurer, always questing. He pretty much created modern drama; he put life itself on the stage. He assailed the conventions of his time. When Nora walks out on her husband at the end of *A Doll's House*, they said the slamming of that door echoed all over Europe. After that he wrote a play called *Ghosts*.'

The title echoed in Skip's mind. 'What ghosts?'

'Not the haunted house kind, the real kind – the hidden past invading the present. Ibsen exposed the sins concealed beneath a veil of respectability. What sins? Well, let's just say one word: syphilis. It was the public outcry against *Ghosts* that made Ibsen write *An Enemy of the People*. Because that's what he was, you see. Ibsen was the real Dr Stockmann.'

Skip, worried about the word 'syphilis', said cautiously, 'Would I understand his plays if I read them?'

'They're in the house. Why not try?'

She screwed up her mouth. 'Nah. Marlo's the smart one.'

Roger cuffed the side of her head.

'Yeow! What was that for?'

'You're an uneducated little barbarian, my darling, but you're not stupid. Quite the reverse. You're brilliant. You can be anything you want to be. And be warned: I'll be behind you with a cattle prod, just to make sure.'

'Uh-huh.' Skip scooped up her handful of stones again, clenching them tightly, so tightly they dug into her palm. Tears had filled her eyes; she must hold them back. No one had ever cared before what she might become. No grown-up had told her she was brilliant.

The walls of rock had turned purple now; the water below was almost black. Birds clucked and cackled unseen among the trees.

'I like being in your house, Roger,' Skip said.

'And I like having you there. Do you know what Ibsen said about living in a community? No man, he said, is ever free of responsibility for the society in which he belongs, or without a share in its guilt. This is just the beginning. It's time I became a citizen of Crater Lakes again.'

Skip wondered if Roger was mad like Karen Jane. He had to be, didn't he? How could he have lived in secret all these years? What had it been like? Was he lonely? Was he afraid? She threw a stone into the glassy mirror below. 'Do you ever wish you didn't come back?'

'It's my home. I've been such an alien in the world, spinning the globe, ending up here and there. I've travelled, and for what? You get sick of hating the place you come from, apologising for it, covering it up. Is this worse than England? I thought there was a world out there. But what if Crater Lakes is the world? What if everybody comes from Crater Lakes?'

Skip didn't understand, but she didn't want to say. All she wanted was for Roger to keep talking. What was it like to have a father? She hoped it would be like this.

'Life is a circle,' Roger added, after a moment. 'We want to come back to the place where we began.'

'But didn't they hate you? You were the enemy of the people.'

'It was a part I played. There can be others.'

'That part, Brooker's part, was your last role with the Players, wasn't it?'

'Actually I never did it on the night,' said Roger. He smiled sadly. 'Events, shall we say, took an unfortunate turn, and before I knew it I was in a Baby Austin, bound for Melbourne and a big ship that took six weeks to get to England. Sad. I'd so wanted to play Dr Stockmann.'

'You'd be better than Brooker,' said Skip. 'You'd have to be.'

'Hey! You two coming in for dinner?' Jack had appeared at the pond's edge below. Skip grinned and threw a stone to splash him. She loved him. She loved everyone. In Jack's arms was Mowser, or Purcell.

Shyly, Skip slipped her hand into Roger's as they walked back to the house.

'And what *do* you want to be?' he asked her.

Surprising herself, she answered, 'Your daughter.'

'Oh, Skip!' His voice was soft. 'I think you already are.'

'The Burgomaster's cap!' cried Mrs Novak.

'And here's the staff of office, too!' said Mr Brooker. 'But how in the devil's name did they –'

Mr Singh tried to intervene; Brooker swept him aside. 'Ah! I understand. He's been here to talk you around. Ha ha! He brought his pigs to the wrong market! And when he caught sight of me in the printing room – ha ha! ha ha! ha ha ha! – he took to his heels, eh, Mr Aslaksen?'

A young dentist agreed that this was the case.

The dress rehearsal was far advanced. The stage and the flats behind it had been covered with silver foil; players wore suits of the same material, with silver masks over their eyes, and garden gloves and wellingtons sprayed with silver paint. White chests of drawers and a white wardrobe adorned with light bulbs and bicycle reflectors served as banks of computers, suggesting the printing office in which the scene was set, while the Burgomaster's cap was a space helmet (actually an upturned fishbowl), and the staff of office a toy ray gun made of red and yellow plastic. In his programme notes, Howard Brooker, BA, DipT, spoke of the play's universality. *An Enemy of the People*, he said, was a story that could take place in any time, any place, and citizens of a democracy must be constantly on guard that the tale did not unfold again today, or tomorrow, or the day after.

'This is all wrong. He's ruined it.' Skip, in the dress circle, shut with disgust a shabby greenish volume with the words *Prose Dramas* picked out on the front in faded gold. Following the dialogue was difficult in any case when Brooker had made many cuts and changes and still, with the first-night curtain only twenty-two hours away, remained liable to halt proceedings and rail at the cast for failing what he insisted on calling his 'vision' of the play.

'What's with the book, anyway?' Honza slouched beside her, picking leathery flakes from an arm of his chair. He shifted, squirmed; this was a boy who would never willingly read a book and couldn't understand when others did. 'Let's go down. I want to see what's backstage.'

'Yair. Let's.' Skip sprang up and stuffed the book into her bag. They made for the stairs while Mr Singh and Mrs Novak gaped with horror and Brooker, donning the fishbowl and flourishing the ray gun, strutted back and forth like a jackbooted Nazi. His ridicule of the Burgomaster was in full flight when a door burst open, stage left, and the president of the Lions Club of Crater Lakes boomed like thunder, 'What's the meaning of this folly?'

Brooker, shedding the fishbowl, proclaimed that revolution was about to engulf the town.

'What a whacker,' said Honza, loudly, as he led Skip between the stalls. A small audience, scattered in awkward attitudes across the front rows, scrutinised the rehearsal. Among their number were Mr Novak, who stroked his chin; Pavel, looking bewildered; and an earnest Marlo, who was not required in the present scene. A flight of steps led up to the stage; Honza and Skip, to glares and hisses, ascended it and flitted, stage right, into the wings.

'Looks different from the side, eh?' Skip gazed across the stage, beyond the spacesuits and flaring foil, to dark hollows lined with raw brick. Switches, black and heavy, like levers that might launch rockets or bombs, angled out beside furled-back curtains; winches for the flies looked nautical, and lights flared from a hanging rig above. A red bucket filled with sand declared on the side in black block letters: FIRE. In spite of Brooker, excitement filled Skip. The stage, she realised, was a world of strange magic.

Honza tugged her hand. 'Isn't there a cellar?'

They descended a staircase. Dingy corridors diverged below; pipes ran down the walls like brassy innards. Doors stood ajar to darkened rooms: PROPERTY STORE. GENTS DRESSING. LADIES DRESSING. The screwed-on signs were of lacquered wood, the words painted in chipped bright cursive. Thuds and creakings sounded above their heads and Brooker's rantings echoed weirdly.

'Roger should be playing that part,' said Skip.

They turned a corner. STAGE DOOR, said a sign that pointed towards Crater Gardens, while just before a second staircase, leading up to stage left, was a door on which was taped a quarto page bearing the block-lettered name HOWARD BROOKER. The star's dressing room: that room from which, long ago, a girl called Deirdre Gull had fled in tears into her father's arms.

'Your sister *is* nuts, ain't she?' said Honza.

Skip rounded on him. 'Don't. I've told you: don't.'

'So why's she on with Brooker again, then?'

'She's not. She's *using* him. Don't you know anything? It's one of a woman's arts.' Angrily, Skip pushed open the dressing-room door. She fumbled for a switch. Light glared from a single hanging bulb. The room was mean, low-ceilinged, with a stained pinkish rug filling the space between the clutter. Running along one wall was a chipped, scratched dressing table.

Skip slumped, suddenly weary, into the squeaking swivel chair; her face in the mirror was a potato going green. Against the opposite wall was a rack, empty but for a single spangly spacesuit, with mask, boots and gloves; the wardrobe ladies had made a spare. In the corner by the door stood a large black trunk with a curving, brass-banded top (the treasure chest, perhaps, from a play about pirates); in the other, by the small frosted window that looked into the gardens, a folding screen pasted liberally with flyers for past attractions: *Chu Chin Chow*, Gang Show, Col Joye and the Joy Boys.

Honza sat cross-legged on the treasure chest. 'I hate Brooker.' His bitterness surprised Skip. He never spoke about his mother's affair; he treated their move to the old Dansie house as if it were a lark. But his nonchalance, she saw, was a front. There were things he minded, things that hurt him bitterly.

On the dressing table lay a leather bag with hanging fringes. Skip riffled through it. Brooker's wallet? Better not risk it. Brooker's appointment book? His Silk Cuts? She waved the pack towards Honza. The lighter she found in the bag had been engraved with the words: *To Howard – Love, Deirdre.*

Their smoke wreathed in the air. Skip, eyeing the mirror again, wondered if she was pretty. She didn't look like a potato, did she? Half closing her eyes, she thought, as if the fact lent her a certain mystery, a certain glamour: Col Joye, one of Australia's biggest singing stars, has sat where I sit now.

They could still hear Howard Brooker, one of Australia's biggest whackers, ranting from the stage above.

'What if we could get back at him?' said Honza.

'How?' Skip understood at once the impulse behind Honza's words. She shared it. But it was impossible. 'Everybody loves him. They think he's a genius. Genius, huh! He doesn't care about the play, he just cares about Howard Brooker. It should be Roger taking the stage tomorrow night. He knows every word of that play. Imagine it! He'd blast Brooker out of the water.'

Quiet for once, Honza blew out smoke rings. Distantly, beyond the window, water cascaded in the sunken cave; a sad sound, hollow, like life slipping by. 'What if we switched them?' he said suddenly.

'What are you talking about?' said Skip.

'Stage door's just along there, eh?' He waved a hand. 'And it goes out into the gardens, not the street. Think about it. Wouldn't be that hard to get old Rog in here, would it?'

'So nobody sees? I suppose so. But Brooker –'

'We'd lock him up.' Excited, Honza scrambled off the treasure chest. A big rusty padlock hung from the front of it, a key sticking out from its underside. He turned it, unhooked the lock, raised the trunk's warped lid, and flung across the costume rack the mothballed capes and gowns he found inside. 'Yair, this is perfect. Gag him. Tie him up. Lock him in here.'

Skip mashed out her cigarette. She hated cigarettes. 'This isn't Lummo lying around drunk,' she said. 'We're kids. Brooker's a six foot man. Tomorrow night, there'll be people everywhere –'

'So we knock him out. Better yet, Rog does.'

'Then hide him in that chest?' Skip's chair, as she swivelled, made a protesting howl; the chest, with its oily black exterior and mildewed lining of scarlet felt, looked like some prehistoric creature's vast open mouth. Scarlet vibrated under the buzzing electric bulb.

Her next words were solemn. Honza might never read a book, but his brain could still dazzle her. 'It's brilliant. You're brilliant. Roger wants to show himself to the town again. He'll be in costume.

255

He'll be in a mask. When he goes on stage, people will think he's Brooker – then, slowly, they'll realise. Everyone will see again what a great actor he is.'

Honza rose, grinning, from the treasure chest and flourished, like a prize, the extra spacesuit. 'Might be a bit small, but it'll do. We come here early. Get him in costume, all ready to go on –'

'Hide him, I guess?'

'In this room. In this chest.'

'No, the screen – behind the screen!'

They gripped each other's hands and leaped around in a circle, laughing.

There was only one problem. Skip stopped and slumped. 'But Roger – he'd never agree.' Of course he wouldn't.

But it was then that the voice came: 'That's where you're wrong.'

Skip and Honza jumped. The Ghost of Crater Lakes had a capacity for appearing suddenly, as if he had only that instant flashed into being. For years he had wandered the town at night, flitting through the shadows, avoiding streetlamps; now here he was, emerging from behind the screen, incongruous in a place that seemed defined by Col Joye. In the small room, Roger appeared taller than ever. He was a giant. A thrill went through Skip.

Then doubt gripped her with equal force. The treasure chest yawned redly. Gazing into it, Roger mumbled something. What was he saying? He was born in a trunk, he half whispered, half laughed, in the Princess Theatre in Something-Something, Idaho. To Skip, less familiar with the works of Judy Garland, his words made no sense. She felt alarmed, and touched his hand gently. 'You weren't, Roger. You were born in Crater Lakes.'

He blinked at her, and she asked him why he was there.

'Oh, I wanted to watch the rehearsals,' he said, but without conviction. 'I could sit in the back, couldn't I? In the dark. I can always sit in the dark. I don't have to hide where Deirdre hid – I don't, do I?

Not after all these years.' Turning, he fingered the screen, picking distractedly at the old flyers. Col Joye, in black and white, smiled regardless.

'They're up there.' Trembling, Skip pointed to the ceiling.

'The rehearsals? Yes. Yes.' By now, it seemed, Roger wanted only to escape. In his tumbledown house far out of town, he could seem so sane, so strong. And yet even there, Skip had from time to time come upon him in moods like this: distracted, not quite present. It frightened her – it was terrifying to be reminded that this man she loved like a father could no more be relied upon than her crazy mother. Tears sprang to her eyes and she forced them shut. She counted, digging her fingernails into her palms, until a hand – Honza's – touched her wrist.

She looked around, then ran to the door. Like a phantom, Roger had slipped from the dressing room; he had swung open the stage door and vanished into the night. Was he a dream after all? She turned back to Honza, bit her lip and gripped the boy's shoulders, as if making sure he was solid, rock solid.

# Chapter Seventeen

'How much longer?'

This time it was Skip who asked. Honza shifted his feet again. They stood outside the stage door. Between feathery trees a path led into back reaches of Crater Gardens; down a grassy slope lay the picket fence banding the sunken cave. In the gathering darkness, the grass appeared purple, even black; the fence glimmered with a strange phosphorescence. November evenings in Crater Lakes are long.

'Jack wouldn't let us down,' said Honza.

While they were waiting, they had gone down to the cave, ack-ack with machine-gun sneakers slapping around the spiral; solemnly they had leaned above the scene-of-the-crime wishing well, in which water lapped above a gleaming new grille; they had curved around to Volcano Street and checked the comings and goings at what Mr Novak, who had duties to perform, called the front of house. The town hall clock, the little Big Ben of Crater Lakes, rose against a greyish pallid sky, ticking like a time bomb towards the first act.

Jack should have been here long ago, propelling the Harley illegally along the garden paths, with Roger in the sidecar, concealed beneath blankets. Smuggling him through the stage door would be harder now the Players had all arrived. Some had asked what 'yous kids' were doing, hanging round the back.

'Something's happened,' Skip said to Honza. 'That bloody Harley! I'll bet it's conked out again.'

'Maybe old Rog couldn't go through with it.'

'Don't say that! We've still got time.' They didn't need much. They had stolen the extra spacesuit the night before; Roger would be in costume already. But so much could go wrong. Was Brooker still in his dressing room? Roger should have been hidden in there from the first.

'Heard the news?' The stage manager, a bachelor greengrocer who had his own segment on *Woman's World* each Wednesday ('Tony's World of Veg') and didn't mind a spot of culture now and then, swung out of the stage door, lighting a Benson & Hedges. 'Some reviewer's down from the smoke. Old mate of Howard's – Professor Somebody, from Flinders Uni. Writes for the *Advertiser.* Hah! Howard Brooker's big chance.'

'Chance of what?' said Honza.

Heavily, the greengrocer paced the path. 'He's a terror, Howard. Silver foil and spacesuits! Me, I'm not sorry he's buggering off. Yair, half the town's out tonight. Curiosity, ain't it? That'll work once – twice, maybe. But Ibsen, I asks you! Next time, we need a nice musical. *Guys and Dolls. My Fair Lady.*' His wrist flicked as he gestured with the B&H. 'I'd make a good Higgins, I reckon. Can't be doing with this Russian crap.'

'Ton-*ee*!' A figure appeared in the doorway. 'Where's the dinner for the dining room?'

'They take pills, remember?'

'Pills? What the hell you on about?'

'Howard decided last night. Futuristic, ain't it? All their nutrients in a single daily pill – oh, fuck me dead, where are the bottles?' The greengrocer flung away his cigarette and rushed back inside.

'We're stuffed.' Skip sank down on the steps. 'This should be

Roger's big chance – and with the bloke from the *Advertiser* there, too! And now it's not going to happen. Nothing will.'

Honza sat beside her. He might, Skip sensed, have slipped an arm around her, but didn't quite dare; instead, he just laid a hand on her shoulder. 'It's not so bad,' he said. 'Stupid play, anyway.'

'Shows how much you know!'

Headlights passed brightly beyond the gardens; from the pub across the road came a chorus of voices; from closer, a birdcall. No: a whistle. The signal! Could it be? Skip, rushing forward, almost collided with Jack as he emerged around a leafy corner. 'He's here?'

'I cut the motor. Rolled her in.'

'Bloody took your time,' said Honza.

'Kids in cars. They held me up on the road into town. Tried to start a ruckus.'

'You're all right?' Skip's throat clenched with fear.

'Them kids ain't. Thought they was just taking me on, didn't they? But Mr Dansie jumps out the sidecar – flings off his blankets, roars, and they was off! Reckon they thought he was a monster from outer space. But we was left in a ditch.' His black-olive eyes darted this way and that. 'Coast's clear?'

He vanished again; when he reappeared, he was leading a huddled form. The sky shuddered, darkening, as if the earth had jolted on its axis.

'Check the corridor,' Skip said to Honza.

Roger unbent his tall frame. Blankets slipped from his shoulders. In the silver suit, with a foil helmet moulded over his hair, he appeared formidable. A superhero mask concealed his eyes: Dr Stockmann, when he denounced his townsfolk, would fling the mask aside, showing that he, he alone, was the one honest citizen. Gazing at Roger, Skip knew she was lost in something more than love: it was awe. So what if Brooker had made a hash of the play; Roger wouldn't. Tonight, she knew, was the start of something big.

'Trouble.' Honza pushed back through the stage door.

'Don't tell me – Brooker's left the dressing room?' This was Skip's worst fear: they had to get him alone.

'Dunno. But he's locked the door.'

'Damn it.' Brooker might be 'preparing'; often, during rehearsals, he had said musingly, fingers knitting beneath his chin, *'An actor prepares* – now what do we mean by *an actor prepares*?'*, as if the players were pupils in his class. Skip thought quickly. Backstage was crowded. But the corridor that angled around to his dressing room afforded privacy. They might still clock him when he opened the door. And if they knew when he was about to leave ...

'What you doing?' said Honza.

Foliage brushed against the theatre wall. Some yards down shone a rectangle of light. Girls, Skip thought queasily, must have pressed against it in cavemen times, ardent for a glimpse of Col Joye's dick.

She pushed between the branches, peered into the window – then snapped away, blundering into Honza, who had trailed after her, grinning, as if he still thought they were only playing a game. Violently, she pushed him in the chest, driving him back.

'Hey! What was that for? What's in there?'

'Nothing,' Skip almost spat.

Only your mother, she might have said, acting out a scene that took place the last time this play was about to start. But this time Deirdre Novak had taken a different role. Mr Brooker leaned against the dressing table; Mrs Novak was on her knees. Nothing, Skip decided, was more disgusting than grown-ups. If she could never grow up, she would be happy.

'Roger?' She broke back out onto the path.

Where was Roger? Jack's face was immemorial, a native mask, incongruous above his shabby plaid shirt. His voice was hollow. 'Gone. If we'd got him in there straight away, but –'

'He can't!' Skip ran onto the grass. 'Roger!'

'Eh!' Tony's head poked around the stage door. 'What's this carry-on? Curtain up in five. Yous kids get round the front. And you, the abo – hop it. Drink your meths in someone else's doorway, you dirty derro.' The stage manager flicked a hand, but already Jack had melted into the night.

Their plan had failed. Desperately Skip tried to see how the evening could still be saved. But she could think of nothing. Honza, clearly still curious about what was happening inside that window, edged towards the foliage again, but she grabbed his collar and wrenched him back. 'Come on,' she commanded miserably. 'We can watch the play, at least.'

Mr Novak seemed annoyed when they took their places. 'Where have you two been?' he said. Marlo had secured them seats in the second row: splendid seats. Mr Novak looked jowly and sour – hardly relishing, perhaps, the prospect of watching his wife; Pavel, beside him, was nervous, no doubt more for Marlo than for his father or his mother. The young man had tried to slick down his hair, but already it was springing free. Honza sat next to his brother and Skip took the seat further along. In spite of the failure of their plan, Honza's mood was boisterous. Several times he prodded fingers into Skip's ribs to make her laugh; she slapped his hands away.

Red curtains shifted as in a breeze. Skip, twisting around, gripped the back of her chair. The theatre was packed. Curiosity, Ton-*ee* had said, and here was enough to see off tribes of cats. Look: Brian Rigby, pinkly scrubbed, ramrod straight beside a withered wife. Look: Lucy Sutton, ribbons in hair, perusing – no doubt – an award-winning work of children's fiction before the lights went down; the lady librarian, who sat beside Mrs Sutton, would be impressed. Brenton Lumsden, Brylcreemed and bow-tied, hunkered resentfully beside his floral mother. Spying Skip, he glowered and looked away. Further back, faces blurred: line upon line of pale or brownish ovals, tiered behind the brassy dress-circle rail or hovering in the shadows of the overhang that Skip liked to imagine crashing down. What about Auntie Noreen, Uncle Doug? No sign of them. Sometimes, in these last weeks, Skip could almost believe they were dead. Like Barry.

Noise seethed to the columned heights and abated only a little as the lights dimmed. Facing forward again, Skip craned her neck; a big man sat in front of her, obscuring her view with a frizzy hump of head. She had never seen him before: the critic from the *Advertiser*, perhaps? And what did he see? Skip tried to imagine the play through his eyes.

Curtain up on a silver glare. (Laughter.)

Mrs Novak, spacesuited and masked, hair Medusa-like in baking-foil curlpapers, shrilled nervously, 'Well, if you're an hour late, Mr Billing, you must put up with a cold supper!'

The shy clergyman sat at a glass table; robotically he raised a vitamin pill to his mouth. 'It-is-ex-cell-ent. De-lic-i-ous.'

Her husband, Mrs Novak said, insisted on regular meals. The Burgomaster, or president of the Lions Club, entered with his ray gun and fishbowl space helmet; with difficulty, he removed the latter (murmurs rose; there were fears that it was stuck) and boomed, 'Good evening, sister-in-law.'

Skip sighed. It was going to be a long night.

Woodenly, Dr Stockmann discovered the parlous state of the baths; woodenly, he declared that something must be done; woodenly, the townsfolk decided that, on the contrary, nothing must be done – while the audience variously sighed, groaned, cackled, held conversations, or left, politeness forgotten, with loud uptiltings of seats. When Marlo appeared, Skip felt embarrassed for her. Petra was the only character who delivered her lines convincingly. What of it? It's no good being a good actor if everyone else is bad.

A bored Honza had resumed his prodding. Skip had to escape. Pretending she needed to pee, she pushed her way along her row and skulked off down the aisle. On stage, the president of the Lions

Club was saying that the public really didn't need new ideas; it got along quite well with the ones it already had. Off stage, the public was proving the point. Brooker ranted that he was the only one, the only one with a vision for this town.

In the foyer, Skip slumped on a smelly sofa. What a fool she had been! She should have known their plan would never work. Roger could be Olivier himself – and she half believed he was – and it would make no difference. The magic that had made him famous in Crater Lakes had fled long ago and could never come back. A party of cheery men clumped by, pint glasses slopping on the swirly carpet; they were bringing back beers from the pub across the way.

She shambled outdoors. The night was warm and the darkness now entire; yellow pools shimmered under the streetlamps. She made her way past the institute, past the town hall, along the path that curved back into the gardens. Where was Roger? Perhaps he walked the streets. *Night stalker, come … Night stalker, quick.* He was the real hunter; the rest of them were amateurs.

She paced the grass, then hurled herself down on her back. Pounding filled her chest. How could she bear to hate so many things? Stars, barely blinking on this clear night, glared at her indifferently. Everything she wanted seemed, in that moment, so far away: all the mystery, all the love, all the excitement, all the adventure of a life filled perpetually with meaning and wonder.

Muted thunder sounded from the theatre. Was it interval? She had better go back. Wearily, she hauled herself up and across the grass, past the gate that led down to the cave. She would go in through the back way and see Marlo. 'You're good,' she would tell her. That, at any rate, was not a lie.

A lamp burned weakly above the stage door; the leafy path was mauve in the light. As Skip walked down the path, the door swung open. Brooker stood above her, eyes flinty behind his mask. Cumbersome in space boots, he clumped down the steps. Was he raging at the audience's failure to appreciate his vision, his brilliance? Was he sad? Had he expected to be loved?

'Helen Wells,' he said. 'What are you doing here?'

'Got bored, sir. Thought I'd go for a walk.'

'Bored! Do you know how much work I've put into this production? Well, I'm sure you wouldn't care. Don't give a *fuck*, eh? Is that the sort of language you'd use, you and your little mates?'

She said nothing. He raised a cigarette to his lips and drew back long and deeply; he expelled a slow breath. Blue ribbons curled against the darkness. 'No, you wouldn't understand Ibsen, would you?'

Skip wondered if she could push past him.

'I've seen your type before,' he said. 'You think you're a tough little miss, I suppose. You laugh at everything. You roll your eyes and sneer. Well, I can predict your future exactly, Helen Wells. Leave school at fifteen. Job on the checkout. Hoon boyfriend who roars up and down the main drag every weekend. Pregnant at sixteen. Married at seventeen. Wrinkled old hag by the age of thirty. Hah! Make the most of your days in the sun. They won't last. No,' he finished bitterly, 'you wouldn't understand *An Enemy of the People.*'

Skip's throat had tightened, but she forced out her next words hoarsely, hotly. '*You're* the one who doesn't understand it. You wouldn't set it on a space station if you did. Can't you see how stupid that is? Those Victorian rooms stuffed with furniture, that's the whole point.' Roger hadn't told her this: Skip saw it for herself. 'The burden of it! The characters can't get out of their society,' she ploughed on. 'They're stuck in it, like you're stuck in Crater Lakes with Chickenland and Channel Eight and Puce Hardware – and Mrs Novak sucking you off in your dressing room!'

The last words slipped out before she could stop them. When she began speaking, Brooker had grimaced and turned away; now he swung back with an inarticulate cry, perhaps of rage, perhaps of despair, and went to grab her. He had no chance. Sharp rustlings sounded behind him, and a fist, exploding from the foliage, struck Howard Brooker to the path.

Startled, Skip gazed at Roger as he stepped out of the shadows. 'You've knocked him out.'

'Help me,' said Roger. 'We'll drag him into the trees.'

The pub across the way had been busy, and by the time the play resumed, many audience members were drunk and rowdy. Some simply stayed in the pub. Other people had left the theatre too. Mrs Sutton hustled Lucy away: a well-brought-up child shouldn't be exposed to such behaviour. And the play wasn't much better than its audience: 'A most distasteful choice,' the lady librarian would say the next day, as if all that happened had been Ibsen's fault.

Whoops and slow handclaps broke out as the lights went down. Stamping drummed from the dress circle. Where was P. C. Marky when you needed him? Scrunched in K8, as it happened, hoping that nothing worse than a few larrikins were in the offing in what he thought of as the 'second half'. His senior officers, bastards all, were across the road, haunches oozing over vinyl-topped barstools, beer guts sagging over straining belts.

Skip had not gone back to her seat. For the rest of interval she guarded the stage door. Roger, in his spacesuit, waited in the bushes just outside. She must keep him from the others until it was too late for them to stop him.

Just once she had slipped inside to check, as she put it, the lie of the land. The mood backstage was glum. Tonight was to have revived a noble legacy; instead, that legacy had been ground into the dirt.

'Where's Howard?' Mrs Novak wrung her hands. She stood outside his dressing room, but the door was locked and her pleadings through the panels met with no replies; the play's director and star appeared to have vanished. Fearful murmurings rippled among the cast and crew.

'Howard should be rallying the troops,' said Mr Singh, whose father had been in the Bengal Lancers.

Skip told them Brooker was preparing. 'Like Stanis-what-sky. It's his big speech next.'

When the lights went down, Skip had her chance. Briefly, all was dark. She hustled Roger into the wings. They hung back, stage left; she gripped his hand, which was hot through the glove. Next came the scene of the public meeting, when Dr Stockmann, putting his case to the disbelieving townsfolk, lost control disastrously. Every player, and various roped-in children, friends and workmates, clustered on stage; a silver platform rose above the crowd, on which (so the plan went) Howard Brooker was to denounce them all.

Ton-*ee* swished by. 'Satisfied, Howie?' he shot at Roger. 'I told you we should have done *Salad Days*.'

The curtains drew back. Noise from the auditorium swallowed the prefatory dialogue. First Citizen, Second Citizen, Third Citizen, Bystander: nobody listened to what they had to say. Mrs Novak's first line was: 'Do you think there'll be any disturbance?' The Lions Club Burgomaster burst from stage right, ray gun in hand, determined the meeting should go his way.

Roger's moment had come. Skip gasped as his hand slid from hers. Stiff-backed, he strode into glaring light. Faint applause and subdued hissing were required from the townsfolk; jeers and loud hissing rose from beyond the footlights. Dr Stockmann bowed as the crowd let him through.

'How do you do, Katrine?' he asked Mrs Novak.

'Oh, I'm all right. Now do keep your temper, Thomas.' She had not even looked at him. Nobody knew him. He was costumed and masked, with hair pressed beneath silver foil; he was Brooker's height, if better built. Skip – by now relieved, even excited – slipped from the shadows into the back of the crowd.

The scene continued. Squabbles broke out over who was to chair the meeting; the young dentist at last took the role, taking his place ponderously behind a bank of winking, whirring computers. At every turn the crowd – on stage and off – applauded, jeered, and supplied a chorus of whispers.

'I therefore beg to move' – the Burgomaster's ray gun swept the front rows – 'that this meeting declines to hear the proposed lecture or speech …'

Roger missed his cue. 'So I'm not to be heard?' he returned, too late.

The Burgomaster blustered on about the baths and their importance to the economy. Was the town to be ruined for a theory? The dentist said Stockmann must be a revolutionary, trying to bring down the administration. Ibsen's script called for a drunk at the meeting, slurring out jibes; that night, many a drunk in the audience offered more. Everybody had turned on Dr Stockmann.

Skip was barely listening. She had never stood on stage before. Bright lights seared her eyes and the blackness beyond was a fearful void, like space seen from a space station window. Burly men in silver flung the drunkard into the wings.

'Can I speak?' Roger said at last.

Reluctantly, the dentist pressed PLAY on a reel-to-reel tape recorder, bulky as a suitcase, commanding silence with futuristic bleeps and whirs. 'Dr Stockmann will address the meeting.'

Stars flared from Roger's spacesuit as he gravely mounted the platform. There, palms outspread as if to show he had no weapons, he might have been about to say, 'Blessed are the poor in spirit …' or 'Friends, Romans, countrymen …' or 'It is a far, far better thing that I do …' He started softly, paying no heed to guffaws and sighs. Proceeding, his voice grew stronger; silence fell. Players clustered closer. Some exchanged glances. What had happened to Howard? This was not the man they had known until now. Deirdre Novak fixed entranced eyes on the silver form.

Roger, as the doctor, said he had done a lot of thinking. What he had to say tonight was not what he'd planned to say. He had made a discovery more important than the pestilence in the baths. The town's sources of spiritual life were poisoned. (Murmurs and angry voices punctuated the speech.) His whole society was false. The authorities were corrupt. The leading men were fools; they were goats in a young plantation, doing harm everywhere, blocking the path of the free man whichever way he turned. Leading men, he said, should be exterminated like other noxious pests. But they were not the chief danger society faced. There were other, more perfidious enemies of truth and freedom.

'Who, then?' called the players. 'Who is it? Name, name!'

Roger's voice surged, filling the theatre with the force of his conviction. 'Yes, you may be sure I'll name them! For *this* is the great discovery I made yesterday! The most dangerous foe to truth and freedom in our midst is the compact majority. Yes, it's the confounded, compact, liberal majority!' He whipped the mask from his eyes. 'There, I've told you!'

Here it was, back in force after all these years: the talent that had dazzled Sir Laurence Olivier. Shouting, stamping, whistling filled the stage. It came from the players. It came from the audience. It came from every corner of the theatre. Skip's heart swelled. Roger Dansie, cast out in shame a generation ago, had returned in triumph. His talent, in that moment, was a volcanic force, sweeping away all in its path. No one laughed. No one jeered.

Yet all was not well. Deirdre Novak clutched her hands to her chest. She might have woken suddenly, painfully to find herself in a different play, a story of ghosts and hauntings. What went through her mind in that moment? Horror, no doubt, at the irony of fate. Deirdre had done with Howard what she had failed to do with Roger, but the reenactment had gone all wrong. She had tried to return to the past and make it different. Her efforts had been in vain. The past had risen up to destroy her, as it had threatened to do all along.

Roger cried, 'The majority is never right – never, I say! That's one of the social lies a free, thinking man is bound to rebel against. Who makes up the majority in any given country? Is it the wise men or the fools? I think we must agree that the fools are in a terrible, overwhelming majority, all the wide world over. But how can it ever be right for the fools to rule over the wise men?'

Players tried to shout him down, but ringingly he declared that truth was always on the side of the minority.

There was more, but Roger didn't have the chance to say it. Deirdre Novak cried out. She rushed downstage, covered her face, collapsed to her knees. Confusion filled the theatre. Was this part of the play?

All doubts were gone when she turned, pointed and shrieked, 'Roger Dansie – it's Roger Dansie!'

Silence fell. Skip staggered as if somebody had pushed her. A hot rush, like vomit, spread in her chest. Her knees, she thought, would give out beneath her, but she forced herself forward – one step, two steps – pushing through the crowd towards the front of the stage. Something terrible had happened. There was a grenade in the theatre. Somebody had pulled the pin and tossed it, and it hurtled, as if for ever, through the crowded auditorium.

Roger tried to continue, but his voice failed. He stood blinking, face blank. On stage, players had scattered. A yell came from the stalls: 'Dirty bastard!' Then another: 'Bloody poofter!' 'Murderer!' Soon, boos and catcalls filled the darkness; a beer bottle shattered on the stage. Drunkards surged from their seats.

The world became a blur. As the lights plunged to black, Roger leaped down from the platform. Skip grabbed his hand, struggling with him through a jostling forest. They battered out of the stage door. They blundered across the gardens towards the low wall. Where now? Behind them, a crowd had spilled out of the theatre, eager for mayhem.

A voice rasped, 'Over here.' Jack, with the Harley!

They bundled Roger into the sidecar. Strangled gurgling burst from his throat and he shuddered as if in the grip of fever. In Skip's brain the words thudded: My fault. All my fault.

Jack gunned the motor. 'Get behind me and hang on.'

# Chapter Eighteen

'Roger? We're home.'

Skip touched him and he flinched. Curled like a question mark, he cowered in the sidecar, legs drawn up awkwardly, hands clawing his face as if to tear it from his skull. Gently, Jack shouldered Skip aside, speaking soft words she could not make out. Roger's head lolled. He could not respond, and shuffled like an old man as Jack helped him up the veranda steps. Heat, pregnant with summer, hung like fruit in the tangled trees. Insects chorused frenetically in the dark.

'He'll be all right, won't he?' Skip's voice cracked. In the drawing room, she watched helplessly as Jack lowered Roger to a sofa. There could be no hope of getting him up to his room; his legs seemed unable to hold his weight. Jack told Skip to get blankets and she raced upstairs. Moonlight flickered goldenly at the window as she ripped the blankets from her own bed.

Outside, car doors slammed shut. When Skip returned to the drawing room, Mr Novak was bent over the sofa. He silently took the blankets. Roger was convulsing – in the grip, it seemed, of a seizure. Jack poured brandy. Marlo, still in costume, peeped through the tasselled curtains; Pavel, head hanging, stood beside her. Honza was the only one who looked at Skip. He seemed frightened. Mr Novak took the glass from Jack and held it to Roger's lips.

Roger tried to speak. Where was the voice that had dazzled Olivier, that had thundered to the furthest seats in the King Edward VII Theatre? All that remained was a reedy gasping, as if the force that had infused him was gone, never to return, spirited away like lost time.

'Has he been like this before?' said Marlo.

'Not quite this bad.' Mr Novak smoothed Roger's forehead. Long moments passed before he grew quiet. Tears pressed intolerably in Skip's eyes. When Mr Novak turned towards her she felt the accusation swing back like a pendulum, poised to toll the hour.

He said simply, 'It was too much.'

Patterns in the carpet leaped out under the lights. The clock on the mantelpiece thudded metallically, Baskerville howled somewhere in the dark, and a voice that seemed to swell from the air said, 'My fault. All my fault.'

Skip thought the words had come from her own throat, and was startled to realise they were Honza's. He burst out in sobs; she went to him, and her own tears followed swiftly as she wrapped her arms around him. His shoulders were thin and shook violently. Honza was not the oblivious boy he seemed. Strings of snot swung from his nose and she didn't care.

'My poor children!' Mr Novak encircled them both in his warm, soft embrace. 'The fault is mine. I should never have let Roger stay in this town. I was selfish. I wanted him here. We've got to get him away.'

Skip brushed her eyes. 'Away? But where?'

'He has a cousin in Sydney. Malcolm McKirtle's an ABC scriptwriter. More than once he's urged Roger to go and live with him. It's a big city.' Mr Novak looked sadly at his friend. Roger appeared to be sleeping now, though from time to time he shivered and his teeth chattered. 'He'll be all right by the morning, I hope. Then I'll take him. It's a long way. Dangerous, what with his health. But I've no choice. He'll never be safe in Crater Lakes.'

'I'll take him.' It was Pavel who spoke.

'You?' said his father.

'I've been thinking, you see. Oh, I suppose you think I'm not much good at that. Marlo's helped me see things more clearly. Roger's helped in his way. Everything that's happened here in Crater Lakes has helped. But mostly I had to understand for myself. I've got things straight now. It's time for me to go.'

'No.' Mr Novak understood at once. His face was ashen as he stared at his son. 'You've been called up. It's your duty.'

'Are you going to tell me about the fight against communism?' When Pavel stepped forward, Skip saw, to her surprise, that he was taller than his father. 'You ran away when you were my age,' Pavel said. 'Now it's my turn. I'm not going to end up like Baz. And for what? I've been thinking about this war. I didn't understand it before. And now I reckon I do. I'm running away, and not because I'm a coward. I'm running away because I'm brave.'

Mr Novak nodded. Perhaps at another time he would have argued, but now he knew it was no good. Crumpled bags hung beneath his eyes and his jowls were grey and pendulous. He said quietly, 'Where will you go? What will you do?'

'Sydney, like you said. You can hide out in the big city. Give yourself a different name.'

'And I'm going with you,' said Marlo.

'But your exams …?' said Pavel, astonished.

She went to stand beside him. 'Maybe I've put too much trust in exams. It's time to trust in life.'

Skip remembered her plan to escape with Marlo to the shabby glamour of Kings Cross. That had been a fantasy, she realised, but now perhaps the fantasy would come true. Already there were three bound for Sydney: Pavel, Marlo, Roger. And what if there were a fourth? There had to be. Hope surged in Skip's chest, then plummeted again, as she saw in Marlo's eyes the answer to a question that had not yet been asked. And, Skip knew, she would never ask it. Of course not: Skip Wells was a child, just a child. Marlo Wells was a child no longer. Time is a terrible thing. Blankly, Skip surveyed the drawing room: the green stripy wallpaper; the shelves of leathery books; the mirror over the mantelpiece, framed like an old master; the glimmering varnish of the grand piano.

'Let's get ready,' Marlo said to Pavel. 'We'll need to pack for Roger too.'

But the chance was lost. As they went to the door, an explosion rocked the room. Skip gasped, crouched. A brick had crashed through the window. Glass lay scattered on the carpet, the curtains whipped back and forth, and a cheer sounded from outside.

Honza was the first to move, rushing out to the veranda, though his father called him back. The boy put a foot through a rotted floorboard, stumbled into a wicker chair; he kicked, cursing, but was just in time to see two silhouettes scrambling away towards the open gates.

'Bastards! Come back!' Limping, Honza made it into the long grass just as one, two, three, four motorbikes burst as if from nowhere and revved across the lawn. They swirled around him; the riders, monstrous insects in their flashing helmets, bellowed in triumph. One slapped the side of Honza's head. Gasping, Honza sank to his knees as the bikes accelerated away.

Skip at once was beside him. 'Are you hurt?'

Stunned, Honza could say nothing, but rose unsteadily to his feet. For a moment the boy and girl clung together, trembling; then, looking up, they saw a line of cars racing towards them down the road. And not just cars: among them was Sandy Campbell's Greyhound. The whole population of Crater Lakes, it seemed, had descended on the old Dansie house. Vehicles screeched to a halt. Drunken men lurched into the night. The coach doors squealed open.

'Quick,' said Skip. 'We've got to warn the others.'

But there was no time. They had barely regained the veranda before the attack began. Boots slammed through the grass. There were ululations, shrieks and chants as torches seared the darkness. They plunged inside the house with barely a moment to spare. Rocks rained down on the roof. Pavel and Marlo secured the locks but footsteps thundered all around. Fists hammered on the doors. Somebody swung up to the second-storey veranda. Baskerville, in the garden, howled and gnashed. Skip hoped he would rip out somebody's throat. She crouched with Honza under the piano as a desperate Jack, shotgun in hand, drove off the first wave of attack. Blasts boomed above the melee.

'Maniac!' voices cried. 'Fucking abo maniac!'

Quiet descended slowly after that. Skip and Honza, after some moments, crawled out from beneath the piano. The drawing room was a shambles of dust and glass. A missile had gashed the piano's lacquered top, and the mirror over the mantelpiece had cracked and fallen in shards to the floor.

'It's the OK Corral!' Pavel released Marlo from his arms. 'Where's Wyatt Earp when you need him?'

Jack was bleeding from a cut to the face.

'My God.' Marlo went to him. 'Let me help you.'

'No. Leave me.' He dashed blunt hands against the blood. 'Them buggers will be back soon enough.'

The lights flickered twice, then guttered out. 'Damn, they've got the generator. Find candles,' Mr Novak told Skip.

'What about Roger? We have to move him.'

Mr Novak had stayed with Roger all through the attack. 'He's out cold now. Cold as if he were dead. Damn, damn.' His voice shook as if on the verge of sobs. 'But those cowards wouldn't touch him. Let them try.'

'Hello?' The new voice came from the veranda. A torch played through the darkened drawing room, its yellow beam buffeting the piano, the clock, a brick on the floor, and catching blindingly in the mantelpiece mirror. Cautiously, a figure stepped through smashed windows.

'Get back!' Jack brandished his shotgun.

'Now put that down, eh?' The voice was male, young – afraid, but attempting to hide it. The torch hit Pavel's face and he squinted. 'For Christ's sake, Pav, can't you control your abo? He's pushed his luck one time too many. I'm going to have to run him in, I'm afraid.'

'What? We're under attack.' Pavel crunched forward over powdery glass. 'Look at this place! It's a war zone. And what the hell are you doing about it, Marky Bonner?'

P. C. Marky held firm. 'Shooting at people is against the law.'

'And them bastards out there? I suppose it's not against the law to trash people's houses?'

'Ye-e-s,' Marky admitted. 'But Pav, people are upset. Can you blame them, after what yous lot pulled tonight? I don't know if you're a poofter too or your dad is or what's going on, but that bloke shamed this town in front of the world. Don't worry,' he added, weary now, as if making a concession more generous than circumstances could warrant, 'I've called for reinforcements.' Reinforcements: Marky liked that word, it seemed. 'But we're going to have a hell of a time seeing that lot off. Pissed out of their brains, half of them. We can't arrest them all. Sandy Campbell reckons they just want ...'

'Want what?' Mr Novak said coldly.

Marky sniffed. Perhaps he knew he was playing an ignoble part. Perhaps it galled him, but he had no choice. 'They want Mr Dansie to leave town. If yous can ... make him go, that's all. Then they'll go home.'

'Call yourself a cop!' Sneering, Pavel slapped Marky in the chest. Torchlight veered wildly through the dark.

Skip tried to push between them. 'Pav, don't. The bugger's not worth it.'

'Come here, Constable Bonner.' Mr Novak remained calm, beckoning Marky towards him. 'See, here on the couch? There's your enemy of the people.' He gestured down to where Roger lay corpse-like. 'To think they still hate him so much, after all these years!'

'He's not – ?' Marky's voice cracked.

'No, he's still breathing. Don't worry, we'll take him away in the morning. He won't be back here again. Would you believe he loved this town? Nothing went well for him after he left. So he came home. I believe he's a legend in some quarters, a myth. The ghost of Crater Lakes! For a long time Jack and I were the only ones who knew about him – really knew, I mean.'

'Where's the abo?' Marky said doggedly. 'I'm running him in.'

'We both love him, you see,' Mr Novak went on.

Marky's face twisted. He looked as if he would gladly turn and run; instead, struggling, it seemed, to keep his voice level, he said, 'I'll say Mr Dansie's leaving town, all right? You make sure he does, and I won't press charges against the abo. But he'd better give me that gun.'

'Do as he says, Jack.' Mr Novak's voice was soft. 'But I'm telling you, Constable Bonner, if anything else happens here tonight I'm holding you responsible. You're not a kid playing cops and robbers now.'

'You reckon I don't know that?' Marky, trying – too hard, it seemed – to be a man, snatched the shotgun out of Jack's hand. Quickly, efficiently, he emptied the ammunition. 'Count yourself lucky no one's been hurt. Christ, what were you doing, putting that crazy bugger in the play? People in the Lakes have always felt strongly about Mr Dansie. He's, he's a –'

'Yes?' said Mr Novak. 'Tell me what he is.'

Marky shook his head and said, 'He's a murderer.'

'Not quite,' Mr Novak replied with dignity. 'And remember this: whatever Roger is or was, he's done his time. He's paid – and paid, and paid. Must he keep paying for the rest of his life?'

'Get out, Marky,' Pavel said.

'I'll tell them he's going,' Marky said again, and made his exit, shotgun in hand. Jack, defeated, melted into the dark.

Skip turned to Honza. 'Come on. Let's get candles.'

The candles gave the room an unearthly beauty. At the piano, Mr Novak played Fauré, Debussy, Satie. The notes sounded like echoes of another world. Different music drifted in from outside. Honza, who had been scouting, said that parked cars were banked up for a hundred yards down the road. Food and kegs of beer had been ferried in; people had lit bonfires; Sandy Campbell fried sausages on a fork while 'Eagle Rock' blared from car radios and kids danced.

Several times they had heard excited voices close by or footsteps creaking across the veranda. Skip, brandishing a shard of broken glass, had seen off a group of boys who tried to look through the window. But there had been no further attacks. The clock beat like a metronome. The night had entered its long middle, when all should be sleeping and the world still.

'Won't they go?' Marlo said to Pavel. 'They must.'

'That lot? They haven't had their show.'

'But when we bring out Roger, what then?'

'We'll drive away. That's all.'

'Until some kid chucks a stone. It won't end well – it can't.'

Pavel kissed her temple. They sat apart from the others, tangled together, but not uncomfortably, in a single deep armchair. Scratchy horsehair burst through split leather. Marlo had changed out of her silver suit. She was sad and happy. Life lay before her like a strange highway leading to a place she had never been. Her suitcase stood in the hall; Olly Olivetti, in his green zippered case with the single black stripe, waited beside it expectantly.

But Pavel's next words did not surprise her. He said, 'I can't take you to Sydney. You know that, don't you? This is a crazy night. It's not real. Those exams of yours, you've got to do them.'

'How can you say that, here in Roger's house? This is the place where everything changed. Nothing can be the same for us again. Not now.' But Marlo, as she spoke, felt something flutter inside her, something trapped and frightened, and wondered what was right and what was wrong and how she could know the difference. What would Germaine do? she wondered. But Marlo wasn't Germaine. She was herself: there was nobody else she could be. The strange highway was one she had to pass down alone.

'We've had a good time, haven't we?' Pavel was saying. 'I'm no hero. I'm not brave or smart. If it wasn't for Mr Dansie, I'd be off to the army, not Sydney. Oh, Marlo! You'll meet people. You'll do things. You don't need me. You're so beautiful. You're so smart. I love you.'

She picked at a paint splash on the knee of his jeans. 'And I love you,' she said and began to cry.

# Chapter Nineteen

*Where am I?*

Brenton Lumsden woke with a snort. His head had fallen forward, constricting his windpipe. Knives stabbed his forehead and his bladder felt as though it would burst. Silver-blue moonlight played at wide windows. Snores and grunts rose all around; others on the Greyhound still slept, splayed at odd angles across sticky vinyl seats. The air was a sludge of stale aromas: smoke, beer, sweat, belches, farts.

Lummo's big feet slapped down the aisle, crushing a Foster's can underfoot. He was the only kid on the coach. The others were grown men, mates of Mr Campbell's, except for some old slut of a barmaid who had let the blokes grope her. One of her tits, a mound of mottled flab, hung half out of her dress. Lummo snapped his eyes away, ashamed. Mr Campbell, in the driver's seat, slumped back like a murder victim; a dark-stained upper set, drooling spit, hung from his gaping mouth. There was a sound like a raspberry.

*Aw, Mr Campbell!* It smelled like rotten eggs.

Lummo had to piss real bad. Holding his breath, he reached over Mr Campbell's beer gut, jabbing at levers until he found the one that released the door. Gasping, he zigzagged down the high steps, nearly turning his ankle. Fuck. Fuck-fuck-fuck. His stream drummed and drummed against the Greyhound's flank. Afterwards his dick throbbed as if he had spunked himself, and the pounding behind his eyes doubled in force. He laid his forehead against the coach's chilly side and rolled it back and forth. Was he going to chunder?

Fewer cars lined the road now. Coppers had moved some drivers on; others had got bored and buggered off. What had they expected? Lummo imagined the poofter coming out while they pelted him with rocks. Mr Campbell had reckoned they would give him until morning. 'Can't have his sort in Crater Lakes,' he had said to Marky Bonner, and Marky Bonner knew it was a threat.

The old Dansie house rose, grim and silent, against the pale moon. Lummo, curious, restless, scuffed his way between screening trees. Something had to happen: that much he knew.

His mum would kill him when he got home. Let her. Stupid old twat. When uproar broke out in the theatre last night, he had been glad to lose her. Slipping into the Greyhound just before it roared off down Volcano Street, he felt a sense of victory. Since the Show, everyone had laughed at him, jeered at him. Even his so-called mates – Kenny and Greaso, those bastards – had turned their backs on him. Now look at him! He had stuffed himself with sausages cooked over the campfire. Blokes had given him tinnies and he'd glugged them back. Mr Campbell lent him a lighter so he could light everyone's smokes. 'And have one for yourself too, eh?' The lighter still lay in Lummo's pocket and he fingered it fondly like a rabbit's foot. Mr Campbell had told jokes. There was one about a girl called Fuckarada; everybody damned near pissed themselves. Lummo told the one about 'Would you bum off Brooker for an apple?' as if he'd made it up himself, and they liked that too. Fuck the kids at school. Lummo was one of the blokes. The old slut mussed his Brylcreem, pulled off his bow tie, kissed his lips. Blokes played two-up and he tossed the coins. 'Come in, spinner!'

Lummo scouted around the house. Would the poofter ever come out? He looked into one side window, then another. *Stickybeak*, Mum would say. What could he see? Dust. Filth. Mum would have a fit. He tried a door at the back. Shut fast. Bugger it, he would get in somehow. There were broken windows at the front, but he didn't fancy clambering over jagged glass. He was more likely to get caught there, too. What about upstairs? Feeling like a hero, he grabbed a pillar of the back veranda, balanced on a rickety railing and hauled himself up, then thumped down on the decking above. The long rear of the property stretched away: sheds, stables, wreck of a barn, horror-movie trees. A loose strut of the balustrade lay beside him and he picked it up. Might need a weapon.

Crouching low, careful of creaky boards, he made his way to a glassed-in door and peered inside. No sign of anyone. Had the bastards slipped away?

The room contained a big old-fashioned bed. Curled asleep on the bed, grey in moonlight, was a fat stripy cat. Lummo hated cats. On cracker nights, the Lum's Den's favourite game had been to catch one, stick a banger up its arse, and light the fuse. What about that mother cat with kittens at school? He'd fixed that one, hadn't he? He shuddered with pleasure as he remembered the cat, its spine broken, trying to crawl back under the portable, dragging itself on its front paws, while the back ones trailed uselessly behind and the kittens bleated, *mew-mew-mew*. Best laugh ever. For weeks afterwards a delighted Lummo had imitated the paddling front paws and the pathetic cheeping kittens.

He slammed his stick into a panel of glass. The cat looked up sharply. 'Here, kitty kitty.' Still the knives drove into Lummo's forehead, and as he reached inside the door and turned the handle he sliced his wrist on the jagged glass. 'Fuck.' Blood ran from his wrist as he stumbled inside. The cat stared at him, but didn't move.

Lummo raised his stick.

Skip heard the smashing glass.

She had woken, minutes earlier, with a guilty start. All through the night she had imagined its end: Roger and his guards (as she thought of them) emerging in mournful procession; the crowd silent, strangely awed, as the Land Rover rolled away, never to return. She had vowed not to sleep; no break must come between night and morning. But eventually she had fallen into a heavy doze, head on arm, legs drawn beneath her in a dusty armchair. Someone had covered her with a blanket. When she opened her eyes again, she saw the others still asleep in the tea-coloured light: Marlo and Pavel, his arms around her shoulders, her head resting on his chest; Honza, by the piano, curled up with Baskerville; Mr Novak in a stiff-backed chair, head nuzzling his chest like a pigeon's in its coop. Only Roger had moved. He had gone. Skip felt disoriented, as if their vigil of a few hours before had been a dream or a story she had heard. Empty glasses and plates lay all around. On a low table stood a chess set with pieces still in play.

She got up and went to the window. Far off, through the trees, glimmered the Greyhound. All was quiet. She stretched, yawned, and passed into the hall. Moonlight spilled down the wide staircase, exposing threadbare carpet and missing banister rails. She climbed the stairs. Where *was* Roger? Perhaps he was looking his last on the old Dansie house. She must find him. She would hold his hand and tell him, as if she believed it, that everything would be all right; then he would hold her in his arms and she would cry and not be ashamed. In the murk of the upstairs corridor, she softly called his name.

She heard a crack, a clatter. She stiffened. Breaking glass? Wide awake now, she turned her head this way and that. Her heart pounded hugely in her chest. She heard a cry, then a howl. Mowser? The sounds had come from a far room. Gasping, she raced towards it, to find the frenzied cat engaged in battle with a rolling, writhing Brenton Lumsden. Lummo, blood flowing from his wrists and arms and face, grabbed Mowser by the neck. The stick swung back in his hand, ready to strike.

Skip hurled herself on the bed, knocking Lummo sideways. The stick clattered down and Mowser leaped free, hissing, tail upright like a chimney-brush, every strand of fur aquiver with fear and rage.

'Bastard!' Fury gave Skip strength. For desperate moments she grappled with Lummo. They rolled across the squeaking bed. He bit her ear, gouged her eyes. She slammed her knee into the boy's crotch and he twisted away, lowing like a cow, and crashed off the bed's high edge.

Lummo gurgled like a huge, hideous baby. Skip dropped at once onto his squelching belly, dug her fingers into his hair, dragged up his head and pounded it against the floorboards. His fat rippled like an earthquake as he bucked her off. He sprang up. 'I'll kill you,' he cried, but blood from a deep scratch on his forehead flowed into his eyes. When he reached up to wipe it away Skip saw her chance, charged, and pushed him in the chest. He reeled back through the door to the veranda. He slammed against the railings. Rotten wood gave way and he fell.

Skip leaned, panting, over the balustrade. Lummo lay spreadeagled in a prickly bush below. She could hardly breathe. Somehow, in the fight, she had twisted her foot. Pain shot from her ankle. Wincing, she made her way back into the room. She sank down on the bed. The covers were smeared with blood. She sobbed and sobbed and wished she could stop.

Lummo, meanwhile, peeled himself clumsily out of the bush and pushed himself to his feet. He took a few steps, threw up, then leaned against a column of the veranda, gulping air. Had he fought against a girl and been defeated? Never. In the darkness beneath a smashed window he made out a pile of kindling, an eight-gallon drum and a heap of rags. As soon as he saw it, his decision was made. Brenton Lumsden must not be defeated. Nothing else mattered.

He picked up the drum and shook it; liquid sloshed inside. Efficiently he unscrewed the cap and upended the contents over the rags, the kindling, and the floorboards all around. The reek of kerosene filled his nostrils, turning his stomach again, and he swallowed back a fresh tide of vomit.

The cigarette lighter Mr Campbell had given him was still in his pocket. Lummo lit a dripping rag and tossed it down, almost burning his toes – he sprang back, laughing – as the flames rushed up. Revenge, yes; but even as the boy saw flames wreathe around the columns of the veranda he felt a sense of pointlessness. What recompense could there be for being Brenton Lumsden? He thought of his mother combing Brylcreem through his hair, demanding that at all costs 'my Brenton' grow up to be a nice young man. He knew he never would. He thought of his father, who had shot through, sneering at 'Billy Bunter' and saying, 'Christ, Valmai! You'll never make a man out of that fat poof.' That was years back, and the time since then had only proved his father right. Lummo hated himself. He would never be a man. He was a fat poof. He breathed in kero and smoke. The lighter dropped from his hand. Tears ran down his bloodied face. He wanted to curl up somewhere safe. He wanted his mother, but she didn't come.

Then bellowing filled the air, and Baskerville was upon him.

As the claws ripped him, as the jaws snapped and tore, Brenton Lumsden knew he was finally getting what he deserved. Weakly he tried to cover his face with his pudgy hands. He screamed and screamed. Nobody heard. Nobody came. The flames by now were deafening. Glass shattered. Burning beams crashed down.

\* \* \*

Nothing lasts in Australia. It had only been a matter of time before the tinderbox that was the old Dansie house, this flimsy imposition on an alien land, succumbed to the fury of fire. Orange-red leaped like sudden flowers; in moments, flames took hold in the shabby back rooms, licking with animal fervour at the rotted timbers, the old curtains and hangings, the stiff dark papers that still sagged in strips from too many walls. Grey treacherous fingers coiled beneath doors, then clouds pumped from every doorway crack. Nothing could stop the fire from spreading. Smoke cascaded down the shadowy hallway.

It was Marlo who raised the alarm. Strange dreams had flickered through her sleep, dreams of water, air, earth; now she dreamed of fire and started awake, hot-faced and trembling. What was that smell? Pavel stirred, complaining, as she pulled away from him. Blearily, she stepped into the hall. She cried out. Filling her gaze was the cloud, a wall of advancing black-grey-white. Magma, red and rippling, gleamed from the back of the staircase.

Marlo remembered little of what came next. First they careered through the smashed front window, as if from one life into another. Here was Honza; here was Pavel; here was the darting, miaowing cat. Roger, still in his spacesuit, arrived suddenly among them from somewhere – had he been out in the grounds, perhaps, when he saw the spreading fire? – and helped Mr Novak, who coughed and stumbled. Others were there too: Marky Bonner, rushing forward, desperate to show leadership in the crisis; Sandy Campbell and his mates from the coach, scratching their heads and saying 'Streuth!' and never thinking to run for a hose, a bucket. It would have done no good anyway; the house was already gone.

Smoke rose from the gables and every upstairs window in dark, choking gouts by the time Doug Puce's van tore to a halt at the roadside. The passenger door burst open, and charging forward came Noreen Puce. In the weird glow of firelight, she might have embodied the spirit of an ancient femininity. Her skinny husband, struggling behind her, could do nothing to hold her back. Wild-eyed, she swivelled this way and that, before she found the object of her fury.

Sandy Campbell turned, grinning, as if this were some jape, then howled in astonishment as the enormous woman descended upon him and pummelled him with rock-like fists. 'Bastard!' she cried. 'Them's my kiddies was in that house – my kiddies, you murdering bastard!' Someone, no doubt, should have tried to intervene. But they could only look on, astonished, as all the force of Queen Noreen's rage erupted over the man who had been her most loyal courtier. He fell to the ground. Still she assailed him.

Meanwhile, Marlo sank into the grass. It was cool, wet with dew. Pavel was beside her, holding her tight. All that night she had dreamed of dying. In dreams of water, she had been drowning; in dreams of air, she had dropped without a parachute, green paddocks rushing up from below; she was buried in the earth; and then she was Joan of Arc, bound to the stake as flames roasted her flesh. But Marlo knew she was not the one burning.

'Skip!' The scream leaped from her like blood from a severed artery. She sprang up again, her gaze sweeping across the lawn. Where was Skip? Once more, in agony, she cried her sister's name. All around her, others shouted too. The cat revolved in howling circles on the lawn. Marlo, suddenly decisive, knew what she must do. She rushed back to the house. Even now there were tunnels between the flames, smoky corridors she could push her way through. She had no choice. She had to find Skip.

Sudden strong hands grabbed her. She cried out and struggled, but it was useless. 'Let me,' the man was saying. 'If anyone's going to die in this house, it'll be me.' And, with no time to waste, he flung her aside. All around the lawn, screams and shouts rang out as Roger Dansie plunged back into the house.

Marlo could only imagine what happened next: Roger, like a silver vision, charging through the smoke; Roger calling and calling, hurtling into one black, noxious room after another; Roger thundering up the stairs, two at a time, as already the carpet smouldered underfoot. On the upper floor, the air was thick with smoke. From bedroom to bedroom Roger stumbled, gasping. He called Skip's name again, screamed it over the gathering roar. Nothing could be saved from his burning house. But the child: the child.

From the end of the corridor came a cry.

Afterwards, Skip could not remember when she first realised the house was on fire. With Lummo gone, she had lain on the bed in tears, face sticky with blood that she half believed was hers; then, all at once, the thick, choking clouds surrounded her and she scrambled up, taking only two steps to the door before her ankle buckled. She cried out. Pain shot up her leg, then there was no pain, only knowledge. Heat closed around her. Here was the end.

But it was not the end. Skip had no dream of a saviour, but one came all the same: a silver spaceman, battling through the blackness and calling her name. He scooped her into his arms.

Skip huddled against Roger's chest as he carried her down the corridor. Thump, thump: she could hear his heart. Dimly she was aware of the clouds growing thicker, darker, hotter; down, down the stairs they went, reaching the landing just as the stained-glass window exploded around them in scorching shards; below lay the hall and the door and the lawn outside that shimmered like water beyond the front veranda. Charred wallpaper coiled down, and ancient paintings crashed to the floor. Did Roger, in this moment, think of his mother descending these stairs in glittering jewels while a child gazed up at her in dazzled wonder? Gone, all gone. It was the end of the world, but a new world lay ahead.

As they descended, Skip could see that the flames downstairs were brighter and the smoke still thicker. Roger's breath was stertorous and he thumped unsteadily down one stair, then another. Down, down. His heart, keeping time, echoed like a drum. 'Not much longer,' Skip tried to say, just as a sharp crack filled the air. Gazing up, she saw a heavy beam, brightly burning, suspended for one timeless moment against the high ceiling. Her warning cry caught in her throat, and she could only gasp as the beam smashed down, striking Roger's back. He barely cried out, only plunged forward, his arms releasing her as he fell.

Skip rolled helplessly down the stairs. Heat suffused her arm and she looked down, almost detachedly, to see her shirtsleeve burning. She slapped at it weakly. Flames played across the hall ceiling, which billowed as if it were a sail. Skip had landed at the foot of the stairs, looking up; behind her lay the open door, the bags – Olly Olivetti and all – still waiting beside it, naively trusting, it seemed, in the adventure that had been promised for that day. Midway up the stairs lay Roger. The beam that pinned him was vast and heavy as the mast of an old ship. Skip crawled up the staircase towards him.

He shook his head. 'Go!'

She would not. She raised herself to her feet. Pain stabbed her ankle and she fell at once; she was a wounded bird, struggling to fly. So instead she pulled herself up the stairs. She had no choice. Already flames surrounded Roger; she crawled to him, tugged his hand violently as if, were her faith only strong enough, she could wrench him free. She knew she could not, but she would never leave him. He was her father and she loved him more than life.

With all the strength left to him, Roger pushed her away. His back was twisted strangely, his legs lying useless. 'I can't ... I can't – go!' he cried again.

She gasped, 'I can't leave you!'

His voice was barely audible against the roar, the cracking and crashing of the blazing house. What was he saying? Skip missed most of the words. But not their spirit. That was graven on her heart and always would be. She must go, he rasped out. She must, for him. He said they were like each other, Roger Dansie and Skip Wells. For all that was different about them, under the skin they were the same. But Skip's life, Roger told her, would not be like his. She was free to fly. He had crashed back to the ground, but she would not. He had tried and failed, but she would not. His Skip? Never! The world lay before her. She must take it, make it her own. 'Don't die for me,' she heard him say. 'Live! Go into the world and live … for me.'

Her tears flowed and flowed. 'No! You can't make me leave you – I won't.'

For the last time his voice rose. 'Skip, obey your father – go!'

'Roger, I can't live without you – don't make me!'

'It wasn't your fault. Remember that. None of this was your fault.' For one last moment he gripped her hand. 'Now go – go into the world and be my daughter. Quick. Now. Go –'

'*Daddy!*' The cry might have come from a small child, but the word was one she had never before had a chance to speak. How she loved him! He *was* her daddy, he had to be; because if, for each of us, there is a family of the heart – heedless of history, deeper than blood – Skip had found hers. She was Roger's daughter, nobody else's. But how, then, could she leave him in a burning house? And how could he not hold her, hold her to the end?

'I love you, Skip.' Firmly, he pushed her away. Aghast, she stumbled back, in the very moment when the ceiling fell.

When Skip emerged from the flames, half crawling, Marlo flailed forward to embrace her. And in the dazzled moments that followed, there they all were, the little band who had held out that night against a whole town of enemies: Skip and Marlo, Pavel and Honza, kindly Mr Novak. Some might have seen another figure, too: Jack, barely visible against the dark trees. Yes, they were all there: the family of the heart, minus one.

Clutched in Skip's arms was Olly Olivetti.

* * *

The fire burned and burned, consuming the old building in less than an hour. When the fire brigade arrived, far too late, the house that had once been the grandest in Crater Lakes was a ruinous, smoking shell. Townsfolk lingered, cowed but curious; P. C. Marky did his best to move them on. Smoke traced a black, ragged zigzag against the brilliant dawn.

# Chapter Twenty

'Hey, Mowser.'

Skip had been trying to call him Purcell but kept slipping back: he looked so much like Mowser. Insistently he butted his head against the heel of her hand; his purr was loud as a lawnmower. She sat on the decking outside the sleepout, legs dangling from the edge, swinging a little. Darkness had fallen hours before, but summer heat still lingered over the garden.

Footsteps sounded on the decking. 'Still up?'

Marlo sat down beside her. She wore jeans and a T-shirt and had knotted a leather strap around her wrist. She flicked back her hair; it had grown long and unruly, like Germaine's. Skip felt a plunge of sadness. Light from the sleepout window painted the sisters a shimmery, burnished gold. They sat for a time in silence.

At last Marlo said, 'I'm wondering what to say.'

'So am I.' They had said it all already. Yes, Skip knew why Marlo had to go. Yes, Skip would be all right. No, Auntie Noreen wasn't so bad, was she? No, Skip would never end up in Puce Hardware.

That afternoon they had gone to the cemetery. Heat had spilled from a pale unclouded sky, and the sticky tang of eucalyptus coiled around them like a soporific. Tombstones tumbled whitely downhill; below, the town lay like a map, its wide unbusy streets in a flat grid. The sisters stepped into a grove of melaleucas. Sunlight spangled them through leathery leaves as they kneeled together. The grass around the grave grew in dry clumps, and ants swirled officiously over the brown, cracking earth. Only months had passed since Roger's death, but already this last of the Dansie graves was joining the others, becoming history: the royal line of Crater Lakes was extinct, like the volcano that loomed above the town.

On the decking, Skip stroked Purcell. 'All packed?'

'All packed.' Marlo put an arm around her sister's shoulders. 'What's it like, back at school?'

'It's different this year. Without Brooker ...' Should she mention Brooker? They had heard enough about him to last them all their lives. Since Deirdre Novak ran off with the schoolteacher, Auntie Noreen had spoken of little else; the subject, indeed, seemed to cheer her up. Hadn't she always said Deirdre Gull was a whore? So much for her airs and graces! Even Valmai Lumsden's mood had lifted a little as she turned to themes other than poor Brenton's trials at the hands of his plastic surgeon. Deirdre Gull, Mrs Lumsden declared exultantly, had been just the sort of woman to keep a vicious dog.

'Make sure you study,' said Marlo. 'It's our only way out, you know.'

'Of Crater Lakes? I know.' At another time, Skip might have been annoyed by the reminder, but not now. Already, it seemed, she saw Marlo in the morning, suitcase in hand, climbing the steps of Sandy Campbell's Greyhound; she saw herself watch as it drew away. Skip knew she should be happy, not sad. Marlo's matriculation exam results had been the best in the state. To Skip, it was no surprise. Marlo Wells would have done brilliantly, Mr Brooker or no Mr Brooker. Reporters – photographers, too – had come from *The Advertiser*, from the *Crater Lakes Times*. Beaming, Auntie Noreen told them she had always encouraged Marlo's studies. She seemed genuinely proud of her niece's success. And so was Skip.

'You done real good, Marlo,' she said, her voice thick.

'"Done real good"? Oh, Skip!' Marlo gestured towards the Novak house. 'That boyfriend of yours is a bad influence.'

'He's not my boyfriend!' Why did everyone think he was?

'You'll watch out, won't you? You can have fun with a boy like that, that's one thing –'

'Like you did with Pav?'

'Just be careful.'

'I'm thirteen! Honza's a mate, that's all.'

It was Sunday, but no lights from the Sanctum burned through the trees; no music, no laughter, no clinking of glasses rippled towards them down the dark rise. Mr Novak, so everyone said, had let everything slide since his wife went away. They had taken him back at the town hall – nobody else could do all the things he did – but still he was in a bad way and everyone knew it. Valmai Lumsden, gleefully, had used the word 'breakdown'. Honza, for his part, had become a moody, silent boy.

'What did Pav's letter say?' Skip said now.

'Not much. They're at a camp in Queensland. Basic training's nearly done; they'll be shipped out soon. Oh, and he's sure his mum will come home.'

'You reckon she will?' said Skip.

'What can Howard give her? Hardly London, Paris, Berlin.' *An Enemy of the People* had earned Howard a droll review in *The Advertiser* – '"Director's Theatre" Comes to Crater Lakes' – but South Australia was not exactly rich in opportunities for experimental drama. This year Howard was teaching at Prince Alfred College. There, scandalising the stuffier parents, he might mount an avant-garde production or two – *Waiting for Godot* or *Hair* or *The Effect of Gamma Rays on Man-in-the-Moon Marigolds* – but Marlo couldn't imagine him getting much further; and Deirdre, no doubt, would tire of him soon enough. 'Life in a little flat in Adelaide won't hold its appeal for long. I'll bet Vlad doesn't even reproach her, not once. He'll let her come home as if nothing had happened and they'll carry on as they always did. That Sanctum crowd will be back; a bit of scandal will just make Deirdre more of a legend. She belongs in Crater Lakes. Yes, she'll come home.'

'I hope Pav does.' Skip had one secret she had never told her sister: if she loved either of the Novak brothers, it was not Honza but Pavel. She thought of them racing to the Jump together and plunging ecstatically into the green cool water. 'Are you still mad at him?'

'For going into the army? I should be. He could have been an outlaw on the run, and what is he?'

Skip knew the answer. 'A tool of American imperialism.'

'But he was bound to be, wasn't he? He's that sort of boy. Good old Pav,' Marlo added in a gentle voice, and smiled. She could hardly talk: she had admitted it more than once. Kings Cross had been a chimera. Marlo would spend the next years studying literature at the University of Adelaide. Later, perhaps, she would find herself in other universities far away. Who knew where it would end? Germaine had studied literature, too. And look at her.

The house behind them was silent; Channel Eight had finished for the night, and their aunt and uncle had gone to bed. From the dark grass an insect tickered. What sort of insect made that noise? Distantly a dog barked, and they both thought of Baskerville.

Skip had been at the Novak house when Marky Bonner came to take the dog away. 'You realise that's a dangerous dog?' the young man said in his best official voice. Mr Novak, so strong until then, had collapsed, sobbing and sobbing, and no words could allay his grief.

Now Marlo stood and stretched. 'Long day tomorrow. I'd better get to bed, and so should you.'

Skip didn't want her sister to go. 'You'll tell me,' she said, 'when you see Karen Jane?'

'Of course. Regular reports.'

'And Olly, you're sure about Olly?'

'He's yours, I told you. My scholarship will run to a new typewriter. Make good use of him, won't you? You're smart, Skip. Maybe, just maybe, you're the writer in the family.'

Skip smiled. 'Will you read *The Female Eunuch* on the way back?'

'With Sandy Campbell driving? You bet.'

'Read it out loud. Marlo?' One last sally. 'You won't go mad, will you?'

'I won't if you won't. Deal?'

Skip, to her delight, felt her sister's fingertips splay softly on her crown. Yes, they had a deal. They would live. They would grow. She thought of the old days in Glenelg, in the room above the garage. Hadn't they been happy there, with the tree that creaked by the window and the rolling waves beyond? Those days seemed so far away. But they would be happy again. Marlo's footsteps faded across the decking.

Skip thought about time. Why must it pass so quickly? Why must everything change? On Roger Dansie's gravestone the dates revealed that he had died in his fortieth year. To Skip, he had seemed ageless. Of course, she knew he had once been a callow boy; he must have been, or his tragedy could never have happened. But there had been something eternal in him, something permanent, that she had glimpsed when his voice rang out from the stage of the King Edward VII Theatre. Hadn't he been a great actor, even if he was only famous in Crater Lakes? She pictured his grave, overgrown already under the melaleucas. And what, she wondered, had happened to that eternal part of Roger? Had it gone, gone for good?

Purcell, miaowing, bounded down from the decking.

'What is it, Mowser – something out there?'

Tonight there was only a crescent moon, but the stars sparkled brilliantly. Skip got up and followed Purcell into the dark. Cats really were curious, like everyone said. She feared that one day he, too, would go away and not come back.

'Mowser?' She couldn't see him.

A voice came in reply: 'That's not his name.'

Startled, Skip stumbled back as a dark figure approached. In his arms was Purcell.

'Saw your light on. Thought I'd say hello. I walk around a bit at night, you know. Can't sleep.'

'But where have you been?' No one had seen Jack after the day of the fire. To Skip, the scene had the quality of fantasy. She hadn't heard the gate opening; had Jack climbed the fence? His eyes caught the dim light and glittered; his face looked more than ever like a mysterious ancient carving.

'Oh,' he said, 'I went away for a while. Worked on a property up north for a bit. But Mr Novak there' – he gestured to the house – 'reckons I should come back. It's yours, he reckons. Yours fair and square.'

'What's yours?' said Skip.

Purcell struggled in Jack's arms. 'Getting down already, you big lump? And that's all the welcome I get! Always a squirmy one, this one,' he added, straightening up as the cat flickered away. 'Mr Novak's making sure them lawyer blokes play right by me. Even us blackfellas have rights these days – well, one or two. And Mr Dansie left it to me fair and square.'

Skip said, understanding, 'He left you the house?'

'Not much to leave! But the land, what his dad didn't flog off, that's mine. It was a big property, the Dansie place, and there's still a lot of it left. Them back paddocks have been rented out for years. Mr Novak reckons just the income from that's enough to keep old Jack in comfort.'

'But that's marvellous!' cried Skip, delighted.

He shrugged. 'Still, so what? I'd rather have Mr Dansie back, like the old days.'

Jack turned to go and Skip felt suddenly desperate, as if she had failed him somehow. If only she could make it up to him! She touched the sleeve of his shirt. 'I'm sorry. It was all my fault.'

His voice remained level as he turned back. 'You reckon?'

'Roger died trying to save me.'

The black man shook his head. 'He didn't try – he did save you, love.'

'He said not to feel guilty. But I have to, I must.'

'Silly girl! Don't you know Mr Dansie was already dead? He'd been dead for years. You brought him alive again, just for a while. Yair, he saved you. But you saved him too.'

'Sorry,' Skip could only say again. 'I'm sorry.'

Jack cupped a hand to her face. The hand felt like soft leather. 'Me, I get it into my head he's still out there, stalking the streets. Poor bastard. I want to find him and make him come home.'

'I loved him.' Skip's tears were flowing now.

'And he loved you.' Jack drew her towards him. His embrace was deep and long. His shirt smelled of smoke and dust. Sinking against him, Skip felt as if she were coming home after too long away. Her world was so fractured. She had given up so much. And here, for the merest fragment of time, was something solid, something complete. The sky with its dark and its distances arced above them, infinite, studded thickly with stars.

'You know,' he said, as they drew apart, 'I reckon I saw that dog tonight.'

'Baskerville?' said Skip. 'Where?'

'Somewhere. He's around.'

Constable Bonner, to his ignominy, had never succeeded in running in his dangerous dog. Baskerville had taken off. How such a big dog could hide out, and for so long, nobody knew; attempts at capturing him had come to nothing, but by now sightings had been reported all over the district. Farmers had found sheep with their throats ripped out; more than one chicken coop had been breached in the night. Already, in stories told about him, Baskerville had grown twice as large and twice as fierce. In fifty or a hundred years' time, Skip suspected, he would still live on, a tale to frighten children.

Jack said they must see each other again.

'But where will I find you?'

'Oh, love! You'll always find me.'

As Jack slipped away into the dark, Skip remembered the day she had seen him standing by a lonely country roadside; then, as now, he seemed to embody worlds of loss greater than any she could begin to imagine. Did he have a surname? Did he have a family? How old was he? Once she had asked him how he came to be the only Aborigine in Crater Lakes. He shook his head. That was the way it was, the way it always had been. He could not remember his parents; raised in a Church of England orphanage up north, he had been sent down to work on the Dansie property when he was still little more than a child. His story left Skip humbled. She thought of her own family, flawed as it was, and realised she was lucky.

She heard, faintly, the click of the side gate. Returning to the sleepout, she stood on the decking and looked up at the stars. She breathed deeply. Her biggest trial was about to begin: life without Marlo. It would be hard, she knew, but not, perhaps, so hard as she had feared. These last months had taught her one thing. She was strong. She would survive.

Skip, Skipper: captain of the ship.

The crescent moon cut, clean and dazzling, against the velvet sky. In the night, in the country, you could feel the earth turning: the motion of time, telling us that everything, all we love and all that makes us suffer, must come at last to an end. We are all travellers through the darkness of space, tumbling with the stars and planets back to the place where we began.

She swung open the screen door. Purcell lay on the counterpane. Settling himself in for the night, the cat licked a furry paw with his quick pink tongue. Must he always lie in the middle? She lunged at him, rubbed her face into his tigery flank. How she loved him! Auntie Noreen had complained about the cat, even made threats, but Skip knew she didn't really mean it. She was all talk. Perhaps she always had been. No, Skip wasn't frightened of Auntie Noreen; lately, in spite of herself, she was even a little fond of her.

'Goodnight, Purcell,' Skip whispered.

She was too wide awake to join him in bed. If only Honza would come tapping at the window! But she didn't think that would happen. Honza – Honza, of all boys! – had become quiet and withdrawn. Maybe she should take the initiative and tap at his window instead. She decided that she would. Soon.

She paced the floor. The sleepout had seemed empty and barren since the day Auntie Noreen burned Barry's things. Skip, in the months since, had made no Airfix models and found no posters to replace Paul Newman or Jackie Stewart; and she knew she would never win a sporting trophy. But nonetheless the room was beginning to seem like her own.

Under the window stood a table and chair. The table was a folding one Skip had found in the garage; Auntie Noreen, surprisingly, had donated a chair from the kitchen. On the table sat three things: Olly Olivetti, without his case; a fresh ream of quarto; and an Anglepoise lamp Skip had saved from the blowhole. Uncle Doug had got it working again.

She switched off the overhead light, turned on the lamp, and sat at the table: her desk, as she called it. There was something comforting in the pool of yellow light. It was a magic circle, shutting out the world outside.

On the window ledge above Skip's desk lay three books she had found at the library: a sleek black Bible-like volume bearing the title *Famous Plays of To-day*, the first of which was *Journey's End* by R. C. Sherriff; *Seven Famous Plays*, in a yellow jacket, by the writer she had once thought was called Henry Gibson; and a little ragged olive-coloured book, *Man and Superman* by Bernard Shaw. She was reading the Shaw; she found it hard going, but Marlo said many things were difficult when you started but not if you kept at them. Skip would read all the plays in which Roger had appeared and imagine his performances. Perhaps Mr Novak would help her. He could remember; she could imagine. Later, perhaps, they would find other plays, newer plays. Marlo could help.

Early that evening, Skip had been practising typing on Olly. His carriage had travelled far across to the left; a sheet of paper curled around the platen with nothing on it but lines of letters, nonsense words, and the name SKIP WELLS repeated many times. Now she ripped out the page, screwed it up and tossed it into the dark beyond the lamplight. Rolling in a fresh sheet, Skip leaned over the carriage. Olly's smell was delicious: ink, grease, metal. She felt sad and happy at once. In eight hours' time, or seven, the Greyhound bus would roll away down Volcano Street while Skip stood on the pavement with her aunt and uncle and watched; for a few seconds, Marlo would wave, and then she would be gone. For a sudden, intense moment, Skip longed to rush to Marlo's room, embrace her, sob with her. But she wouldn't. She blinked and wiped her wrist across her eyes.

Olly's new page glared in the lamplight. What should Skip write? She had no ideas; then she looked at her library books and knew. There was a trick to everything, and so there was to this. But it was more than a trick: it was magic. You didn't copy the stories others had written already. You steeped yourself in the spirit of those stories and that spirit would guide you. Time passes and things change; but in many ways, too, they remain the same. In age after age there are wars and soldiers. There are men and there are supermen, or those who think they are. And there are enemies of the people. Imagine, say, a man cast out from his community, when all the time he was the one who could have saved it. She touched, like a talisman, the yellow Ibsen, and typed with care the words: ACT ONE.

Her cat slept peacefully as the keys clicked.

# Author's note

Those familiar with the state of South Australia may imagine they recognise Crater Lakes. They don't. The town is fictional, as are all the people in it.

Some things are not of my invention. 'Fuckarada' and all the jokes told by Sandy Campbell and others are, without exception, real jokes I heard when I was young. Ditto the numerous profanities, insults, taunts. And Brenton Lumsden, or a boy not unlike him, really did do that to the mother cat.

*An Enemy of the People* is quoted from the translation by E. Marx-Aveling, daughter of Karl, which appears in William Archer's 1890 edition of Ibsen's *Prose Dramas*. The Crater Lakes Players would, in all likelihood, have used that version; there are later versions which nowadays may be regarded as superior, including those by Arthur Miller, Peter Watts and Christopher Hampton.

'Mowser' was a strip cartoon – in its way, a work of genius – created by the British artist Reg Parlett (1904–1991). One of my happy childhood memories is of sitting with a stack of *Lion* comics and reading episodes of 'Mowser' one after the other. Dr Lyall Watson's article about future population growth, 'Standing Room Only', from

*Eagle,* 21 October 1967, is reprinted in Daniel Tatarsky's *Eagle Annual: The Best of the 1960s Comic* (2009), pp. 181–2.

Sir Laurence Olivier and Vivien Leigh made a famous and tumultuous theatrical tour of Australia and New Zealand with the Old Vic company in 1948. It figures in all Olivier and Leigh biographies, and a whole, quite splendid book has been written about it: Garry O'Connor's *Darlings of the Gods: One Year in the Lives of Laurence Olivier and Vivien Leigh* (1984). Olivier really was on the lookout for new talent. In Adelaide, he discovered Keith Michell – to become famous for his portrayal of Henry VIII on British television – and sent him to train in England; Australian actor Peter Finch, later Leigh's lover, also came into the Oliviers' orbit during this tour. Another notable Olivier connection, Sir Laurence's later wife Joan Plowright, evokes life at the Old Vic Theatre School in London in the late 1940s in her memoir *And That's Not All* (2001).

Many people helped me write this book, sometimes without knowing it. I am grateful to John Wright for introducing me to the Arthur Collection, an archive of historic photographs in the State Library of South Australia; Garry Costello, who taught me to read 'Henry Gibson' – and, in a sense, all the other books I've read; Deborah Madsen, who gave me, long ago in another life, the content of several pages; Antony Heaven, who has never lived in Crater Lakes but understands it – and helps me understand it, too; Mary Nash, who is in every line; Ravi Mirchandani, Margaret Stead, Toby Mundy, James Roxburgh, and all at Atlantic Books; Clara Finlay, who has made this book much better than it otherwise would have been; and Sara Menguc, without whom it would never have appeared at all.

I have not written this book because I hate Crater Lakes. Often I wish I could have spent my life there.

I haunt it, like Roger Dansie.

# Note on the Author

David Rain is an Australian writer living in London. Formerly a lecturer in English Literature at Queens' University, Belfast, he presently runs the MA in Creative Writing at Middlesex University. His debut novel, *The Heat of the Sun*, was published in 2012 by Atlantic Books.